Rosie Goodwin has work[...] years. She has children, a[...] husband, Trevor, and their four dogs.

A ROSE AMONG THORNS

ROSIE GOODWIN

headline

First published in Great Britain in 2009
by HEADLINE PUBLISHING GROUP

First published in paperback in 2010
by HEADLINE PUBLISHING GROUP

4

Cataloguing in Publication Data is available from the British Library

ISBN 978 0 7553 4226 6

Typeset in Calisto by Palimpsest Book Production Limited,
Grangemouth, Stirlingshire

Printed and bound by CPI Group (UK) Ltd, Croydon, CR0 4YY

HEADLINE PUBLISHING GROUP
An Hachette UK Company
338 Euston Road
London NW1 3BH

www.headline.co.uk
www.hachette.co.uk

For Geoff and Janet Hancocks who believed in me
and always told me . . . one day!

Also for

John William Smith
27 March 1942–16 June 2009
A dear brother-in-law who will never be forgotten.

Acknowledgements

As always, my sincere thanks to the following people: Flora Rees, Kate Byrne, Maura Brickell, Jane Morpeth and everyone at Headline for their unfailing support and enthusiasm.

Joan Deitch, my lovely copy editor.

Peter Lee, for invaluable help with research.

My lovely children and family for their patience and understanding.

My readers for all their lovely messages and reviews.

And last but never least, for my husband, Trev . . .

PART ONE

Nuneaton, July 1870

A Ring o' Roses

Chapter One

A ring, a ring o' roses,
A pocket full o' posies
Atishoo, atishoo,
We all fall down!

As the voices of the children wafted through the partially open bedroom window, Clara Mallabone wiped the sweat from her brow with the back of her hand. Then, wringing out the rough linen cloth in the dish of cold water at her side, she again sponged the feverish forehead of the poor soul lying in the great brass bed.

Clara's back felt as if it was breaking. It had been the early hours of the morning when Arthur, Sarah Churm's distraught husband, had woken her with his banging on the cottage door and, since then, Clara had scarcely left Sarah's side.

Clara had delivered many a little soul into the world, but now she was gravely concerned. Something was wrong. Sarah's baby should have been born long ago.

The terrible screams that had rent the air as darkness turned to light had now quietened to dull whimpers, and as each new contraction wracked Sarah's poor body, her grip momentarily tightened on Clara's wiry hand. But still no baby was forthcoming. When Clara realised that there was nothing more she herself could do for Sarah, she had sent Arthur, who was terrified now, in search of the doctor. There was no clock in the bedroom and so Clara had no way of knowing how long he had been gone, but to her tired mind and body it seemed like hours. She offered up a silent prayer that the doctor would come soon, for Sarah was almost at the end of her endurance.

For now, the young woman seemed to have slipped into a fitful doze, so gently untangling her thin fingers from the clammy grip, Clara crossed to the cottage window and, stretching her aching back, gazed hopefully up the lane that skirted the quarry. There was still no sign of Arthur or the doctor's pony-tub cart. She tutted to herself, but then as her eyes fell on the children playing unconcerned on the grass outside the cottage, a smile twitched the corners of her lips.

There was her firstborn, Thomas, the ringleader as usual. He made a handsome sight with his springing dark curls and deep blue eyes. At twelve years old he was a rough and tumble sort of lad, always into scrapes and mischief, with the confidence to survive anything. Sometimes she worried about him. Although she loved him dearly, she was also honest enough to admit to herself that Thomas had a selfish streak. On the other hand, Jack, her youngest, was Thomas's opposite and gave her constant cause for concern for another reason: if anything, he was too much the other way and would have given away his last penny. Her eyes searched amongst the children until she found him; as usual he was close to Melissa. Melissa Churm, or 'Sassy' as she was affectionately known, was Sarah's eldest child, a beautiful eight year old with dark hair, deep brown eyes and the looks and nature of a little angel.

Jack totally worshipped Sassy and followed her around like a little lap dog, but even at Sassy's tender age it was obvious where her affections lay. She idolised Thomas, and although they were only children as yet, this bothered Clara. Jack was much quieter and more

4

slightly built than Thomas, although to her mind he was equally as good looking, but because of his limp and shy personality he lacked Thomas's confidence.

Close to Sassy's other side were William and George, the girl's two younger brothers. Sassy was like a little mother to them, constantly wiping one runny nose or another or tending to some minor scrape or bruise. Clara had a huge soft spot for Sassy. One of the greatest regrets in her life was that she had never been blessed with a daughter, but if she had, she would have wished her to be the mirror image of Sassy in body and mind.

A sudden cry from behind her pulled Clara's attention back to the room, and hurrying over to the bed, she found Sarah awake again.

'There, there, lass,' she soothed, wiping the damp curls from the woman's sweating brow. 'Happen the doctor will be along any minute now, I'm thinking.'

Sarah's sunken eyes seemed to be silently pleading with Clara to end her torment.

Pulling back the sheet from the young woman's enormous bulging stomach, Clara offered up yet another prayer, but this time one of thanks for, at last, the baby's head was just beginning to show. But her thanks quickly turned to panic, as Sarah's body suddenly seemed to lift from the bed as another mighty contraction ripped through her. Her eyes were rolling back into her head and Clara knew that she could wait no longer. Quickly now, she seized the knife from the dish at the side of the bed.

Taking a great breath to compose herself, Clara then leaned over Sarah and did what had to be done.

Almost before she'd had time to return the bloodied knife to the dish, the child slithered from Sarah's body. It was a boy! And a bonny one too, but no newborn cry filled the room. Grasping the infant by the ankles and taking up the knife again, Clara quickly separated the child from its mother, then holding him aloft she delivered a resounding slap on his backside. There was still no sign of a cry, and despairing now, she laid him at his mother's feet and frantically began to blow her own breath into his tiny lungs. After what seemed like hours, he suddenly coughed and let out a thin wail. Great tears of relief began to roll unchecked down Clara's workworn cheeks, and after wrapping him quickly in a clean white towel she had laid ready, she placed him in the crib to the side of the bed. Now that he had drawn breath, she must turn her attention back to Sarah.

It was just then that the door flew open and Arthur and the doctor rushed into the room. Clara had never been so grateful to see anyone in her whole life. She had great faith in Dr Massey. He was scarcely taller than herself – small and thin with a handlebar moustache and greying hair – but as Clara had been heard to say on more than one occasion, 'He has a heart as big as a bucket.'

Scarcely glancing at the child in the crib, Arthur made straight for his wife's side, for it was obvious to all present that Sarah was very ill.

Patting Clara kindly on her shoulder, murmuring, 'Well done, my dear,' Dr Massey quickly washed his hands then began to press gently around Sarah's still swollen abdomen.

Frowning now, he turned and suggested tactfully, 'Perhaps you should take Mr Churm downstairs and make him a good strong brew?' Nodding at the now unconscious form upon the bed, he said quietly, 'If I'm not very much mistaken, there will be another birth in this house today.'

Clara's mouth dropped open in amazement but, quickly composing herself, she took Arthur gently by the elbow and led him from the room. Within minutes she was back up the stairs to help the doctor, but it was almost an hour later before the second child, a beautiful little girl, was born.

As she slipped lifeless into the world with the cord wrapped tightly around her tiny neck, it was obvious to them both that no amount of smacking or blowing could bring life back into this tiny being. Taking her from the doctor's hands, Clara held the still little body to her breast, her warm tears splashing down onto the perfect little face.

But for Sarah, the ordeal was not over. She had lost a tremendous amount of blood, and although Dr Massey worked with a will to stem it, still it gushed from her relentlessly.

Exhausted now, he at last stopped his efforts and sank onto the side of the bed.

Clara placed a comforting hand on his arm as he sadly shook his head.

'There's nothing more I can do.' He knew when he was beaten. 'Her life is in God's hands now. Please will you fetch her husband up to sit with her?'

Clara made her way down the steep wooden staircase and sent Arthur up to his beloved wife, then composing herself as best she could, she dashed round to her adjoining cottage to prepare a hasty meal for Walter, her own husband, and the children. After swiftly chopping some vegetables and a scrag end of beef, she placed them all in a large metal pot, added water, herbs and barley, then flinging some more logs onto the now dying flames, she placed the pot into the heart of the fire.

When Walter came in some half an hour later and began to sluice himself down from the bowl of water Clara had ready for him, the table was laid, not just for their own family, but for Sarah's children too. A crusty loaf of bread was sliced ready in the middle of the table, next to a frothy jug of milk.

Walter was thick with grime from his shift at the Haunchwood Colliery, and tired to the bone, but at the sight of Clara, his face broke into a loving smile.

There were those who said that Clara and Walter made an odd couple, and happen they did, for Walter was a great bear of a man, whilst Clara was a mere scrap of a woman. But for all that they shared a solid, loving marriage. Walter totally adored his Clara, for what she lacked in stature she more than made up for in kindness.

'I'm going to have to leave you to feed the bairns,' she told him with a tremor in her voice. 'Sarah is very ill. She gave birth to twins this afternoon. One of each, but the little girl were stillborn.'

Walter's smile was instantly replaced by a look of great sadness. He was fond of the Churm family and could only imagine how devastated Arthur must be feeling.

Patting her bottom with a gentleness that belied his great strength he said, 'Then off you go, love. I'll serve up all the children and put 'em to bed here if need be.'

Clara needed no second bidding, and almost flew next door. Arthur was where she had left him, hunched in the chair at the side of the bed, his eyes fast on Sarah's face. He looked like a soul in torment and was grasping his wife's pale hand tightly in his own as if he were trying to pour his own strength into her.

Lifting the crib, Clara carried the tiny boychild downstairs into the small scullery. There she washed and fed him with a drop of milk from a pap bag, then with the newborn's comforts seen to, she made Arthur and herself a strong brew of tea. After carrying his upstairs to him she placed it carefully at his side, but he was unaware of her presence. His eyes never once left Sarah's face, and the tea remained where Clara had placed it, untouched, as she slipped away to wait by the fire should he need her.

It was deep night now. Dr Massey had long since departed but still Arthur sat at Sarah's side, gripping her hand, willing her to live as she fought the battle between life and death.

Clara had settled all the children into her own cottage with Walter watching over them. She fed and changed the newborn and then washed his tiny, lifeless sister before laying her in a drawer in the front parlour.

Clara's heart was heavy as she settled into the fireside chair and began to doze. Sleep was just coming to claim her when suddenly a heartrending wail filled the air. It was a cry of such torment that Clara knew that she would never forget the sound for as long as she lived.

Hot stinging tears welled in her eyes and ran unchecked down her cheeks. She had no need to climb the stairs. She already knew that for Sarah Churm the battle was over, and Death was the victor.

Chapter Two

The skies above the cottages perched high on Tuttle Hill were leaden and overcast, and a misty drizzle had begun to fall, almost as if the heavens wished to join their tears to those of the mourners assembling in the lane for Sarah Churm's funeral.

All morning, neighbours had been in and out of Clara's cottage, bringing homebaked pasties and pies as their contribution to the funeral tea. Inside, all was hustle and bustle, with every available surface seemingly covered with food.

In the adjoining cottage, Walter was nailing down the lid of the simple wooden box that served as poor Sarah's coffin. The remaining mourners were now waiting outside after having entered the small parlour one by one to pay their last respects.

It was Walter who had contacted Bob Capener, the local carpenter, and instructed him to make the coffin, for Arthur was in no state to organise anything.

The sight of Sarah lying in that cold box had affected Walter mightily. Sarah had been a beautiful woman and death had failed to rob her of her beauty, and the sight of the tiny baby tucked close to her side only added to his sadness.

All through the night of her death, Arthur's heartrending sobs had echoed in the lane and into the deep quarry bordering the cottages, reaching even to the canal beyond that ran through the green leafy fields of the Warwickshire countryside, but come morning the sobs had stopped abruptly and since then Arthur had sat, like a man possessed, in silent torment.

As he banged in the last nail, Walter had an uncanny feeling that Arthur wished he could have passed on too, to be with his wife.

Clara herself had laid Sarah out before reverently closing her eyes for the very last time and placing two shiny pennies on her eyelids. And now the tiny infant, whom Sarah had never held in life, lay alongside her mother in death.

Passing Arthur, who sat, as he had for days silently next to the coffin, Walter paused, but unable to find the right words, he squeezed his shoulder and made his way next door to change into his Sunday best.

All along the row of cottages, the curtains were drawn together as a mark of respect, and although a small crowd was now gathered, silence prevailed; even the birds had stopped singing as if they too sensed the deep air of sadness.

A huge pile of simple wild flowers had been placed outside the cottage door, ready to go with the horse and cart that would carry Sarah and her baby to their final resting-place.

Entering his own cottage, Walter found the mood no brighter. The children were seated on the wooden settle, alongside the fire, confused and silent. As his eyes met Sassy's, his big heart went out to her. She was holding her new brother, still as yet unnamed, closely to her. Arthur had refused to even look at the child, but Sassy had hardly let him out of her sight since the morning following his birth, and her great sad eyes touched Walter deeply.

Clara would not be attending the funeral, preferring to stay and look after the children whilst it took place.

11

She also had the task of transferring all the food into next door, once Sarah's body was removed from the parlour, and laying out the funeral feast in readiness for the mourners when they returned.

Grandmother Cox from the end cottage was also staying to help, as the two-mile walk to Chilvers Coton Church would have been too much for her old legs.

Thomas had gone out early this morning with strict instructions to be back in plenty of time but, as usual, he was late. After glancing at the mantel clock, Clara tutted in annoyance. The procession was almost ready to begin and still there was no sign of him. He was probably off playing with the gypsies who were at present residing in the aptly named Gypsy Lane, and if she knew anything about him, he would have lost all track of time.

'Eeh, that lad,' she muttered, for although she loved him dearly, her elder son was a law unto himself.

Just then, the clip-clop of the horse's hooves on the hard-packed earth of the lane was heard. The children's heads all turned to stare at Clara and she hurried over to them with her arms opened reassuringly.

'Is that the cart come to take me mammy to the church-yard?' whispered William, his frightened, bewildered eyes tight on Clara's face.

Her heart seemed to twist in her chest. 'Aye, it is, pet,' she answered gently as she gathered the child to her.

'Tell me again where heaven is, Clara.'

Clara had to swallow the great lump that had once more formed in her throat before she could answer him. This was another job that had fallen to her, to explain to Sarah's children about their mother's death.

All eyes were upon her as for what seemed like the umpteenth time in these last days, she began to explain as best she could.

'Well, as I told you, your mammy was very poorly

12

and in a lot of pain, so God took her home to heaven and now she'll be a beautiful angel in the sky.'

Although William quite liked the idea of his mammy being an angel, he would much sooner she was here with them.

'How *long* will she be gone?' His eyes were full of unshed tears that glistened on his lashes.

'I've already told you, hinny,' Clara soothed. 'Once you go to heaven, you can't come back.'

The tears that had threatened now began to pour down his pale cheeks and soon young George's sobs joined with his brother's.

Of all the children, only Sassy remained dry-eyed as she sat cradling her tiny brother, for she was the only one amongst them who could even begin to comprehend the terrible finality of death.

Grandmother Cox was moving amongst them all like a mother hen, a huge white hankie flying from the runny little noses to the wet cheeks.

'Happen death is a lot for these little 'uns to understand,' she said, and Clara nodded wearily in agreement.

By now, Sarah's coffin had been respectfully placed upon the cart, ready to begin its journey to the pretty village church in the parish of Coton where the young woman had been born and bred. By the time all the flowers had been placed on and around the coffin, hardly an inch of wood was showing, and as the cart moved off, the mourners formed a train behind it and fell into solemn step.

William and George's sobs had now subsided to whimpers.

Clara's eyes caught those of Grandmother Cox across the heads of the children. 'Eeh, this has been a rare week an' no mistake,' she muttered.

The old woman's head bobbed in agreement, but then

she declared optimistically, 'I'm thinkin' things can only get better now, for surely they couldn't get any worse?' But almost before the words had left her mouth, the door was suddenly flung open with a force so great that it almost danced from its heavy metal hinges, and the little cottage seemed to shake.

Every head in the room snapped up as one. The sight that met their eyes caused old Grandmother Cox's mouth to gape so wide that the wrinkles in her ancient face almost disappeared.

Thomas's shaking body filled the doorway. His eyes were bulging from his head, and from where Clara stood it appeared that every hair on his head was standing on end. His breath was coming in great shuddering gasps, and though his lips stretched from his teeth and his mouth repeatedly opened and shut, not one sound escaped from him.

Leaping across the room, Clara grasped her firstborn by the shoulders. 'By, lad,' she scolded loudly, 'you gave us a rare old turn then and no mistake. What in God's name is wrong with yer?'

Obviously deep in shock, Thomas could only shake his head. Although Clara alternately begged and threatened him to tell her what was wrong, still he stood, his great blue eyes staring ahead as if incapable of speech.

It was apparent now that the boy was hysterical, and realising that she must bring him out of this state, and quickly, Clara brought back her thin arm and swung it forward with a vengeance, to land a resounding smack on her son's cheek. The poor lad's head rocked on his shoulders, and his whole body seemed to jerk. Then, with a great sob, he threw himself into Clara's arms.

Grandmother Cox hastily pushed a glass of water into Clara's hand and, raising it quickly to Thomas's lips, his mother attempted to pour some into his quivering mouth.

14

Most of the cold liquid dribbled down his chin onto his rough linen shirt, but some found its mark and, coughing and spluttering, Thomas leaned against his mother until the sobs began to slightly subside.

Clara clutched him to her protectively, then as he quietened, she held him at arm's length and looked deep into his eyes. 'Now then,' she soothed. 'Calm yourself and tell me what's wrong.'

He pointed shakily to the open doorway.

'It were there, Mam. I saw it!' His expression pleaded with her to believe him.

'All right, all right, lad, calm down. *What* did yer see?'

Gulping deep in his throat, he attempted to explain. 'I knew I were late back, so when I arrived and saw them putting the coffin onto the cart, I hid behind the bushes across the lane.' When no scolding was forthcoming from Clara, he licked his dry lips and continued, 'I knew you'd be sore at me for not getting back afore the funeral started, so I stayed put till the cart moved off.'

Clara nodded encouragingly.

'Well, it was then I saw it.' He was visibly trembling again now.

'Saw *what*?' A note of impatience had crept into Clara's voice.

'It was an angel, Mam.' And seeing the look of disbelief cross her face: 'It were, Mam – it were, I swear it! As the men carried the coffin out, an angel suddenly swooped down and flew across it.'

Clara stared at her son incredulously as Thomas grasped her shoulders in frustration.

'It's the truth, Mam. She were wearin' a white dress and she had great wings, an' after a moment of hoverin' above the coffin, she flew up into the sky wi' Mrs Churm in her arms.'

'Happen you've been listening to me talking to the

little 'uns,' Clara said kindly, untangling herself from his trembling fingers, but Thomas was adamant.

'No, Mam, no!' he stated. 'I swear it were an angel.'

Clara was just about to begin arguing the point again when she felt a firm hand grip her elbow. With a strength that belied her wizened old frame, Grandmother Cox then unceremoniously dragged her across the room to stand beside the deep stone sink.

The old woman's eyes seemed to be flashing fire. 'You just go steady on him, me gel,' she said, and Clara glared back indignantly.

'But didn't yer hear him?' she demanded. 'As if we've not enough on our plates this day, without all this wild talk and a hysterical son to deal wi'.'

'You just listen here.' The old lady's bony finger was wagging furiously, almost in Clara's face. 'You are Yorkshire born and bred, an' have different sayings and beliefs to us as were Warwickshire born.' Drawing herself up to her full height, she tapped the side of her nose. 'Happen that lad *did* see an angel, for there's many a strange thing happens 'twixt heaven and earth as we can know nowt about, so you just go easy on him now.' And then turning from Clara, she snatched up a huge meat pie and without another word hobbled from the room to take it into the cottage next door, leaving the younger woman with her mouth agape and speechless for one of the very few times in her life.

Thomas meanwhile was standing with his head bowed. He knew what he had seen, and from that day until the day he died, no one would ever convince him otherwise.

The mourners stood at the side of the grave, the misty drizzle lending a chill to their bodies that matched the chill in their hearts. Walter held fast to Arthur's elbow, for he had a feeling that if he should release his grip, then Arthur would surely leap into the open grave to join Sarah.

'*Ashes to ashes, dust to dust*,' the vicar's voice droned on. But so concerned for this placid, kindly neighbour standing close to his side was Walter, that the words of the service were lost to him. Although he stood in the pretty churchyard of Chilvers Coton, Walter's thoughts were back in the cottage sat high atop Tuttle Hill with Arthur's children and Clara. Closing his eyes he offered up a silent prayer, not for Sarah this time but for the poor motherless mites, for what was to become of them, if Arthur didn't pull himself together?

His thoughts turned to Clara. If he knew anything about it, his wife would be running around like a headless chicken by now, preparing the funeral tea. And he had no doubt it would be a feast to be proud of. His Clara was renowned for keeping a good table and was able to make a meal out of scraps. So lost in thought had he become, that when he pulled himself back to the present, the service was over and the mourners were leaving the graveside.

Vicar Rigby walked solemnly around the grave to offer his condolences and shake Arthur's hand to which Arthur responded woodenly, his eyes never leaving the simple coffin in which lay the love of his life. With a kindly nod at Walter, the vicar too then strode away towards the church.

It was time to begin the journey back, and as Walter spotted the gravediggers coming across the churchyard towards them, shovels in their hands, he guided Arthur away and led him back to the waiting horse and cart.

Surprisingly, as the mourners plodded back to the cottage, the drizzle stopped and a watery sun appeared in the sky. It was almost as if, now the summer had also paid her respects, she wished to return to her full glory.

The procession moved slowly, skirting Nuneaton town centre and passing into Swan Lane, where the homes of the town gentry were built. As they went past one such house, a curtain was pulled aside and Walter spotted the doctor who had attended Sarah gazing out at them.

When Walter caught his eye, Dr Massey smiled sadly at him. Clara had told Walter how hard he had fought to save Sarah's life. Dr Massey was a much-respected and well-loved member of this close-knit community, and Walter knew that there had been many a time when he had waived his fee to help those who had fallen on hard times. Raising his hand in salute, the doctor then let the curtain fall back into place, and the procession moved on past the Old Abbey before turning to begin the final lap of the journey.

As they finally approached the cottages after the last steep uphill trek, a haze rose from the fields and flowers, and summer returned as if rejoicing that on this day, 12 July 1870, Sarah Churm was finally free of earthly pain.

The funeral tea was one that would be talked about for many a long day, and now some two hours after the return of the mourners, the tables, which had almost sagged beneath the weight of the food, were covered with empty platters and crumbs.

Most of the people had departed after offering their final condolences to Arthur. Outside in the lane, the men who still remained were enjoying a smoke of their pipes and a glass of home-brewed ale, while in the small parlour the women drank tea and gossiped quietly amongst themselves.

At present, Clara was back in her own scullery, and Grandmother Cox had long since departed to the comfort of her rocking chair, for a well-earned late-afternoon nap. It had been a long day for the old woman, just as it had been for Clara, but for the latter it was far from over yet. Her arms were deep in the stone sink, washing up the many dirty pots that Sassy was carrying in to her from next door, a trayful at a time.

Miriam, Arthur's sister, was seated in the comfortable old rocking chair in the corner of the room, cradling the newborn baby in her arms and rocking to and fro. Raising her arm from the sink to wipe the sweat from her eyes, Clara glanced across at her and her gaze softened. They made a pretty picture, this childless woman and the innocent infant, and yet again, for the countless time this week, Clara had to question the unfairness of life. Here was Miriam, a gentle-natured woman, to all intents and purposes far better off than herself or indeed any of the folks in the cottages, but without the one thing she craved most in the whole world, a child of her own. And there was Arthur with a bonny newborn son, at whom he couldn't even bear to look. Even as she pondered on this, an idea was born in her mind, and returning to the dirty dishes she chewed on her lip thoughtfully.

Next door, Ben Ratcliffe, Miriam's husband, was pouring himself another glass of ale from the stone jug at the end of the table. He then cut some wedges of apple pie from the remains of the food and pressed them into the hands of George and William. 'There now, lads,' he said kindly. 'Happen that'll fill a hole till teatime.'

The two little boys stared back at him, subdued.

'Come on now,' he encouraged. 'Get yerselves off outside to eat your pie. A bit o' fresh air will do you the world o' good.'

It seemed wrong somehow to keep them in any longer, for after the miserable start, the sun was once again gloriously hot. Ben had a great fondness for his nephews and he stood in the open doorway watching them walking slowly down the lane, their small shoulders stooped with sorrow. They were good lads. One of the biggest regrets of his life was that he and Miriam had never been blessed with a child, particularly a son. Still, he supposed if it wasn't meant to be then it wasn't meant to be. He was well aware that he did still have a lot to be thankful for. He had a fine wife and was the owner of a handsome smallholding in Bermuda village, some three miles from Tuttle Hill. Although he worked long hours, he enjoyed being his own master and his hard work was paying off, for his business was thriving.

As the boys disappeared around the bend in the lane, he sighed heavily then left the doorway and went to join the men assembled outside.

Chapter Three

As usual, Jack was close on Sassy's heels, helping her to collect up the many dirty pots that were strewn about. His eyes frequently sought hers, his young heart sore to see her so unhappy and quiet. He would willingly have taken the burden from her shoulders to his own if he could have; for although he was only one year older than Sassy, he felt a great need to protect her.

Inside, Arthur sat hunched in the chair at the side of the empty grate, staring into space.

Still also amazingly subdued, Thomas was sitting across the lane from the cottages, staring into the quarry, his mind still full of the vision he had witnessed earlier. As Clara left the door with her arms full of clean pots it was a shock to see him there. Once she had given the children leave to go outside to play, Thomas would normally have been the first to be off, like a shot from a gun.

Clucking her tongue in bewilderment, she entered Arthur's door, her mind on Thomas. 'Angels indeed,' she said to herself, and hastily began to transfer the shining cups and plates back onto the old oak dresser that took up almost half of one of the walls. Her own cottage was now back to some semblance of order, but there seemed no point in trying to tidy up in here properly until the rest of the mourners had gone. She was longing for a moment to herself now that everyone was seen to, so crossing to the back door of the cottage she slipped quietly out into the yard.

As she walked towards the shared privy at the bottom of the path, she looked across the gardens at the back of the cottages. Each one looked much the same, full of fruit bushes and vegetables. Each one that is, except Sarah's, for hers had a feature that made it stand out from the rest. In the far corner was a circular bed full of rosebushes. Clara could well remember the day that Sarah had stood over Arthur while he planted them. It was not long after they wed. She could remember Arthur laughingly pointing out the impracticality of planting flowers where vegetables could be grown, but Sarah had been insistent.

'*One day*,' she had teased him, '*we'll have a fine family, and they'll play "A Ring, a Ring o' Roses" around this flowerbed.*'

Shaking her head sadly as the fond memories crowded back, Clara let herself into the whitewashed lavvy, with its squares of newspaper tied with a piece of string, hanging from a nail in the wall. In there she could think, and at this moment she had a lot of thinking to do, for before this day was over there was one particular problem to be solved, and as yet she had no idea how to tackle it.

When she re-entered the cottage some time later, she found the Widow Bonner just pulling on her long black gloves, her smart hat set at a jaunty angle on her head. She was murmuring something to Arthur, and Clara wondered why it was that although the woman appeared genuinely concerned, something about her felt fake.

'Eeh, me an' my suspicious mind,' she scolded herself, but the sight of the fashionably dressed woman bending so close to him gave her an uneasy feeling.

Widow Bonner was a handsome woman, Clara couldn't deny. She had been surprised to see her arrive back here shortly after the funeral, for as far as she knew, apart from seeing Sarah and Arthur at church each week on a Sunday, the Churms hadn't really known her that well.

The Widow Bonner had been left very comfortably provided for when her husband had died some three years earlier. But even so, it was no secret that it was her money that had bought their smart house in the best area of town, for she was the sister of John Stanley, who owned the thriving brickworks close to the Haunchwood Colliery. He was a self-made man and had ensured that his sister was comfortably provided for, and from then on she had looked down on everyone who was less well off than herself, even though she had originally come from nothing. And yet the husband she had chosen was a normal working-class man. It was said that she had married him for that very reason, since Elizabeth liked to feel that she was the one in control. She had never for a single day let the poor soul forget that she had married beneath her, and although no one could deny that she was an attractive woman, it was rumoured that she had led him a hell of a life, for her nature did not match her looks. The union had produced two children, Louise and Matthew, and while she had ruled her downtrodden man with a rod of iron, it was well known that she spoiled her children shamelessly.

Eventually, she straightened from Arthur to look haughtily down her nose at Clara, and after nodding curtly in her direction, she swept from the room in a swish of dark purple silk skirts.

'Good riddance,' muttered Clara beneath her breath. She couldn't abide people who looked down on others. As she related to Walter later that night, 'She reminded me of a big spider stood over a fly. Arthur is too good lookin' fer his own good, that's the trouble, an' now Sarah is gone he'd be a good catch for any woman.'

And Walter replied laughingly, 'Happen you have a bad mind, my love.'

'Happen I do. Aye, well, we'll just see then,' said Clara, and from then on her dislike of the Widow Bonner was born.

Now, as she slipped into the lane, she saw that the last of the mourners had left the cottage and were on their way home.

Only Walter, Ben and old Jimmy Wainthrop were still standing quietly talking, and as she passed them, Jimmy left the other two and unsteadily approached her.

'Why, me schweet gel,' he slurred. 'That were a fine feasht an' no mistake.' He hiccuped merrily, and his Sunday-best cap, which was already hopelessly askew, slipped to an even more precarious angle. 'Mind you,' he held his glass out hopefully, 'another glass o' yer fine ale wouldn't go amissh.'

Laughing, Clara snatched the glass from his outstretched hand. 'I'm thinking you've already had more than enough, Jimmy Wainthrop. An' if I'm any judge an' you don't get yerself away home right this minute, you'll find yerself in serious trouble wi' yer missus.'

He flashed her a gappy grin before replying, 'Yer could be right. Happen I'll do that, Clara.' And singing merrily to himself, he now lurched off down the lane.

The children had been fed and scrubbed and were now tucked up in their own beds for the first night since their mother's death. Clara looked around and, content that the Churms' cottage was neat and tidy, she crossed to the large black-leaded cooking range and lifted the heavy brown teapot. After pouring out a steaming mug of tea she carried it across to where Arthur still sat at the side of the fire and pressed it into his hands. Although he took it from her, she had little hope of him drinking it. She had not seen a thing pass his lips all day.

'Will there be anythin' else you're wanting, lad?' she asked, and when no reply was forthcoming she tried again.

'I'll keep the baby wi' me tonight so as you can get some rest, eh?' Still no reply. Sighing now, she crossed the room and lifted the latch of the door.

'Goodnight then, lad,' she said and, deeply disturbed, she stepped out pulling the door to behind her.

It was a beautiful evening. The stars were winking in the sky and the night owls were hooting softly, Clara allowed herself a few minutes' breathing space before she went back into her own home. She hadn't had time to put her plan into action, as Miriam and Ben had had to leave earlier to see to their animals, but Miriam had promised to come back tomorrow as soon as possible. Clara closed her tired eyes for a moment and offered up a silent prayer. 'Forgive me, Lord, fer what I'm about to do, but happen it'll be for the best.'

She took a last look at the peaceful countryside. It was fourteen years now since Walter had brought her here as a bride, but still she never tired of gazing out across the fields and wide open spaces. After being brought up in the smoky mill towns of Yorkshire, this quiet little spot had appeared as heaven to Clara. She was just about to go inside when she heard the sound of weeping. Looking up, her eyes rested on the slightly open window of Sassy's bedroom.

Clara's heart went out to her. She knew only too well that of all the children, Sassy would be the one most affected by their mother's death. Once things settled down a bit, it was she at the tender age of eight years old who would have to become the woman of the house. As if that wasn't enough, the child must feel that she had lost her dad too, for Arthur seemed to be so locked up in his own grief that he couldn't even help himself, let alone his children. If only it were Arthur crying, she thought. To her mind it was unhealthy, the way he was bottling things up, and Clara felt that if only he could give way to his tears, then perhaps his healing could begin.

When she said as much to Walter that evening he nodded in agreement. He too was deeply disturbed about the man's withdrawn state.

'But try not to worry, love,' he told her, squeezing her reddened hands gently. 'If he's no better tomorrer I'll try and get through to him.'

Smiling gratefully at this dear man, Clara kissed him. She had great faith in her husband and felt that if anyone could get through to Arthur, he could.

Walter had already changed and fed the baby and so now, lifting the crib as if it were no heavier than a feather, he proceeded to carry it upstairs to place it at the side of their bed. 'Come on, my love,' he said quietly. 'Get yourself up to bed now. If anyone has earned a good night's sleep this day, 'tis you.'

Only too happy to oblige, Clara did as she was told.

Chapter Four

It was in the early hours of the morning when the first muffled cry brought Walter and Clara starting awake. Before Clara could get her bearings or even bring her legs to the side of the bed, the cry was followed by a wild moan, and then another.

Walter was struggling into his longjohns, seeming to dance in his haste to put them on. Wrapping a warm woollen shawl about her thin shoulders, Clara leaped from the bed and the two almost collided as they both reached for the bedroom door at the same time.

Throwing it open with a force that flung it back against the whitewashed wall, Walter beat Clara across the landing and rushed into his son's room. Jack was sitting wide-eyed, his knees tight up to his chin with his arms wrapped about them, gazing across at Thomas, who lay awash with sweat in a tangle of damp sheets, still fast asleep but thrashing about as if in the throes of a fit. The only light in the room was that of the moon shining through the tiny leaded window, and as Walter approached the bed, Clara rushed back to her own bedroom and after a few attempts, because of her shaking hands, she finally managed to light the oil lamp and hurry back with it to Walter.

As the light spilled on Thomas's face, Walter said, 'The lad's having a nightmare.'

Placing the lamp on the little chest of drawers that stood between the two beds, Clara wrapped Jack in her arms. 'It's all right, lad,' she soothed. 'Yer brother's just

27

havin' a bad dream, but he'll be fine now. You lie down and go back to sleep, eh?' Kissing him affectionately, she laid him back and pulled the blankets up to his chin. Reassured now that his mam and dad were there, Jack obediently closed his eyes again.

Crossing back to the other bed where Thomas continued to writhe and whimper, Clara looked at her husband. 'What shall we do?'

Scratching his chin, Walter thought for a minute. 'I think we should wake him – but easy, like.'

Leaning across the bed, Clara took Thomas by the shoulders and gently began to shake him. For some seconds her efforts seemed to have no effect, but then without warning his eyes suddenly flew open and he sat bolt upright in the bed. For a short time he didn't know where he was, but then his eyes rested on Clara, and for the second time in less than twenty-four hours, his stiff body went limp as he fell into her arms.

'I *did* see her, Mam . . . the angel. I swear I did.'

As Clara's eyes met Walter's above the child's head, Grandmother Cox's words rang in her mind. *There's many a strange thing happens 'twixt heaven and earth as we can know nowt about.*

Clara soothingly rocked Thomas to and fro, as the scent of roses drifted in through the bedroom window from the garden next door, filling the room, and she wondered if the old lady might not just be right, after all.

The next day dawned clear and bright. Thankfully, once Clara had managed to settle Thomas back down, the rest of the night had passed uneventfully. Even the baby had not whimpered, and although Clara was grateful for a much-needed rest, this gave her cause for concern. Her eyes settled on the infant, now changed and fed and lying placidly in his crib.

Since the day of his birth, the child had not cried once, and although he took his feeds when offered, Clara feared that all was not as it should be. She had only ever known one other baby such as this, and that had been many years ago when she lived back in her native Yorkshire. A neighbour of her mam's had given birth to a child with much the same temperament as the one that now lay before her, and as he had grown it had become apparent, to use her mam's term, that 'he was not quite right in the head'. Still, if the idea that had grown in her mind came to fruition today, then his birth could have been for a reason after all, so turning from the crib, she set about preparing the family's breakfast.

Walter had been long gone to start his shift at the pit, and although she had started to get up with him as she usually did, he had told her to have a lie-in. When she protested, he only tucked the blankets more closely about her.

'No, love,' he'd said. 'You stay where you are. I can see to me own snap tin today.'

Leaning back, Clara had smiled up at him. 'All right then,' she had agreed. 'I'll just 'ave another ten minutes or so.' But somehow, the ten minutes had turned into over an hour, and now as the porridge began to bubble she hastily sliced the bread that the lads would take to school for their lunch. When the sandwiches were filled with cheese, she wrapped them into two clean muslin cloths and placed an apple and a plum on the top of each package. She then went to the bottom of the stairs and called Thomas and Jack for their breakfast.

When the meal was over, which was a quiet affair by usual standards, Clara took up a comb and, wetting it at the sink, she slicked down first Jack's hair and then Thomas's, then catching his chin, she tipped her elder son's face up to hers. He frowned at her nervously as she gently patted his damp curls, which were already springing back into their own unruly style.

'Listen, lad,' she said quietly. 'I'm sorry if I was a bit sharp with you yesterday. Happen yer did see an angel. I've had time to think on it now.'

When he nodded his head vigorously in agreement, Clara went on, 'Well, if yer did, then it was nothing to be afraid of. I dare say it had come to guide poor Sarah to heaven, an' if anyone ever deserved a guide then it was she, 'cos she were a good lass, weren't she?'

He nodded again.

'Then happen you were privileged to see it, and shouldn't be scared – but proud, like.'

A thoughtful expression crossed the boy's face. He could see the wisdom of his mam's words and after some seconds his face broke into its usual cheeky grin. Wrapping his arms tight about her, he planted a sloppy kiss on her cheek.

'Away wi' yer now,' laughed Clara, pushing him playfully from her, and Thomas, much more his usual self again, picked up his lunch from the table and crossed to the door to join Jack, who stood waiting, impatient to be off.

Once they entered the lane, they found George and William waiting for them as usual, but no sign of Sassy. Clara raised her eyebrow at William in silent enquiry and pointing at their cottage the boy told her, 'Me dad ain't gone to work, so Sassy is stayin' to watch him, like.'

Clara forced a smile. 'Perhaps that's for the best today then, eh?'

When William nodded uncertainly she waved her hand at him, saying, 'Get yerselves away then, or you'll be late for school. An' don't get frettin' about yer dad. I'll see to him an' Sassy, an' I'll have a nice meal ready for yer when you all get back.'

Almost in step, the lads set off down the lane on their journey to Shepperton School, close to the church in Coton, where only yesterday Sarah had been buried.

By his own admittance, Thomas was not overly keen on school, much preferring to be off on some jaunt or another. Jack, on the other hand, loved it, as did Sassy, and could never have enough of the books that their teacher, Mrs Ransom, would sometimes allow them to bring home. The teacher was a generous-hearted woman who took a great interest in all the children that attended the little school. Always ready with a kind word or a smile, she was a much-loved member of the community.

Clara watched until the boys reached the end of the lane where they all turned as one to raise their hands in a final wave. Smiling, Clara waved back, thinking how strange it felt, not to have Sarah standing beside her doing the same. But as the children passed from view, Clara's smile faded and her eyes now fell on the door of Arthur's cottage.

'No work, eh?' She bit on her lip, concerned. If he didn't snap out of it soon, he would lose his job. There were always men waiting for the chance of a permanent place, and his gaffer at the pit would only make allowances for his bereavement for just so long.

Taking the few steps from her own door to Arthur's, she lifted the latch and walked in. As Sassy looked up from the sink where she was washing the breakfast pots, Clara's heart missed a beat, for she looked so like Sarah that it gave the woman a rare old turn. The boys had deep chestnut hair with blue-grey eyes like their father, while Sassy's hair was a striking dark brown and hung almost to her waist in thick, glossy ringlets. At present it was tied into the nape of her neck with a blue ribbon, but when it was worn loose it was a sight to see, although if asked, Clara would have had to say that it was Sassy's

31

eyes that were her main feature, for they were a deep dark brown, thickly fringed with dark lashes. Today, however, as they met Clara's they were red-rimmed and puffy from crying.

Without a word, Sassy pointed towards the open fire-grate, and Clara was shocked to see Arthur sitting exactly where she had left him the night before, still in his Sunday-best suit, unshaven, almost as if he were carved in stone. His thick dark hair was uncombed and his lovely blue-grey eyes had a blank look to them – yet still he managed to look handsome.

As Clara stared at him, Sassy came and stood beside her and slipped her damp little hand into hers.

'Me dad won't eat, Clara,' she whispered fearfully. 'Nor he wouldn't go to work . . . an' he wouldn't talk to George or William neither when I got 'em ready for school.'

Clara sympathetically patted the small hand that was gripping her own, almost as if it were a lifeline. 'Don't worry, lass,' she soothed. 'Your Uncle Ben and Aunt Miriam will be here soon. Happen yer Uncle Ben will talk him round. Yer have to remember, it's early days yet, an' he's suffered a grievous loss.'

Sassy turned back to the pots in the sink, her young heart heavy. She knew what Clara said was true, but hadn't they all suffered a loss? They had lost their mam, hadn't they? And one of the new babies. This morning she had nearly shouted at her dad when he ignored George and William, and even at her tender age, it had come to her then that her dad was a weak man. Why didn't he realise that they were hurting too, and needing him now more than ever?

It was then that they heard horse's hooves in the lane, and seconds after the cart stopped outside, Aunt Miriam and Uncle Ben entered the room.

Miriam's eyes went first to Arthur and then to Clara. She raised her eyebrows questioningly, but Clara could only shrug her shoulders. Gesturing towards the open doorway, the two women went outside into the lane.

'Has he not moved all night?' Miriam asked.

Clara shook her head. 'Not according to Sassy.'

'It can't go on like this; something has to be done to shake him out of it,' Miriam said worriedly.

Clara agreed, but could offer no solution, and after a few minutes more she left Miriam to begin her own daily chores, with a promise that Miriam would come around for a cup of tea later in the morning. It was then that Clara intended to put her plan into action.

By the time Clara had made the beds, swept the floor and tidied the cottage in general, it was well past eleven o'clock, so pushing the sooty kettle into the heart of the fire to boil, she measured out the tea from the caddy into the big brown teapot. She had just made the tea and laid out two cups when Miriam appeared in the open doorway.

Miriam was not what Clara would have classed as an attractive woman by any means, and yet her kindly nature made people see beyond the plain face to the true beauty that shone from within.

Entering, she immediately crossed to the crib and gazed down at the child lying there. She glanced across at Clara as if for permission to pick him up and, receiving an answering nod, she stooped and swept the baby into her arms.

Minutes later, when they were both seated at the big oak table with their tea at a safe distance before them, Clara knew that the time had come to put her plan into action, for another chance such as this might never come again.

33

Taking a big swig of tea, she looked at Miriam over the rim of her cup. 'He's a right bonny lad, don't yer think?' she said.

'Oh yes! Yes, he is indeed!' The words almost burst from Miriam's lips, and she hugged the baby to her adjusting his shawl.

''Tis him I'm most concerned about at present,' Clara confided.

Miriam looked at her questioningly and seizing the opportunity, Clara rushed on, 'I pray to God as I'm wrong, but I have the feelin' that somethin's not quite right somewhere. I've only ever known one baby as placid as him, an' to put it kindly, as that baby grew up, he were . . . a bit slow, like.'

Miriam shook her head rapidly in denial. 'Oh Clara, surely not?'

Clara explained about the child's difficult birth, before comparing him to her own two sons at that age. 'Our Thomas were the worst,' she chuckled. 'He were a right greedy little bugger, mek no mistake. I always said to my Walter, yer could have piped a cow's udder into that little devil and he'd still have yelled fer more, fer there were no fillin' him. Still ain't, fer that matter.'

All the while she was watching Miriam closely to gauge her reactions, and as she had hoped, her disclosure made Miriam draw the child closer to her. Happy in her mind now that she was doing the right thing, she continued slyly, 'I really can't see as how Arthur will cope wi' this little mite, an' the other three young 'uns an' all. But then who would take to him, if me suspicions are right?'

For a few moments, silence reigned. Miriam might have been alone in the room; she was obviously deep in thought and Clara had a feeling that her plan was working.

Suddenly pushing back the chair, Miriam carefully placed the sleeping baby back in his crib, and with a look of excitement on her face, she hurried to the door saying, 'Thanks for the tea, Clara, but I've got to speak to Ben about something. I'll be back in a while.'

'All right, lass.' As Miriam disappeared through the door, Clara chuckled to herself and, rising, she carried the two cups to the sink.

Ben was at the bottom of the garden chopping logs. His shirt was off and sweat was running down his strong back. As he saw Miriam flying down the path towards him, he stopped the axe in mid-swing and lowered it to the chopping block.

Miriam's words were tripping over each other in their haste to be told and for a while, as he tried to calm her, he couldn't understand a word she was saying. Eventually, however, she calmed down a little and when he grasped what she was proposing, his mouth gaped wide in amazement.

'Why, love!' His face expressed his wonderment. 'Arthur would never agree to that.'

Miriam shook her head, and seeing that she was not to be put off, he drew her into the shelter of the wide hawthorn hedge that hemmed the bottom of the garden and there they talked, heads close together, for almost half an hour.

Unknown to them, Clara was viewing all this from her kitchen window with a twinkle in her pale-blue eyes. Everything seemed to be going just as she had hoped.

Almost an hour later, Miriam re-entered Clara's scullery. Clara was darning in the chair at the side of the crib, and as Miriam approached she smiled in greeting.

Her friend seemed nervous. 'Ben's trying to talk to Arthur,' she told her.

Clara nodded. 'Well, let's hope he does some good then,' she said quietly and returned to her darning. Miriam once again lifted the baby from his crib and as she settled into the old rocking chair with him, the two women slipped into a companionable silence, each lost in their own thoughts.

Next door, Ben was squatting before Arthur, trying his hardest to get some reaction from him. But no matter what he said, the man just stared blankly ahead, lost in his grief. Ben was deeply frustrated. If only Arthur would look at him, answer him, or indeed do anything that would show he had even heard him!

'Oh, *Arthur* man,' he pleaded, running his hands agitatedly through his thick brown hair. 'Come on, yer have to snap out of it.' He had been trying so hard to get through to his brother-in-law that he had almost forgotten Sassy's presence in the room, but now as his eyes lit on the girl, standing pressed tight and scared against the sink, his sympathy suddenly turned to anger. Hadn't the poor child suffered enough, without having to witness this?

Crossing to her quickly, he put his arm about her quivering shoulders and led her to the front door.

'Off yer go, love,' he said kindly. 'Go down the lane and cool off a bit, eh? I'll speak to yer dad an' see if I can sort him out, eh, pet?'

When Sassy stiffened slightly in his arms, he gently pushed her through the open door. 'Go on now, lass, do it fer me,' he pleaded. An idea that might just pull Arthur from his present state had sprung to mind, and he didn't want Sassy to witness it.

Although it was obvious that she didn't want to go, she set off obediently with a heavy tread, and when she was some way down the lane, Ben turned resolutely to Arthur.

'Right then, me lad.' Grasping Arthur beneath the armpits, he almost dragged him from the chair. Once Arthur was standing, he led him through the back door and urged him on until they reached the bottom of the garden. Not until they had reached Sarah's beloved rose-bushes did Ben allow him to stop, and then he swung him about to face them.

'There now.' His voice had a hard edge to it now as he ordered, 'Look at them, Arthur. Sarah's roses – do yer remember how she loved 'em, an' tended 'em?'

Still no response. Ben was desperate now. It hurt him to see his brother-in-law so low. Reaching out, he plucked a full open rose from one of the bushes and waved it in Arthur's face. As the sweet scent of the flower reached the man's nostrils, Ben could have sworn that he felt him react, and encouraged now, he went on, 'Arthur, me man, Sarah would be brokenhearted if she could see yer like this. She loved you, an' she loved the little 'uns an' all. *Surely* you owe it to her to go on, even if it's only for their sakes?'

Arthur's hand hesitantly reached out to take the rose from Ben's shaking fingers. As his eyes lingered on it, Ben saw recognition in them for the first time since his wife had died. Offering up a silent prayer of thanks, he grabbed Arthur and pulled him close, and as their cheeks touched, the two men's tears mingled and fell together, as Arthur let out his pent-up feelings in a cleansing explosion of grief.

Chapter Five

When Sassy returned from her stroll almost two hours later, it was to see her dad shaven and changed, sitting at the table with Ben, eating a meal that Miriam had prepared for him. As she entered the room, he looked up and smiled at her, and her young heart leaped with relief. Although his eyes were red-rimmed and his fingers shook, she felt he had returned to them again, and she flashed a look of pure gratitude towards her Uncle Ben.

Next door, Miriam was standing nervously at the side of the table as Clara kneaded a pile of dough on the floured surface.

'Clara . . .' She gulped deep in her throat before summoning up every ounce of courage she had and saying, 'What do you think Arthur would say if Ben and I were to offer to take the baby for a time?'

As Clara raised her eyes to Miriam's her hands became still.

'Just for a time of course,' the woman gabbled on. 'To help him out, like.'

Clara dropped her eyes back to the dough and now her hands began to knead the mound in front of her again as she replied calmly, 'Well, I can't say what Arthur would think, but it sounds like a damn good idea to me – if you think you can manage him, o' course. Happen I should have thought of it meself. What does Ben think to yer idea?'

'Oh, he's all for it, but I haven't put it to Arthur yet. I thought I'd ask your opinion first.'

Clara rested her floury hands on the table. 'Then, now you have, perhaps you should put it to him. I'm thinking the poor bloke has a lot on his plate to deal wi' at present, without having to worry about an infant an' all.'

She chuckled, feeling well pleased with herself, as Miriam turned and hurried excitedly from the room. If Arthur agreed, then at least some good would have come from all this heartbreak. If Miriam and Ben took the baby, he would want for nothing, and a childless couple would have their greatest wish fulfilled. Oh! She hoped it would work out – then poor Sarah's death would not have been all in vain.

Next door, Miriam spotted her niece as she entered Arthur's kitchen, saying casually, 'Clara's baking and she thought you might like to give her a hand, Sassy, pet.'

The child nodded eagerly; she loved to help Clara with her twice-weekly baking sessions. Needing no second bidding, she headed for the door, rolling her sleeves up as she went.

Miriam then seated herself at the table with Ben and Arthur, and after receiving an encouraging nod from Ben, she put the proposition to Arthur. He listened intently as she spoke and when no answer was immediately forthcoming, she took his hand across the table.

'It was only a thought, love,' she said sadly. 'We wouldn't dream of taking your lad unless you were willing.'

For some minutes, her brother sat deep in thought, while Miriam and Ben held their breath, but then he looked up slowly to gaze from one to the other. 'I think it's a fine idea,' he said. 'Happen you two could give him more than I ever could, an' as I'm back at work tomorrer, our Sassy will have enough on her plate carin' for the other two.'

Miriam could scarcely conceal the look of pure joy that crossed her face.

'There's just one thing I'd ask of you though,' he went on.

Both pairs of eyes looked at him questioningly and at that moment in time they would have agreed to anything.

'Sarah was set on calling him James if it were a lad, after her dad.'

'Oh yes, that's a lovely name,' Miriam agreed enthusiastically.

'Then it will be as you suggest,' Arthur stated. 'I'll start collectin' his things together. Most of 'em are round at Clara's. The poor little mite has spent most of his time there since . . .' Unable to go on, he lowered his head.

'We'll take such great care of him, I promise,' Miriam whispered softly.

'Aye, I know you will, love, I know.' And so saying, he quietly left the room to climb the stairs for the first time since Sarah's death.

The children had long since returned from school, and with their bellies full of the tasty meal their Aunt Miriam had cooked for them, they were now playing in the lane – all, that is, except Thomas, who was late as usual.

The cart was piled with the baby's belongings, including his crib, and Ben was keen to return to his smallholding. He had neglected it for days and was aware that the animals would be waiting to be fed.

William and George had been fairly unconcerned about their brother's imminent departure, but Sassy had taken it badly. Now her eyes were even redder and puffier than they had been this morning, for in the days following the birth she had come to love her baby brother dearly.

Aunt Miriam hugged her fiercely as she looked down

40

into her sad little face. 'You'll see him every week, Sassy, I promise,' she whispered. 'And we will still come every Sunday afternoon, just as we always have.'

Sassy nodded numbly, and seeing that Ben was growing impatient, Miriam scrambled aboard the cart to sit beside him. Clara handed the child up to her, wrapped in one of the shawls that Sarah herself had knitted for him, and Miriam held the child tightly to her breast. Then with a wave they were off, and as the cart trundled down the lane, Sassy felt that she had lost yet another person she loved.

Thomas finally arrived home as dusk was settling, sporting a big black eye, and he soon received yet another injury as Clara cuffed him soundly around the ear.

'Eeh, lad,' she said furiously. 'Look at the state o' you. You've been fighting again, ain't yer?' When Thomas hung his head and didn't deny it, she sighed deeply and wagged her finger in his face. 'I'm tellin' yer now, fightin' will be the death o' you,' she warned, then slipped away to check on the family next door, before settling down to enjoy a glass of ale with Walter before retiring to bed.

She found Sassy sitting at the side of the fire with her head deep in a copy of *The Coral Island*, a thrilling adventure book that Mrs Ransom, her adored teacher, had sent home with Jack for her to read, to help take her mind off things for at least a short while.

Sassy had scrubbed George and William in the tin bath that hung on the wall outside the scullery door, and now they were both fast asleep upstairs in the double bed they shared.

'Me dad is asleep an' all, an' has been all afternoon,' she solemnly informed Clara.

Clara was pleased to hear it. She was a firm believer

that sleep was a great healer, and to her mind that was just what Arthur needed right now.

'Is there anythin' that you need doin', lass?' she asked softly.

The girl's head moved from side to side.

'Right then, in that case I'll be away. You just bang on the wall should you need me.' After assurances from Sassy that she wouldn't stay up too much longer, she dropped a kiss on the glossy dark head and headed back to the promised glass of ale.

As the door closed behind her, Sassy smiled to herself. Eeh, she loved Clara, and wondered what her family would have done without the kindly little woman this week. Trying not to think about her mam, her eyes dropped back to the book in her lap, and promising herself that she would only read to the bottom of the next page, she again lost herself in the exciting story.

Clara was snuggled next to Walter on the wooden settle. His arm was comfortable about her shoulders as she kicked off her old slippers and held her aching feet out to the warming glow of the fire. Even though it was midsummer, most of the cottages kept a low fire burning, for the stone walls could strike a chill.

Clara recounted to him Ben's struggle with Arthur earlier, and Walter listened intently as she told him of Miriam's suggestion to take the baby. Although he heartily agreed that it was for the best, knowing Clara as he did, somehow the story didn't quite ring true. Turning his wife's face to his, he tipped her chin up and looked deep into her eyes.

'*You* wouldn't happen to have had anything to do with putting the idea into Miriam's head, would yer, woman?' There was a twinkle in his eyes.

'Why, Walter Mallabone, I can't *think* what you're

42

implying,' she said, blushing. Then she chuckled, and as their shoulders touched, their laughter joined and echoed from the walls of the cottage for the first time in days.

Eventually Walter stood up and pulled Clara to her feet, and as he did so, his hand slid down to pat her bottom suggestively. 'Come on, woman.' He winked cheekily. 'I reckon our bed's callin' us.'

Laughing, she slapped his hand away. 'Why, you randy old bugger you. Be off wi' yer.' But even as she spoke, she was following him to the bottom of the stairs. There she paused to turn and glance about the humble home that was her palace, and solemn again now, she offered up a silent prayer that the worst was over and that things could now return to some sort of normality.

PART TWO

New Year, 1874

Gypsy Magic

Chapter Six

It was New Year's Eve. Tomorrow would be the start of a brand new year – 1874 – and Sassy was feeling very excited. Putting down the copy of *Through the Looking Glass and What Alice Found There* that her dad had bought her for Christmas, to go with *Alice's Adventures in Wonderland*, she stood on tiptoe to peer at herself in her own looking-glass.

Oh, it's going to be a grand party tonight, she thought happily. Her dad had promised her that tonight, for the first time, she could stay up right until the New Year was seen in. At midnight, Walter would carry in a piece of coal on a shovel, passing right through the cottage, letting out the old year and seeing in the new, and then, while Jimmy Wainthrop attempted to tap a tune on the piano that had been dragged from the corner of the parlour, they would all join hands and sing 'Auld Lang Syne'. Crossing to the window, she lifted the curtain aside and peeped into the lane. The snow had stopped falling, and as she gazed across the quarry to the fields and the spinney beyond, she caught her breath in wonder. The stars were twinkling high in the sky, and the light they cast on the freshly fallen snow made it sparkle as if it had been sprinkled with diamonds.

All along the row of cottages, Sassy could hear doors opening and shutting, and laughter floating on the air, along with echoing shouts of, 'a Happy New Year!'

Hurrying towards the bedroom door, she took one last

glance at herself in the mirror. She was wearing the dress that the Widow Bonner had given to her some months earlier. It had belonged to Louise, the widow's daughter, and had been much too big for Sassy, but Clara had done wonders with it. A tuck here and a tuck there, and now it fitted a treat. It was a rich deep blue in colour and set off Sassy's colouring to perfection. It was also of a far superior quality to anything she had ever owned, and because it was so pretty, Sassy had saved it for weeks, even after Clara had altered it, especially for tonight. About her neck she wore her mother's silver locket, which her father had given to her some weeks after Sarah's death. The locket had belonged to Sarah's mother before her, and had been the only piece of jewellery that Sarah had ever owned, save for her wedding ring, which had been buried with her. Because it had belonged to her mother and her grandmother, Sassy treasured the locket dearly and it only saw daylight on high days and holidays.

Although she was only twelve years old, whenever she wore it, Sassy would finger the finely engraved silver lovingly and dream of a day when perhaps she too would have a daughter to pass the locket on to.

Taking the stairs two at a time, Sassy rushed down to join in the merriment. The parlour, only ever used on special occasions, had a cheery fire burning brightly in the grate and the best chenille tablecloth had been folded all along the length of the heavy oak sideboard. It was now laden with frothy jugs of ale and bottles of home-made wine, which friends and neighbours would help themselves to as they passed from one cottage to another.

George and William were scrubbed and in their pyjamas. It was already well past their bedtimes, but Arthur had agreed that they could stay up a little later tonight and they were now both clutching a large glass of homemade lemonade in one hand and one of Clara's delicious mince pies in the other. Their heads were close together and they were giggling. There were some in the room who had already had more than enough wine and ale than was usual, including Arthur, which the boys found highly amusing.

As Sassy's eyes followed the boys to her dad, she too giggled. It was good to see him looking so carefree for a change. Unbidden, a happy little bubble of excitement rose up in her again, and her eyes came to rest on Thomas, who was standing close beside the window, gazing out across the quarry to the fields beyond. He put Sassy in mind of a caged animal, for he only ever appeared to be truly happy when he was out in the open air. Be it hail, rain, sun or snow it made no difference to him, just so long as he could be wandering. Clara often commented that Thomas should have been born a gypsy, like the ones with whom he spent so much of his time.

As always, at the sight of him, Sassy's heart beat faster. At sixteen, he was already taller than Walter, standing almost six feet tall in his stockinged feet. His body was heavy but muscular, and with his unruly mop of black hair and blue eyes, there was not a single girl hereabouts who didn't have her sights set on him.

A gentle hand on her elbow caused her to drag her eyes away from Thomas, and turning she found Jack smiling shyly at her.

'You look really beautiful, Sassy,' he told her.

Sassy blushed a deep red. 'Thank you, Jack.' He had recently gone to work on the farm with his Uncle Ben, and the time spent out in the fresh air had lent colour to his cheeks. Sassy envied him in a way for having a job. Had it not been for the fact that she was needed at home to look after the family, she might have been working herself by now. But then she didn't begrudge caring for her brothers and her father.

With her hair brushed until it shone hanging loose about her shoulders, and wearing the beautiful dress that showed off her just blossoming figure, Jack could hardly drag his eyes away from her.

Out of the corner of her eye, Sassy saw her dad ushering the boys towards the stairs and as she left Jack's side to help tuck them into bed, his gaze followed her across the room.

His gaze was not lost on Clara, and she clucked her tongue worriedly. It was already obvious where Sassy's affections lay and they certainly weren't with Jack, more was the pity. Still, determined that nothing should spoil this special night, she turned back to the women who sat hunched close together, enjoying a good old gossip and soon, for now, she forgot about everything else.

One of the items of gossip on the agenda was the widow, Elizabeth Bonner, absent tonight, though a frequent visitor of late.

As Clara whispered wickedly, 'She's trying to sink her hooks into Arthur, you just mark me words.' Which caused yet another fit of giggling to erupt amongst the women.

'But why would she want him? He ain't got two brass farthings to rub together,' one of them commented.

'No, he ain't, that's true,' Clara retorted indignantly. 'But she's got enough money fer both of 'em an' he's a good-lookin' bugger. What's more, she were married to a working man afore.'

Just as Sassy had anticipated, it was indeed a grand party. By the end of the night, the furniture was pushed right back against the walls and with old Jimmy Wainthrop, as usual the worse for drink, belting out some popular tunes on the piano, everyone was enjoying a good old knees-up. Even the elderly Grandmother Cox, who would normally long since have been away to her bed, suddenly hitched up her long skirt to display her bony, boot-clad ankles, and after pulling Arthur into the centre of the room, she then proceeded to do an Irish jig with him, which caused a wave of hilarity to sweep the room.

As the clock on the mantelpiece struck twelve, a hush fell as Walter performed the solemn duty of letting in the New Year, then with this done, hilarity again reigned and everyone formed a large circle as best they could in the small confined space, to join hands and sing 'Auld Lang Syne'.

Rushing to Thomas, Sassy grabbed him by the hand and dragged him into the circle while Jack held fast to her other hand and the merriment continued.

It was now almost one o'clock in the morning and the last of the merrymakers were leaving, some having to be helped away amongst much laughter and shouting. Sassy's face ached from smiling and she was sure that this had been the best night of her whole life.

Clara helped her to carry the dirty glasses and plates to the sink, where she dumped them unceremoniously in a great pile, telling Sassy in a thickened voice; 'Leave 'em there, lass. They'll keep till the mornin'.'

This sent Sassy into another fit of the giggles; she had never seen Clara, as Walter called it, 'tiddly' before. The woman's hair, which she usually wore in a tight bun at the back of her head, had come loose, and wisps were now floating all around her glowing cheeks, which together with her unsteady step and overly bright eyes, gave her a comical appearance.

A sudden rush of love for this kindly woman, who for nearly four years had been as a mother to her, swept

51

through Sassy, and she hugged her fiercely. The hug was returned, for although Clara had always had a great fondness for this child, over the last years, it had grown into a love that matched that which she felt for her own children.

By the time Walter managed to drag Clara away, the snow, which had lain like a clean white sheet in the lane at the beginning of the night, was now slushy underfoot from the many comings and goings. With her dad's arm about her shoulders, Sassy giggled as they watched the couple stagger to their own door. It was difficult to say who was helping whom. Both had had more than their fair share of ale and wine throughout the night, and as they clung together, slipping and sliding, their muttered oaths hung in the air.

'Ouch, Walter Mallabone!' whittered Clara. 'Keep yer clod-hoppin' feet to yerself, will yer? You just walloped me ankle.'

'No, I did not, woman,' Walter denied indignantly between hiccups. ''Twere you as kicked mine.' And so it continued until at last they reached their door and disappeared from sight.

Still laughing, Arthur and Sassy stood for some seconds, looking past the slushy lane to the view beyond. As their laughter died they slipped into a companionable silence, broken eventually by Sassy, who whispered, 'It's been a grand night, ain't it, Dad?'

Arthur nodded his head in reply. 'It has that, my lass, it has that. Now let's hope the year to follow will be as good, eh?'

Sassy awoke the next morning to the sound of her dad raking out the fire. She stretched her legs out as far as she could and then pulled them back almost to her chin, wrapping her arms tight about her knees. Rolling into a tight little ball beneath the warm blankets, she allowed her mind to drift back over the night before, and even before she was properly awake, she was smiling, for the warm happy feeling was still there. Today her Aunt Miriam and Uncle Ben were bringing James, who was now almost four years old, to spend the whole day with them. Not only that, but her Aunt Miriam had promised to cook the New Year's Day dinner, so Sassy could have the whole day to herself.

Her mind full of these cheery thoughts, she eventually left the comfort of the cosy bed, and pushing her feet into the slippers that Clara had bought her for Christmas, she gathered up the shawl that lay on the nearby chair and wrapped it tightly about her. Her brothers' bed was empty and their day clothes were gone, which meant they were probably already downstairs having breakfast. Reaching the window, she drew back the curtains. Overnight the glass had frozen and was so heavily patterned with ice that it was impossible to see through it. Leaning close, Sassy blew her warm breath on it until a corner began to melt, and then quickly wiping it with the cuff of her cotton nightgown she cleared a little space, just enough to see through.

The sight that met her eyes caused her to gasp in wonder, for overnight the snow had begun to fall again and the slushy lane was now once more transformed into a thick white carpet. Snowflakes were gently falling and just for a moment Sassy bit her lip in consternation.

What if Aunt Miriam and Uncle Ben couldn't get through, she fretted, but then squaring her shoulders, she turned away. She didn't want anything to spoil this happy mood that was upon her, and anyway, knowing them, they would get here, come hell or high water. They had never broken a promise as yet.

Hurrying across to the china jug she tipped some water

into a matching bowl, and after pulling her nightgown over her head, had a hasty wash in the icy water. Then after dressing and tidying the beds, she went downstairs to join her dad and the boys. It was almost eleven o'clock before Aunt Miriam, Uncle Ben and James arrived, although by then, the snow was now so deep that the Churms didn't even hear the approach of the horse and cart. Aunt Miriam burst in first with James, who was almost twice his size in his many layers of clothes, in her arms.

'Eeh,' she laughed as she approached the fire. 'It's enough to freeze the hairs on a brass monkey out there.'

Sassy took James from her while Aunt Miriam hurried back outside to help Uncle Ben in with the huge hamper full of goodies from off the back of the cart.

Uncle Ben then led the horse off down the lane where he could be comfortably stabled for the day in Grandmother Cox's huge outhouse. Arthur and Sassy had long since washed the pile of dishes left overnight in the sink, the oak table was once again cleared and scrubbed, and Aunt Miriam was unloading the hamper on top of it. There was a large leg of pork, still warm from the oven even after the journey, a huge ham, dishes of various vegetables, all prepared ready for cooking, and a large apple pie, along with mince pies and so many other treats that Sassy found it hard to keep her mind on what she was doing – which was peeling off the many layers of clothes on James, one by one. All the while she was doing this, his blue-grey eyes never left her face. He was a handsome little chap, the double of his brothers in looks, but sadly Clara's prediction had proved to be true, for although he was a bonny child, as he grew it became apparent that he was, as Clara put it kindly, 'slow'. He hadn't walked until he was two and a half years old, and even now at almost four, he could say only a very few words. But for all that he had a trusting, smiling temperament and Miriam and Ben adored him.

When at last his outer clothes were piled on the chair at the side of the fire, Sassy pulled him into a warm embrace, then holding him from her, she smiled at him lovingly. The child returned her look straight-faced. His mouth was opening and shutting soundlessly, reminding Sassy of a goldfish in a glass bowl she had seen once at the fair. When Miriam saw what was happening, she hurried to his side and encouraged, 'Go on, James, you can do it.'

The child's head turned for an instant to gaze at Miriam, but then turning back again he looked deep into his sister's eyes and, obviously trying very hard, he opened his mouth. 'S . . . Sassy,' he said haltingly.

The look that lit Sassy's face was one of pure joy. 'Oh James, you *clever*, clever boy!' She laughed through her tears, as the little chap proudly puffed out his chest.

Uncle Ben was back by now, and soon the preparations for the New Year's Day dinner were under way. When Sassy offered to help, Aunt Miriam turned from the stove and shook a wooden spoon at her.

'Where are George and William?' she asked mock sternly.

'I dare say they'll be sliding about on the canal by now or making a snowman,' replied Sassy.

'Well then, young lady,' said her aunt kindly, 'you get your warm clothes on and go and join 'em, 'cos as I told you, this is your day off.'

Beaming all over her face, Sassy did as she was told, and was soon making her way through the deep snow down the lane towards the canal. She had a feeling that Thomas and Jack would be there too, for there were four sets of footprints leading away down the track. One set was much bigger than the others – Thomas's, she thought, and was proved to be right when, as she rounded the bend in the lane, she saw him on the heavy rope swing that hung from the great oak tree, sailing from one side of the canal to the other. He made a comical sight, for as his weight shook the tree, great clods of snow were falling onto him and his dark hair looked as if it had turned white. Sassy was standing enjoying the scene before her when there was a flash of movement to her side and she was just in time to see a small grey rabbit appear from the snow. He had obviously left his burrow unaware of the weather, and as the snow stuck to his twitching little whiskers, he turned about, shook his bobtail as if in disgust, and quickly disappeared back the way he had come.

Grinning to herself Sassy looked at the figures at the bottom of the hill. George and William were slipping and sliding about on the icy canal, more on their bottoms than on their feet, and Jack, who was unable to join in because of his lame leg, was finishing off a large snowman that George and William had started.

Sassy felt deeply sorry for Jack; she of all people knew how much his limp troubled him. Clara had recently spoken to the local cobbler about making him a built-up boot for his short leg, and although the man had never attempted such a thing before, he had taken Jack's measurements, and sent word to Clara that the boots would be ready early in the New Year.

Sassy was looking forward to the arrival of these boots almost as much as Jack was. She felt it could make a big difference to his confidence, and she loved Jack dearly, almost as a brother. After standing for some seconds enjoying the picture that they made as the boys frolicked and larked about, she then carefully picked her way towards the merry crowd. It was when she was almost upon them, that she noticed two other figures approaching from the opposite direction, along the towpath. One was a tall, dark-haired youth, of about the same height as Thomas, and the other a girl of much slighter build who looked to be around her own age. It was the colour of their clothes that caught Sassy's eye first. Even at this distance they were attired in clothes the like of which she had never seen before. They had almost reached the rope swing when Thomas caught sight of them and his pleasure was plain to see. He immediately leaped from the rope and landed sure-footedly almost at their feet.

After shaking the boy firmly by the hand he then turned to the girl and enclosed both her small hands in his large ones before bending to whisper something into her ear. Seconds later, their laughter joined and rose into the chilly air.

Sassy had now reached Jack, who had temporarily abandoned his attempts at finishing the snowman, and was gazing across the iced-over canal, as much interested in the newcomers as Sassy was. George and William, however, after a cursory glance at the brightly clad pair, turned their attentions back to each other and the snowball fight they were involved in.

As Sassy saw Thomas's pleasure as he spoke to the girl, a funny unknown feeling seemed to flutter in her heart, and she didn't like it. It seemed to wipe away all the other happy feelings of the last few days in a minute.

The girl's eyes had now left Thomas's and fastened on her, and turning from her, Thomas smiled and beckoned Sassy to join them. She picked her way unsteadily across the icy canal until she stood opposite the girl.

'Sassy,' Thomas beamed. 'This is Ellie and Jez, her brother.'

Jez flashed an admiring smile at her, revealing a set of gleaming teeth that appeared even whiter against the swarthiness of his skin. His hair, which Sassy guessed must have reached way past his shoulders, was tied into the nape of his neck, where it sprang into jet-black curls, and from one of his earlobes hung a small golden ring. Despite the bitter cold, Jez wore no coat, only a full-sleeved shirt, which was covered by a multi-coloured embroidered waistcoat, and on his muscular legs he wore trousers that were so tight, Sassy wondered how he managed to walk without splitting them. The thought brought a smile to her face and she had to stop herself from giggling. But if she found Jez's looks amazing, when her eyes settled on Ellie, she found herself totally fascinated, for never in her young life had she seen anyone so beautiful. Standing there beside her in her drab dark coat, Sassy felt colourless by comparison.

Ellie seemed to possess an almost fragile beauty and held herself proudly as if she was well aware of it. Her thick straight black hair fell way below her waist and shimmered as brightly as the large golden hoops that hung from her ears. Her skin, lighter than her brother's, was olive-coloured, and she had huge luminous dark brown eyes. About her slim shoulders she wore a deep blue cloak that reached to her knees, and from beneath the cloak billowed a full-length crimson skirt, the colour brilliant against the contrast of the snow.

So dark and so colourful were the two standing before her, that to Sassy they appeared foreign. By now Thomas and Jez were deep in conversation, and Sassy realised with a start that Ellie was studying her as intently as she had studied her. The smile she flashed Sassy was warm and full of fun, and her eyes twinkled with mischief. Sassy had, in fact, already guessed at the identity of the two even before Thomas had introduced them, for on the rare occasions when Sassy did manage to get him to herself for a few minutes and draw him into conversation, his talk would invariably turn to his gypsy friends.

Although Sassy had formed a picture of them in her mind, nothing he had said could have prepared her for actually meeting them face-to-face.

It was just then that a cry of distress rent the air, and Sassy was so bewitched by the gypsy girl that she turned her head almost impatiently from her, to find the cause of the noise. On seeing George, who was sprawled upon the canal and howling lustily, she sprang onto the ice, the gypsies forgotten, and within seconds was kneeling at his side. He was wailing loudly as huge tears coursed down his cheeks, and pointing to his ankle.

Sassy tried to soothe him as Jack, who had reached him almost as quickly as she had, gently prodded and turned the injured foot, while William looked on white-faced. When Jack raised his eyes eventually he winked at George.

'It's all right, lad,' he soothed. 'There don't appear to be nothin' broken. Happen you just twisted it as you fell, eh?'

George nodded tearfully and, greatly relieved, Sassy stood up. With Jack's aid, she pulled her brother to his feet, then together they helped him to hobble to the bank of the canal. By now his sobs had dropped to hiccuping sniffles and he was feeling very sorry for himself.

'I tell yer what,' said Jack kindly. 'How about I piggy-back you up the hill, eh?' Without further ado he bent over, and with Sassy and William's assistance, George clambered onto his back, already much happier at the prospect of his ride.

Sassy had misgivings about whether Jack could manage the climb. The ground was treacherously slippery but, despite his limp, Jack was a strong lad and set off with a will. By the time they had almost reached the bend in the lane, they were all once again in good spirits, and as if suddenly remembering his brother, Jack stopped and turned back.

'Hi, Thomas!' he shouted.

Still deep in conversation with the gypsies, Thomas glanced up.

'You'd best be joinin' us. If you're late fer dinner again, Mam'll skelp yer backside.'

The older boy flapped his hand impatiently. 'Tell her I'll be there in a minute,' he said, and turned back to his friends, Jack and his dinner already forgotten.

Jack shrugged. 'What's the bettin' he'll be late then?' he sighed, and turning about he continued his climb.

Sassy raised her hand in a final salute to Ellie and the girl returned it. Then almost struggling to keep up, she followed Jack. They were nearing the next bend in the lane that joined the path leading to the Punch Bowl Inn, when old Jimmy Wainthrop came staggering towards them. They heard him before actually seeing him, for he was singing merrily to himself. The snow was once again falling, not in gentle flakes this time, but in thick white sheets, and Jimmy looked like a snowman. His cap was thickly covered with it and he had fallen down so many times that it was hard to see the colour of his clothes.

'I wouldn't like to be in his shoes when he gets in,' Jack whispered. 'If I know Connie he'll be havin' a taste o' the rollin'-pin this day.'

Sassy grinned, picturing the scene in her mind.

What Jack said was true. Many a night, Connie Wainthrop could be heard raving at her husband when he arrived home the worse for drink, following one of his binges. Although Jimmy was a likeable rogue, Sassy felt sorry for Connie. It was a well-known fact that Jimmy liked a flutter and more than the odd pint, which meant that the poor woman had to try to feed and clothe their eight children as best she could with the odd bit of money that didn't pass over the bar of the Punch Bowl.

As they continued, the group grew quiet. The snow was coming down with a vengeance now and it took them all of their time and effort just to stay on their feet. They were all short of breath when at last the cottages on Tuttle Hill came into sight.

As they approached, Sassy stared at the handsome horse and trap that was standing outside her door and her heart sank to her boots.

It appeared that the Widow Bonner was paying them a visit again. Sassy supposed she ought to feel grateful. The Widow always came bearing gifts, and yet somehow, she never felt easy in her presence and just couldn't seem to take to her. Perhaps it was because her smile never seemed to reach her eyes – until she smiled at her dad, that was, and then they became almost hungry.

Ah well, Sassy chided herself. Me dad would never look the side she's on anyway, and somewhat reassured, she now lifted George from poor Jack's aching back and ushered him to the door, flashing Jack a grateful smile.

Chapter Seven

On entering the room, Sassy felt a little easier when she saw that the Widow was pulling on her gloves and preparing to leave. Sassy smiled at her politely as she pushed George towards the fire and the woman coldly acknowledged her. Then turning back to Arthur after the distraction of the children's entrance, her smile once again warmed. 'So, shall I see you at church on Sunday then, Arthur?'

He nodded. 'Aye, you will. Weather permittin', o' course.'

Inclining her head towards the others in the room she now swept towards the door and with a final nod at Miriam who was silently holding it open for her, she left with a swish of her fashionable silk skirts.

The snow was almost blizzard-like now, and when Miriam eventually managed to close the door, she leaned against it.

'Phew!' she laughed and everyone joined in, not sure if they were laughing at Miriam's struggle with the gale or the woman's departure.

Next door, Jack was pulling his wet boots and socks from his feet and Clara was busy putting out the New Year's Day dinner, which made the lad's stomach grumble with anticipation at the smell of it.

Clara was much the worse for wear today. Her head felt woolly and her tongue seemed to be cleaving to the roof of her mouth, although this had brought forth no sympathy from Walter. 'Serves yerself right, woman,' he told her self-righteously. As Jack told her of George's mishap on the frozen canal, she tutted, asking, 'Is the little 'un all right?'

Jack laughed. 'Oh aye, Mam, he's as right as ninepence. I reckon it just shook him up more than anythin'.'

'That's all right then,' she said, as she battled the huge roast from the stove to the table. 'But where's our Thomas?'

Jack glanced worriedly at his dad, as if aware of the storm about to break, and Walter raised his eyebrows. When Jack didn't immediately answer her, Clara glared at him suspiciously.

'Well, lad, did yer not hear me?' she barked. 'Has the cat got yer tongue or sommat?'

Without meeting her eyes, Jack replied, 'No, Mam, the cat ain't got me tongue, an' the last I saw o' Thomas he were down by the canal.'

'Why didn't he come back wi' you lot then?' Clara was not to be put off so easily.

'He were talkin' to some friends and said to tell you he'll be back shortly.'

'*What* friends?'

Taking a deep breath, Jack mumbled, 'I er . . . I reckon they were gypsies.'

Clara almost dropped the carving knife in her indignation, and seemed to swell to twice her size. 'I'll box that little bugger's ears, you just see if I don't,' she declared. 'I've told him no good will come o' mixin wi' the likes o' them, but will he listen to me? O' course, he won't, 'cos the little sod thinks he knows the lot.' And with that she attacked the joint, muttering to herself whilst Walter and Jack wisely held their tongues. They both knew better than to mix with Clara when she had a mood on her.

Although Walter held his peace, he too was deeply

concerned about Thomas. He had hoped that once the lad began work with him at the pit, he would calm down a bit, but if anything he had grown worse lately, and each day as he followed the pit ponies into the bowels of the earth, Thomas looked like a man going to his doom. He always walked ahead in the mornings as Walter followed on with Arthur at a more leisurely pace. Walter was painfully aware that Thomas had missed a lot of shifts lately and the gaffer was becoming impatient. There were always men willing to take his place as he had pointed out to Walter. And yet no matter how many shifts he missed, still on pay day he would tip his mam's share of his wages onto the table, which caused Walter even more cause for concern, for where was he getting his money from? And it was not only that; lately he seemed to be always sporting a black eye or other minor injuries. Walter had wisely kept Thomas's absences from work from Clara as yet, but he knew that eventually she would find out and the thought caused him to quake inside. Knowing his fiery little wife as he did, he had no doubt that all hell would be let loose.

It was a somewhat subdued trio that sat down at the table for the New Year's Day dinner, for Thomas was usually the one who kept the conversation going. Once or twice Clara's eyes rested on Jack and she could only wonder at the difference between her sons. They were as different as chalk from cheese, not perhaps in looks, but in nature. There was Thomas on the one hand, not a bad lad really, but never happy except when wandering. And Jack on the other hand, never more content than when sitting at the fireside. It amazed Clara that two so different boys could have come from the same womb. Then to take it to the other extreme, there were George and William next door, so similar in every way that they could have been two peas in a pod. Eeh! she thought to herself. Life's a funny thing.

They were just about to start their pudding when Thomas suddenly appeared and stamped the snow from his shoes before joining them all at the table.

'About time too,' Clara snapped. She fetched his dinner from the oven and slammed it down in front of him and then they all concentrated on their food.

During the afternoon the weather worsened, and Miriam and Ben decided to leave earlier than expected. They were gravely concerned that if they left it much later, they would never make it back to the smallholding. The snow was falling faster by the minute, and it turned out that they did right, for by the time evening had set in, it had drifted halfway up the door.

George and William needed no urging to their beds that night. The festivities of the last few days had caught up with them and their eyes were closing even as Sassy tucked the blankets about them. She stood for some seconds, gazing fondly down on them as they snuggled closer together. George was now fully recovered from his fall on the canal, although he had certainly made the most of all the fuss and attention it brought him. He'd had poor William running around after him, fetching and carrying, much to everyone's amusement, all afternoon. Now, after taking one last peep at them, Sassy crept across the room and closed the bedroom door softly behind her.

Arthur was battling his way through the blustering snow to the henhouse that stood in the shelter of the hawthorn hedge at the bottom of the garden, to throw some corn to the hens and hopefully collect some eggs for breakfast. It was a job that he usually enjoyed, and on many a fine night, he could often be seen, sitting beside Sarah's beloved rosebed, quietly drawing on his pipe. His mind would then drift back to happier times as he gazed up the hill to the five-sail windmill that stood atop it, seeming to stand guard over the little row of cottages. It was a fine windmill, one of only very few of its kind in the whole of the country, but tonight Arthur could hardly see his hand in front of him, let alone the windmill, and so after attending to the hens as quickly as possible, he hurried back to the comforting warmth of the little scullery.

After stamping the snow from his boots and hanging his hat and coat on the nail on the back of the door, he crossed to the table, where Sassy was sitting reading by the light of the paraffin lamp.

Pulling out a chair, he joined her. 'If this keeps up all night, I reckon we'll have a job to get to work tomorrer,' he commented. Sassy nodded in reply. A silence then settled on the room until some time later when Sassy closed the chapter on Tweedledum and Tweedledee and let out a loud yawn.

Her father gently prodded her arm and nodded towards the stairs. 'Go on, young lady.' he ordered. 'Get yerself off to bed. I'll finish off down here.'

Flashing him a grateful smile, Sassy planted a kiss on his cheek before heading off up to her room.

Within moments she was undressed and pulling on her flanelette nightgown that her dad had left wrapped around a stone hot water bottle and, shivering, she jumped into her bed and pulled herself into a tight ball. In no time at all the gentle snores coming from George and William next door lulled her off to sleep, and her dreams were full of a beautiful black-haired gypsy girl dancing around a campfire.

The snow continued to fall for another two whole weeks. Although the men managed to get to work, their days were much longer. They had to leave earlier in the morning and were arriving home later in the evening tired to the bone, not only from their long shifts but also from their journey through the deep snow.

For now, the local families had sacrificed their Sunday morning church services, preferring instead to stay within the warmth of the cottages. Sassy missed the outings, her only consolation being that there was a temporary absence of the Widow Bonner. Thankfully, it seemed that even she was unwilling to face the elements.

Sassy and Clara had also stopped their weekly visits to the market. They were lucky enough to still have plenty of fruit and vegetables stored from the summer or stewed and bottled in the cold stone cellars beneath the cottages.

Clara developed a cold and soon it turned into a terrible hacking cough. Walter was all for calling the doctor out but Clara would have none of it.

'Wastin' yer money on him indeed,' she muttered. 'Grandmother Cox'll mix me a cough potion as will have me right as rain in no time.'

Knowing better than to argue, Walter wisely held his tongue.

However, Clara did reluctantly agree to Sassy lending a hand about the cottage.

'Just till I'm back on me feet, like,' she croaked, and Sassy was only too happy to oblige; there was nothing she wouldn't have done for this kindly neighbour. She knew that she owed Clara a debt she could never repay. It was Clara who had taught her to wash, clean, iron, and keep house in general. In fact, under Clara's guidance, Sassy was now a very good little cook in her own right, although it hadn't always been so. There had been many a time in the weeks following Sarah's death that Clara, seeing the child out of her depth and almost at the end of her tether, had herself taken over the running of the Churms' home with never a word of complaint, and Sassy would never forget this.

Following the snow came the rain, and bitterly cold days that brought them almost to the end of January. Sassy had washed their dinner pots up and was now standing at Clara's sink washing hers. She enjoyed the excuse to be in the Mallabones' cottage at this time of the day, for it meant that she got to see Thomas when he returned from his shift at the pit. But tonight she was disappointed when Walter arrived home alone.

'Where's the lad then?' asked Clara, staring at her husband, and when he looked shifty and mumbled something in reply, she shook her head in exasperation.

'That lad,' she clucked disapprovingly. 'Stick his dinner in the oven, Sassy, and if it dries up then it's his own bloody fault.'

Sassy did as she was told and there it remained until it was so dried up it was inedible. Thomas had missed yet another shift as Walter was well aware, but still he couldn't bring himself to tell Clara and dreaded the day when she must surely find out, 'cos it was only a matter of time now.

Jack was sitting at the table, his day's work behind him. He had been employed by Sassy's Uncle Ben for some time now, and counted himself very fortunate. Ben expected a fair day's work for a fair day's pay, but he was a good boss and would never ask Jack to do anything that he wouldn't do himself.

When the pots were all dried and put away, Sassy crossed to the heavy oak table and poured them all out a strong cup of tea, and they had just sat down to enjoy it when a knock came on the door.

'Get that would yer, lass?' Clara asked, taking a spoon of her cough medicine and, placing her cup down, Sassy went to the door. When she opened it, Bill Stubbs the cobbler was standing there. Almost pushing past her out of the pouring rain, he hurriedly entered the room.

Poor Bill was soaked to the skin, and as he pulled off his dripping cap he said, 'How do,' to Walter, and flashed a cheeky wink at Clara.

'It's rainin' cats and dogs out there,' he puffed as he crossed to the table and dropped a large, somewhat wet brown paper parcel on it. 'There you are then, gel,' he said proudly. 'They've took some doin' 'cos I'll admit I ain't never done anythin' like it before. But even if I do say so meself, I reckon you'll be pleased with 'em.'

Clara eyed the parcel warily. This must be Jack's long-awaited boots; the boots that she prayed would make a difference for him.

Jack eyed the parcel equally as warily. Half of him had looked forward to their arrival, hoping that they might improve his limp, but the other half had whispered, '*What if they make you look even worse?*'

By now Clara had unwrapped the parcel to reveal two sturdily made black leather boots. One was just an ordinary lace-up ankle boot, but the heel and sole of the other was built higher, although it had been so skilfully done that at first glance no one would have spotted the difference. As they were passed from hand to hand for examination, everyone had to agree that Bill had done a grand job. However, after some minutes Clara looked straight at Jack.

'Well, that's enough admirin' them. The proof o' the pudding is in the eatin',' and so saying she dumped the boots into Jack's hands. 'Come on, lad,' she said encouragingly. 'There's no time like the present, an' happen Bill here would like to see if all his hard work's been worth it, eh?'

Bill nodded in agreement and a ripple of laughter passed through the room as poor Jack's face flushed a deep beetroot red. Knowing there was no point in arguing, Jack slowly pulled on his new footwear and carefully began to lace up the boots. By the time he had done so, a silence had fallen on the room and he could feel all eyes on him. His mind was in turmoil; he wished he were a million miles away. What if he couldn't walk in them? What if he fell? And in front of Sassy too. As he looked at her, he saw her expression, which was full of sympathy – willing him to try – as if she could read his thoughts.

Knowing there was nothing else for it, Jack took a deep breath and stood up holding fast to the table's edge. He stood for a short time, getting the feel of them, for the boots felt strange on his feet. But stranger still was the fact that he was standing on a level. Usually when he stood, his shorter leg immediately pulled him to one side, making one shoulder appear much lower than the other. Sassy's eyes had never left him, so taking another deep breath, he let go of the table and walked slowly but surely to the sink.

When he finally turned about to face them, he dared not speak, his heart was too full. To Clara it was almost as if a miracle had occurred. Here was her boy, standing straight and upright for the first time in his life. Gone was his lopsided gait, and now the lad appeared almost as tall as his father. Walter was making a great show of blowing his nose. Clara and Sassy were crying openly and even Bill Stubbs had a lump in his throat. Crossing to Jack, Clara took both his hands in hers. And for the first time, she found she had to look up to him.

'You're a sight fer sore eyes, son,' she whispered. 'An' yer need never feel any less than what you are again; you're a fine handsome lad.'

Jack could only nod as he pulled his mam into a fierce embrace.

When Bill Stubbs eventually left some time later, with

more than a few pints of Clara's home-made ale beneath his belt, his pocket was also considerably heavier. Not only had Clara paid him his price for the boots, but she'd added a little extra, all the while insisting that they were worth double the price. And Sassy, who saw the money change hands, could only agree. Jack appeared like a changed lad, and clumped up and down the kitchen with his head held high for the rest of the night. As word spread of the difference his boots had made to Jack, Bill Stubbs's little cobbler's shop in Nuneaton town centre was soon so busy, both with ordinary customers, and those with bunions and other oddities looking for specially adapted boots and shoes, that he had to take on an apprentice to help him.

Chapter Eight

Sassy brushed her glossy brown hair till it shone and, picking up a crimson velvet ribbon, she tied it firmly into place at the back of her neck before turning her head to admire it in the mirror. Last week had been her thirteenth birthday, and the ribbon had been a present from Clara. Today was market day, a day she always looked forward to. Usually she and Clara went together, but today Sassy had insisted that she would go alone. Clara's cough was now much better, but she was still not completely right as yet, and as the girl had pointed out, 'Go out in this damp an' you'll be back where you started.'

Although Clara grumbled, she saw the sense in what Sassy said, so she had begrudgingly made out a list of the things that she needed, hoping that the child would be able to read it. Clara had always been insistent that her own children should have schooling, but was far from a scholar herself.

Now, with her coat firmly fastened against the February winds, Sassy lifted a large wicker basket, checked that she had Clara's list safe in her pocket and briskly set off. Although it was bitterly cold, today the rain was holding off and Sassy made the journey in good time. As the muddy lanes gave way to cobbles, her footsteps slowed while she glanced at the many little ribbon factories that stretched down either side of Abbey Street. She loved to walk past them; sometimes if their doors were open she could peep inside to where the women sat, hard at work at their looms, surrounded by ribbons of every colour and style, from the finest gauze to the richest velvet. When the ribbons were finished, some would find their way to the hat factory that stood at the end of the street, but the majority of them would be transported to Coventry or Atherstone, where they would be used to trim the bonnets of the gentry. Nuneaton women were renowned for turning out ribbons of the finest quality.

Sassy felt that if she hadn't had to become the woman of the house she might now have been working in one of these little factories herself; each time she peeped inside, she could almost imagine she was looking into a rainbow. They appeared very glamorous and romantic to her young mind, although the women inside could have indeed told her a different tale, of long, back-breaking hours spent bending over their looms. Beyond the ribbon factories was the cattle market, where often of late she and Clara would spot her Uncle Ben and Jack bartering after some beast or another. Besides cows, chickens and pigs, her uncle was now also breeding sheep and was doing well. By autumn he was hoping to buy yet another two fields to add to his thriving little business, and if this came about he had promised that George and William could join Jack and himself.

It seemed strange to Sassy to think of the lads working, and yet she knew that many much younger than they had already been earning their living for some time. Arthur had actually kept them at school much longer than was usual, for it had been Sarah's greatest wish that her children should be well educated. Because by the standards of most people hereabouts they were a small family, Arthur had been in the fortunate position of being able to afford it, as Clara had with her two lads.

Sassy had been forced to forgo schooling, as was

expected of the eldest daughter when her mother died. But she had been fortunate because Mrs Ransom and Jack always made sure that she never lacked reading material, and that, coupled with the fact that George and William had always been happy to share their own lessons with her of an evening, had ensured that at thirteen, Sassy was more educated than most, just as Sarah would have wished.

Today as she entered the cattle market, her eyes cast about, but there was no sign of Uncle Ben or Jack. A hundred different smells and noises assailed her all at once. The large pens were full of animals, from chickens to great flare-eyed bulls that pawed the ground indignantly. Everywhere she looked, men were arguing noisily, and Sassy took it all in with great enjoyment, for market day was one of the highlights of her week. As she finally passed on to the stalls beyond, she came to the pie stall, where she and Clara would normally stop to indulge in a tray of faggots or a bowl of hot peas. Seeing her approach, the pie man gave her a friendly wave.

'Where's your mate today, then?' he shouted pleasantly.

'Indoors with a nasty cough,' Sassy told him, and after exchanging a few words she moved on. Somehow, without Clara there to share them, the faggots and peas didn't hold the same appeal. Taking the list from her pocket, she smiled to herself. Clara would never be classed as a scholar, judging by the many spelling mistakes.

Soon Sassy's basket was full of her purchases and, deciding that there was nothing to be gained by lingering, she headed home. When she finally turned into Tuttle Hill, all the while moving the heavy basket from one arm to the other, she was feeling more than a little deflated. Without Clara's cheerful gossip she hadn't enjoyed the outing nearly as much as usual.

74

It was then that a sudden movement in the spinney to the side of the lane caught her eye. Setting down the heavy basket, she stopped to rest for a while and saw Thomas, Ellie and Jez suddenly emerge from the trees.

Sassy's mouth gaped in amazement, for Thomas should have been at work. As if reading her mind, he took a furtive glance up and down the lane, before slowly approaching her.

'I can tell what yer thinkin',' he said, and before Sassy could reply he went on, 'You're thinkin' as I should be at work, ain't yer?' His worried gaze held hers. 'Look, if me mam finds out I ain't, there'll be hell to pay, so yer won't tell her as you've seen me, will yer, Sassy?'

Deeply perplexed, Sassy stared back at him.

Sensing her dilemma, Thomas took a step closer. 'Look, if yer just don't mention that you've seen me, you ain't tellin' no lies, are yer?'

Sassy saw the truth in this, and sensing now that she wouldn't betray him, he flashed her a grateful smile.

'I'll tell yer what,' he said coaxingly, 'I promised you a visit to the gypsy camp, so how's about yer come back wi' us now?'

The words had barely left his lips before Ellie and Jez, who were now standing on either side of her, eagerly added their invitations to his. Although Sassy knew she should go straight home, she longed to accompany them. Her mind was racing; she had actually finished her shopping much more quickly than usual today, and Clara wouldn't be expecting her for at least another hour or even two, if she were to stretch it.

Unable to resist, Sassy nodded and allowed Thomas to take the heavy basket, and within minutes, the four of them were laughing and chatting freely, as they left the lane and crossed the fields that would take them on a short-cut to the gypsy encampment.

It was a visit that Sassy would never forget, for as they finally walked into the camp, it was like entering another world. Hostile eyes turned in her direction and she had the feeling that if she hadn't been in the company of Thomas, Ellie and Jez, she would have been shooed away.

There were brightly coloured bow-shaped wagons for as far as her eyes could see. Children were playing around a campfire, clad in a remarkable assortment of clothes. Their hair was unkempt and uncombed, and they were so grubby that Sassy could hardly tell the boys from the girls. About their unshod feet roamed two large brindled hounds, with every rib showing. As the four passed, the dogs' ears pricked up and low growls emitted from their throats, but thankfully they stood their ground and didn't approach them. Deeper into the camp, a small sinewy man appeared from behind a wagon. He wore a flat cap on a tangled mass of hair and his skin was so dark that he put Sassy in mind of a chestnut. When he first saw her, he eyed her quizzically, but then as his eyes fell on her companions he relaxed and touched his cap in salute as they moved on.

Eventually they arrived at a beautifully painted wagon, beside which sat a tall woman, steadily stirring what appeared to be some kind of stew in a huge metal cooking pot over a fire.

'Sassy, this is me mother, Pearl.' Ellie introduced the woman proudly. The woman turned her head to peer closely at their visitor and Sassy couldn't help but be shocked at the difference between mother and daughter, for Ellie's mother looked like an old woman. She was painfully thin, her gaunt face deeply lined and ravaged by her life on the open roads.

She nodded at Sassy, but didn't speak. As Sassy was to learn, the Romany women didn't easily talk to strangers, and because they were so closely guarded by their menfolk, mostly preferred to speak to their own kin. As time wore on, Sassy was amazed at the way the gypsies seemed to accept Thomas almost as one of their own. Wherever they went, curious eyes followed her about, although no one paid any heed to him, and it came to her that he must be spending more than a little time here to have earned such acceptance. Throughout her tour of the camp, Ellie kept up a running commentary, pointing out things of interest and happily answering Sassy's neverending questions.

If only Sassy could have known it, Ellie was as entranced with her as she was with Ellie, and as they strolled about, a warm friendship was forming between them that was to entwine their lives for many years to come. To Sassy, everything about that brief stolen time was magical.

Presently they came to the edge of a huge lake in a clearing amongst the trees. There seemed to be horses everywhere she looked, and despite the bitter cold, some of the gypsies were actually stripped to the waist, knee-deep in the water, vigorously scrubbing every inch of their precious horses. The sight made Sassy giggle. After seeing the grubby, ragamuffin children, it seemed more than a little strange to see the men taking such good care of the livestock. But as Thomas pointed out, the horses were in fact more valuable to them.

'Come the spring, when the gypsies leave this place they'll make their way to Appleby Fair. It's one o' the biggest horse fairs in England, and there the horses will be sold,' Thomas informed her. 'They are the main income of the gypsies and therefore valued above all else.'

In a field that edged the clearing were even more horses. Some were tethered, grazing on what little grass they could find amongst the mud, others were being trotted patiently up and down, as they would be when put on display for sale at Appleby Fair, and some were being furiously galloped to and fro by bare-backed gypsies, who held fast to the shining manes.

A smell of horse dung and horseflesh floated on the air and Sassy was so enchanted with it all that she felt she could have stood there and watched for ever. But by now she was well aware that time was drawing on, and she knew that this brief stolen interlude must end. Bidding goodbye to Jez and Thomas, who were deep in discussion on the merits of a certain pony, she followed Ellie slowly back through the camp, trying hard to lock every little sight and sound safe into her mind. At the edge of the site as she clung tight to Ellie's hand, her eyes were shining. 'I'll never forget this visit,' she whispered.

'Let's hope it's the first o' many,' Ellie answered warmly and, nodding, Sassy hurriedly headed home, their friendship sealed.

It wasn't until she was within sight of the familiar cottages that the first pangs of guilt set in. Sassy was not a girl known to go off willy-nilly, and were Clara ever to find out where she had been, Sassy knew she would feel the length of her tongue and no mistake. But it seemed that day as if the gods were smiling on her, for on entering Clara's cottage there was no sign of her, and surmising that she must be in the lavvy, Sassy offered up a silent prayer of thanks. Hastily emptying Clara's purchases onto the table, along with her few coppers change, she then rushed guiltily next door as if the very hounds of hell were at her heels.

Sassy was not the sort to complain at her lot. If sometimes her life appeared a little dull she only had to close her eyes and she could imagine that she was back in the exciting atmosphere of the gypsy camp. Clara soon recovered fully from her cough and cold, the shared weekly visits to the market were resumed, and as February turned to March, life returned to its normal pattern.

By now, as Thomas had told her, the gypsies were preparing to leave for their yearly pilgrimage to Appleby Fair in Cumbria, and Sassy felt sadness at this. Since her stolen visit, Sassy had only ever seen Ellie at a distance, and always accompanied by Jez for, as she now knew, the gypsy girls were not allowed to leave their camp alone, unless it was to sell the wooden pegs they made or the little bunches of lucky heather they gathered from the fields. Still, come winter they would return, and the thought gave her comfort. And so came the day when Thomas informed her dejectedly of their leaving, and if Sassy had felt sadness at their going, he appeared completely devastated.

It was the following evening as Sassy was dishing up the evening meal that a loud commotion was heard to come from next door at the Mallabones'. Arthur raised his eyes questioningly to hers, but Sassy could only shrug her shoulders in answer.

Thomas had just entered the cottage to find Clara waiting for him, red in the face with rage.

'Is it right what I'm hearing then?' she shouted, her fists pressed so tight to the table they were white.

Thomas eyed her nervously. 'Happen if yer tell me what it is you've heard, I might know,' he answered quietly.

'I've heard as you've been missin' yer shifts an earnin' yer money bare-knuckle fightin' wi' them bloody gypsies. I've also been told as you've been seen in the company o' one o' the girls from the knockin' shop in Regent Street.'

Walter was cringing in the chair at the side of the fire.

He'd known of the missed shifts but this business about a loose woman was news to him. Not that he was surprised to hear it. Thomas had had a bit of an eye for the ladies for some time now, and because of his dark good looks he never seemed to lack female company. Even so, a girl from the brothel? He knew that the day he had dreaded had finally arrived, and almost held his breath as he waited for the lad's answer. However, the reply when it came was not what he had expected. Thomas had stood with his chin almost on his chest during Clara's tirade, but now he raised his head – and both Walter and Clara were shocked to see that his temper matched hers.

As he faced her, his eyes flashing, he appeared for the first time to be a man instead of a lad.

His voice held a terrible calm. 'Aye, it is right, what you've heard, but I'm tellin' yer now, so listen hard.' He paused as if to add strength to his words. 'I tips me money up onto this table come pay day, same as everybody else, no matter how it's come by. An' what if I do earn a few bob bare-knuckle fightin'? There's blokes from hereabouts earn their livin' that way, if yer did but know it. Furthermore, it ain't like I'm pickin' fights wi' any Tom, Dick or Harry from off the streets, is it? I'm fightin' like-minded men. So I'll tell yer now, if yer try to tell me how to live me life just *one* more time, I'll go an' bloody *live* wi' 'em.'

Clara's shocked eyes were almost starting from her head, for never in his life had her son ever spoken to her like this before. Sensing that he meant every word he said, she was struck dumb and could only gape at him soundlessly. Then turning abruptly on his heel, Thomas strode from the room, banging the heavy door behind him with such force that it was left shuddering on its hinges.

Clara knew better than to ever mention the incident again, and from the outside, life appeared to return to normal. Every payday, as promised, the wages were tipped onto the table, and Clara without a word would take down her tin from the mantelpiece and place the money inside it. But she felt as if a part of Thomas had already gone from her. The carefree lad she had scolded, but always loved, somehow felt distant from her, as if his soul were indeed already in some far-off place with the gypsies. And as she sometimes watched him staring moodily from the cottage window, a cold hand would close about her heart.

Chapter Nine

In April, George and William celebrated their birthdays only ten days apart, and Clara laughingly joked that although a year and a few days divided them, they might as well have been twins. As they became older, instead of growing away from each other as most brothers did, they never seemed to be more than an arm's length apart. The boys shared a birthday party halfway between their birth dates, and Sassy and Clara baked cakes and pies and it was a joyous occasion. A whole troop of little Wainthrops duly arrived, clad all in their Sunday best and bearing gifts, along with a few other friends from school. Surprisingly, the Widow Bonner presented them both with a beautifully bound book each. George's was a book of trains, which he adored. He loved to go and watch the great steam engines chug their way through Weddington, and William's was a book about ships. Within fourteen days of receiving it, William's book appeared to be years old, for it was hardly ever out of his hands, and much read. It became a joke that one day he would surely become a sailor, for just as the ribbon factories had appeared glamorous to Sassy, so everything about the sea fascinated the lad, and although before receiving the gift he had never really liked the Widow Bonner, he now found he looked on her quite kindly. However, the same could not be said for Sassy, and it was one day when she and Clara were enjoying a cup of tea together that she dared to say as much. They had carried their chairs outside into the lane, for it was a mild day, and the wild primroses peeping from beneath the hedgerows made a pretty picture.

'Widow Bonner called again yesterday,' she said quietly, all the while watching Clara from the corner of her eye for her reaction.

'Oh aye?' said Clara.

Sassy began to feel uncomfortable. Perhaps it was just she who had a suspicious mind, yet she couldn't let it rest and after another few minutes' silence she blurted out, 'Clara, do you reckon Mrs Bonner's set her cap at me dad?' There, it was said. And she didn't regret it, for she set a lot of store on her friend's judgement.

Clara sat on in silence for what seemed like ages to Sassy, outwardly calm but inwardly in turmoil. She loved this lass as her own, and whilst her own thoughts on the Widow Bonner had for some long time run along the same tracks as Sassy's now, she had no wish to worry the child.

Eventually she said, 'Look, lass, I'd be lyin' if I were to tell yer I thought yer was wrong, but . . .' she held up her hand quickly at Sassy's crestfallen face, '. . . what I will say is this, yer dad is still a fine handsome man, an' I could name more than a few women who'd gladly step into yer dear mam's shoes. But if he ain't showed no interest in them, he ain't hardly going to bother wi' a woman far above his own class, now is he?'

As Sassy thought on this, she scowled. A few months ago she might have agreed with Clara, but now she wasn't so sure. Her father actually seemed to look forward to Elizabeth Bonner's visits, whereas before he had hardly given her the time of day. Sassy knew that he was lonely but could only hope that if he did decide to marry again, he would look further afield than her.

It was then that Connie Wainthrop appeared from her

cottage, and stepping into the fresh air, she breathed deeply. She looked tired and low spirited, and Clara shouted, 'Eh Connie, what's up, lass? Yer look fit to drop.'

Connie nodded. 'I am that, Clara. Five o' the little 'uns is bad – fevers, sick, the lot! An' now two on 'em's developed a rash an' all.'

Clara placed her cup down and strode down to her, saying over her shoulder, 'You stay where yer are, Sassy, in case it's somethin' catchin', while I take a look at 'em.' And so saying, she disappeared indoors with Connie.

It was some time later when Clara returned. By then, Sassy had washed up the cups and returned the chairs to their proper place by the table.

On entering the kitchen, Clara clucked her tongue worriedly. 'Happen yer should keep the lads away from the Wainthrop brood for the time bein',' she said. 'Because if I'm right in me thinkin', I reckon they's all comin down wi' the measles.'

As it turned out it was already too late to heed the warning because when the lads arrived home from school later that afternoon, they both appeared flushed and unwell.

'There ain't no school tomorrer,' William informed his sister. 'Mrs Ransom says over half the school's off wi' measles an' we're not to go back till further notice.'

Sassy nodded numbly, scared to her stomach that their bright eyes and flushed faces could be the start of it. She was proved right, and by the next morning, they were both so ill that they didn't even want to venture from their beds. Terrified, Sassy flew next door to fetch Clara, who immediately confirmed her worst fears.

'Aye, happen they've got it all right,' she said. 'And so has the rest o' Connie's brood. Every last one on 'em's down wi' it now.' Seeing Sassy's frightened eyes she patted her hand kindly. 'Don't worry, lass,' she smiled. 'They're both good strong lads. Once the rash is out, they'll be right as rain afore yer know it. Meantime, keep 'em warm an' give 'em plenty to drink.'

Sassy nodded.

'I'll be back every hour or so,' promised Clara, 'but if yer need me before, I'll be at Connie's. That poor bugger's got her hands full wi' them lot an' no mistake.' And giving Sassy a final reassuring smile, she hurried away.

When Arthur arrived home that evening, it was to find the fire burned low and no dinner on the table, for Sassy had spent the whole day rushing up and downstairs for cold compresses and drinks for the fretful invalids. Arthur pitched in to help and at last the lads dropped into a restless sleep. By morning they were both so covered in spots that it would have been hard to fit a pin on an unmarked place on either of them. But while William, as Clara predicted, did indeed seem a little cooler, George was still feverishly hot and crying out in his sleep as he thrashed about the bed. Clara took it in turns with Sassy bathing his hot little body, but as William seemed to improve almost by the hour, George, if anything, seemed to grow ever hotter.

When Arthur arrived home that evening, Sassy flew down the stairs to meet him.

'Dad, Dad,' she caught his hands in her own, 'I think we should send for the doctor. George is burning up.'

Arthur glanced at William who, although still far from well, was sitting tucked up snugly in a blanket at the side of the fire reading his precious book. He then followed Sassy upstairs to find Clara bending over the small child on the bed.

'I reckon yer will have to call the doctor out tomorrer if he's no better,' she said anxiously. 'No amount o' this cold spongin' seems to be doin' any good, an' now we've had to close the curtains 'cos he's crying as the light's hurtin' his eyes.'

When Sassy hurried from the room to fetch yet another bowl of cold water from the pump, Clara drew Arthur from the bed and whispered, 'He has it bad, man, just as does two o' Connie's.' Then she quietly left the room, leaving Arthur gazing anxiously down at the child on the bed.

That night, William slept in his dad's bed while Arthur and Sassy sat either side of George, taking it in turns to see to his needs.

It was deepest night, and neither of them had slept a wink when a terrible scream pierced the air from further down the lane. Sassy had not heard such a cry of utter torment since the night of her mother's death, and she saw her deepest dread mirrored there, in her father's eyes.

First thing the next morning, Bob Capener was seen entering Connie Wainthrop's cottage. When he left a short time later, he held not one, but two sets of measurements in his hands. Poor Connie's heartbroken sobs seemed to follow him down the lane as he departed to set about making the two little boxes. George was no better and Sassy now was frantic.

'Hurry, Dad,' she pleaded, as Arthur struggled with his braces. 'If we can just get the doctor early enough, he might make George the first call.' Little could she know that the doctor had not seen his bed at all that night, for Connie's two were not the only ones who had fallen to the epidemic.

However, Arthur need not have hurried, for just then there was a loud knock on the door, and after flying down the stairs two at a time to answer it, Sassy found the doctor standing there.

Seeing the look of confusion on her face, the doctor

pushed past her, smiling kindly. 'I received word from Widow Bonner that George needed a visit, and as I was in the area I thought I'd call in,' he explained.

Although Sassy had harboured unkind thoughts about her before, had the widow been in the room right then, she would have thrown her arms about her and kissed her soundly, although she did wonder how Mrs Bonner could have known of George's illness.

Dr Massey thoroughly examined George, watched over by Arthur and Sassy who were standing close together at the side of the bed, as if they were trying to steal comfort from each other. When he had finished, he stood up and, stretching wearily, he addressed Sassy.

'You're doing very well,' he praised. 'Just keep up the cold sponges and keep trying to get some drinks into him.'

Sassy nodded eagerly, and after snatching up the damp cloth, she bent to the bed to do as she was told. Catching Arthur's eye, the doctor gestured at the door and together they descended the stairs. William was watching them from huge frightened eyes from his place at the fireside, so speaking in a whisper so as not to alarm the child still further, the doctor told him, 'I'm afraid he's at his worst, Arthur. There's nothing more I can do, apart from what Sassy's already doing.'

Arthur looked stricken as Dr Massey placed his hand on his arm. 'The fever should break within the next twenty-four hours.'

'And then what?' Arthur's eyes pleaded with him to give him the answer he longed to hear, but all the doctor could say was, 'Then it's in God's hands. The child will go one way or the other.'

Dr Massey left the cottage with a heavy heart. In the last two days he had witnessed enough heartache to last him a lifetime. At that moment he bitterly regretted the

87

decision to ever enter his profession; in this situation, he felt completely useless.

As if sensing the severity of his brother's illness, William became fretful and Arthur had to spend much of the day downstairs with him, not wanting him to deteriorate. And so the task of caring for George fell mainly on Sassy, with Clara helping as much as she could whilst she ran between Connie's cottage and Arthur's. She didn't know who needed her most, for poor Connie was inconsolable, as was Jimmy. Although he was known for his love of ale and a gamble, he was a good man at heart and had taken the deaths of his little ones badly.

Come the evening, William had finally fallen into a fretful doze deep in Arthur's bed. Arthur himself was taking a much-needed rest in the chair at the side of the fire, while George alternately shivered and sweated on his bed, thrashing about until the sheets were damp with sweat. In the lane a deep dark silence had settled as the stars looked down on the struggle between life and death that was once again taking place in the little cottage.

Clara planted a kiss on Sassy's head, as she sat close to the side of the bed, gripping George's hot little hand in her own. 'I'll just go an' pinch an hour's kip while he's quiet,' she whispered.

Sassy nodded absently, her eyes never leaving George's.

'If the fever shows any sign o' breakin', yer fetch me straight away.'

Sassy nodded again as Clara tiptoed from the room.

She wasn't aware of falling asleep, but eventually Sassy slipped into an exhausted doze. Somehow sensing a change in the room, her tired eyes struggled to open and as she looked towards the bed she saw George, who was calm now, smiling at her with recognition.

'Oh, pet,' she whispered joyously. 'You're awake.'

His eyes, which were still feverishly bright, bored into hers. 'Th . . . there was an angel here, Sassy.'

She had to lean to catch his words, for he was very weak.

'She stood by the bed an' smiled at me, an' she were beautiful.'

'No, sweetheart,' she whispered, as she stroked the damp hair from his forehead. 'You've been very poorly and had a dream.'

The child shook his head fretfully. 'She *were* here, honest.' His eyes were begging her to believe him, and not wishing to upset him further now that the fever had at last broken, she smiled.

'All right then, love,' she soothed. 'You tell me all about it in the morning, eh? When you've had a good sleep.'

Reassured that she believed him, the child was just about to close his eyes again when suddenly his little hand tightened in hers. 'Sassy!'

'Yes, love?' She blinked to hold back the tears of relief.

'I . . . I love you, Sassy,' he whispered.

Bending, she kissed him gently. 'I love you too,' she said, and as she laid her head on the pillow at the side of him, their hands joined and she again fell into an exhausted sleep.

A gentle shake on her shoulder pulled her slowly back to consciousness to find Clara and Arthur standing on either side of her. The light was filtering through the cotton curtains, and little dust motes were dancing in the air. She was just about to excitedly tell them that George's fever had finally broken when something in their faces stopped her. Her little brother's hand was still clasped in her own, but whereas before it had almost burned her, now it felt deathly cold. Moving her eyes slowly from Arthur and Clara she brought them to rest on George. He lay pale and still beside her. There was a smile of pure joy on his face, and even as her heart tried to deny it, Sassy knew in that moment that he had gone from her for ever.

Too stunned for tears as yet, she choked disbelievingly, 'He can't be gone – he *can't*.'

Clara was gently trying to pull her from the bedside, but keeping a tight grip on George's hand, Sassy wriggled away.

'He said there was an angel,' she sobbed.

Clara nodded sadly. 'Well then, lass,' she whispered, 'happen there was. He's at peace now, and perhaps it were yer own dear mam as came to fetch him.'

As Sassy gazed down on him, the wisdom of Clara's words slowly sank in, and bending her head to this adored little brother, she sobbed as if her heart would break.

And so it was yet again, that some days later, the same horse and cart that had carried Sarah to her grave now came to pay the same service to George. But he did not go alone; three small coffins travelled together on their final journey to Chilvers Coton Church, and there in a small grave that had been dug as close to Sarah's as was possible, George Churm was laid to rest with his mother and baby sister.

Arthur Churm was a changed man for all time. He had managed to rally around after the death of his wife, but this latest cruel blow seemed to break his spirit completely. Sassy found it hard to believe that George was really gone for ever, and only Clara's comforting words about him being with their mother got her through. But William was beside himself with grief, for never had two brothers been closer than he and George, and everywhere he looked he seemed to see him.

He would disappear for hours at a time, only to be

found sitting silently beside the small square of earth that was his brother's grave. One beautiful summer morning, Sassy woke to find his bed empty. Her father had left for his shift some time since and so she hurried downstairs. On entering the scullery she saw a single sheet of paper with her name written on it propped against the milk jug on the table. With trembling fingers she took up the note, and yet even before reading it, she had guessed its contents. It read simply:

Dear Sassy,

I have gone to sea, don't worry about me. Sorry, but I can't stay without George. I will write.

I love you,
William xxx

As the note fluttered to the floor she sank onto the hard wooden chair, and it was there that Clara found her some time later, dry-eyed and staring off into space. When Clara finally got out of her what had happened, she clutched the girl to her breast; hot scalding tears poured from her eyes and she angrily berated a God who could place yet another burden on such young shoulders. But then as she calmed down, she tried to comfort herself and Sassy.

'Eeh, lass, you've had more than yer fair share o' sorrow,' she cried. 'But happen William needed to get away. There were too many memories here for him, but he's a big lad for his age. He'll fare well, you'll see.'

When she received no answer from Sassy, only a blank wooden stare, she shook her again gently. 'Look, lass, you ain't lost him. He'll be back when he's come to terms wi' what's happened. An' things can only get better now, fer they surely couldn't get any worse, could they?'

Once again, Clara was proved to be wrong, when only weeks later Sassy entered the cottage after paying a visit to George's grave to find the Widow Bonner sitting there.

Arthur sat silently at the table but Elizabeth Bonner was in a triumphant mood.

'Ah, Sassy,' she gabbled, the moment she entered the room. 'Good news after all the bad.'

Sassy gazed at her suspiciously.

'Your father and I have just decided that we are to be married!' She appeared like a cat that had got the cream. As far as she was concerned, she had waited far too long for Arthur, but after this latest tragedy he was like putty in her hands, glad of someone to care for him again and to take charge of everything.

Sassy's startled eyes flew to Arthur, praying to find a denial there, but her father merely nodded in dumb agreement.

Sassy suddenly wished, not for the first time in these last weeks, that she too had been buried with George.

Chapter Ten

In the shade of the windmill, Sassy sat eyeing the beautiful view before her. The fields appeared like a patchwork quilt, all embroidered in soft shades of green, and the canal, which could clearly be seen from this point, sparkled as the sun reflected on it.

Today was her father's wedding day, and it was almost as if, after organising everything else over the last few weeks, Elizabeth Bonner had also commanded the weather to be perfect.

Sassy knew that Clara would scold her when she returned to the cottage, for she was now dressed in a lovely fine cord burgundy dress with the hint of a bustle, just right for a young miss like herself, and it was wicked to sit on the grass in it like this. The dress had been supplied by Elizabeth, as was the suit that her father would be struggling into even now. As a surprise gift, Clara had decked Sassy's straw bonnet with velvet ribbons to match the dress and yet surprisingly, though the outfit was such as Sassy had only ever dreamed of owning, it brought her no joy. Her eyes scanned the landscape that she loved. She knew every nook and cranny for miles about, and the thought of leaving all that was familiar was frightening.

It was hard to believe that this day had finally arrived, for since Elizabeth had announced their engagement, everything had passed in a blur of preparation. Nothing in the cottage was considered good enough for Elizabeth to want in her home, so the task of disposing of the furniture had fallen to Sassy. The huge oak dresser that had been her mother's pride and joy, after many protests, now took pride of place in Clara's scullery. Aunt Miriam had taken other choice bits for her own cottage. Recently, Uncle Ben had extended it to match his still-growing business, and the extra furniture came in very handy. Connie Wainthrop had taken almost everything else that was worth taking. All that was left in the cottage now were the beds that Sassy and Arthur had slept in the night before, and various bits and bobs that Sassy hoped the new tenants would be glad of. This morning she had swept out the little house from top to bottom, and then left her father to prepare for his wedding, while she herself dressed at Clara's. Once the new dress was donned, Clara had tied the ribbons of Sassy's bonnet tight beneath her chin and smiled encouragingly at her.

'Eeh, lass,' she had whispered. 'Me only fear now is that you'll outshine the bride, for yer look as pretty as a picture.'

Sassy had smiled bravely back. 'You'll not think that when you see Louise,' she replied. 'If you think this outfit's smart, you should see hers. It's like something out of a fashion book.'

It seemed that Louise Bonner had taken an instant dislike to her stepsister-to-be, and had been quick to point out that her outfit was of far superior quality to Sassy's. On hearing this, Clara had tutted in annoyance.

'Huh, she'll not put you to shame, not even if she's decked in jewels,' she'd mumbled indignantly. 'Yer can't make a silk purse from a sow's ear, no matter how yer dress it.'

Sassy had smiled sadly at this. Now that she was about to leave Clara, it had come to her just how much she would miss her, and feeling the need for a few minutes to herself, she had crossed quickly to the cottage door.

'I'll just leave you to get ready then,' she'd said chokily over her shoulder, unable to look Clara in the eye. Her throat was tight and she had the feeling that if she started to cry now, she might never stop.

'Aye, all right then, lass,' Clara said easily. 'But don't be gone long, and don't crease yer dress up, mind.'

Once Sassy had pulled the door to behind her, Clara stood lost in thought. She had said very little to Sassy, but she had her own thoughts on this wedding. As she'd commented to Walter, 'I can't think what Arthur's thinkin' of, takin' to the likes o' her.'

Walter had gazed at her wisely. 'Well, lass, it's his decision an' there's nowt yer can do to change it.'

'Well, I bloody well know that, don't I?' she barked. 'But I'll tell yer somethin' . . . I reckon Arthur is makin' the biggest mistake of his life, an' happen he'll rue the day he ever agreed to this weddin'.'

Walter had held his tongue, but if truth were told, he couldn't have agreed with Clara more.

Now, in the cottage, Clara glanced at the clock and realising that the time was fast approaching when they must leave to begin the journey to the church, she hurriedly set about getting her men all dressed in their Sunday best and fit to be seen. Thomas was already complaining loudly at the tightness of his tie and pulling at his collar uncomfortably, but Clara slapped his hand away, exclaiming loudly, 'Leave yer tie be, lad! An' fer God's sake go an' get a comb through yer hair.'

Thomas did as he was told, complaining bitterly. He didn't know why they had to attend this wedding anyway. Some of his gypsy friends were camped at Mancetter at present and he would far sooner have spent the day with them. Jack, on the other hand, stood quiet and ready to go. He was feeling the loss of Sassy even before her departure, and was finding it as hard as Clara to picture life in the lane without her. Since the arrival of his new boots, there were more than a few lasses looking his way, but for Jack, there was still only Sassy.

Meantime, realising that the time was drawing on, Sassy finally stood from her seat in the swaying grass and began to brush the creases from her new dress. Then with a sigh and a final glance at the familiar landscape, she carefully made her way to the bottom of the bank. Rounding the hawthorn hedge that sheltered the back gardens of the cottages, she stood for the last time to gaze upon her mother's rosebed. Most of the roses were long past their best, but seeking amongst them, Sassy found two just coming into full bloom, and after plucking them carefully from the bush, she walked sadly up the garden path and into the cottage.

Arthur was standing straight and upright with his hands behind his back in front of the empty grate, and as Sassy looked at him in his fine unfamiliar clothes, she could well see why Elizabeth Bonner wanted him so, for he made a handsome sight. However, he did not appear excited, as a man about to be wed should be. As Clara was heard to mutter later in the day to her husband, 'He looks more like a man goin' to his doom than his bride.' Which made Walter give her a swift dig in the ribs that momentarily managed to shut her up. Arthur's head was down and he seemed to be lost in thought. When Sassy approached him and gently slipped a crimson rose into his buttonhole, his eyes became bright with unshed tears.

'You are all right about me marrying Elizabeth aren't you, Sassy?' he questioned her, and before she could answer he rushed on, 'I get lonely you see.'

She smiled and nodded, unable to speak, and pinned the second rose to her own dress. As she followed her father to the door, she turned to take a final look about the little cottage that was the only home she had ever known. In recent years it had seen more than its fair share of tragedy, but Sassy could well remember all the happy times she had known there too, and her heart was heavy as she pulled the door to behind her for the last time.

It was a sombre crowd that made its way to Chilvers Coton Church, with hardly a word spoken on the journey, as most of them were lost in their own thoughts. When they finally arrived, Sassy and Arthur stepped down from the cart and Miriam, Ben and James hurried to meet them. As always, at the sight of James, Sassy's mood lifted. He was now the only brother she had, apart from William who had still sent no word of his whereabouts. The little lad threw himself into her arms with delight.

'Sassy, p . . . pretty,' he stammered as Sassy beamed at him. His speech was progressing far better than the doctor had forecast. Miriam and Ben spent endless patient hours with him, encouraging and praising, and it seemed like almost every time Sassy saw him, he had learned a new word.

'You clever boy.' She hugged him fondly then taking his hand firmly in hers she moved on, closely followed by Clara, Walter, Jack and Thomas, who was still pulling fretfully at his tie and grumbling to himself all the way.

Uncle Ben was Arthur's best man, and now ushered the groom away to take his place at the altar, in readiness for the arrival of the bride. Sassy was left with Miriam and James to tread a more leisurely pace through the churchyard to the church door where they met Louise and Matthew, Elizabeth's children.

'So, the big day has finally arrived, eh?' Matthew said with a smile as he fell into step beside them.

Sassy nodded. She saw Louise glowering at her from

the corner of her eye, but at least this boy seemed friendly enough.

When they were almost at the church doors, Sassy looked across at her mother's grave and offered up a silent prayer that, despite her own misgivings, Elizabeth Bonner might make her father half as happy as her mother had. Then taking a deep breath, she entered the church.

When Elizabeth Bonner finally arrived on the arm of her brother, who was to give her away, it was admitted by everyone present that she looked truly beautiful. She was wearing a fitted gown of the richest velvet Sassy had ever seen, in a beautiful shade of green that perfectly matched her eyes, and a tiny little velvet hat that barely covered her shining upswept hair.

As she stood at Arthur's side in front of Vicar Rigby, they made a very handsome couple. As the service progressed, Elizabeth's eyes hungrily sought Arthur's, but he stood staring blankly straight ahead, and even had to be gently prompted by Ben when it came to his turn to take his vows. Eventually it was done, and the vicar solemnly pronounced them man and wife.

Once outside the church, while the wedding guests milled about the newlyweds to wish them well, Sassy slipped away, unnoticed by everyone but Clara, hurrying among the tombstones to her mother's resting-place. There, Sassy plucked the rose from her dress and laid it reverently on her grave.

Elizabeth's fine horse and trap then transported herself, Arthur, Louise, Matthew and Sassy back to what was to be the couple's new home. Sassy felt strangely out of place in such a fine transport, and as if sensing her discomfort, Matthew smiled kindly at her. But Louise scowled sulkily at her, and in that moment Sassy realised that the other girl was no happier about the wedding than she was.

The rest of the wedding party, which included Clara and her family, who had been invited at Arthur's insistence, closely followed the trap. That was the only thing that he had made a stand on in the whole of the preparations, for he knew, just as Sassy did, that it was Clara, over the last difficult years, on whom his family had come to rely. Elizabeth, who had chosen to entirely forget her own humble beginnings, was less than pleased at the thought of such common folk sitting at her table, but now that Arthur had finally agreed to marry her, she didn't want anything to make him change his mind at the last minute and so grudgingly agreed to it.

When eventually they arrived at Elizabeth's home in Swan Lane, and Arthur helped her down from the trap, Sassy was daunted by the grandeur of it. She had known that Elizabeth lived but a stone's throw from Dr Massey's house, and she had thought his home was beautiful, but this place made their cottage on Tuttle Hill appear almost like a hovel. It was so high that Sassy imagined it was almost touching the sky. It consisted of four storeys, the fourth storey being the attic, the servants' quarters. The outside was heavily timbered in black and white, and had high sash-cord windows, which were covered in snow-white lace curtains, so thick that it was impossible to see through them. Elizabeth and Arthur immediately disappeared inside to make sure that everything was in readiness for the wedding feast, but Sassy, feeling completely out of her depth, refused Matthew's polite offer to accompany her inside and, instead, stood waiting for Clara to arrive as she wrung her hands nervously.

She didn't have to wait long. Soon the more modest horse and cart arrived, and Clara hastily alighted. She had no wish to be there and had only come because she knew that Sassy wished it. But now as she stood at the girl's side gaping up at the beautiful house, the enormity of the change of circumstances that Sassy was facing suddenly struck her.

'By heck, lass,' she whispered in awe, 'it's like a bloody palace, ain't it?'

Sassy gulped nervously. 'Let's go inside and see, eh?'

Nodding, Clara followed her up the path.

After entering the front door they found themselves in an enormous hallway. On the floor was a rich crimson carpet that reached from wall to wall, so thick that their feet sank into it. The velvet flock wallpaper was a matching crimson and gold, and a beautifully ornate staircase swept up one side to a galleried landing.

It was as they were openly gawping that a young girl, who was later to be introduced as Maisie, hurried to meet them. Dressed in a starched white cap and apron she dropped a curtsy – which caused Clara to gape even further – then ushered them into a dining room the like of which neither Sassy nor Clara had ever seen before. A huge mahogany table stretched almost the whole length of the room, covered in starched white napkins and gleaming silverware. The china was so wafer-thin that Clara was almost afraid to touch it, let alone eat off it, and covered in a rich gold-leaf design. Three huge silver candelabra were placed at intervals all along the table's length, and green tapered candles sat in them, so unlike the common wax candles that Clara was used to using that she was totally fascinated by them. Epergnes full of fruit and flowers made the table look very festive. The main colour scheme in this room was green, and everything in it seemed to match, from the thick green carpet, to the ornate wallpaper and the curtains, which were tied back by thick golden ropes.

Elizabeth was seated at one end of the table and Arthur at the other, and as the young maid called Maisie pulled their chairs out for them, Clara and Walter hastily sat down, feeling decidedly out of place. Sassy noted that Louise was batting her eyelashes and flirting shamelessly with Thomas, but he was having none of it. Elizabeth had obviously noticed too and Sassy was amused to see her glaring at the girl.

As Clara eyed the huge array of silverware in alarm, Maisie quickly bent to her ear.

'Start at the outside and work in,' she whispered discreetly and Clara flashed her a grateful smile. She had never seen so many different knives, forks and spoons at one setting in her whole life before.

Eventually all the guests were seated and the wedding feast began. No one could have faulted the meal. Course followed course, each served from huge silver dishes and platters, until Sassy thought she would burst. Then it was time for the speeches. Her Uncle Ben stood up and uncomfortably uttered a few words, as did Arthur, but there was no toast made to the bride and groom. Elizabeth had signed the Pledge and would not allow alcohol in her house, even on her wedding day. And so it went on until at last the guests began to depart with handshakes and good wishes to the newlyweds.

Clara was amongst the first to leave. Although the house was luxurious, she couldn't wait to get back to the comfort of her own cottage, and by now Thomas was almost straining at the leash to get home and out and about. Arthur was standing at the door next to his new wife, and Clara grasped his hand fondly.

'I wish you all the best, lad.' Her voice was sincere. 'And don't forget where we live. If ever you should need us, we'll always be there for yer.'

Elizabeth's cold eyes met hers and she smiled, but as Clara was to tell Walter later that night, the smile was false.

'Thank you so much for coming,' she said imperiously. 'Arthur has me to take care of him now. As for him needing you, well . . . I doubt that very much, don't you?'

Clara stared back at her stonily. 'Let's hope he don't, eh? But as Arthur knows, there's some things as is more important than worldly possessions.' And so saying she marched down the elaborately tiled path to the front gate without a backward glance, closely followed by her family.

Once outside, Clara and Sassy faced one another, hands clasped tight together.

'Right then, lass.' Clara's throat was full. 'What I said to yer dad back there goes for you an' all. I'll expect a visit at least once a week, mind.'

Sassy nodded dumbly. She didn't trust herself to speak because she knew if she did the lump in her throat would erupt into tears. Walter and Thomas were already on the cart, and she saw Thomas strumming his fingers impatiently on the wooden rail.

'Goodbye, Thomas.'

It was almost as if he had forgotten her presence already, but he pulled his thoughts back to the present and turning to her, he raised his hand.

'Oh, bye then, Sassy.'

Sassy's heart twisted in her chest. Jack had not yet mounted the cart, but stood close to Clara's side, his eyes as bright as Sassy's. Leaning over to her, he pecked her self-consciously on the cheek.

'Hark at me mam now,' he said sternly. 'If you should ever need us, yer know where we are.'

And then the Mallabones' cart was rattling off down the lane leaving Sassy feeling as if the bottom had dropped out of her world.

By now the rest of the wedding guests had departed, and the pony and trap had once again returned and now stood waiting to take Elizabeth and Arthur to the railway station where they would catch the train to Bournemouth for their two weeks' honeymoon. Sassy had barely had a minute alone with her father all day, but as they stood facing each other in the plush hallway, he said tenderly, 'You take good care of yourself, love, till we get back.'

Sassy nodded. The trunks were all loaded onto the trap and Elizabeth was standing tapping her foot in the doorway.

'Come along then, Arthur, we'll be late for the train,' she said commandingly, and so with a final quick kiss for Sassy, he hurried to join her.

'Now then, Maisie, you have all my instructions, and I want them carried out to the letter, do you understand?' Her eyes were fast on the maid, and the girl dipped her knee.

'Yes, ma'am,' she replied, keeping her eyes downcast.

Turning back to Arthur, Elizabeth told him sweetly, 'I have instructed Maisie to put Sassy's things up on the fourth floor for now. I thought she might feel more comfortable up there, but of course, if she doesn't like it, when we return she can move to another room.'

Arthur opened his mouth to object but Sassy hurriedly told him, 'It's all right, Dad. I'll be fine there, honestly.'

Nodding with satisfaction, Elizabeth pulled on her gloves and strode out of the house with Arthur jogging uncertainly behind her.

After closing the door on her mistress, Maisie leaned back against it and let out a long-drawn-out sigh.

'Well, that's the back o' *her* for a couple o' weeks,' she beamed at Sassy. 'Happen we'll get some peace now, eh?'

When Sassy grinned in reply, Maisie took her hand and led her to a doorway right at the end of the long hallway. 'Come downstairs an' meet Ada the cook,' she invited. 'Wi' Miss Louise an' Master Matthew stayin' wi' their uncle, it's gonna be almost like a holiday for us too.'

As they entered the kitchen, which was bigger than

the whole of Sassy's beloved cottage put together, Sassy had her first glimpse of Ada the cook and almost immediately felt that here she would find yet another ally.

Ada, a huge red-faced, homely-looking woman, was sitting in a chair at the side of the fire, a big mug of tea in her hands and her feet stretched out before her.

'Hello, love,' she welcomed Sassy. 'Don't mind if I don't get up, will yer? But me poor feet are on fire. This is the first time I've been off 'em since six o'clock this mornin'.'

As Sassy flashed her an answering smile, a look passed between Ada and Maisie that seemed to say, '*We'll get no trouble from this one,*' and in that moment Sassy received their unspoken seal of approval. With the mistress out of the way, Ada was all for leaving the dirty pots until morning, but seeing that the poor woman was almost dead on her feet, Sassy rolled up her sleeves and after filling the huge stone sink with hot water from two kettles, she set to with a will. It was a pleasure to wash the beautiful china. She had never handled anything so fine before, and soon, with herself washing and Maisie drying, the enormous table that stood in the middle of the kitchen was covered in clean shining tableware. The large meat tins that had roasted all the various joints were then left to soak overnight and Sassy now sat between Ada and Maisie, enjoying a well-earned cup of tea. It was well into the evening by now, and although Sassy didn't usually go to bed this early, she couldn't help a great yawn escaping her. It had been a long day and she was tired out. Noticing the yawn, an uncomfortable glance passed between Ada and Maisie, but as the mistress had given her strict instructions, Maisie knew that she must carry them out.

Taking Sassy's arm she said quietly, 'Come wi' me, miss, and I'll show yer to yer room.'

'Maisie, *please* don't call me miss,' Sassy said immediately. 'My name's Melissa but everyone calls me Sassy.'

Glancing as if for support at Ada again, Maisie nodded. 'All right then – Sassy it is,' she agreed. 'But there's something I must tell yer.' The maid blushed. 'It's just that, well . . .' The poor girl faltered. 'It's just that when the mistress said that she was puttin' you up on the fourth floor, she should 'ave told you that you'll be sharin' my room wi' me up in the attic.' When no argument came from Sassy she continued hastily, 'Me an' Cook don't agree wi' it. We think you should have yer own room on the third floor, along o' Master Matthew an' Miss Louise. But the missus made me put yer stuff in my room. Perhaps you could argue it out wi' her when they get back like, 'cos me an' Cook think it's right unfair, don't we, Ada?'

Ada nodded in strong agreement.

'It's quite all right, Maisie,' Sassy assured her. 'I'd rather be up there with you, honestly,' so, feeling slightly better, Maisie led her to her room.

During the next two weeks, Sassy got to find her way about the great house, and although every room, except the attic rooms, was beautifully furnished, she missed the comfort of the little cottage. However, there was one room that proved to be a constant source of joy to her, for Elizabeth's fine house boasted its own small library. Sassy spent every spare minute she could in there; she had never seen as many books all together in one place before.

Maisie found her in there one morning and looked enviously at the book Sassy was reading. 'It must be wonderful, to be able to read and write,' she sighed, and when Sassy stared at her enquiringly she hurried on, 'I never got much chance to go to school.'

'Would you like me to teach you?' the girl asked, and Maisie's eyes grew round with excitement.

'D'yer really reckon yer could?'

'I don't see why not,' Sassy told her. 'I'll take some pens and papers up to our room and every night before we go to sleep I'll teach you, starting with the alphabet.'

'That would be wonderful,' Maisie agreed, and so it was decided.

During the first week of her father's honeymoon, Sassy visited Clara three times. On two of the visits she got to see Thomas briefly, which cheered her somewhat although Clara seemed less than pleased with him, for as she confided in Sassy, 'Since them bloody gypsies have been back, he's missin' his work again, I'm sure on it – but what can I do about it, eh?' She was also highly indignant when Sassy told her that she was sharing an attic bedroom with the maid.

'That bloody stuck-up snob,' she said furiously. 'You just wait till yer dad gets back – he'll be none too pleased, I'm telling yer. I don't know why he bloody married her in the first place. I mean, let's face it; he were hardly jumpin' fer joy on the big day, were he? It's as I said to my Walter, 'twere more like a blooming funeral than a weddin'. I reckon he were havin' second thoughts afore she even got him to the altar.' Then as her indignant eyes caught the twinkle in Sassy's, she suddenly threw back her head and they fell together giggling like two schoolgirls.

It was following this visit, as Sassy was making her way back to Swan Lane, that she again came upon Ellie and Thomas. This time Jez wasn't with them, which Sassy found strange, knowing that he normally accompanied his sister everywhere. Still, her delight at seeing Ellie soon made her forget all about Jez, and the girls were both soon lost in conversation as they told each other of all the events that had happened to them since their last meeting. All too soon, the time passed and they parted to go their separate ways. Sassy was lifted at the sight of her friend, and as she was now on good terms with Ada and Maisie, she began to feel that perhaps things were not going to be as bad as she had feared, after all. Ellie had informed her that unfortunately this was only to be a short stay, but even so Sassy's heart was lighter than it had been for many a long day and she went on her way with a spring in her step.

Chapter Eleven

Sassy's newfound peace of mind was destined to be shortlived, for the following week when Elizabeth swept into the house on her return from honeymoon, it was more than apparent to all present that things were not as they should be. Arthur appeared downcast, and when she barked at him to hurry and fetch in the trunks, he wearily turned to do as he was told. Even when Arthur discovered that Sassy was sharing an attic bedroom with the maid, he offered up no argument. Although Sassy was quite happy where she was, and loved her father dearly, she suddenly felt angry with him for being so weak as to bow to her new stepmother, but she bit her tongue and said nothing.

The return of Matthew and Louise caused yet another stir. Louise soon made it quite clear that as far as she was concerned, Sassy was no more than another maid. Matthew tried to make Sassy feel welcome, but this caused still more hard feelings towards her and Louise's dislike of her new stepsister quickly grew to a deep dark jealousy.

Arthur began his new job at Elizabeth's brother's brickworks in the office, as befitted his new status, but he missed the comradeship of his workmates at the pit. Yet strangely, of all the people in the house, Elizabeth was perhaps the unhappiest. After waiting so long for Arthur, she had realised on the first night of their honeymoon that although she wore his ring and now bore his name, his heart still belonged to his first love. Even as he took her body with a passion that matched her own, he had cried out almost as a man in torment, one word: '*Sarah!*' and Elizabeth's rage had been terrible to witness. She had always prided herself on playing second fiddle to no one, and she would never forgive him. The worst of her hatred was directed at Sassy. With every day that passed, the girl seemed to look more and more like her mother, and Elizabeth realised that every time Arthur set eyes on her, he must almost be able to see Sarah.

Luckily, all was not bleak for Sassy. A warm friendship had sprung up between herself and Maisie, and soon the little attic bedroom that they shared became Sassy's haven, as well as Maisie's schoolroom. Just as she had promised, Sassy spent a few minutes every evening teaching Maisie her letters, and the girl turned out to be a willing pupil. Already she could recite the alphabet by heart and she was even reading little words now, a fact of which she was inordinately proud.

Ada had also taken a great shine to Sassy, and as Elizabeth never entered the kitchen apart from bringing in the menus, Sassy found another sanctuary there. Most of her time in the house was divided between the two rooms and the library – when Elizabeth was out visiting. Instinct warned her to conceal her friendships with both Maisie and Ada, for if her stepmother knew how happy they made her, the girl was certain she would find a way to spoil it.

Sassy rarely saw her father, even preferring to dine in the kitchen with Maisie and Ada, which was just as well because she knew that Elizabeth would not have wanted her eating with the family. If this troubled Arthur, he held his tongue rather than face his wife's scathing wrath. The same could not be said for Matthew, who was heard to have a blazing row with his mother one day whilst Arthur was at work.

'I think it's appalling that you've stuck Sassy up in the attic rooms with the servants,' he told her in no uncertain terms.

'Don't be so silly, darling,' she placated him. 'Sassy is happy up there, otherwise she would say something.'

He shook his head in angry denial. 'Oh no, she wouldn't. She's not the sort of girl to cause trouble – and why have you got her cleaning? I thought we had Maisie to do the household chores.'

'Sassy *likes* to help,' Elizabeth simpered, and turning on his heel, her son stormed from the room. But he wasn't done yet – not by a long shot.

And so the months slowly passed, and Sassy's life formed a pattern. Sometimes she wondered if she should suggest getting a job, as other young women her age did, but she dismissed the thoughts almost immediately. Elizabeth was a snob, and whilst she was quite happy for Sassy to help out around the house, she would not like it to be known that her stepdaughter had gone out to work.

Her trips to see her aunt and uncle became ever more frequent. They were always pleased to see her and were also glad of the help she gave whenever she visited them. As the smallholding grew from strength to strength, there were always jobs that needed doing and Sassy was more than willing to lend a hand. James and Jack also looked forward to her visits, and it would have been hard to say which of the two adored her most.

Each night, tucked up in their little beds in the attic, Maisie and Sassy would gossip about the things that had happened during the day – although in fairness, Sassy usually had more to tell. Maisie only had one afternoon a week off, and on that afternoon she always visited her family who lived in one of the humbler cottages that backed onto Abbey Street. Sassy had learned during these conversations that Maisie actually came from a very large family, consisting of four brothers, five sisters and her mother and father. She spoke fondly of her siblings and her mother, and often had Sassy in fits of giggles as she relayed some of the mischievous pranks that the little ones got up to. Every week when she paid her visit home, she would stop at the little corner shop and spend a shilling of her wages on candy for them. This was their only treat, and Sassy guessed that she probably tipped the rest of her wages up to her mother. As the weeks passed, Sassy began to feel that she almost knew the children, even though she had never met them, and she began to envy Maisie. There was no word of William, and as Maisie chattered on about one or another of her siblings, Sassy missed him terribly.

Sometimes she found it strange that Maisie rarely mentioned her father, and assumed that the girl chose to live in because of her large family. But on that score she was soon to be proved wrong. By now, she had become almost expert at avoiding both Elizabeth and Louise. It was easier that way, rather than take the constant spiteful snides, but it just so happened that one day as she had just left the library to take a book to her room, she came across Elizabeth berating Maisie for leaving a smear on the sitting room's impressive black marble fireplace.

'I'm sorry, ma'am, I'll correct it right away,' apologised Maisie, but Elizabeth was having none of it.

'Oh no, you won't, girl,' she snapped. 'You'll do the whole thing again from top to bottom.'

'But, ma'am,' implored Maisie, 'today's me afternoon off, an' if I don't leave soon, me mam won't have no money for the little 'uns' meals.'

Elizabeth eyed her icily. 'Then if your mother's so important, perhaps you'd rather go back and live there?

I assure you there are any number of girls who would be more than glad of your position, don't you agree?'

Maisie visibly paled beneath her mistress's sarcastic smile. 'Oh, no, no, ma'am, I'll start again, just as you say.'

For some reason that Sassy couldn't yet understand, Maisie seemed terrified by the threat of being forced to live at home again. The poor girl was just about to start the whole of the job again, when Sassy stood up to her stepmother for the first time.

'Leave that be, Maisie,' she commanded. 'Go and get yourself ready an' I'll redo the polishing.'

Elizabeth was so angry that she looked like she was about to explode. 'How dare you give my servants orders in *my* house!' she spluttered.

Sassy stood her ground. 'I dare,' she said quietly, 'because it's Maisie's afternoon off, and as she said, her mam's relying on that money coming.'

Elizabeth was temporarily speechless with rage, but before she could utter another word, Sassy continued, 'Of course, you could make her stay and do it, but then I wonder what the congregation at church would think, if they knew that the highly respected Elizabeth Churm had deprived some poor little souls of their evening meal?'

Sassy turned back to Maisie and took the cleaning rags from her shaking hands. Then, with a determined tilt to her chin she faced Elizabeth and asked, 'Well, Stepmother – does she go or does she stay?'

Desperately trying to regain control of the situation, Elizabeth nodded at Maisie. 'Go,' she ordered shortly.

Poor Maisie was astonished that Sassy had dared to make a stand against this formidable woman, but even so she flew from the room.

Face to face now, with their mutual dislike more than obvious, they eyed each other.

'Well, you *will* do it now, and make a good job of it – or else,' Elizabeth hissed.

Sassy nodded. 'Oh, I'll make a good job of it, all right.' The words were quietly said. 'After all, I've had more practice at skivvying since coming to this house than I ever had when I ran our own cottage.'

Elizabeth's mouth gaped at the cheek of the girl. Normally she kept out of the way, and never answered back – so what could have got into her? She opened her mouth to answer but then thinking better of it, she lifted her skirts and flounced from the room in a rustle of silk.

As Sassy and Ada were sitting companionably in the kitchen that evening, waiting for Maisie to return from her trip home, Sassy told her of what had gone on earlier in the day. Ada laughed until the tears ran down her fat old cheeks. Sassy laughed with her, but presently she became serious.

'I couldn't understand it,' she said, more to herself than Ada. 'It was almost as if Elizabeth were threatening to send her home. I mean, I can understand that they must be overcrowded, but if I were Maisie, I'd much sooner be with them than here, 'cos she sounds to have a grand family.'

The smile vanished from Ada's face.

'Look, love,' she said uncomfortably, 'perhaps there's more to it than meets the eye.' Meeting Sassy's curious gaze, Ada held up her hand. 'All I'll say is this. I knows you've had yer share o' sorrow an' upheaval, but there's allus some poor soul worse off than yerself, an' happen Maisie's one of 'em. Happen when she's ready she'll tell you of it in her own good time. I've said too much already.' She settled deeper into the chair, and her posture more than told Sassy that for now at least the matter was closed.

The two girls were tucked deep into their beds and Sassy was just slipping into a comfortable doze later that night when a slight noise from the other bed caught her attention. She strained her ears, and presently the noise came again. It was Maisie crying. Should she ignore it? Sassy was unsure what to do. She lay quite still listening to the muffled sobs, until finally she could stand it no more, so getting down from her bed, she quickly crossed the cold linoleum floor and, pulling back Maisie's blanket, climbed in beside her and held her fast until Maisie's sobs began to subside. She asked no questions. Ada's words were loud in her mind – '*she'll tell you in her own good time,*' she'd said – and they proved to be true when some time later, Maisie's voice came out of the darkness.

'I'm sorry about that, Sassy,' she whispered.

'It's all right, Maisie, we all need to let our feelings out sometimes.'

She could feel the other girl nod. 'It's me dad, yer see.' Her voice held fear. 'That's why I don't want to live at home, like.'

'You don't have to tell me,' Sassy whispered, but now the girl shook her head.

'No . . . if yer don't mind listenin', I'd like to.' She sighed deeply before slowly continuing, 'I do have me brothers an' sisters at home, but perhaps I gave yer the wrong picture.' Her voice was so low that Sassy had to strain to hear her, and the silence that followed, although it was in fact only seconds, seemed to stretch for long minutes.

'It started a few years back,' Maisie began at last. 'Till then we was poor, but we was happy; even if our bellies weren't allus full, we was happy.' She repeated it, almost as if trying to convince herself as much as Sassy. 'Anyway, round about then, me dad started callin' in at the pub on

114

his way home from work, an' slowly his drinkin' sessions got longer an' longer an' him an' me mam started to row.' She paused as if picturing the scene in her mind, and then taking a deep breath she went on, 'At the time, me mam was turnin' nippers out nearly one a year, an' what wi' that an' me dad's drinkin', things seemed to go from bad to worse. Then one night, we young 'uns were all in bed an' in comes me dad, steamin' drunk.' She stopped again, then: 'Well, in no time they was goin' at it hammer an' tong, an' the next thing we hears is me mam screamin' fit to waken the dead. We were too scared to get up, but next mornin' she had two black eyes as would have put a boxer to shame – an' that were the start of it.'

Sassy caught her breath in horror. She had suffered her fair share of heartache, but this was the first time she had heard of brutality like this.

'After that,' Maisie went on, 'it were downhill all the way. He never hit the little 'uns but he started on us older 'uns, and I knew then I had to get me two sisters out o' there. So, before I got meself this position, I found posts for them first. We all go home once a week. If we don't tip up us wages, then me poor mam gets used as a punchbag, an' even though the mistress is hard, I'd a hundred times sooner be here than there wi' *him*.'

'But why does your mam stay with him?' Sassy asked. 'Why doesn't she just leave him?'

Maisie laughed bitterly. 'It's easier said than done. Where would she go wi' all the nippers? An' what would they live on? No, Sassy, as me mam says, she's made her bed an' now she must lie on it. An' I'll tell yer somethin' else an' all – after seein' me dad's behaviour, I ain't *never* goin' to get married.'

'Oh, pet.' Sassy was deeply upset. 'You mustn't say things like that. Not all men are like your dad, an' one day you'll meet a decent man, just like *my* dad.'

Maisie snorted. 'Huh,' she said. 'Your dad ain't violent, admitted, but he has his faults an' all.'

'What do you mean?' Sassy asked in quick defence.

'What I mean is this, your dad's not violent but he's too much the other way, wi' no will of his own. The mistress rules him with a rod of iron, yer have to admit, an' sometimes I wonder why he ever married her in the first place, for she wears the trousers in this house an' no mistake.'

A silence fell between them as Sassy pondered on Maisie's words, and tried to absorb the impact of her judgement of Arthur as a weak man under his wife's thumb. The two girls lay close together as if drawing comfort from each other, and when at last they both drifted into sleep, Sassy knew that never again would she view life through the innocent eyes of a child.

Since the day Sassy had defended Maisie to Elizabeth, an uneasy truce had sprung up between them, but the same could not be said of Louise. As Sassy's fifteenth birthday approached and she slowly blossomed, Louise grew even more jealous of her and at every opportunity she tried to slight her. The two girls were almost the same age, but in both looks and nature were totally different. Sassy's figure was gradually gaining curves, while Louise could only be described as plump, which she hated, but not enough to give up the many sweetmeats that she devoured. These also gave her spots, while Sassy's complexion was as clear as a bell. Sassy had maintained her kind and giving nature, but Louise was sly and envious of everything that Sassy did or owned; the latter had long since acknowledged to herself that she and Louise would never be friends. Thankfully, the same could not be said for Matthew. Sassy sensed that she had found a true friend in him and often wondered how a brother and sister could be so very different.

Her visits to Aunt Miriam and Uncle Ben were a welcome release for her, for although the house she had now lived in for almost two years was as luxurious as any in the town, it lacked the homely, happy atmosphere of the smallholding, and so her visits became even more frequent. It was as she was heading there on a blustery January day that she bumped into Matthew. She was just passing the Cock and Bear Inn at the end of Swan Lane when she saw him; he didn't immediately see her as his head was bent low against the bitingly cold wind. When he did finally spot her, he called out a greeting. He liked Sassy and often wished that it were she and not Louise who was his sister. Since Sassy's arrival, he had often taken her side against Louise. He considered his sister to be a snob and had little time for her.

For some time now, Matthew and his mother had been locked in a bitter dispute regarding his future. Elizabeth wished him to join his Uncle John in the family business, but Matthew, although fond of his uncle, had his own ideas: it was his burning ambition to go to medical school and become a doctor but Elizabeth had flatly refused to fund him.

Sassy guessed where he had been when she saw that her stepbrother had two huge medical journals tucked beneath his arm. Dr Massey had probably lent them to him; she knew that he was encouraging him in his ambition and felt that the lad had all the makings of a good doctor.

Smiling, she nodded at the books. 'I dare say you're rushing home so you can get your nose stuck into that little lot, eh?'

'You're not far wrong there,' he quipped back, but as

his smile faded she saw the sadness in his eyes. 'I just wish Mother could accept that this is what I want to do.'

Sassy's warm heart felt for him; reaching out, she squeezed his arm gently. 'I reckon you'll get there in the end,' she said, 'an' when you do, you'll make a fine doctor – I just know it.'

'I can always hope, can't I?' he shrugged, and then his mood lifting slightly, he asked, 'Where are you off to anyway – to see your aunt and uncle?'

'Yes, I am, an' if I don't get a move on they'll have a search-party out looking for me.'

'Right, I can take a hint.' Matthew grinned and raised his hand in salute before setting off in the direction of home.

Sassy watched him as he strode away. She thought it was nothing short of a shame that Elizabeth was so against his chosen career. A doctor was a fine vocation. But then, as she had come to discover, Elizabeth was a law unto herself and woe betide anyone who went against her.

Chapter Twelve

When Sassy arrived at the smallholding, her spirits lifted as always. James almost bowled her over as he sprang at her in his joy at seeing her, and again she had to admit that even now, compared to Maisie, she had a lot to be thankful for. One of the pigs had just delivered a large litter of piglets, and as the little boy tugged her towards the sties to see the new arrivals, Jack, who was gazing across the wall at them, beamed at her.

'You made it then.'

Sassy returned his smile and nodded. James was almost beside himself with excitement at the little piglets but after standing and admiring them for some time, Sassy finally managed to disentangle her fingers from his, and leaving him in Jack's capable hands, made her way to the farmhouse where Aunt Miriam was waiting for her.

It was teatime when she arrived back at Swan Lane, frozen to the bone. Even though she had worn warm gloves, and tucked her hands into a muff, her fingers were blue with cold. She had just let herself in the front door, when a commotion coming from the library caused her to stare in amazement. Elizabeth was screaming like a fishwife and it sounded as if John, her brother, usually a kindly man, was giving as good as he got. Matthew's voice could also be heard, arguing. Not wishing to be caught eavesdropping, Sassy hurried noiselessly along the long hallway and down into the kitchen. Maisie and

Ada were standing as close to the door as they could get, doing their best to hear what was going on. As Sassy entered, they raised their fingers to their lips and uttered, 'Shush,' in unison. Shivering, she tiptoed across to hold her hands out to the welcoming warmth of the fire. It was some ten to fifteen minutes later when they heard the two men walk out of the library, pulling the door resoundingly to behind them.

Maisie and Ada were hopping from foot to foot in frustration, but luckily they didn't have to wait long for their curiosity to be satisfied. Voices murmured in the hall, then the front door closed. Shortly afterwards, they heard Matthew's footsteps approaching the kitchen door. The second he entered, the three women saw that something wonderful must have happened, for he was barely able to contain his excitement and his eyes were shining.

Clasping Sassy round the waist, he quite unexpectedly swung her off her feet and planted a great wet kiss on her cheek. Then he did the same to Maisie which caused a huge blush to spread from her neck right up to her hairline. When it came to Ada's turn, the old cook had to settle for a kiss and a hug. Even in his jubilation, Matthew could never have lifted her, let alone swing her around. His mood was infectious and by the time he dropped breathlessly into the chair at the side of the fire, the whole room was in an uproar.

Sassy caught his hands and shook them impatiently. 'Well, come on then, if you've some good news, share it, eh?'

He was beaming like the Cheshire Cat in *Alice*. 'All right then, I will,' he said. 'Uncle John has just had a big quarrel with Mother and told her that I should be allowed to go to medical school.' He gazed from one expectant face to another. 'Anyway, the outcome of it was, she wouldn't budge, and eventually Uncle John said that if she won't pay for me to go, then *he* will.'

As the meaning of his words sank in, Sassy cried, 'Oh Matthew, that's wonderful news! Didn't I tell you things would come right in the end?'

He nodded happily. 'Yes, you did, but I didn't expect it to happen this quickly. You must be a witch.'

Elizabeth, still furiously pacing the library, heard the merriment coming from the kitchen and gritted her teeth with rage. She was used to getting her own way, and the confrontation with her brother and her son had gone sorely against the grain.

The following weeks passed in a blur of activity as Matthew prepared for his departure to London. Although Elizabeth was still furious that her brother had taken Matthew's side against hers, she finally accepted that her son did indeed intend to go, and so, ever conscious of her place in society, she began to rig Matthew out with new clothes from top to bottom. She even supplied him with a beautiful set of fine leather journals that left the boy gasping with pleasure. She realised now that he would not be swayed from his choice of career, and so decided that if he were to be a doctor, then he must be the best. And St Bartholomew's Hospital Medical College was the finest place to study, she had been assured by Dr Massey. At last, albeit grudgingly, she even gave him her blessing, knowing that the alternative would be to lose him for ever.

In the hustle and bustle of all the preparations Sassy's fifteenth birthday came and went with the minimum amount of fuss. Clara baked her a cake, which Sassy was delighted to share with them all, particularly Thomas, who to her eyes grew ever more handsome. Ellie and Jez were still camped in Nuneaton and Sassy

121

had enjoyed quite a few chats with them recently, and even another visit to the camp, which held just as much enchantment as the first time. As always when with his gypsy friends, Thomas had seemed to come alive, a fact which didn't slip Clara's notice, although she wisely said not a word to him on the matter. His threat was always in her mind and while the gypsies dwelled in Nuneaton, Clara lived in fear.

On the other hand, Walter was growing gravely concerned about his firstborn, and one evening when Clara had retired for an early night he took the opportunity to talk to him.

'Yer know, son, I'm a bit worried about how much time you're spending wi' these here gypsy friends o' yourn.'

When Thomas opened his mouth to protest, Walter held his hand up. 'Just hear me out, will you, lad?' he asked. 'I ain't meanin' to scold yer, an' happen yer old enough to do as yer please now, but just go steady, eh? Everyone knows gypsies ain't folks to be trifled wi' – especially their womenfolk – an' yer spendin' an awful lot o' time wi' that gypsy lass, from what I can see of it. If you ain't careful, old Saul will be holdin' a shotgun to yer head an' forcin' you to make an honest woman of her.'

'Huh! I ain't got no intentions o' getting married,' Thomas said scathingly.

'I dare say you ain't,' Walter replied sagely. 'I know you've got an eye fer the ladies an' there's nowt wrong in that. Yer a good-lookin' lad. All I'm sayin' is, just go careful, eh?'

As Thomas turned on his heel and carried his candle up the steep wooden stairs, his lip curled. His father was an old stick-in-the-mud. Why shouldn't he enjoy spending time with Ellie? She was a right pretty lass and he was a normal hot-blooded male.

His thoughts now turned to Sassy and he frowned as he blew out the candle. She had never made a secret of the fact that she was besotted with him, and he knew that his parents would be delighted if he was to take up with her, but somehow he couldn't get his thoughts beyond Ellie, although Sassy was turning into a lovely young woman. Clambering between the cold cotton sheets, he soon drifted off to sleep with pictures of Sassy and Ellie dancing behind his closed eyes.

At last the day of Matthew's departure arrived. His trunks were loaded onto the trap, and the fine grey cob that pulled it stood pawing the ground, impatient to be off. Every single person from the household was standing outside to wish him well and see him on his way. Having already said her goodbyes, Ada now held her starched apron to her streaming eyes. She had cooked for him since he was knee-high to a grasshopper, and had lost count of the times she had baked him his favourite cakes. She had a huge soft spot for Master Matthew and would miss him sadly.

Arthur took his stepson's hand firmly in his and wished him all the best, as Maisie stood by blushing furiously. She too had a soft spot for Matthew, and raised herself on tiptoe to shyly peck him on the cheek. And so it went on until all the goodbyes were said.

Conflicting emotions were rushing through Sassy as he at last climbed up into the trap. One half of her was jubilant that this gentle youth was having his greatest wish fulfilled, the other selfish side was crying out. She already knew how much she would miss him, for he had stood up for her against Louise and Elizabeth more times than she could count in the last two years, and with his going she would lose a treasured ally.

The house seemed strangely quiet after his departure

and, restless, Sassy pulled on her warm coat and hat and set off for the afternoon to Miriam and Ben's, where at least she was sure of a warm welcome. As she made her through the bitterly cold winds, she drew more than the odd admiring glance. She was now a very attractive young woman, just as Clara had predicted she would be. Yet strangely, Sassy was totally unaware of how pretty she was, and still retained an air of modesty which, if only she could have known it, made her even more alluring.

As always, her visit to the smallholding went a long way towards lifting her flagging spirits, and when she finally returned to Swan Lane she felt lighter of heart. For the sake of her father she determined that even without Matthew to back her against Louise's spite, she would continue to try and make that cold house into a home.

It was early in April as Sassy was returning from the market that she bumped into Thomas. His head was down, and his hands were thrust deep in his pockets, looking for all the world as if he had the weight of the universe on his shoulders. He was so deep in thought that Sassy was almost upon him before he even noticed her. As always, at the sight of him, her heart began to beat faster.

He had been handsome as a lad but now he appeared almost godlike to her and she totally adored him.

'Penny for your thoughts,' she said, and his startled eyes flew up to meet hers.

'Oh, hello, Sassy.' His voice held a dejected note.

Sassy's heart sank to her boots. 'Is something wrong?' she enquired worriedly. 'Clara's not bad, is she?'

'No, gel,' he quickly reassured her. 'I'm just a bit low, like. Happen it's 'cos me pals are movin' on shortly.'

Knowing how Thomas loved the company of his gypsy friends, after her visits to the camps she could well understand why. They held a curious fascination for her too. 'Never mind,' she said kindly. It hurt her to see Thomas unhappy. 'You know as well as I do that they'll be back in a few months' time.'

'Oh aye, I know yer right,' he agreed, 'but it gets harder an' harder to see 'em go. Life round here is not exactly excitin', is it?' As he answered her Sassy couldn't help but stare at his swollen cheek, and aware of her eyes on it, Thomas slowly raised his hand to stroke the offending bruise.

'Don't get frettin' over this. I got it havin' a bit of a play-fight wi' the lads,' he explained self-consciously.

She chewed on her lip. Surely Thomas was a little old to be play-fighting now? Still, knowing that he would not take kindly to being questioned, she bit her tongue. There was something about him today that made her feel uneasy, yet she couldn't quite put a finger on why. After walking on together for some way in silence, they eventually reached the fork in the road that would take them their separate ways.

There he paused, and as he stared at her intently, she blushed. 'It's more like March weather than April, ain't it?' he said. 'How's about we go an' sit in the copse fer a while, out o' the wind?'

Sassy stared up into his handsome face. He was eyeing her appreciatively and she suddenly felt as if all her birthdays and Christmases had come at the same time. She nodded, tingling with pleasure when he took her hand and led her towards the copse. Once beneath the canopy of trees she gasped with delight. A carpet of bluebells stretched for as far as the eye could see, and the scent of them almost took her breath away.

'It's a pretty sight, ain't it?' Thomas murmured as he

turned her to face him. 'Though I have to say, not half as pretty as you, Sassy.'

When his lips met hers, a mixture of emotions fluttered to life in Sassy's stomach. This was the moment she had waited for, for as long as she could remember, and her heart was pounding with joy. His kiss slowly became more demanding and when he undid the ribbons of her bonnet and let it fall to the ground, Sassy made no protest. His hands were stroking up and down her back now, leaving a trail of fire. Then they were clumsily fiddling with the buttons of her coat and Sassy helped him to undo them. And then he was kissing her again as he inched her long skirts above her knees and although she knew that what they were doing was wrong, terribly, dangerously, wonderfully wrong, Sassy gave herself to him trustingly.

When Thomas breathlessly rolled off her some time later, Sassy lay staring up at the sky through the trees. She supposed that she should feel ashamed of what she had just allowed him to do, but then surely this was his way of telling her that he loved her? They would be married one day, so what did it matter?

'I . . . er . . . suppose we'd better be goin'.' Thomas rose and hastily began to button his flies.

Sassy scrambled to her feet and hurriedly straightened her skirts before snatching up her bonnet while Thomas discreetly looked the other way. Strangely, he felt distant now, but she supposed he was feeling embarrassed.

They walked to the edge of the copse in silence then with a curt nod he told her, 'Right then, I'll be off. I'll see yer, Sassy.'

As she watched him striding away, her heart was singing, but could she have known it, Thomas was feeling bitterly ashamed of himself.

* * *

The next morning, Sassy was still floating on a cloud of happiness and after helping Maisie with the breakfast dishes, she hastily donned her warm clothes and dropping a peck on Ada's wrinkled cheek, she lifted her basket, which contained two jars of Ada's delicious homemade jam. 'I'll see you both later then,' she shouted over her shoulder, and Ada and Maisie's voices replied almost in unison. 'Not if we see yer first, yer won't!' which sent her through the door with a wide smile on her face. This was wiped away almost immediately as she nearly collided with Louise, who was just leaving the drawing room. Catching sight of Sassy dressed for outdoors, she eyed her disdainfully from top to toe.

'Oh, we're off to see the commoners again, are we?' she sneered, and eager to avoid a confrontation, Sassy hurried past her without a word. This only infuriated Louise the more.

'Well, if you're so intent on visiting riff-raff, I hope you'll have a bath when you come back – *and* check your hair for lice,' Louise added spitefully to her retreating back.

Her words caused Sassy to come to a shuddering halt. No one – but *no one* – would insult Clara to her. Containing her temper with an effort, she slowly turned to face her stepsister.

'I don't know why *you* should worry so,' she said sarcastically, as her eyes flashed fire. 'For even if I did bring back lice, they would never live on you. Even nits are fussy, you see, an' avoid bad meat.' And so saying, she then turned from Louise who was red in the face and gently closed the front door behind her, leaving the other girl speechless with rage.

As she marched up Swan Lane, Sassy held her head high. She could feel Louise's eyes boring into her back from the hall window, and knew that if looks could kill, she would have dropped down dead on the spot there and then. Not until she had rounded the bend in the lane did her steps falter. Since Matthew's departure, the girl had picked and sneered at Sassy, every opportunity she got. Now it was beginning to wear her down. Some time ago, Aunt Miriam had invited her to move into the smallholding with them, and Sassy had to admit that the idea was sorely tempting, but at the end of the day, she was reluctant to leave her father and felt that she must stay for his sake.

She missed Matthew sorely, although the two letters she had received from him were full of London and the new friends he had made. She was almost ashamed to admit that she envied him. He obviously had no regrets on his choice of career and she had no doubt that when he did eventually come home, he would be a fine doctor. Until her encounter with Thomas yesterday she had begun to feel that her own life was going nowhere, with nothing but her visits to her aunt and uncle and Clara to look forward to. But of course, all that was changed now. Thomas loved her and no doubt soon he would be ready for everyone to know. By the time she was almost halfway up Tuttle Hill her spirits were high again.

It was now two years since William had left, but still on each visit to Clara, she always hoped that she would have word of him, for if he should write, his letter would go to the little cottage they had lived in, and Clara had promised to keep it safe until her next visit. As yet, no letter had ever come and sometimes Sassy felt that William could have vanished from the face of the earth. Still, as Clara was wont to say, 'Hope springs eternal to the human breast,' and this was the case with Sassy, for even when despairing she never gave up hope that one day the letter would come. And then added to that there was also the hope that she might see Thomas again, of course.

Her arrival at the cottage was timely as Clara had just sat down to a cup of tea before beginning the weekly chore of stripping the beds. Her face as always lit up at the sight of her, and nodding to the chair opposite, which Sassy gratefully sank onto, she pushed a mug and the big brown teapot across the table to her.

'How are yer then, lass?' she asked kindly. She knew that since Matthew's departure, Louise had set out to make things even worse for Sassy, and as she often said to Walter, 'Big as she is, I'd love to throw that spoiled lass across me lap and spank her fat arse,' which caused Walter to smile, for Louise would have made two of Clara.

Once the tea was poured, Sassy leaned back in the chair and smiled. Through the back door she could see the dolly tub, the washboard and the mangle all stood ready for action in the back yard.

'I reckon you'll dry the washin' today,' she commented, ''cos the wind's enough to cut you in two.'

'Aye, yer could be right.' Clara looked at the trees swaying in the wind through the cottage window. 'But let's both have another cuppa before we start, eh?' And leaning across the table, she poured them both out another cup.

'So how is everyone then?' enquired Sassy.

'They're all well,' Clara replied. 'I have to say though, our Thomas is right down in the dumps 'cos his gypsy pals are movin' on any time now, an' as yer know he's never happier than when they're about.'

Sassy nodded. She was longing to tell Clara that Thomas had made his intentions clear to her, but until he agreed to it she had decided to remain silent. She knew only too well how much Clara worried about his association with the gypsies, and hated to see her so concerned. If only she could have told her that she needn't worry any more.

It was just then that her eyes fell on a metal box on top of the sideboard.

'Is that one of the men's snap tins?' she asked, and Clara frowned.

'Why, damn me,' she said, shaking her head. Crossing to it, she threw back the lid then gazed down in bewilderment at the bread and cheese packed tight inside.

'It's our Thomas's.' She looked across at Sassy, perplexed. 'I've never known him to forget his snap before.'

'He was probably a bit late setting off an' passed it without thinking,' Sassy soothed, although she too found it a little strange because it was a well-known fact that Thomas had an insatiable appetite. Hoping to take Clara's mind off it, she stood up and, removing her bonnet and coat, she headed for the stairs door.

'Come on then, let's be having you,' she teased. 'Get that dolly tub filled while I go and strip the beds.'

Snapping shut the lid on the tin, Clara nodded. 'Aye, all right then, lass.' Lifting the huge black kettle from the fire, she hurried outside to the dolly tub as Sassy skipped lightly up the stairs.

She entered Walter and Clara's room first, and after pulling back the blankets and the eiderdown, she expertly stripped the white sheets and pillowslips from the bed. Rolling them into a bundle, she carried them down to Clara, who immediately began to furiously dunk them up and down in the hot soapy water with her wooden tongs and dolly stick. She then ran back upstairs and neatly made up the double bed with fresh white linen. By the time she arrived back downstairs, Clara had already rinsed the first sheet and was putting it through the mangle. Catching it as it fell through, Sassy trod down the garden to the line and pegged it out securely. The sheet came alive as the wind caught it, and Sassy stood and watched in fascination, for it appeared to be dancing as the wind blew it first one way then another. As her eyes then strayed to the garden of the cottage next door, they came to rest on her mother's rosebed. There had long since been new tenants living there, a young couple with a large family. They seemed pleasant enough but it was more than obvious that they found no joy in gardening, for the rosebed looked sadly neglected. Sassy felt a great sadness at this, as it had been her mother's pride and joy. It was then that Clara popped her head out of the back door and called to her.

'Come on then, lass, an' get the lads' beds stripped. It's bloody freezin' out here, so it is.'

Chuckling again now at Clara's red nose, Sassy hurried past her and went back upstairs. She had stripped Jack's bed and had turned to do the same to Thomas's when an envelope propped on the chest between the two beds caught her eyes. One single word was written across it – *Mam* – and as Sassy slowly carried it down to Clara, a terrible sense of foreboding gripped her.

Clara had her back to her as Sassy approached and was scrubbing a double sheet up and down on the wash-board. Sassy had to say her name twice before Clara heard her. The woman turned her head questioningly, but then as her eyes dropped to the envelope in Sassy's outstretched hand the colour seemed to drain from her face, which made her red nose stand out all the more.

Straightening, she dried her rough hands on the coarse cotton apron that covered her work dress, and nodding towards the door, she swept through it, leaving Sassy to follow her.

As they stood face to face, back in the warmth of the kitchen now, Clara pointed to the envelope.

131

'Read it to me, lass,' she commanded quietly.

Sassy opened it and after taking out a single sheet of paper, she began to read aloud.

Dear Mam,

I have tried to accept my life as it is, but I can't stand being in one place, and so I have gone to travel with my friends. I will send you some money regularly and I will write. Forgive me because I don't mean to hurt you.

Your loving son,
Thomas

Sassy's face was as pale as Clara's and her voice, by the time she had read the note, had dropped to no more than a whisper. The women stared at each other, both deep in shock.

The silence seemed to stretch on and on. Both of them seemed incapable of speech, but then suddenly the colour flooded back into Clara's cheeks, and raising her fist she banged the table with a force that lifted even the heavy brown teapot.

'*No!*' The word held such torment that tears sprang to Sassy's eyes. Clara was like a woman possessed. But before she could utter so much as a single word, Clara sprang towards the door and sprinted off down the lane, leaving Sassy to follow her as best she could, the cottage door bouncing on its hinges behind them.

Although Sassy was only a third of Clara's age, she couldn't keep up with her, for if Old Nick himself had been snapping at her heels, Clara couldn't have gone any faster. She knew that the gypsies had been camped in Hartshill Woods from bits that Thomas had dropped out over the last weeks, and it was there that she now headed, determined that her son wouldn't leave with them if she could stop it. Before they were even halfway there, they were gasping for breath and Clara had a terrible stitch in her side, but still she ran on, stumbling and tripping over the muddy fields, the wind whipping her hair from its pins until it hung about her shoulders, giving her an almost witch-like appearance.

At last the woods came into view and, frantic now, Clara threw her legs across a rough wooden fence that edged a field and almost fell across it. A roughly knocked-in nail caught at her skirt and pulled a great tear in it, but she seemed hardly to notice as she stumbled on. Soon they reached Oldbury Lane and, still running, they flew along it until they reached the bend that would bring them to the gypsy encampment.

At last, side-by-side they rounded the bend – and the sight that met them stopped them in their tracks. They were too late. Tree-studded horizons seemed to stretch into infinity before them, but all that was left of the gypsy camp were piles of cold ashes, heaps of dung and grass crew-cut by the teeth of many horses. It was as if the sounds, colours and life of the gypsy camp had vanished into thin air. As the terrible truth sank into Clara that her beloved lad was really gone from her, she slipped to the ground, and while the mud soaked greedily into her skirts, she covered her eyes and sobbed as if her heart would break. Meanwhile Sassy stood gazing on the scene before her, too numb to even offer her dear Clara comfort.

They made a sorry sight as they retraced their steps, each leaning heavily on the other. When they reached the comfort of the cottage, they kicked off their boots and sank onto the wooden settle, hands clasped tight together as if to draw comfort from each other. The mud on

Clara's skirts had been dried by the bitingly cold winds and now stood out stiffy from her legs. The fire had long since gone out, and the sodden sheets lay in a wet heap where she had left them. But still they sat on, and it was there that Jack found them some hours later. It was he who remade the fire and brewed them both a strong cup of tea. He was greatly distressed to see his mother so upset, and his heart ached as he saw the effect that Thomas's leaving had had on Sassy. Jack had guessed some long time ago that Thomas's heart was with the gypsies, and had hoped that once Sassy realised it, she might have looked his way. After almost lifting Clara into her room to wash and change, he then turned his attention to Sassy who had finally risen from the settle and was slowly buttoning her coat.

'I'll walk yer back, Sassy,' he offered, but she shook her head firmly.

'No, Jack, it's all right, I'd rather go alone, thanks.'

He began to protest but she held up her hand. 'No, really.' Her voice held a plea now. 'I'd like a bit of time to meself, an' I'm all right really.' She certainly didn't look all right to Jack, but realising that she was in no mood to argue, he nodded.

'All right then, lass, if you're sure,' he said quietly.

'Aye, I am.' Lifting her basket she left the cottage without a backward glance, leaving Jack to stare after her from painfilled eyes.

Once outside, instead of taking the path that would lead her home, she skirted the cottages and, on leaden feet, slowly climbed the hill to the windmill. Ever since she had been a little girl, Sassy had loved this place. She could almost imagine that she was on top of the world here. But today the panoramic view gave her no joy. Although the wind tugged at her skirts and threatened to whip her bonnet from her head, it was a clear day and Sassy could see right across almost three counties. The view seemed to stretch for ever, and straining her eyes, she saw the chimneypots of Caldecote Hall reaching through the trees that surrounded it, before they came to rest on the old Roman road. Her eyes ran along the length of it as far as she could see before returning to seek amongst the many lanes that wound through the emerald-green fields laid out before her. But no matter where she looked, no colourful gypsy caravans could be seen and a deep feeling of loneliness closed around her heart. She could almost imagine that she was the only person on earth.

A lone fox suddenly broke from the bushes at the bottom of the bank, and glimpsing Sassy standing there, he paused and glared at her through his sly yellow eyes. Then, as if realising that she offered him no threat, he trotted across the lane to disappear into the thick undergrowth, leaving Sassy to wonder, as his bushy tail vanished from view, if he had ever been there at all.

Images of her mother, her baby sister, George, William, Matthew and now Thomas drifted through her mind, for at that moment it felt as if everyone she loved was being taken from her one at a time, and although her eyes were dry, inside her heart was crying.

Somehow, after what had happened between them yesterday, Thomas's going seemed the cruellest loss of all. She had no idea how she could face life without him. Ever since she had been a very little girl, he had been her shining star and without him, her world suddenly seemed as dark as deepest night.

PART THREE

Summer, 1878

At Holly Bush Farm

Chapter Thirteen

On a perfect summer's day in July in the year 1878, Ben stood admiring his newly built barn. He was so delighted with it that he was hopping about almost as much as James – greatly to the amusement of everyone present.

'What do you think of it now it's finished then, Sassy?' he asked for the third time.

His delight was infectious, and Sassy smiled indulgently as she answered yet again, 'Why, it's a grand barn, Uncle Ben.'

Jack caught her eye and grinned. It was nice to see her smile. She had seemed so sad lately. James was holding Ben's hand and was jigging around with excitement. The boy loved to see his family happy, and sensed Ben's pleasure. Although he was slow in many ways, they had soon discovered that James had an uncanny knack of being able to pick up on people's moods, and because of his sensitive, gentle nature, his own mood would usually then match theirs.

It was a splendid barn, of solid timber construction and boasting two storeys. The lower floor was large enough to house most of the growing herd of cows during the winter, and the upper storey was divided into halves. One half would serve as a hayloft and the other had been made into living-quarters, consisting of a sitting room and a small bedroom. Ben hoped that soon he might be able to employ someone who would make use of these rooms, using the washing facilities in the farmhouse, where they would take their main meals with the family; the earth closet was discreetly tucked away at the end of a path, and everyone had a chamberpot under their bed.

He and Jack now had to work much longer hours to deal with the growing business. Over the last couple of years, Ben had managed by employing casual labour to help out here and there, but now he desperately needed another permanent, resident pair of hands that he could rely on, fulltime. He had already offered Jack the new living-quarters, but the lad, acutely aware that his parents were still feeling the loss of Thomas, had turned him down, although it would have saved him a lot of travelling to and fro to work. He was happy to make the sacrifice as he felt that his parents were not yet ready to cope with his leaving too.

During the months since Thomas's departure, Clara had slowly come to accept his going. She had no choice, but Jack knew that she still missed him sadly, as did Sassy, and as he looked across at her now, smiling at her uncle and James's antics, his heart lightened. He never gave up hope that once she realised Thomas was truly gone for good, she might then look on him at last.

Ben went striding into the barn with James still clutching his hand, and as she watched them go, Miriam smiled at Sassy.

'Look at the pair of 'em,' she laughed. 'It's hard to say which is actin' the daftest, ain't it?' But her voice held pride. Her Ben had worked long and hard at this business, and she of all people knew just how much he deserved to get on.

Although Sassy's smile matched Miriam's, inwardly she felt a twitch of concern. Lately, Miriam was looking pale and seemed to have lost some weight, but when Sassy had mentioned this, her aunt shrugged it off.

'Oh, I'm fine, love,' she'd assured her. 'It's just that

there never seems to be enough hours in the day, but once we get some more reliable help, I'll be able to slow down a bit.'

Sassy felt a pang of guilt. She would happily have moved in tomorrow as things were still no better back in Swan Lane. In fact, sometimes Louise was so spiteful that Sassy would almost decide to do just that – and it was only the thought of her father, who appeared even more downtrodden than ever, that stopped her.

Ben and James had by now disappeared from sight into the barn, although their laughter still floated on the air.

'Come on, love.' Miriam swiped the sweat from her brow with the back of her hand. 'Let's go and get us a nice cold glass o' lemonade, an' then we'll have a sort-out, an' dig out some bits and pieces for the living-quarters, eh? It's enough to bake you out here in this heat.'

Sassy followed her aunt into the welcoming coolness of the cottage and by mid-afternoon they had almost everything they needed to furnish and equip the rooms above the barn. Jack carried the furniture over for them and by teatime, the empty rooms were transformed. Fresh, clean cretonne curtains hung at the windows, which boasted a breathtakingly pretty view over Bermuda village in the distance, and various useful items were all neatly stacked away in a small oak cupboard. An easy chair, slightly worn but still comfortable, stood in one corner of the small sitting room, and in the other corner was a solid little table with a highly polished brass oil lamp, all ready for lighting. In the bedroom, the bed was made up with crisp linen sheets tucked around the flock mattress, and it had a bolster and warm blankets. Miriam stood with her hands on her hips as she surveyed their handiwork.

'There then, that's not bad even if I do say so meself.' She winked at Sassy happily, and tired but satisfied with their afternoon's work, they linked arms and made their way down the stairs back to the cottage to prepare the evening meal. When Ben and Jack later climbed up to see what Sassy and Miriam had been up to all afternoon, Ben was delighted.

'Why, lad, they've done ruddy marvels!' he exclaimed, gazing around at the two little rooms, which now looked cosy and inviting.

Jack nodded in agreement.

'All we need now is somebody reliable to move in, to help us out,' muttered Ben.

Jack held his tongue. He already had someone in mind, but didn't want to mention it to Ben until he'd had time to find out if they would be interested. For some weeks now he had been waiting for the barn to be finished and now that it was, he could hardly wait for next market day – for then, if the opportunity arose, he intended to speak to the person who just might meet all Ben's requirements.

It was late afternoon by the time Sassy set off for home. She took her time. The heat had cooled a little now and it was pleasant to stroll through the fields with nothing but her thoughts for company. Like Clara, she had now begun to accept the fact that Thomas had left, the difference being that she still hoped he would return, while his mother seemed to believe that he never would.

When she arrived home she was worn out, so after tucking into the hearty meal that Ada had kept warm for her, she grabbed a book from the library and climbed the back stairs to bed for an early night. Tomorrow was one of her days to visit Clara, and she wanted to be up bright and early.

The sun streaming through the curtains woke her the next morning, and looking across to Maisie's bed she saw it neatly made up with her nightgown folded on the pillow. She must have crept about the room as quiet as a mouse when she rose. Sassy hadn't heard a sound, and hastily rising now, she quickly washed, dressed and brushed her hair. On entering the kitchen, she guiltily found that breakfast was long over. 'Why didn't you wake me? You know I always like to help you with the dishes,' she said to Maisie.

The little maid grinned. 'That's exactly why I didn't,' she replied. 'Yer looked fair frazzled last night, an' I thought a bit of a lie-in would do yer good.'

Sassy smiled at her friend's thoughtfulness, and once again thanked God for her. Without Maisie and Ada, life in this loveless house would have been pure misery.

She set out on her familiar route somewhat later than usual, and by then the sun was riding high in a cloudless blue sky. The walk didn't hold quite the same excitement now that there was no chance of glimpsing Thomas, but still she loved Clara just the same and never missed a visit. The wild flowers growing in the hedgerows made a pretty picture, and every now and then she would stop to pick one. By the time the cottages came into sight, she had plucked a huge bunch for Clara.

The doors of the cottage and all the windows were flung open to allow the cool air in, and as she entered and placed her flowery offering on the table, Clara turned from the sink to smile at her.

'Ah, so yer here then. I was just beginning to wonder if you'd make it today.'

'Maisie never woke me and I slept in,' Sassy explained apologetically.

Clara nodded in approval. 'Good fer her,' she declared. 'Yer should be allowed to do it more often. It seems to me yer little more than a bloody skivvy in that place.'

Not wishing to set Clara off on that score again, Sassy hastily told her all about her Uncle Ben's new barn.

Although Clara listened she seemed strangely distracted, and by the time she had placed two tumblers and a glass jug full of lemonade on the table, with a little beaded muslin cover to keep off the flies, Sassy knew that something was amiss. Taking Clara's hand in hers, she asked softly, 'Is something wrong?'

Clara pulled herself back to the present with an effort. 'Not wrong exactly, lass, but I do have somethin' for yer.'

When the girl raised her eyebrows, Clara dug deep into her pinny pocket and pulled out two envelopes, one of which she brandished at Sassy. 'This came to next door yesterday on the carrier cart,' she said quietly. 'It's for you, an' I reckon it could be from William.'

Sassy felt the colour drain from her face. She had waited so long for this letter, yet now that it had finally come she was afraid to open it.

'Go on, take it, lass,' Clara urged. 'You've been waitin' for it long enough, God knows, an' it ain't goin' to bite yer.'

With shaking fingers Sassy did as she was told. The envelope had obviously been some long time in the post and was grubby and well-handled. The ink was smudged in places, and it bore a foreign stamp that Sassy couldn't recognise. Her heart was beating so fast now that she feared it would jump from her chest. Slowly, she slit it open and drew from it a single sheet of paper. As her eyes flew to the bottom of the page they filled with tears. 'It *is* from William!' she cried excitedly and Clara beamed at the look of relief on the girl's face.

'There y'are then, lass. I allus said it would come, did I not?' she said, but when Sassy still continued to gaze at the long-awaited letter, she snapped, 'Well, come on then, the suspense is killin' me. Read it out loud.'

Sassy cleared her throat and began:

144

Dear Dad and Sassy,

I hope this note finds you both well, as I am. I am working aboard a cargo ship as a cabin boy. I am sending this letter from America and so far I have visited three countries. I'm sorry for the way I ran off, and hope you have both forgiven me. I love the sea life and when we next dock in England, I shall come home to see you both. Give my love to Clara and all next door.

Yours affectionately,
William xxxx

When Sassy had finished reading the letter, she and Clara stared at each other in silence for some moments, both with tears streaming down their faces, but presently Clara dried her eyes with the back of her hand.

'Bugger me,' she said throatily.' 'Who would have thought it, eh? An' won't you two have some catchin' up to do when he comes home!'

Sassy smiled through her tears. 'We certainly will,' she agreed. 'William doesn't even know that Dad married the Widow yet. He obviously thinks we're still living in the cottage.' Not for the first time, she fervently wished that they were – but now was not the time to feel sad. If someone had presented a fortune to Sassy at that moment, it couldn't have meant half as much to her as the grubby letter. She gripped it tightly. Her relief at knowing William was safe and well was enormous, and although she had not long arrived, she could now hardly wait to get home and share the news with her father. Still, he wouldn't be home from the brickworks until late afternoon, so she would just have to contain her excitement until then.

'Just fancy William bein' in America, eh?' She could

hardly believe it. She herself had never been out of Nuneaton and in that moment she envied her brother's exciting, adventurous life.

Clara looked at her indulgently. 'Aye, well happen now yer can stop worryin' about him. If his letter's owt to go by, he certainly sounds happy enough.'

'Yes, he does, doesn't he?' Sassy happily agreed. She appeared so light-hearted that Clara dreaded what she must do next, but knowing that Sassy must be told, she cast about in her mind for the best way to do it. Coming up with no easy answer, she decided to just come straight out with it.

'That weren't the only letter that arrived yesterday,' she said hesitantly.

Sassy's eyes were instantly on her face. 'Was the other from Thomas?' It was hard to keep the eagerness from her voice.

Clara nodded. 'Aye, it was, lass.'

The tone of her voice warned Sassy that something was not right, and she felt a little bubble of apprehension form in her stomach.

'He's not ill, is he?'

Hearing the deep concern in the girl's voice, Clara quickly shook her head.

'No, no, lass, it's nowt like that. In fact, from what I can make of it, he's fightin' fit. He sent me a ten-bob note – he won a purse in a fight.'

Thomas was fast becoming renowned as one of the best bare-knuckle fighters in the county, and in fairness it had come as no surprise to either of them. They had both had their suspicions on that score for some long time, and whilst neither of them liked it, they had no choice but to accept it.

'What is it then?' Sassy was growing impatient; if something wasn't right, she needed to know.

'Well, it's . . .' Clara's clammy fingers opened and closed. This was one of the hardest things she had ever had to do, but she forced herself to go on. 'He's sent word that he's married Ellie, the gypsy girl.' There, it was out.

Clara had had a night to come to terms with it, but the look of shock that crossed Sassy's white face and the tears that sprang to the girl's deep brown eyes made her wring her hands in consternation.

Sassy was struggling to take in what she had just heard. It couldn't be right. Thomas had loved *her*. He *must* have, or he would never have . . . She stopped her thoughts from going any further as she sat there in stunned disbelief. Clara meanwhile hurried around the table and took her in her arms. After some moments of silence, Sassy gently disentangled herself.

Gazing up at her, she said quietly, 'It's all right, Clara. If I'm honest, I think I've always known underneath that one day this would happen. Right since the day I met Ellie down by the canal when George had his fall on the ice.'

Clara stared at her questioningly.

'It was just something about the way his face lit up when he saw her.' In her mind's eye Sassy could still see the scene as if it were yesterday. 'I knew even then that there was something growing between them, but being young, I didn't want to accept it.'

Clara clenched her fists, and if Thomas had been present at that moment she would have clouted him there and then. From where she was standing it was a bloody shame. Sassy had never made a secret of her feelings for Thomas. And yet there was her Jack who worshipped the very ground she walked on and Sassy had never even looked on him, only as a brother. But taking that aside, her son's news had still managed to shock Clara. There was something about it that just didn't ring true. Thomas was a wild one, and no matter how hard she tried, Clara couldn't envisage him as a married man. Gazing towards the open window where the curtains were gently blowing in the breeze Clara tutted as she once again questioned the unfairness of life.

Chapter Fourteen

On market day, Jack was up with the lark. It was another bright clear day, and by breakfast time he was strolling among the pens in the cattle market, his eyes seeking this way and that. He had a number of things to get for Ben today, plus one thing that Ben had no idea of as yet. As his eyes scanned the outskirts of the pens, his eyes finally lit on the person he was seeking, and he hurried to get to the youth before anyone else should.

'Mornin' there.' He smiled amiably and the youth nodded. 'I'm lookin' for a good milkin' cow. I was wondering if you'd help me choose one then help me get it back to the smallholding where I work?'

The lad looked at him but said nothing.

'There's five bob in it for yer if yer do, an' yer could be back here fer dinnertime.'

'That sounds fair enough,' the youth said, and Jack held out his hand, which the lad took and shook firmly.

'Jack Mallabone,' he introduced himself.

'Aaron Lee.'

Without further ado they walked deep into the heart of the cattle pens and the search began. Jack was more than able to spot a good cow himself, otherwise Ben would never have trusted him to do it, but this morning he was keen to see what the youth would pick, so he kept his distance and left the lad to choose. He'd had his eye on this youth for some time now, for he seemed to have a way with beasts. Once, Jack had seen him calm a very irate bull and finally lead it to a pen, when all others had failed, and this had greatly impressed him. Every market day, rain or shine, the youth could be found hovering at the edge of the pens. His reputation with the animals was becoming recognised amongst the local farmers now, so it was usually not long before someone set him on for the day, which was why Jack had arrived particularly early.

The youth examined almost every cow systematically with an expertise that greatly satisfied Jack, and finally, after almost an hour and a half, he pointed to a creature with soft brown eyes.

'If you're askin' my opinion, I'd go for her,' he said. 'She's docile, healthy, got good teeth, an' I reckon she'd give yer a good milk yield.'

'I reckon yer right,' Jack said, and turned to begin haggling with the farmer who owned her. After some bartering a price was finally agreed and the money changed hands, followed by a firm handshake.

Jack was well pleased with the purchase, and taking the beast by the rope that tied her, he led her through the cattle pens to the outskirts of the market. Pointing to the horse and cart that were tethered there, he handed the rope to Aaron. 'Right then, I'll just go an' get the rest o' the feed. You tie her to the back o' the cart an' I'll be back in a jiffy.'

Some short time later, with the rest of his purchases piled into the back of the cart, and the cow firmly secured, Jack and Aaron climbed aboard and set off for home. When they finally reached the outskirts of the town, Jack drew the horse to a halt and, reaching beneath his seat, fetched out a large stone jug of cider. It was now well past mid-morning and the heat was becoming unbearable. 'I reckon we've earned a drop o' this, don't you?'

Nodding his agreement, Aaron grasped the offered jug and took a long swig before handing it back to Jack.

Aaron was an attractive youth whom Jack judged to be about his own age. He was tall and fair-haired with a well-built frame, and if it hadn't been for the ugly portwine birthmark that covered nearly all one side of his face, he could have been classed as handsome. Jack had already guessed that Aaron was very self-conscious. Whenever he looked at him, the lad had a habit of turning his head so that only the clear side of his face could be seen. But he was an amiable, quiet youth and Jack had already taken a great liking to him. While Jack took a drink, Aaron climbed down from the cart and went to check on the cow, which he stroked and whispered to. Jack watched silently, more sure than ever that he was doing the right thing. He waited for Aaron to climb back aboard, then clicking his tongue at the horse to move on, he asked casually, 'Live local then, do yer?'

'Aye I do.' Aaron kept his eyes straight ahead as he replied. 'I lodge in a room in town.'

'Yer don't live with yer parents then?' prompted Jack.

Aaron shook his head. 'Don't have none.'

It was obvious that Aaron was going to say no more on that subject, so Jack continued cautiously, 'In that case then I might just have a proposition to put to yer that could be of interest to yer.'

Aaron looked at him questioningly.

Seeing that the youth was interested, Jack continued, 'O' course, it's not down to me, but it just so happens that me gaffer's built a fine new barn with livin'-quarters above, an' he desperately needs another pair o' hands to help about the place. Whoever got the job would get the rooms an' all. The work is getting too much fer just the two of us, yer see. Have a think on what I've said and let me know how yer feel about the idea, eh?'

For the rest of the journey, Aaron did just that. He had taken a liking to Jack and the offer sounded tempting. Up to now he had taken work wherever and whenever he could, but the thought of a permanent job was pleasing.

As they entered Ben's fields some time later, Aaron looked about him. The smallholding was obviously well kept and the animals all looked healthy and well fed. By the time they pulled into the yard it appeared almost like heaven to him.

On hearing the cart pull up, Miriam hurried outside, wiping her hands on her apron. She'd been baking and her nose was covered in flour, which gave her a comical appearance. As she caught sight of the cow tethered to the back of the cart, she walked round to inspect it. After giving the beast the once-over, she smiled delightedly at Jack.

'Why, you've chosen a right little beauty here,' she praised.

Jack shook his head. 'Afraid I can't take the credit fer this 'un. It were Aaron here who had the final say. But I have to agree with yer, I reckon he chose well. He has a good eye fer beasts.'

Almost as if it were an everyday occurrence to have strange visitors to her home, Miriam took Aaron by the hand and shook it warmly.

'This is Aaron Lee.' Jack introduced him and as Aaron nodded at her, he blushed so deeply that the clear side of his face almost matched his stained one.

'In that case then, Aaron, I reckon you deserve a nice cold drink,' she said matter-of-factly.

Poor Aaron was speechless with embarrassment. Usually people's eyes flew to his birthmark, but this kindly woman appeared to have not even noticed it.

Just then, Ben came striding from the barn with James

on his shoulders giggling loudly. They had been stacking hay into the new loft in readiness for winter, and resembled two haystacks. If Ben had been asked, he would have been forced to admit that James was more of a hindrance than a help. But the little chap was so loved by them all that no one ever had the heart to send him away.

On spotting the little gathering to the side of the cart, Ben now gently lifted James down and patting him on the backside, ushered him towards Miriam.

'Go on, be off with yer,' he instructed. 'Go an' help yer mam finish her bakin'.'

Still giggling, James obediently took Miriam's hand and followed her into the cottage.

Jack then introduced Ben to Aaron, and Ben carefully examined the new cow.

'You've done well, lad,' he told him approvingly. 'I couldn't have chosen better meself.'

Once again Jack quickly explained that Aaron had chosen the beast. He then told him that Aaron might be interested in a full-time post and left them to discuss it while he joined Miriam and James in the cottage.

Some time later, Ben and Aaron came in and, addressing Miriam, Ben asked, 'Would yer mind takin' Aaron over to see the livin'-quarters in the barn, love?'

'Of course I will, an' gladly,' she consented. 'Follow me, pet.'

Without a word Aaron did as he was told.

When Miriam threw back the door to the small sitting room and bedroom above the barn she was apologetic. 'It ain't posh,' she hastened to tell him. 'To tell the truth, it's furnished with bits an' bobs from the cottage, but it's clean an' I hope it'll be comfortable enough.'

Aaron said nothing, but his eyes took it all in. Crossing to the only window in the tiny sitting room, he looked out at the view. After gazing for some minutes, during which time Miriam became anxious, he slowly turned to her.

'It's lovely,' he said quietly.

Miriam beamed from ear to ear. 'So do you think you could be comfortable here then?' she asked.

'I've never had nothin' the like o' this to meself in me whole life,' he told her and, well pleased, Miriam led him back down the stairs and across the yard to the cottage.

In no time at all, the deal was done, and Aaron departed to collect his belongings and bring them to his new home. He turned down the offer of using the horse and cart since, as he pointed out, his possessions were few. The only thing that he wouldn't agree to was sharing his meals inside with the family.

'But there's no kitchen in the living-quarters,' Miriam objected.

When Aaron shrugged she quickly came up with a solution. 'Well, it needn't be a problem, lad. I can carry your meals over to you on a tray.' She had sensed a great sadness in this young man and hoped that once he had settled in and got to know them, he would get a bit more confident and join them in the cottage.

After he had left, Ben praised Jack for his initiative. Already, he had a feeling that this quiet youth would be an asset to the smallholding.

During the very first week, Ben's intuition was proved to be right. One of his prize cows was in labour and all afternoon, while Aaron and Jack had been about other business, Ben had stayed with her. Now as dusk set in and she still showed no sign of calving, Ben was growing concerned. Once James was safely tucked in bed, Miriam joined him in the barn. Jack had long since left and Aaron was upstairs in his living-quarters. Miriam was as worried as her husband when she saw how distressed the beast was.

'Still no sign of the calf?'

Ben shook his head despairingly, keeping a safe distance. The poor beast was now obviously in great pain and kicking out.

'I'm a bloody fool, I am,' he chided himself. 'I should have seen things weren't right and fetched the veterinary earlier on.'

It was then that a light appeared above them, and Aaron came down, carrying a candle. Taking in the gravity of the situation at a glance, he immediately took control.

'I need a bucket o' hot water quickly, please, missus,' he instructed, and without question, Miriam hurried away to do as she was asked.

When she returned and placed it down, he rolled up his sleeves, then turning to them both, in a voice that brooked no argument, he told them, 'Get yerselves off to bed. All these bodies millin' about the place is makin' her nervous.'

The lad was so confident that Ben took Miriam by the elbow and led her away, somehow sure that he was leaving his beast in good hands – and how right he was. When he rose at daybreak the next morning and hurried to the barn, he found not only the mother, but two hand-some calves, all doing well, with Aaron fast asleep in the hay beside them.

James's delight at the new arrivals was a pleasure to see, and from then onwards Aaron became his hero. He would follow him about like a little puppy and almost became his shadow. On occasions, Miriam scolded him, afraid that Aaron must be tired of James always dogging his footsteps. But strangely, Aaron seemed to like it and Miriam couldn't help but notice that when Aaron was in the company of James or the animals, he became a different lad. Where he was quiet to the point of taciturnity with them, in James's company he would talk quite freely and their joined laughter was often to be heard about the place.

One evening, Miriam carried across Aaron's tray with his supper covered with a snowy-white cloth. She was about to knock and place it outside his door as she usually did, when she noticed that the door was slightly ajar, so balancing the tray on one hand, she tapped, and receiving no answer, she then pushed it open. There was no sign of Aaron, so she placed the tray on the small table next to the chair, and was about to leave the room when something on the windowsill caught her eye. Crossing to it she lifted a small carving of a pig. It was so beautifully made that she could almost have imagined it breathed. Every single detail was perfect, right down to its little corkscrew tail. She was so lost in admiration, that for a moment she was unaware that Aaron had entered the room and now stood beside her. When she finally sensed his presence, she started guiltily, and quickly placed the pig back in its place.

'Oh, I'm so sorry, love,' she apologised, 'I wasn't meanin' to snoop, but this just caught me eye an' I couldn't help but admire it.'

Aaron smiled and she was relieved to see that he had taken no offence.

'It's all right,' he assured her. 'Yer can have it if yer like, I've plenty more.' Crossing to the chest, he drew one drawer open and began to take out a number of small carvings, each one as perfect as the last. There were pigs, sheep, cows, ducks and quite a few more. Miriam was totally amazed, and as she fingered them she couldn't help but stare at him.

'Whoever made all these?' she asked.

Aaron laughed nervously as he quickly began to replace them in the drawer.

'Oh, they're nothin' much. I just like to whittle away at a bit o' wood in me spare time.'

'*You* made them?' she gasped.

Flushing darkly, he nodded.

'Well, lad,' she said, 'I reckon you have a special gift there. Perhaps yer should have made this yer livelihood, eh?'

Aaron shook his head. 'Nah, I like workin' wi' live beasts best,' he replied, and her face softened.

'I bless the day you came to us, lad,' she said gently. 'You're a pleasure to have about the place.' And so saying, she turned and left the room, leaving Aaron with an unfamiliar warm glow in his heart.

It was approaching James's eighth birthday and he could hardly contain his excitement. Sassy was bringing Maisie to a special tea-party, and Miriam was baking him a 'royal' cake. The Victoria Sponge had become all the rage, as the Queen apparently loved it and often ate it at her retreat, Osborne House on the Isle of Wight. The cake was all the boy had talked about as he followed Aaron from one job to another, much to the older youth's amusement. When eventually Aaron stopped and sat on a bale of hay for a breather, the child stood in front of him, and suddenly his small face became serious. After studying Aaron's face intently for some moments, he slowly lifted his hand and gently stroked the portwine stain that disfigured it.

'Poorly,' he said softly.

Aaron didn't pull away. 'Aye, lad,' he said. 'Poorly,' and wrapping his arms about the little lad, he hugged him to him. 'I reckon as you an' me have somethin' in common. Somewhere in our makin' we were left a bit less than perfect, weren't we?'

As if James understood, he solemnly nodded.

'Ah well, we'll have to look out fer each other then, won't we?' said Aaron, and they stood cuddled close together, enjoying their newfound bond.

Unnoticed by either of them, Miriam had observed all this and not wishing to intrude, she slipped quietly away. There was a huge lump in her throat. She had always sensed that there was a great sadness in Aaron, but as he never talked of his past, she had no idea where he had come from.

From that day on, she would have entrusted James's very life to him. She also sensed in him a great kindness and determined that if ever he would let them, they would become his family, for something deep inside her told her that this was what the lad may have lacked.

At last James's birthday arrived, and as Sassy and Maisie made their way up the rough lane towards the smallholding, Maisie was almost as excited as the little lad. This was a rare treat for her and she intended to make the most of every second. Elizabeth and Arthur were away on their summer vacation, and Ada had added her pleas to those of Sassy's.

'Oh *please* come, Maisie,' Sassy had implored, and Ada had joined her.

'Aye, go on, love,' she'd encouraged, 'Go an' get yer glad rags on. There's nowt spoilin' here, an' a day out would do yer a power o' good. Yer know the old sayin' while the cat's away the mouse shall play. So be off with yer an' make the most of her ladyship bein' gone.'

And so Maisie had finally agreed, although in truth, she hadn't needed too much persuading. As Sassy glanced at her now, she smiled. Maisie was skipping along and with her hair loose, as Sassy had insisted on, and her eyes sparkling, she appeared almost pretty. As they entered the yard, James flew to them excitedly and launching himself at Sassy, he covered her face with wet sticky kisses.

'*Cake, cake.*' He was jigging about with glee and pointing into the kitchen, so in a merry mood Sassy and Maisie laughingly allowed him to drag them through the door to admire it.

It was a happy occasion. Ben and Jack both came in for an hour during the afternoon to witness the cutting of the cake. The only one absent was Aaron, who still insisted on eating his solitary meals in his room. However, although he didn't attend the tea-party as such, at about four o'clock a gentle tap came on the open kitchen door. As they all glanced up from the little train set that James was playing with, they saw Aaron uncomfortably shuffling from foot to foot.

'Ah, come on in, love,' beamed Miriam.

'No. I won't, thanks,' he muttered, averting his face. 'I just brought this for James.'

As James sped towards him, Aaron awkwardly held out a small parcel untidily wrapped in brown paper, and James gleefully undid it. The contents brought a hush to the entire room. Aaron had carved two tiny calves, joined only at the hoof, almost identical to the newborns in the barn. James gazed on them with a look of wonder on his small face. It was Miriam who first noticed that Aaron and Maisie's eyes were locked tight together and they were so intent on one another, it was almost as if there was no one else in the room. A little ripple of joy flowed through her. She had only ever seen that look on one other person's face in the whole of her life, and that person had been her Ben on their first meeting.

If she knew anything about it, she was witnessing a sure case of love at first sight, and the thought made her feel warm inside.

It would have been hard to say who realised they were staring first but Aaron suddenly flushed a deep crimson and Maisie, looking very flustered, turned her eyes to the carving that James was gripping in his sweaty little hand. Miriam's smile stretched from ear to ear. However, her instincts warned her of the old saying, that the course of true love never did run smooth. Still, never mind, she told herself. She quite fancied playing Cupid, and she could see now that Aaron's coming had been for more than one reason.

Aaron had by now scuttled away, and Sassy and Ben were admiring James's fine present. Maisie's eyes went to the doorway and followed his hasty progress across the yard to the barn. When she noticed Miriam gently smiling at her, she blushed so rosily that even her ears glowed.

The rest of the afternoon passed pleasantly enough, although Miriam was amused to find Maisie somewhat subdued. It was as they were all washing up the pots that she asked the girl innocently, 'So what did you think of our new helper then?'

Maisie gulped and couldn't meet Miriam's eyes. 'He seems all right,' she muttered, and smiling to herself, Miriam continued with her washing up.

The girls left when it was time for James to go to bed. On their way home, Sassy had one more visit to make. As well as being James's birthday, it was also the anniversary of her mother's death, and just as she always did on this day each year, Sassy had picked a bunch of Sarah's favourite wild flowers to lay on her resting-place in Coton. Ignoring the rose bushes in the garden of her stepmother's house in Swan Lane, the girl had collected as many rambling roses as she could find, to perfume the bouquet. Miriam had put them in the larder for her, in a pail of water, to keep them fresh and out of the July sunshine.

Maisie considerately waited at the church gates, while Sassy went to pay her respects. As she stood in silence, staring down at the simple grave, anyone seeing her standing there could have been forgiven for thinking that she was Sarah's ghost, for with each year that passed, Sassy grew to look more and more like her mother. Her eyes then strayed to her brother George's little grave, and a sad smile played around her lips as she remembered the happy times they had shared. Then, her goodbyes said for now, Sassy slowly turned away and left her loved ones to rest in peace.

Chapter Fifteen

As the summer passed into autumn, Sassy noticed that Maisie's visits to the smallholding were becoming more frequent. Often now on her afternoon off, she would dash home to tip up her wages to her mam and then hurry on to join Sassy at her aunt's, where she would arrive breathless and panting. It had taken Sassy some time to guess why the visits had become so popular, but one night, after Sassy had finished reading aloud a few pages of *Jane Eyre*, as had become their bedtime ritual, and they were enjoying their evening gossip, Sassy had innocently mentioned Aaron. 'It's a shame about his birthmark, isn't it?' she said, and Maisie had instantly come to his defence.

'There ain't nowt wrong with his face,' she fired up. 'In fact, I'd have to say he's about the handsomest lad I've ever met.' Instantly she could have bitten her tongue off, and flushed a deep crimson in the dark.

As realisation dawned on Sassy she cried, 'Oh Maisie, I'm so sorry, I didn't mean to say anything against him! Aaron is a fine lad, and you should know I'm not the sort to condemn anybody just 'cos they aren't perfect.'

Maisie was immediately contrite. 'No, I'm sorry, I know you wouldn't, Sassy,' she apologised and a silence settled on them for some minutes.

Then, feeling the ground cautiously, Sassy continued, 'You have a liking for him, don't you?'

Her friend remained stubbornly silent for a while longer but then, knowing that she could trust Sassy, she admitted, 'Aye I do. But nowt can ever come of it.'

'Why ever not?'

'Fer lots of reasons.' Maisie sighed regretfully. 'One bein' I could never wed. Who's to say he wouldn't turn out the same as me dad? And secondly, even if I would have him, he ain't hardly goin' to look at the likes of me, is he? I ain't pretty like you.'

It was Sassy's turn to be annoyed now. 'Who says you're not pretty? And anyway, Aaron would be lucky to get someone as nice as you, 'cos as Clara would say, you've got a heart of pure gold.'

Maisie was very touched by Sassy's kind words. 'Ah well, gel,' she whispered, 'we'll have to wait and see, won't we?' She then turned over quietly and burrowed deep beneath the bedclothes, and Sassy knew that, for now, the subject was closed.

In September, the days began to cool and winter coats and bonnets were fetched out of wardrobes.

One blustery cold day, Sassy climbed Tuttle Hill for her regular visit, and on entering Clara's kitchen she sensed at once that the woman had something to tell her, for her eyes were sparkling with excitement.

'Eeh, you'll never guess what, lass,' she chuckled. 'Our Thomas is headin' this way fer the winter, an' he wrote to say he's comin' to see me and his dad. Walter's like a dog wi' two tails, an' so am I, pet. I can't wait to tell our Jack when he gets home this evening.'

Sassy's heart sank into her boots. Now she must face Thomas as a married man. Still, not wishing to take the pleasure of his visit from Clara, she managed to raise a brave smile and say, 'That's grand then.'

Suddenly realising how insensitive she had been, Clara

mumbled, 'Eeh, I'm an unfeelin' old bugger, I am. I'm sorry, lass – I never meant to hurt yer feelings.'

'Don't be so daft,' Sassy said. 'I'll be as pleased to see him as you two will. I'll be able to tell him all about William, for one thing. He's bound to be interested.'

Clara nodded but deep down she felt sad. Although Sassy hid it well, Clara knew her as well as the back of her own hand, and was aware that she still had feelings for her wayward son.

During the rest of the visit, both of them studiously avoided mentioning his name, and for the first time ever, Sassy was almost glad when she had to set off for home.

By now, Aaron was as invaluable to Ben as Jack was, and he blessed his nephew for finding him. As the weeks passed, the lad settled in so well that he began to seem like a part of the family. Much to Miriam's delight, he now even shared the odd meal in the kitchen with them, for sometimes James, who adored him, would become fretful if he refused, and Aaron would have done anything to spare his feelings.

Miriam noticed that on the days when Maisie was due to visit, Aaron always seemed to find something that needed doing around the cottage or the barn. Her plans at playing matchmaker had been put away for the time being. Things were going along nicely without any interference from her, and so for now she was quite happy to sit back and let nature take its course.

In October, Sassy, Maisie and Ada received some good news. Elizabeth announced that Louise would be spending Christmas with a friend, and that she and Arthur would be away for the holiday in a hotel at the coast.

Sassy felt guilty about feeling so happy at the news,

since it meant that she wouldn't get to spend Christmas with her father. But in the end she decided that it was a small price to pay if it meant a break from Louise.

It was as she was leaving the house the next day, almost bursting to share her news with Clara, that her father found her in the hall.

'You've heard the news then, about Elizabeth and me being away for Christmas?' he said. Sassy nodded.

'And you don't mind too much? I feel very bad about leaving you here.'

'Then don't, she said cheerily, thinking how sad he looked. 'I shall be fine. I'm going to spend Christmas with Aunt Miriam and Uncle Ben, and I want you to enjoy yourself.'

Arthur thought there was very little chance of that, but refrained from saying so as he looked down at his daughter. 'Off out, are you?' he asked now, and Sassy grinned.

'Yes, I'm off to see Clara.'

'I won't keep you then, but Sassy . . . if ever there is anything you aren't happy about, you will come and talk to me about it, won't you? I know that you and Louise don't get on that well and—'

'Everything is just fine. There's no need to worry about me,' she assured him as she kissed his cheek, and skipping towards the door she slipped out onto the tiled path. He watched her go with a pensive expression on his face.

As she set off up the familiar lane, she was humming happily to herself, and by the time the cottages came into view she was in high spirits. The fresh air had brought a rosy glow to her cheeks and that, added to her sparkling brown eyes and shining hair, had more than the odd cap raised to her in passing. She ran the last few steps to Clara's door, and flinging it wide, burst into the kitchen to tell Clara the good news, only to stop abruptly when she saw Thomas and Ellie seated at the table.

Wishing with all her heart that she could just sink through the floor, but pulling herself together quickly, Sassy offered them a smile. As Thomas rose to greet her, a jumble of emotions tore through her, for since seeing him last, he seemed to have grown even more good looking. His lip was split on one side and slightly swollen, but for all that, he was still the most handsome man she had ever seen. As he came around the table to take her hands he looked slightly uncomfortable.

'Well, you've grown for sure,' he said softly. Since he had last seen her she had filled out, and now appeared very much a young woman.

'Congratulations on your wedding,' she said, addressing them both, unsure of what to say.

He glanced over his shoulder at Ellie.

'Thanks.' He looked at his wife, then went on, 'We . . . er . . . have somethin' else to celebrate an' all now.'

As Ellie slowly rose from the table, Sassy's eyes settled on her swollen stomach and she gasped. 'Why, you're having a baby!' She looked so shocked that the gypsy girl laughed.

'It's either that or a bad case o' the wind,' she joked.

Sassy looked at Clara in bewilderment and although at one time, Clara would have been the first to admit that she wasn't happy with Thomas's choice of a wife, still now that a grandchild was in the offing, she couldn't help but be pleased.

'It's due at Christmas,' Ellie informed Sassy proudly.

'Then I hope all goes well for you,' Sassy said sincerely, but inside she was crying. Ever since she had been a little girl, whenever she had dreamed of being a mother herself, Thomas had always been the father – and now she finally knew that this would never be. Ellie would bear his children, not her, and the thought caused her such pain that it was all she could do to force herself to stand there.

The rest of the visit passed in a blur of polite chit-chat, until eventually Sassy stood up and declared that she must be going. When Clara protested and asked her to stay, Thomas stood up and said quickly, 'Actually, we should be gettin' off an' all, Mam.'

'Ah, but can't yer hang on just long enough to see yer dad an' our Jack?' Clara pleaded.

'I can't today, Mam,' he said firmly. 'I've a fight tonight an' there's a good purse restin' on it. I'll see Jack an' me dad as soon as I can, all right?'

When Clara dropped her eyes, he smiled reassuringly at her.

'Look, Mam, I love what I do, so happen yer should be glad fer me.'

Knowing that there was no point in arguing, Clara nodded resignedly. 'All right then, lad, but just go careful, eh?'

'Of course I will.' He pulled her into a hug, then turning to Sassy he planted a brotherly kiss on her hair and taking his wife by the arm, they left amidst pleas from Clara that they would come again soon.

When they had finally disappeared down the lane, Clara topped up the teapot from the great black kettle on the fire and plonking herself down next to Sassy, she said thoughtfully, 'Our Thomas don't seem exactly over the moon about the fact that he's about to become a dad, does he? In fact, he don't seem too happy about bein' a married man, if you were to ask me. What do you think?'

When Sassy bowed her head, Clara frowned. 'Are you all right, lass?'

Sassy nodded. 'Why wouldn't I be?' She was blinking

to hold back the tears that were pricking behind her eyes. 'I just hope this grandchild turns out to be a little girl. I know you always wanted one.'

Clara nodded in agreement. 'Aye, I did at one time,' she admitted. 'But then I got you.'

Sassy only needed an excuse to let out her feelings and now she fell into Clara's outstretched arms and sobbed as if her heart would break for all the lost dreams.

That night, as Clara related Thomas and Ellie's visit to Walter, he could see that she was all upset about something. Jack had been in bed for some time, tired out from his day's labour, and now she sat by the fire with Walter.

'I know Sassy still has feelings for our Thomas.' She shook her head sadly. 'If only it had been our Jack she'd set her heart on. He's never had eyes for anyone but her, and yet the lass can't see it.'

Walter, comfortable in his chair, drew deeply on his pipe. He hated to see his wife upset, for although she presented a brash front to everyone, he knew better than anyone that inside she was as soft as dough.

'Well, yer know, love, yer can only leave life to take its course,' he said wisely.

Seeing the sense of his words, Clara felt comforted. She picked up her mending and they fell into a familiar, companionable silence.

As Christmas rapidly approached, Ada announced her intention of spending the holiday with her sister and her family in Leeds. As she pointed out, if Maisie and Sassy were off at the smallholding, there wouldn't be much to do here. Miriam had invited Ada to join them all, but though grateful for the invitation, Ada was a firm believer that Christmas was for families and was now looking forward to her trip. Maisie grew more and more excited

168

as the time got nearer, and Sassy had a sneaking feeling that it was because she would get to see a little more of Aaron.

They were all hoping that the snow would hold off a while longer, but the first two weeks in December were bitterly cold, and Ben was forever forecasting, 'We'll have it today, no doubt about it.' Fortunately, up to now he had been wrong.

Aaron was still something of a mystery to them all. Over the last few months he had come out of his shell to a certain extent, but they still knew nothing of his background and, if the subject was broached, he would clam up. Miriam had long since stopped prying, knowing that if ever the moment was right, he would tell them in his own good time.

She would be cooking for nine people on Christmas Day, for besides herself, Ben, James, Sassy, Maisie and Aaron – who had agreed to join them for James's sake – Walter and Clara and Jack had also agreed to come. Although it meant a lot of extra work, Miriam was greatly looking forward to it.

With Aaron's help, James had collected some holly and it was now dotted about the sitting room, almost everywhere she looked. On the last market day before Christmas, Miriam asked Aaron to buy a Christmas tree from the stall there. The custom of buying and decorating a Christmas tree had started in 1841, when Queen Victoria's late husband, Prince Albert, brought a tree over from Germany and the Royal Family were portrayed standing around it. Now as James impatiently awaited the older boy's return, he could barely contain his excitement. 'Aaron come soon?' he kept asking, and before Miriam even had time to answer he would trot off back to the window and peer down the lane for a sign of him.

Miriam smiled on him indulgently; he was the sun in

her sky, and never a day went by when she didn't thank God for this child.

At last, on one of his frequent visits to the window, James cried, 'He's coming! Aaron's coming!' And before she could stop him, he had flung the kitchen door wide open and was impatiently hopping from foot to foot as the horse and cart slowly trundled down the lane. Aaron had barely had time to draw the horse to a halt, when James sped towards him.

'Tree, tree!' He clapped his hands, his little face full of joy. Piled on the back of the cart, amongst all the sacks of feed, was a beautiful Christmas tree. Aaron pulled down the tailgate at the back of the cart, and James was clumsily trying to climb aboard it. Laughing, Aaron gave him a leg-up. However, as the child gleefully began to drag the tree to the back of the cart, he suddenly became still and stared perplexedly at a rough sack, hastily tied with string amongst the food sacks. The sack appeared to have a life of its own and was wriggling and squirming about. Miriam too stared in amazement.

'Why, whatever's in that sack?' she asked Aaron, as the lad squirmed under her gaze.

'To tell the truth, it's James's Christmas box from me,' he muttered.

'So fetch it down then, and let's have a look at it, eh?'

Wondering now if he had done the right thing, Aaron joined James on the cart and handed down the squirming gift, then jumping down to stand beside it, he lifted his arms and swung James down too.

The child was so mesmerised by this wriggling package that he was now standing quite still, his eyes fast on it.

'Well, come on then, James,' ordered Miriam, as intrigued as the child. 'Open it up and let's see what Aaron's bought you for Christmas.'

Needing no second bidding, the child bent to do as

he was told, and clumsily untying the string, he then took the sack by a corner and tipped its contents onto the frozen hard-packed earth of the yard, sending the indignant chickens clucking in all directions.

It would have been hard to say who was the most amazed or delighted when suddenly a little black and white bundle of fur, relieved to be free of his prison, launched himself at James, and immediately began to furiously lick his face and wag his tail.

It was a tiny little sheepdog puppy, and it seemed that this must surely be another case of love at first sight, for James's screams of delight were so loud that they brought Ben and Jack hurrying from the barn.

Aaron's eyes were tight on Miriam's face as he realised that perhaps he should have asked her permission before buying such a present. But he needn't have worried; she appeared to be almost as delighted as James. Even Ben and Jack were laughing at the antics of the two little ones.

'I weren't meanin' to buy it,' he apologised hastily. 'But this chap at market was sellin' a whole litter of 'em, and said he'd drown any as didn't sell.'

Miriam once again sensed the kind heart beneath the shy exterior.

'I think it's a fine present,' she assured him gaily. 'Though I have a feeling now that nothin' we've bought him will match it.'

As their eyes returned to the two frolicking on the ground their laughter joined. James and the puppy were so wrapped up with each other that they appeared almost oblivious to the presence of anyone else, and from that day on, 'Oscar', as the puppy was duly named, and James were inseparable.

Christmas morning finally arrived, and Jack, who had spent the night at the farm, set off bright and early with the horse and cart to pick up first his parents, and then Sassy and Maisie on the way back.

Ben and Aaron had been feeding the animals, for even on high days and holidays, this was a job that must be done. It was as they were replacing the various feedsacks in the corner of the barn that Aaron disappeared up to his rooms, and came down clutching three clumsily wrapped packages.

By now, Ben was standing quietly in the barn doorway, hands on hips. Recently he had acquired a further two fields, and now the rolling acres for as far as he could see were all his.

Aaron came and stood beside him, enjoying the peaceful view with his master.

'The snow's held off well, ain't it?' Ben commented presently.

Aaron nodded in agreement. 'Aye, it has, but I reckon it'll come today before teatime.' He gestured at the sky. 'It ain't quite so cold today, an' that's usually a sure sign. There's always a calm before a storm, an' the sky looks full of it.'

Ben didn't argue. Lately he had come to respect Aaron's judgement on many things, for the lad seemed to be almost as one with the elements and the beasts.

They stood shoulder-to-shoulder for some short while longer, but then realising that the time was drawing on, Ben finally said, 'We'd best get us glad rags on then, lad. Jack should be back soon with the guests.'

As he was about to stride away, Aaron's hand on his arm stayed him.

'Here, I've somethin for yer,' he said shyly as he pushed a large parcel into Ben's arms. He had only ever had one other person in his whole life to give presents to, and for the past three years she had been far below the ground – a fact that still caused him constant pain.

172

'Eeh, lad.' Ben measured the weight of the gift in his hands. 'You've got me curious now. I can't fer the life o' me think what this could be.' Laying the heavy parcel carefully on the floor of the barn, he untied the string and turned back the paper. The sight that met his eyes made him catch his breath, for an expertly carved sign lay before him. It was oblong, and all around the edge of it was carved a pattern. The words *Holly Bush Farm* were etched deep into it, but so smoothly that even as he ran his hands wonderingly across it, he couldn't feel the grain of the wood. A heavy chain was attached to the top two corners, all ready for hanging it, and Ben was so taken aback that for a moment he was struck dumb.

'It were James's idea,' Aaron offered almost apologetically. 'It were him as noticed all the signs on the farms one day, when he came to market with me.'

When Ben continued to silently stare at him, Aaron said anxiously, 'Well, it were him as asked why we didn't have one, which got me to thinkin'. Then as we were gatherin' the holly for his mam, I noticed as how we've a fair share of holly bushes about the place.'

There was still no comment from Ben, and Aaron was stuttering now in his embarrassment as he ended breathlessly, 'I've done casual work on a fair few farms about Nuneaton, an' some o' them ain't half the size o' this place, so I thought as how perhaps it's time it were recognised as a farm instead of a smallholdin'. But o' course, it's *your* place an' I won't be offended if yer don't want to use it.' Relieved now that the explanation was out of the way, he hung his head and waited for Ben's reaction, which when it came, caused his head to snap back up.

Ben appeared almost as excited as James had earlier on opening his present, and grasping Aaron's hand firmly in his own, he shook it up and down. 'I'll tell yer what, lad,' he cried happily, 'this is one o' the *best presents* I've ever had, an' I thank you. I've been so busy building up the business that I've never given it a thought. But I'm telling yer now, first chance I get, this sign will be hung, an' every time I pass it, I'll remember it was *you* who turned this place from a smallholdin' into a farm.' Then, as if he had forgotten that Aaron was standing there, he snatched up the sign and almost ran to the kitchen, for he could hardly wait to inform his wife that in the last few minutes she had become the mistress of a farm.

When Aaron followed some short time later, he found Miriam basting a huge leg of pork, and waiting until she had popped it back in the range oven, he then handed her her gift. Smiling widely, Miriam wiped her hands on her apron and quickly undid it. Her delight was evident, for inside was the little carving of the pig that she had first admired on his windowsill.

'Oh, thank you, pet!' Ignoring his embarrassment, she planted a big sloppy kiss on his cheek then hurried off with her treasure to put it in pride of place on the mantelpiece.

James had one more present. It was an enormous bag of all his very favourite sweets, from bull's-eyes to candy sticks, and Miriam guessed that Aaron must have hand-picked every one. The little boy's eyes lit up greedily at the sight of them and she almost had to snatch the bag from him before he had a chance to devour them.

'Oh no you don't, me lad,' she laughed. 'At least not till after yer dinner.'

She was just wondering how she was going to keep them off him when the horse and cart was heard pulling into the yard, and James, with Oscar yapping excitedly at his heels, flew out to greet his visitors, his sweeties for now forgotten.

* * *

As it turned out, the birth of Holly Bush Farm was not the only birth that was celebrated on that special day, and Clara was bursting with her own good news.

'I'm a grandma!' she shouted as she bustled into the kitchen. 'Just as we were leavin', Jez, Ellie's brother, came to tell us that she had a baby girl in the early hours o' this morning.' Her delight was infectious and Miriam hugged her warmly.

'Why, that's wonderful news, Clara!'

'Aye, it is. They're goin' to call her Florica – it's a gypsy name meanin' flower. I would have preferred the name Florence meself, but then it's their business, what they call her.'

Although delighted at the news, Miriam immediately glanced at Sassy, but the girl was busying herself laying the cutlery out on the table. Sassy had had time to come to terms with the idea, and was relieved that the birth was over and that mother and baby were doing well. Since her mother's death, although the news of a birth brought joy, it also awakened a fear in her, and loving both Thomas and Ellie as she did, she couldn't have borne it if anything had gone wrong. Seeing that everyone was now clambering about Clara for details, she discreetly slipped out into the yard and wrapped her arms about herself as she stared up into the grey sky. Florica was such a pretty name, she thought, and felt a pang of yearning for a child of her own. In her mind, she pictured a baby girl in her arms, could smell the sweet scent of her. Rose, she would have called her – Rose Sarah Mallabone – but now that would never be . . .

Shedding a last and secret tear, she turned back to rejoin the Christmas Day cheer at Holly Bush Farm.

Chapter Sixteen

The cosy kitchen was humming. Everyone was in good spirits and seemed to be talking all at once. Everyone, that is, except Maisie and Aaron. The latter remained struck dumb, for ever since Maisie had entered, wearing a pretty grey gown that Sassy had helped her to sew, Aaron was finding it hard to keep his eyes from straying to her.

It was a merry bunch that finally sat down to dinner, and soon they were all tucking into a meal fit for the Queen herself – God bless her. Ben said Grace and then the feast began. There was a huge leg of pork, covered in crisp sizzling crackling, and a great piece of beef, so tender that it melted in the mouth. The first course was then followed by a brandy plum pudding, handsomely decorated with some of the holly that Aaron and James had cut. The Mallabones and Aaron had all stirred the mixture in honour of the Three Kings, and Clara had popped in two threepenny coins, which she had scrubbed first. These landed in Maisie and James's portions, much to their delight. Finally, Clara's deliciously light mince pies were passed round, sampled and highly praised.

Throughout the meal, little Oscar constantly nipped at everyone's ankles for attention, and scrounged more than the odd titbit, until eventually, his little tummy bulging, he staggered to the fireside and fell fast asleep.

A toast was then drunk to the birth of Holly Bush

Farm, and the glasses refilled and raised again to welcome little Florica Mallabone into the world, and if anyone noticed that Sassy was rather quiet, they tactfully refrained from mentioning it. During the course of the afternoon, as they all sat enjoying each other's company at the fireside, the baby's head was wet so many times with Miriam's homemade wine and ale, that the little soul could have drowned in it. It was James who first noticed the snowflakes falling past the darkening cottage window, and pointed them out to his dad.

'You were right then, lad,' Ben told Aaron.

'Aye, I thought it would come today.'

By four o'clock, as dusk was fast falling, Ben reluctantly rose and stretched.

'Ah, well,' he said, 'I suppose I'd better go and see to the beasts before it gets too dark.'

Miriam was deep in conversation with Clara and Sassy but now she raised her head to ask, 'Do yer need any help, love?'

'Nah, you stay in the warm, pet.' He stroked her hair affectionately as he passed. 'Happen it'll work up an appetite for me tea, eh?'

Everyone laughed. They were all still full to bursting from dinner, but as he headed for the door Aaron beat him to it.

'I'll see to the animals, Ben,' he offered. 'You stay with yer guests an' have an' evenin' off.'

Ben shook his head. 'No, lad. This is your day off as much as anyone's.'

But Aaron refused to take no for an answer, and so eventually, Ben settled back into his armchair, and stretching his feet to the glowing fire, sighed contentedly.

Miriam had listened to all this with one ear cocked, and seeing a chance to get the two young people together, she waited until Aaron was pulling his work boots on before asking innocently, 'Are yer sure yer can manage on yer own?'

'Oh yes, missus,' he replied but, turning to Maisie, Miriam suggested, 'Why don't you go an' give him a hand, love? Two pair o' hands is always better than one.'

Maisie obediently began to pull on her cloak, bonnet and gloves, and without a word followed him out into the snow. When Miriam turned back to the fireside, she found Sassy and Clara grinning from ear to ear.

'You crafty little bugger,' teased Clara. 'I reckon there's a bit o' matchmakin' goin' on here.'

Miriam widened her eyes innocently. 'Why, Clara, I can't *think* what you mean,' she said, and as Sassy and Clara fell together laughing, her mirth joined theirs, and Walter, catching Ben's eye, shook his head at the deviousness of women.

After the warmth of the kitchen, it was bitingly cold outside, and Maisie shivered as she and Aaron stood in the yard, their eyes adjusting to the darkness. During the afternoon, they had become slightly easier in each other's company and now they stood shoulder to shoulder, admiring the view before them. The world appeared to be virginal white, for a thick carpet of snow, as yet unspoiled, lay glistening as far as their eyes could see. However, the silence didn't last long, for suddenly a huge rat shot past them, with one of the fat farm cats close on its heels. The cat's eyes gleamed wickedly in anticipation of his Christmas feast and as Maisie and Aaron grinned at the departing figures, the ice between them finally melted.

Side by side, they began the job of feeding all the animals, right from the chickens to the cows, and eventually when the needs of all the beasts were satisfied, they returned the various feedsacks to their rightful place in the corner of the barn. The snow was falling thickly now, and as they finally faced each other in the shelter of the barn doorway, Aaron asked shyly, 'Would you like to go back in, or will yer come upstairs fer a while?'

Blushing furiously, Maisie shrugged her shoulders. 'I suppose we may as well go upstairs,' she muttered. 'I'd like to see yer rooms.'

Nodding, Aaron led the way. Once inside, he quickly crossed to light the lamp, and as it spilled its gentle light across the little room, Maisie gasped in admiration, for with his carvings about the place it appeared cosy and inviting. Aaron was obviously proud of his home, and spreading his hands to take it all in, he smiled at her. ''Tain't bad, is it?'

'It's really lovely,' Maisie whispered as she looked about her enviously.

'How come you ain't at home with yer family?' he asked.

Maisie laughed bitterly. 'Huh, if it weren't fer me brothers an' sisters, I'd never go back at all.'

When he frowned and looked at her questioningly, she continued, 'Me dad's a drunkard. Just lately, me ma ain't much better 'cos she's hittin' the hard stuff an' all now.'

Aaron said nothing for a while, but then as Maisie stood, seemingly lost in thought, he said, 'I suppose it's better than havin' no family at all, like me.'

Instantly full of compassion, Maisie stared at him, horrified, but he hastened to reassure her.

'I ain't said it to get yer sympathy,' he told her. 'But it probably explains why I love this place so much 'cos it's the first time I've ever had a home o' me own.'

Maisie couldn't comprehend how awful it must be to have no family at all, and asked tentatively, 'Where were yer brought up then?'

'In the workhouse. I were left on the doorstep apparently, when I was but a few hours old, an' the woman who ran it named me and were the nearest thing to a mam as I ever had.' His eyes found hers, and amazed at how easily he could confide in her, he continued, 'Her name were Mrs Lee and bein' as she were readin' the Bible on the night she found me, she called me Aaron. Apparently it means "a gift from God" and is a name from the Good Book.'

'Aye, it is.' Maisie's heart was aching for him and her eyes were full, as she sensed the deep loneliness in him. As bad as her own homelife had been, she couldn't imagine how awful it must be, to not even know where you had come from.

'How long were you there?' she now asked softly.

Aaron shrugged. 'All me life, till Mrs Lee died three years back, an' then I upped an' left, an' ever since I've worked wherever I could.'

'But I thought most children in the workhouse got adopted out?'

'Aye, they did,' he agreed so quietly that she had to strain to hear him. 'Particularly the lads. The farmers an' their wives would take 'em for workers, see.'

He crossed quickly to the window now and stared out, his soul bleak as he remembered all the times he had been lined up alongside all the other waifs and strays whilst some couple would walk by and choose some other child – but never him.

He remembered one such occasion when a woman had smiled on him, only to then choose the little lad stood next to him, and how he had cried brokenheartedly when she left. It was Mrs Lee who had found him sobbing and she had taken him into her arms and soothed him. 'There, there, love,' she had whispered kindly. 'It's a damn shame people can't see beyond yer face, to the beauty that's inside you.'

Aaron had drawn comfort from her words and from then on she had become like a mother to him.

Whilst he was lost in his thoughts, Maisie had come to stand beside him.

'Weren't you ever picked fer adoption then?' She looked up at him questioningly.

'Huh!' His eyes met hers and the misery she saw there tore at her heart.

'Who would have took me with *this* spread all across me face?' He jabbed at his cheek.

Maisie's mouth gaped in amazement, and almost as if she were noticing the ugly birthmark for the first time, her eyes became angry.

'Well, more bloody fool them then,' she cried, her voice thick with emotion, and before she even realised what she was doing, she raised her hand to his face and gently rested it on the disfiguring stain. 'I'll tell yer somethin', Aaron Lee, I'd hardly noticed this mark till you mentioned it. That's only a small outward flaw, but inside, you have the kindest heart of anyone I know.' Her eyes were flashing. 'An' I'll tell yer somethin' else an' all while I'm at it, an' I ain't ashamed to say it: even with yer mark, yer the handsomest lad I've ever seen, bar none.'

She spoke with such sincerity that for a moment Aaron was too full to speak and his hand came up and covered hers where it lay on his cheek. For what seemed an eternity, they stood gazing deep into each other's eyes, and then just as fate had long ago ordained, his head bent and their lips joined, and both knew, with no words spoken, that this tender kiss was only the beginning.

Sometime later when they re-entered the kitchen, their faces flushed and their eyes bright, Miriam caught Clara's eye and winked delightedly. As she looked around at the people in the room she observed Sassy, who was on her knees quietly helping James to build a house with his little wooden blocks. Despite being eight now, he still enjoyed playing with them.

181

The girl faced an impossible task, for as fast as they built them up, Oscar's furiously wagging tail would knock them all back down again, much to James's delight. It had been a grand day, one that she would long remember, and if only Sassy could have looked as happy as Maisie did at this minute, it would have been perfect.

Much to Sassy's delight, the goodwill feeling of Christmas was to last a while longer, for when Louise returned from her friend's home after the holiday, she was a different person, and although no one could understand it, they didn't question it – and just prayed that it might last. Her skin appeared to have a bloom about it, and there was a sparkle in her eye that no one could fail to notice. It was Ada who finally discovered the reason for Louise's newfound happiness. One morning as she entered the dining room to receive the next week's menus from her mistress, she found the girl and her mother deep in conversation and Louise almost bubbling with excitement.

'Ah, Ada, there you are. I've added a few new dishes to the menu.' Elizabeth handed the list to her imperiously. 'Master Matthew and a friend will be visiting for a few days,' she explained. 'So of course I will expect the best silver and china to be used for the whole of their stay. You will make sure that Maisie sees to it, won't you?'

'Yes, ma'am, I will.' Ada bobbed her knee. 'May I ask when they'll arrive?'

Before Elizabeth could answer, Louise butted in. 'They'll be here on Sunday and are staying until Thursday.'

Elizabeth frowned at her. Louise bowed her head, blushing furiously, but even this silent reprimand failed to wipe the beam of delight from her face. After going through the menus with the mistress, Ada then beat a hasty retreat and toddled back to the kitchen with her news.

'I reckon I've found out why Miss Louise has been full o' the joys o' spring lately,' she babbled before the door had properly shut behind her.

'Well, come on, then,' demanded Maisie. 'Spit it out – let us all in on the secret.'

'I've just been informed that Master Matthew an' a friend will be stayin' next week, an' if I'm not very much mistaken, it's the friend who we have to thank fer Miss Louise's sudden nicer nature.' Ada hitched her ample bosom up beneath her folded arms and looked like the cat that had got the cream, while Maisie and Sassy gawped at her.

'Bugger me!' Maisie said, and whistled. 'So our Miss Louise has a fancy, does she?'

Ada chuckled. 'I reckon you should have picked up on it by now. They say it takes one to know one, an' you've had the same look about yerself fer some time now.'

Poor Maisie suddenly decided that the coal-scuttle was looking low and snatching it up she made a hasty exit, much to the amusement of Sassy and Ada.

As Matthew's arrival drew closer, Louise demanded that the house be cleaned from top to bottom until everything shone. She had ordered a whole new set of clothes whilst in London, and when they arrived, there were new bonnets and new gowns, in the very latest fashions. The biggest shock came, however, one evening as Sassy sat quietly reading by candlelight in her little attic room. There was a tap on the door, and on opening it, she was amazed to see Louise standing there, with her arms absolutely bulging with clothes.

As she stared at her stepsister wide-eyed, the girl

actually smiled at her and, pushing past, crossed to Sassy's bed and deposited the clothes on it.

'There,' she said, in a friendlier voice than she had ever used to Sassy before. 'I've been having a sort out, and thought you might be able to make use of some of these.'

Sassy was momentarily struck dumb.

'I dare say you'll need to alter them a bit,' continued Louise, 'but you're good with a needle. Oh, and by the way, it would be nice if you could eat in the dining room with the family when Matthew and Richard arrive. After all, you are my stepsister.'

Sassy could only nod in agreement, as words still failed her, and when Louise had closed the door behind her, she stood and stared at the pile of clothes on the bed.

When Maisie joined her some time later, she screeched with delight as she held up first one gown, then another.

'Lord love us!' she cried. 'There's a bloody *fortune's* worth o' outfits here.' She sifted through the pile until her hands fell on a pale blue muslin summer dress, all sprigged with tiny pink rosebuds. It was tight fitted into the waist, with a full skirt and pretty long puff sleeves. Snatching it up, she rushed to the mirror and holding it up before her, she sighed.

'Oh Sassy, this is *beautiful*.'

Smiling widely, Sassy came and stood beside her, surveying her friend through the glass. 'Yes, it is,' she admitted. 'But I think it would suit you far better than me, 'cos it sets off your colouring.'

Maisie immediately almost pushed the dress into Sassy's arms. 'Oh, no, no, Sassy.' She was shamefaced. 'I weren't dropping hints or nowt.'

Sassy pushed it right back at her. 'Look, Maisie, there's a whole pile of clothes here, and the colour of this one wouldn't suit me half as much as it would you. Please have it, else I'll be offended.'

Maisie could barely disguise her delight. 'Well, if yer sure, like,' she mumbled.

'I *am* sure, and what's more, that's the first one we'll alter.' And that is just what they did.

On the day that Matthew and his friend Richard were due to arrive, Louise was like a cat on hot bricks. When the pony and trap that had brought them from the railway station finally pulled up outside, she flew into the library. After depositing their bags in the hallway, Matthew and Richard entered to join her, to find her seemingly deeply engrossed in a book, with her skirts very becomingly spread about her on the chaise longue.

Glancing up, she pretended to be surprised to see them. 'Why, Matthew, Richard,' she beamed. 'Surely it's not that time already.' Rising, she hurried to them with outstretched hands, which caused Maisie, who was surveying all this from the hallway, to scurry off glee-fully to the kitchen, where she gave way to a fit of the giggles. On this particular day, Sassy was on a visit to the farm and so it was evening before Maisie was able to relate all the goings-on of the day to her, as they lay tucked up in their beds.

It wasn't until the next morning at breakfast that Sassy actually saw Matthew to welcome him home and meet his friend Richard. Sassy was much happier eating in the kitchen with Maisie and Ada, but as Arthur had added his pleas to Louise's, she finally agreed to join them in the dining room for the duration of the young man's stay. She was delighted to see Matthew again, but it was nothing compared to the look of delight that crossed Richard's face when he first saw her. When she entered the room, Louise and Richard were already seated at the table, having helped themselves from the huge silver salvers of bacon, kidneys, tomatoes and various other foods set out on the sideboard. From the moment Richard saw Sassy he could hardly take his eyes off her, and completely forgetting his manners, he left poor Louise in the middle of a sentence and hastily crossed to where Matthew and Sassy were standing greeting each other at the sideboard.

'Come on then, Matt,' he said jovially. 'I'm hoping you are going to introduce us, man.'

Matthew smiled. 'My pleasure.' Giving a playful little bow, he took Sassy's hand and said gravely, 'Richard, I'd like you to meet my stepsister, Melissa.'

Sassy nodded at him in a friendly manner, but as Richard took her hand firmly in his, his voice was full of admiration as he said, 'No, the pleasure is all mine, I assure you.'

Just when Sassy was beginning to think that he would hold onto her hand for ever and was flushing a very becoming shade of pink, Richard suddenly dropped her hand, and hurrying to the chair next to his, pulled it out for her. Elizabeth was watching all this very closely and she shot Sassy a look of pure contempt. The girl was sure that, if looks could kill, she would have dropped down dead there and then. Luckily, Arthur, Matthew and Richard appeared not to notice, and the meal continued. Louise seemed to have lost her appetite and pushed her plate away pettishly, and from then on she might not have been in the room, for while Matthew and Richard gossiped to Sassy of their ups and downs at medical school, she lapsed into a sulky silence. By the time the meal was ended, it was as though the Louise of the last few weeks had never existed.

Things did not improve during the remainder of the visit. Much to Sassy's distress, Richard hung around her

– and as his liking for her grew, so Louise's dislike of her increased tenfold.

Sassy began to make her visits to the farm and Clara last a little longer. She liked Richard, but saw him only as Matthew's friend. For the few days that the young men were there, she also took on the task of the extra shopping, just to get out of the house as she was beginning to find Richard's attentions extremely embarrassing. It was following one of these trips to the market, as she staggered home beneath the weight of the basket she was carrying that she came face to face with Thomas and Ellie.

Sassy had known that this encounter must eventually come, and although she had dreaded it, once it happened she found it much easier than she had anticipated. Ellie's face lit up at the sight of her and she immediately hurried towards her, with Thomas close on her heels. Being the gentle nature that she was, Sassy found it hard not to respond to her friend's greeting. Motherhood obviously suited Ellie – if anything, she had grown even more beautiful since the last time they had met. Her hair gleamed as the light caught it and her eyes had a softness about them that Sassy had never noticed before.

The gypsy girl had her colourful cloak wrapped tight about the bundle in her arms, and after the initial greetings were over, she gently drew the cloak back to reveal the tiny child held close to her breast. The sight made Sassy gasp in wonder. Florica was easily the most beautiful baby she had ever seen. Her hair was a springing cap of jet-black curls, the colour her mother's, the curls her father's, and her eyes were a deep dark blue that instantly reminded Sassy of the bluebells that grew wild in the woods. As she held her hand out to the tiny girl, Florica gripped one of Sassy's fingers and her heart was lost.

'Oh Ellie,' she breathed, 'she's really beautiful. No wonder Clara is so full of her.'

Ellie grinned delightedly at the praise. 'We've been longin' to show her off to you, but we didn't like to call at the house, not with Elizabeth there. I don't think she'd appreciate our sort knocking on her door, would she?'

Sassy's face clouded. 'I know what you mean,' she said quietly. There it was again – the fact that although she lived in a beautiful house, it had never really been a home.

'I hope one day things will be different.' Her eyes sought Ellie's for understanding, and found it.

'I'm sure they will be,' the girl soothed. 'But in the meantime we'll have to see each other when we can, eh?'

Sassy nodded as her eyes returned to the baby who lay content in her mother's arms. Ellie was now wrapping the cloak closely about the child again and Thomas, taking her by the elbow, urged, 'Come on then, we'd best get this little madam out o' the cold. Happen she's had enough fresh air fer one day.'

Squeezing Sassy's hand, Ellie leaned over and dropped a quick kiss on her cheek.

'Goodbye, Sassy,' she smiled. 'I hope we'll meet again very soon.'

'Goodbye,' Sassy returned. 'I hope we do too, and in the meantime, you take care of that lovely little girl.'

Thomas was still looking very uncomfortable. 'You go on,' he urged his wife. 'I'll just have a quick word wi' Sassy an' then I'll catch you up.'

Ellie nodded obediently and when she was some paces away, he looked at Sassy and told her awkwardly, 'I reckon I owe you some sort of explanation.'

'You don't owe me anything,' Sassy told him, as she drew her shawl more tightly about her.

'The thing is, it ain't how it looks,' Thomas rushed

on. 'I never had no intentions o' gettin' wed, but . . . Well, let's just say Saul found me an' Ellie havin' a bit o' fun, like. We was only kissin' but yer know how strict the gypsies are wi' their womenfolk. Next thing I know, he's organisin' the weddin' an' it were a choice of either goin' through with it or facin' Saul's shotgun.'

'Thomas, I just told you. You really don't need to explain.' Sassy's heart was breaking but she was outwardly calm. *Why didn't you wait for me?* she asked him silently, then unable to stand there a moment longer, she turned about. 'You should catch up with your wife,' she told him abruptly, and without waiting for his answer she strode away.

It was in those moments that her heart finally accepted that Thomas was really lost to her, and though the ache of his loss persisted, somehow she knew that if she must lose him, then she would rather lose him to Ellie than anyone else. But deep down she still loved him and prayed that Ellie would make him happy.

Chapter Seventeen

If Sassy's mood was somewhat sombre when she eventually returned to the house, it was nothing compared to what it was to become, for on entering the kitchen and depositing the heavy basket on the table, she found Maisie red-eyed and flustered and Ada banging about the kitchen with a vengeance.

'Is something wrong?' she asked as she untied the ribbons of her bonnet. It was Ada who answered her.

'*Wrong?*' she ground out furiously. 'I'll say as there's somethin' bloody wrong all right, an' namely it's that little bitch, Louise.'

Sassy sighed. 'Oh dear, what's she done now?' she asked resignedly.

Ada shook her head. 'Why don't you go up to your room and see fer yerself.' The cook was beside herself with rage. 'Go on.' She wagged her finger towards the door. 'Just go an' see. I never thought as even *she* were capable o' such spite. If you ask me, she deserves a bloody good hidin' – and I'll tell yer now, I'd love to be the one to do it!'

Sassy looked at Maisie again, but the girl was so upset that it was obvious she would get no explanation from that quarter, so sighing, she crossed to the door and with one backward glance at Ada, silently entered the plush hallway and headed for the stairs.

Her hand had just rested on the highly polished mahogany banister rail when the drawing-room door opened and she was confronted with Louise, who said not a word, but grinned with such pure malice that Sassy quickly turned from her and hurried up the stairs. Her head was spinning in confusion. She was more than used to Louise's spiteful nature by now, just as Maisie and Ada were, but she couldn't imagine what Louise could have done to upset them so. When she finally slipped through the door to the attic rooms, her feet left the rich deep-pile carpet to echo resoundingly on the bare floorboards. Crossing to the door of the bedroom that she shared with Maisie, she tentatively pushed it open.

Nothing could have prepared her for the sight that met her eyes, and the shock of it was such that she crossed to her bed and slowly sank onto it.

Ever since Louise had given Sassy the clothes that had caused Maisie to squeal with delight they had been busy altering them. First the dress that Maisie had fallen in love with, and then another very pretty blue satin one that Sassy had intended to wear tonight for Matthew's final supper before he returned to medical school. They had worked long hours on those dresses and Sassy knew that Maisie had been longing for an opportunity to wear hers. In fact, she was so thrilled with it that she couldn't even bear to hang it in the wardrobe, but hung it instead on the end of the curtain pole to the side of her bed, where she could admire it each morning on waking. It was still hanging exactly where Maisie had left it, but now it hung in tatters, so slashed and ruined that even the best seamstress in the world could never have put it to rights. The blue satin one that Sassy had intended to wear tonight was in exactly the same state and was in a heap on the floor, while the wardrobe door hung open, with every single item that Louise had given her spewed from it all ripped, torn and slashed beyond repair.

Sassy shook her head in despair. Never in her wildest

dreams could she have believed that even Louise could be capable of doing such a thing. And after the last few weeks, when until Matthew and Richard's arrival, Louise had seemed to be finally warming to her, this act now seemed doubly cruel.

Tears began to run down her cheeks. Now, just as she had had to accept that Thomas could never be hers, she knew too that this house could never be home. She looked forlornly about at the rag-strewn room. The scissors that had obviously been used to wreak the damage lay discarded on the once beautiful blue satin dress, and it was as she sat staring at them that her mood suddenly began to change. Crossing slowly to Maisie's dress, hanging limply from the curtain pole, she fingered the material. Her tears had dried and an unfamiliar cold rage had closed about her heart. Reaching up, she snatched the dress from the hanger and marched determinedly to the door, which she flung back with such force that it banged to behind her with a noise that seemed to echo throughout the house.

Her eyes straight ahead and her head held high, she descended to the ground floor, and there she stood silently until the sound of Louise's simpering laughter floated from the drawing room. She threw open the door, and as Elizabeth, Arthur, Louise, Matthew and Richard looked up in surprise, she advanced on Louise, the tattered dress grasped aloft in her hands.

'You *bitch*!' Sassy almost spat the words at Louise, and the girl was so shocked that for a moment she couldn't even retaliate.

'I've stood your spite and your jealousy since the day I entered this house, but this time you've gone too far.'

Louise was only too aware that Richard was watching this exchange, but before she could say a word, Sassy brought her arm back and flung the tattered dress at her.

'I don't care about the cast-offs you gave me,' she hissed, 'but Maisie worked long hours on this and it meant a lot to her.'

Louise was so embarrassed that she couldn't even retaliate. By now, Elizabeth had risen from her seat, and aware of their visitor and Louise's infatuation with him, and anxious to save the situation, her voice cut in. 'Sassy, I'm sure there's been some mistake. Louise would never do such a thing.'

As Sassy's eyes left Louise for a moment to meet Elizabeth's, the woman balked at the hatred she saw there.

'Don't you *dare* try to cover up for her.' Her voice was ominously low. 'You've stood by since the day I entered this house and watched her try to make my life a misery, and if it wasn't her, then it was you, for as the saying goes "Like mother like daughter". Well, no more.'

A heavy silence had fallen on the room, as Sassy, who was shaking with rage, now turned back to Louise.

'I'm out of this house this very day,' she told her. 'I would rather live in a slum than in this loveless home with the likes of you. You don't have an ounce of kindness in your whole body. But I'll tell you something . . .'

As she bent to Louise, the girl leaned away from her in terror.

'I actually feel sorry for you because you're destined to end up a fat, loveless old spinster.' Turning about, Sassy then left them all staring open-mouthed as she flounced from the room and banged the door behind her.

On entering the kitchen she found Maisie and Ada standing close together, white-faced, at the table. They couldn't have failed to hear the commotion and appeared almost as shocked as everyone else.

'Ada,' Sassy asked, 'would you please pack what clothes I have left into the trunk in my room? My Uncle Ben will fetch them later.'

Tears sprang to Ada's eyes. 'Yes, love, I'll see it's done,' she promised, then crossing to Maisie, Sassy wrapped her tightly in her arms.

'I'm so sorry about your dress, but I'll make it up to you, I promise.'

'No, no, it don't matter about that,' sobbed Maisie. 'Please don't go.'

'I have to. I think I realised long ago that Louise would never accept me living here.' Sassy looked into Maisie's eyes. 'My only regret about going will be having to leave my dad and you and Ada. But you must see I can't stay now. Not after this.'

Sassy took down her hat and shawl from the door. Then turning back to these dear people, she whispered brokenly, 'One day, Maisie, I'll get you out of here too, if it's the last thing I do.'

The young girl raised her streaming eyes to Sassy's and seeing the determination there, she believed her.

'Eeh.' Ada was clearly very upset. 'To think it's come to this,' she muttered. 'An' all 'cos that little madam in there is jealous of you – an' she *is* jealous, you make no bones about it. First she bats her eyes at young Thomas, and now she's got her sights set on young Master Richard, but he's got a soft spot for you instead o' her!'

Sassy flushed and could think of nothing to say, and now Ada leaned closer. 'He's a fine young man,' she whispered. 'I reckon you could do a lot worse for yerself. Trouble is, your affections still lie elsewhere, don't they?'

'I don't know what you mean,' Sassy retorted hotly but Ada wagged her head from side-to-side.

'Yer could have fooled me then,' she said sagely. 'Thomas's name only has to be mentioned an' you go all cow-eyed. Trouble is, he's a married man now an' the best thing you could do is accept it.'

'I have accepted it.' Sassy was blinking back tears.

Ada's words had struck home and she knew that the cook was right, but hearing it said out loud hurt so much.

'I'd better be off,' she said lamely, and without another word she let herself out into the hallway.

She was surprised to see her father there waiting for her, his face deathly pale.

'Please don't go like this,' he implored her. 'Surely it can be mended?'

'Oh, Dad, you must know by now that Louise will never accept me living here,' she told him truthfully. 'It's better all round if I leave. And please don't worry about me, I'll be absolutely fine living with Aunt Miriam and Uncle Ben. We'll still get to see each other.'

'*Arthur!*'

They both glanced towards the drawing-room door as Elizabeth's voice reached them, and Arthur looked help-lessly back at his daughter feeling as if he was caught between the devil and the deep blue sea.

'Goodbye, Dad. Take care of yourself.' Sassy kissed him tenderly on the cheek before stepping out into the bitterly cold night.

PART FOUR

Spring, 1879

The Wild One

Chapter Eighteen

Sassy took the pail of milk from Jack in the cowshed, and flashing a grateful smile at him, she carefully crossed the muddy yard, her skirts held high in her free hand.

Jack thought of the birthday present he had carefully chosen for her, tucked safely into his inside coat pocket, and grinned. It was a scarf made of real silk in beautiful autumn colours that would match her eyes. Depending on her mood they seemed to change from amber to darkest brown, and he knew that she would love it.

Today, Sassy was seventeen years old, and as far as Jack was concerned, she was still the most beautiful girl he had ever seen.

Miriam, who was also watching Sassy's progress from the kitchen window, was thinking much the same. Sometimes she worried that Sassy worked too hard. In the year that she had lived with them, she had taken much of the workload on her own shoulders, and her aunt would often tell her, 'Slow down, love. What don't get done today will keep till tomorrow.' But Sassy would just smile and carry on regardless. She was so much a part of the family now that Miriam couldn't imagine a day without her. When she remembered back to the night that Sassy had moved in with them, her blood still boiled with anger, but strangely the anger was usually directed at her own brother rather than Louise.

From what she could see of it, since the day he had

married the Widow Bonner, Arthur had become a weak, foolish man who was content to sit back and see Sassy, still then only a motherless child, subjected to the spite and malice of a jealous stepmother and stepsister. Selfishly, he was too steeped in his own misery, to even begin to realise that Sassy needed him then more than ever. Even now, whenever Miriam thought of it, her homely features would twist with anger.

Still, to look on the bright side, Arthur's loss on the day that Sassy had finally walked out had been their gain. Miriam couldn't have loved the girl any more if she had been her own daughter, and never a day went by when she didn't thank God for her.

Looking past Sassy, who was now almost to the kitchen door, the smile returned to Miriam's face when James, with his beloved Oscar close at his heels, suddenly flew around the edge of the barn and almost collided with Jack.

Laughing, Jack caught the little chap up into his arms and swung him high in the air, which caused James to squeal with delight and Miriam, warm inside again, to think once more what a very lucky woman she was.

As Sassy entered the kitchen, Miriam turned from the window and gave her a loving smile.

'Now mind, love,' she grinned, 'I don't want you doing too much today, 'cos it's yer birthday, and if yer late for yer visit to Clara, she'll have me guts for garters.'

Sassy laughed as she assured her, 'Don't worry, I've every intention of going and getting changed soon.' But then her eyes clouded with concern as she gazed at her Aunt Miriam. Her aunt seemed to have lost yet more weight and was as grey as putty.

'Are you sure you'll manage all right on your own?' she asked anxiously.

Still in a light-hearted mood, Miriam teased, 'Why wouldn't I, madam? You're not indispensable yer know.'

Then, seeing the worried look on the girl's face, her gaze softened. 'Look, Sassy,' she said firmly, 'there's nowt wrong with me. I just wish that you an' yer Uncle Ben would stop fussing.' Pointing to the staircase she said in a mock-stern voice, 'Now go an' titivate yerself an' get off to see Clara – and that's an order.'

Sassy skipped towards the stairs. 'All right then, you're in charge, but I'll be back before supper.'

Miriam held her smile until Sassy had disappeared up the staircase. Then turning slowly to the stone sink, she gripped the edge of it with one hand, whilst the other pressed deep into the pain in her chest. Even though she denied it to everyone else, she couldn't deny it to herself, and this morning for the first time, she had coughed blood into her hanky.

Hearing Jack and James crossing the yard, she quickly pulled herself together and by the time they entered the kitchen she was in the process of pushing a huge cauldron full of rabbit stew over the range. As they entered she threw them a warm smile and no one would have thought that she had a care in the world.

Sassy almost danced up the lane on the final spurt of her journey to Clara's. The last year had not been easy for her; she still felt terribly guilty about leaving her father to her stepmother's mercy, and yet in another sense, she loved living with Miriam, Ben and James, and for the first time since being a child she once again felt part of a family.

One realisation that had come as a shock to her during the past months was finding that Jack looked upon her as more than a sister. It had been Clara who had diplomatically pointed it out to her one day.

'No, no, you must have it wrong.' She had shaken her head in denial but Clara had smiled sadly.

201

'No, lass, I ain't got it wrong. Our Jack has worshipped the very ground you walk on since you were knee-high to a grasshopper. The trouble is, you've never been able to see past our Thomas. But Thomas is spoken for now, as yer very well know, an' if only yer could find it in yer heart to look on our Jack, you'd never lack fer nothing. He'd fetch the moon out of the sky fer you, if yer was to ask him to.'

Sassy was still reeling from the shock of Clara's statement when she later discussed it with Miriam. To her amazement she found that her aunt believed exactly the same. *How could I have been so blind?* she asked herself, and the answer came back loud and clear. *I never saw because just as Clara said, I could never look beyond Thomas.*

She began to look at Jack in a new light, but try as she might, despite his undeniable good looks and kind heart, to her he was still but a poor second to his brother. Although her heart had long ago accepted that Thomas could never be hers now, no one else could hold a torch to him, and she was beginning to fear that no one ever would.

Today, as always, her visit went well. Clara had knitted her a bright red scarf and gloves as a birthday gift and Sassy kissed her soundly with delight at the sight of them.

Clara was now financially better off than she had ever been in her whole life as Thomas still sent her money on a regular basis. He was fast earning himself a reputation as one of the best bare-knuckle fighters in the whole of the county. It would have been hard to walk into any inn for miles around where his name wasn't known, as his reputation now went before him. Clara still worried about him but had finally accepted his choice of living. She also doted on her little granddaughter, Florica, who was now an irresistible little toddler.

On the way home from Clara's, Sassy called in to see Maisie and Ada, who were always delighted to see her. She would slip down the basement stairs and tap on the kitchen door, so that no one saw her. Sassy always saw Maisie at least once a week. The maid still visited the farm on her afternoons off, and Sassy and Miriam had high hopes that eventually she and Aaron would end up together. In fact, she was shocked that they hadn't come together before now. They were so at ease in each other's company that they were a pleasure to behold. But could she have known it, it was Maisie who was holding back because after that wonderful Christmas evening when he had kissed her, she had suddenly held Aaron at arm's length again, although Miriam couldn't understand why. On more than a few occasions, Sassy had tried to talk to Maisie about her feelings for Aaron, but each time the girl would just bow her head and quickly change the subject, so in the end Sassy had stopped trying.

In the time that he had lived on the farm, Aaron had changed almost beyond recognition. He had more confidence and tended not to turn his head from whoever he was speaking to – something for which Sassy felt they had Maisie to thank. The sign that he had carved for Ben now hung in pride of place above the gate edging the land that led to the farm, and no matter how many times he passed it, Ben still got a thrill each time. His little empire was thriving and soon he was hoping to purchase even more fields to add to his already considerable acreage.

And so it was that following her visit to Ada and Maisie, Sassy set off for home late that afternoon in high spirits. Beside the scarf and gloves that Clara had knitted her, her basket also held gifts from Ada and Maisie and a beautiful gold necklace, which consisted of a delicate chain and a tiny golden cross, from her father.

It was a lovely time of day, the sun was fast sinking beyond the trees and Sassy had a wonderful sense of well-being about her when a familiar figure came staggering towards her in the distance. He was singing happily to himself and as usual his cap was all askew, which caused Sassy to smile. She covered double the ground that he did before they finally met. He seemed to be taking one step back for every one he took forward, but eventually as Sassy came abreast of him, Jimmy Wainthrop flashed her a toothy grin.

'Well, if it ain't our likkle Shassy,' he bellowed delightedly. 'How are yer then, me fine gel?'

Sassy laughed. 'I'm very well, Jimmy, and how's yerself and the family?'

'Oh, they's all well,' he grinned. 'But I ain't goin' to be when I getsh home. Our Connie will no doubt flay me alive.'

Sassy tried to keep a straight face as she said, 'Oh dear, Jimmy, that sounds serious. What have you been up to?'

'It weren't my fault,' he hiccuped. ''T were that bloody neighbour o' yourn.' When Sassy frowned at him questioningly he pulled off his cap and began to turn it agitatedly between his fingers. Glancing up and down the lane as if to make sure that no one was within earshot, he whispered, 'I were in the Jolly Colliers an' they're layin' bets see, on a fight Thomas is in next week. Happen it's gonna be a big fight like, wi' the biggesht purse he's ever fought for, so him bein' a neighbour, I had to 'ave a good wager on 'im, didn't I?'

Sassy shook her head in exasperation. 'Oh Jimmy,' she said, 'it's not *me* that you should be explaining to, is it? It's Connie.'

He nodded as he saw the sense of her words. 'Aye, love, I reckon yer right. I'd besht go an' face the music, eh?' Then replacing his cap as best he could, he staggered off in the direction of home, leaving Sassy to bite her lip perplexedly.

That night, as she recounted Jimmy's information to Miriam and Ben at supper, her uncle said, 'Yes, I've heard the same. It were all round the market the other day. They reckon as the purse he's fightin' for will make him a wealthy man if he wins it.'

Miriam tutted. 'Huh, I don't know what the world's coming to,' she said disapprovingly. 'Surely there's better ways of earning a livin' than fightin'?' And though Sassy never said a word, she couldn't have agreed more, and prayed silently that Thomas might come through this encounter unscathed, for if rumour had it right, this time, he would be facing a more than worthy opponent.

Sassy was not the only one concerned about the impending fight. When Walter heard some of the men whispering amongst themselves about it down the mine, his heart turned a somersault in his chest. Jupiter Lane, the man whom Thomas was to stand against, was known to be a ruthless pugilist and had crippled or maimed more than one opponent in his time. That day, for the first time in his life, Walter left his shift early and with heavy heart made his way to where he believed the gypsy encampment to be. He was thick with grime from his work and the gypsies eyed him warily as he approached the brightly coloured wagons. There was an odd assortment of men, from very young to seemingly ancient, standing on the fringe of the camp, and it was these whom Walter approached.

'I'm lookin' fer Thomas Mallabone,' he said.

A wizened little chap stared boldly back at him. 'Are yer now? An' what would yer be wantin' Thomas fer?' His voice was heavy with suspicion.

'I reckon as that's none o' your business, but if yer must know, Thomas is me son.'

The mood of the man altered immediately and stepping forward, he took Walter's hand and shook it heartily.

'Bugger me,' he laughed. 'Then it's right welcome yer are indeed, fer 'appen we're related.'

As Walter raised his eyebrows the old man introduced himself. 'I'm Thomas's father-in-law, Saul,' he said, and Walter gaped. He would never have taken this wrinkled little chap for Ellie's father, not in a hundred years.

'Follow me.' Saul turned about and without further ado, led Walter into the heart of the camp. The sights that met Walter's eyes had much the same effect on him as they had once had on Sassy. His eyes cast about, taking in the great crates of chickens, the mangy dogs, the grubby children and the noises that came at him from every direction. He could feel curious eyes boring into his back and after passing what seemed like literally dozens of painted wagons, Saul finally came to a halt. He climbed the steps of one particularly bright vardo and rapped smartly on the door.

'Ellie,' he called. 'Is Thomas in there, gel?'

Almost immediately, the top half of the door was flung open and Ellie's head and shoulders appeared. She smiled at Walter as if his visiting was an everyday occurrence.

'He's at the lake wi' Jez,' she answered and Saul, nodding at Walter to follow him again, moved on through the camp. When they finally located Jez and Thomas, Saul touched his cap to Walter respectfully and hurried away to allow father and son their privacy. Ellie had shown no surprise whatsoever at Walter's appearance, but Thomas's reaction was exactly the opposite. At the sight of his father, he hurried towards him, grasped his elbow and led him to a quiet spot beneath the trees.

'What's up, Dad,' he asked worriedly. 'It's not Mam, is it? She ain't bad, is she?'

'No, no, lad, don't fear, yer mam's well. It's nowt like that that's brought me here.'

A wave of relief washed over Thomas's face. Then he stared at Walter curiously. 'Well, if it ain't me mam, what is it?'

'It's you, lad,' his father said solemnly. 'Is it true what I'm hearin', that yer to fight Jupiter Lane?'

'Aye, it is,' Thomas replied. 'But it's nowt to worry about. Has me mam sent yer?'

Walter shook his head. 'Good God, lad, yer mam don't even know as I'm here, an' what's more I'd rather she didn't. But do yer know what yer takin' on? Jupiter Lane is a hard man an' no mistake.'

'I know he's hard,' Thomas said, 'but that's why the purse is so hefty. If I win, I'll be set up fer life.'

'But there's some things as is more important than money, lad, like yer wife an' child, and yer mam. What if owt happens to yer? What would become of them, eh?' Walter's voice was imploring now. 'Look, lad,' he pleaded, 'can't yer just give this one fight a miss?'

'I can't back out now, Dad. It's all set up. People have laid bets on it already. But never fear, I can handle Jupiter Lane.' When he saw the worry in his father's eyes, he gripped his shoulder and said, 'Look, Dad, I appreciate yer concern, but yer know I can handle meself. It'll be all right, you'll see.'

Accepting now that Thomas would not be swayed, Walter said wearily, 'All right then. But you just be careful, eh?'

'I will,' promised Thomas, and giving him another brief affectionate squeeze, he led him back to the fringes of the camp in silence. They both seemed to sense that for now there was no more to be said.

Chapter Nineteen

On 1 March 1879, in a field situated between the Royal
Red Gate Inn on the old Roman road and the village of
Fenny Drayton on the border of Leicestershire, a crude
boxing ring was erected. The ring was unusual inasmuch
as it measured thirty-six feet and had been erected in the
dead centre of the field. The fight was due to commence
at noon, but by eleven o'clock, the men on the gates
were beginning to realise that this field alone would never
cope with the crowd.

Spectators were streaming in from all directions, and
the buckets that held their entrance fees were already
overflowing. Throughout the crowds, men with
outstretched caps were busily taking last-minute wagers,
and nearer to the ring, the crowd vied for the best ringside positions. By eleven-thirty the spectators had far
exceeded the confines of the field and were now assembling in the surrounding fields. A hum of excitement
hung in the air and eyes were straining to catch first sight
of the two opponents.

Walter and Jimmy, who were standing close to the
corner of the ring that would house Thomas, gazed in
amazement at the immense crowd that pushed and jostled
them from behind.

'Eeh,' gasped Jimmy, 'I've seen some fights in me
time, but I ain't never seen a crowd to match this 'un.'

Walter nodded in agreement, his mood sombre. He
had never been one for attending fights, but today he

had felt he must come. He had a terrible feeling that his son would need all the support he could get.

As noon slowly approached, an expectant hush fell on the crowd. In fact, so quiet did it become that the only sound to be heard was the birds singing from the trees, and no one would have believed, in passing, that such an enormous crowd was assembled there.

However, the expectant silence didn't last long, for suddenly the figure of Jupiter Lane began to push his way through the milling throng towards the boxing ring. At his appearance a huge cheer went up, so loud that it echoed around the surrounding countryside. At the same time, Thomas, with Jez and Saul close on his heels, approached from the opposite direction, and found that it was almost a fight in itself just to reach the ring. Hands came out in every direction to pat him on the shoulder and the echoing shouts of well-wishers rang loud in his ears.

As he finally drew near to the ring, he saw his father standing there, and as he stretched out his bare hand to him, Walter caught it roughly and stared deep into his eyes.

'You be careful now, lad.' He had to shout to be heard above the noise of the crowd. 'May God go with yer.' He felt a huge constriction in his throat as Thomas gripped his hand in answer. Then bending, he climbed through the thick ropes and entered the ring.

Jez, who was leaning across the ropes, was shouting last-minute instructions into Thomas's ear, and when Thomas finally nodded and turned, he found Jupiter staring at him, hands on hips, across the ring. Jupiter was a great bear of a man, slightly taller than Thomas, and heavily muscled. He was naked, as was Thomas, save for a pair of black shorts. Thomas realised, as he faced him, why his reputation went before him, for he did indeed appear a formidable adversary and if rumour had it right, he had never as yet lost a fight.

Still for all that, Thomas held his head high and faced him confidently, and there they stood, eye to eye, until the crowd again began to quieten.

Eventually, an attendant entered the ring and called the two opponents to the central scratch line, and then when the usual formalities had been observed, as the church clock struck twelve in the nearby village of Sibson, the battle commenced without delay.

In round one, Jupiter caught Thomas a stinging blow to his left cheek, and the cheek opened as if it had been cut with a knife and blood gushed down onto Thomas's bare chest. So the battle continued, and by the time Thomas was called to his corner at the end of round five, it was more than obvious by now that he was faring the worse. Although he had managed to land a left-hander on Jupiter's nose, which had caused it to bleed profusely, the knuckles on Thomas's right hand were bleeding, and a blow he had received to his left eye was already causing it to swell and close up.

Jez washed the eye from the bucket of cold water as best he could, but glaring now across the ring at Jupiter, Thomas swiped his hand away.

'Look, watch out for his left,' implored Jez, and nodding, Thomas again approached the scratch line to commence round six.

The noise from the crowd was almost deafening. Those who had put their money on Thomas were becoming worried and their shouts spurred him on. For every blow that Jupiter rained on Thomas, Walter squeezed his eyes tight shut, for the pain that they caused him was almost equal to his lad's.

Jimmy Wainthrop, who was standing beside him, was hopping from foot to foot in his excitement as his cries rang in Walter's ears. '*Come on, lad, come on,*' he screeched. '*Give 'im what-for, don't let the bugger beat yer.*'

By the end of round ten, Walter's heart was heavy. By now, Thomas's face was almost unrecognisable, but still he squared up to Jupiter valiantly. The cries from his supporters were dwindling even as Jupiter's grew louder, but just as Walter began to think that the fight was all but lost, Thomas seemed to suddenly rally, and by the end of round thirteen, Jupiter staggered to his corner, looking equally as bloody as Thomas.

The crowd, as Thomas now fought his opponent on a level footing, was going wild and their cries could be heard for miles around, but then in round seventeen Jupiter suddenly caught Thomas a glancing blow beneath the chin and knocked him to the ground. A deathly hush fell across the massed crowd. Walter held his breath, his eyes tight on Thomas who lay as if dead, but just as he thought it was all over, the young man slowly pulled himself to his knees and unsteadily stood to face his opponent again. His eyes were hard and his face set, and as he threw himself on Jupiter, his fists flew in all directions, and by the end of the round, Jupiter had to be helped to his corner. When they again came to the scratch line to commence round nineteen, it was almost impossible to tell one from the other, apart from Jupiter's larger build. By now both faces were battered almost beyond recognition and Walter offered up a prayer that this might end. Though he couldn't know it at the time, his prayer would soon be answered.

As the two men sluggishly circled each other, their eyes locked tight, Thomas suddenly threw a blow that landed square beneath Jupiter's chin. Such was the force of the blow that it actually lifted the giant momentarily from the ground, where he seemed to be suspended, as his head snapped back on his shoulders. Then as his head slowly lolled forward, his eyes seemed to roll back into his head, and he fell senseless onto Thomas, taking him with him to the ground as he fell.

Those who had pride of place at the ringside later swore that as Jupiter's weight bore down on Thomas, they heard a loud snap, and as the two fell together in a great heap, silence reigned.

With the last of his strength, Thomas managed to shoulder Jupiter from him and then, exhausted, he pulled himself to his feet and triumphantly raised his raw bloody knuckles high above his head. He knew that victory was his, and because of the pain it had cost, it tasted doubly sweet.

A great commotion broke out amongst the crowd, as caps were flung high into the air, and a huge cheer went up. Thomas was destined not to hear it, for just then a searing pain from his leg shot through him and he crumpled in an insensible heap next to his opponent, his leg sprawled at an unnatural angle beneath him.

When eventually the horse and cart carried Thomas, several hundred pounds richer but deeply unconscious, back to the gypsy camp, it was a jubilant crowd that followed him. Most of them only went as far as the Royal Red Gate Inn on the old Roman road where, by the end of the day as the celebrations continued, they actually managed to drink the cellars dry.

It was lucky for Thomas that he remained unconscious whilst the revelries took place, for it enabled Ellie, once he was delivered back to her, and with her mother's help, to splint and tightly bandage his broken leg, a feat which would have caused him indescribable pain had he been awake.

In the weeks that followed, Thomas became a local hero as news of his victory spread. Although he was now a wealthy man, his win had cost him dearly. His leg had suffered a severe break, and as time passed it became evident that he would never walk without a limp again.

Sassy received news of Thomas's fight from Jack with mixed feelings, and at Ellie's invitation actually visited him at the camp as he recuperated. Her first sight of him shocked her to the core. It was only days after the fight had taken place and his face appeared so disfigured that Sassy believed he would never look the same again. But thankfully, on that score she was proved to be wrong. The cuts and bruises gradually disappeared and healed, although his leg never did.

Life at the farm was busier than ever and as they were approaching Christmas again, Ben proudly took possession of his next two fields.

Jack and Aaron were working longer and longer hours to keep up with the workload, a fact that Ben was happy to acknowledge in their wage-packets. But Jack was finding it hard toil to make the journey home and back each day now, which gave Ben an idea. Jack had just arrived one morning and was about to set to, milking the cows, his first chore of the day, when Ben appeared in the barn doorway.

'Now then, lad,' he smiled. 'I'm glad I've caught you before yer began.'

Jack looked at him questioningly.

'Leave the beasts fer a while, they won't spoil, an' come with me. I've got somethin' I want to show yer.'

Intrigued, Jack obediently followed Ben across the land towards the latest two fields that Ben had purchased.

Ben eventually stopped at a drystone wall, and pointing across the field at an old cottage that stood alone amongst an overgrown garden, he said, 'You see that there?' And when Jack nodded, 'Well, as yer can see, it

213

is a bit the worse for wear, but I think you'd agree it could be lovely if it were done up.'

As Jack stared across at the little dwelling, he agreed, 'Aye, happen it could.'

'Good, I'm glad we're of the same mind on that then, 'cos it's yours.' Ben laughed aloud at Jack's shocked face.

'What do you mean, it's mine?'

'Exactly what I said. It's yours – lock, stock an' barrel. The deeds are back at the farm with your name on 'em to prove it.'

'No, Ben, no. I *can't* possibly take it,' protested Jack, but Ben held his hand up to quieten him. There was a look of determination on his face as he spoke.

'Look, lad, this is mine an' Miriam's way o' sayin' thank you fer all the years o' hard work you've put into the farm. We've talked it over and she's as keen for you to have it as I am. I know it'll take some time to pull it back into shape, but you ain't never been afraid o' hard work, and if I know you, you'll make it into a home to be proud of.'

Then, patting him on the shoulder, Ben said, 'Right, I'm gonna go an' get on now, lad. I'll leave you to have a good look at it, eh?' And turning about, he strode back the way he had come, a wide smile on his face.

After standing for some minutes, Jack eventually scaled the little wall and slowly approached the cottage, hardly able to believe his luck and the kindness of Miriam and Ben.

Just as Ben had said, the cottage was indeed in need of much repair, but after entering the little gate that squeaked on its rusty hinges, and separated the small garden from the field, he was pleased to find as he walked slowly around the outside of it, that the foundations were solid. He then approached the front door and cautiously pushed it open. It led directly into a kitchen, which still held odd bits of furniture, and on closer inspection, Jack soon realised that beneath the thick layers of dust, they could still be very serviceable. A dresser of heavy oak stood against one wall and in the centre of the room was a large matching table, although of the chairs that must once have gone with it, there was no sign. Probably long since stolen or used for firewood, Jack thought. A large cooking range had a fine deep grate set into it. In the far corner, beneath a small window that looked out to a pump in the back yard, was a deep stone sink, with various earthenware pots still arrayed on the shelves beneath it. The whole of the cottage consisted of three rooms: there was no upstairs.

Crossing to the other two doors, Jack pushed the first one open and found a bedroom, dusty and neglected but containing a huge springed bed. There was no sign of the mattress but Jack was delighted to note that the bedhead was probably made of solid brass and only needed a good clean. In one corner he could see daylight through the roof, but again this didn't deter him. He had noticed a number of slates lying on the ground outside and knew that he was more than capable of replacing them. The last room had him beaming with delight, for it was a sitting room of considerable size with a large inglenook fireplace in the centre of one wall. Suddenly in his mind, Jack could see it as one day it would be, all scrubbed and shining, with gay peg rugs scattered about the stone-flagged floors and fresh, clean curtains hanging at the sparkling windows.

There would be a large sofa positioned in front of a blazing fire, and brass fire irons laid across the hearth. His imagination running riot now, he re-entered the kitchen and again his mind took over, for now the dusty cooking range was blackleaded, with copper pans hanging above it, and a large black kettle bubbling on the hob. The dresser would be stocked with china from the market and the scrubbed oak table would boast good solid chairs, whilst either side of the range would be two comfy rocking chairs, padded with soft, gaily-coloured cushions, matching the curtains that hung at the windows.

In the bedroom, the bed would boast a soft mattress, covered with warm blankets and a pretty patchwork quilt. So his thoughts ran on, until eventually he pulled himself back to the present, and was almost surprised to find himself back in the tumbledown cottage. It suddenly came to him that, once the cottage was repaired, he would finally have a home to offer Sassy – and the thought caused a little ray of hope to spring into his heart.

That evening, when all his chores were done, Jack again returned to the cottage, this time accompanied by Sassy and Aaron. The nights had drawn in, and all they could see of it was whatever Jack's lantern shone on, but even so, as they all went admiringly from room to room, they too were impressed with the little dwelling, and determined to help Jack put it to rights.

By the time Jack arrived home that night it was way past eight o'clock and he was bursting to tell Clara and Walter his good news. By rights he should have been worn out, for a long hard day's work was behind him, but the excitement of being the proud possessor of his own home buoyed him up, and knowing that Clara had got over Thomas's leaving, he felt sure that his mother would be pleased for him. However, he found Clara and Walter waiting for him, obviously bursting with some exciting news of their own.

'Eeh, our Jack.' Clara was so excited she could barely keep still. 'You'll never guess what's happened, not in a hundred years.'

Jack laughed good-naturedly, and winking at Walter, he said, 'If I'll never guess, happen you'd better tell me then, eh Mam?'

'Well it's our Thomas.' Clara needed no urging. 'He's decided to settle down in Nuneaton – leave the road, like – an' there's summat else too.'

Jack was intrigued now.

'He's going to buy his own inn.'

Jack's mouth dropped open in stunned amazement. 'You're jokin'!'

Clara shook her head happily. 'No, lad, I ain't – I promise. He and Ellie were here today an' he told me so himself.'

'Well I'll be,' grinned Jack. He knew how much it would mean to his mam to be able to have all her family in Nuneaton.

'That's great news then, an' I've some more for you,' he went on, then proceeded to tell them both about the cottage, and as if two such pieces of news were too much for her to take in all in one day, Clara sank down onto the chair. She would be sad to see Jack go, but he wouldn't be far away. He was a good lad was her Jack and she couldn't begrudge him his freedom, so now she lovingly took his hand across the table, saying, 'That's right good news, lad, an' I have to say as I can't think of anyone who deserves it more than you.'

As Walter added his agreement, a wave of affection for these two dear people swept through the young man.

'As I explained, the cottage needs a lot doin' to it, so yer won't get rid o' me for a while yet,' he said, 'and even when I do go, I'll see you often – I'll make sure o' that.'

'I know yer will, lad,' Clara replied fondly. 'But once the cottage is ready, happen yer should be thinkin' o' takin' a wife to share it, for I don't like the thought of yer goin' home to no meal on the table of a night.' Her eyes were twinkling wickedly, almost as if she could read his mind, and Jack flushed furiously.

'Reckon I'll take one step at a time, Mam. But yer never know what might happen, eh?'

'Yer right, lad, yer don't,' Clara said wisely, and to mark the occasion, she opened a bottle of her delicious blackberry and apple wine. Then they all drank a toast – first to the soon-to-be landlord and then to the proud owner of the cottage at Holly Bush Farm.

Now that he had come to terms with the fact that his leg might never be the same again, Thomas had resigned himself to settling in one place. Although he could still have earned a comfortable living as a fighter, because of his injury, he was no longer so light on his feet now and the fights would have had to be fewer and farther between. Recently he had felt almost envious of Jack. Since childhood, Thomas had always been the stronger of the two, yet Jack's built-up boot had rid him of his limp, and now it was he himself who had a limp that nothing, not even a special boot, could cure. And then there was Sassy. Now there was the biggest surprise, for she had grown into a right canny lass and she had once been his for the taking. Happen if Ellie hadn't come along when she did, he might have ended up with her. But after meeting Ellie there had been no one else for him, although he still wasn't sure how he felt about being married. Thomas wasn't really the settling-down type; he had too much of an eye for a pretty face. Still, the thought of owning his own inn pleased him, and although Ellie was not enthusiastic about having to remain in one place, he felt that once she was the mistress of her own establishment, she would settle in time.

Over the next few weeks, Thomas viewed quite a few

local inns, but always found fault. Some were too big, some too small, but fortunately he was now in the position with the wealth of his accumulated purses in his pocket to be fussy. Eventually word came to his ear that the Jolly Colliers Inn in College Street was for sale, and so the very same day he set off to view it.

When he returned to the vardo, with a broad beam on his face, Ellie knew without him saying a word that he had finally found a place that would match up to all his needs. He could hardly talk of anything else. The asking price was such that it would leave him with more than enough left over to fully stock the cellar.

However, before the next day dawned when he intended to take Ellie to view it and agree a price, his wife had a surprise of her own to tell him, and this she did as they lay close together that night in their cosy bed in their vardo.

'Thomas,' she whispered softly from the darkness. 'How many bedrooms did yer say the inn had?'

'Three,' his voice came back to her. 'An' all built on the back o' the inn overlookin' the canal.'

'Aye, well happen we may need 'em all, for I'm thinkin' if this is a boy I'm carrying, he'll need a room as well as Florica.'

When Thomas did not immediately answer her, Ellie lay, almost holding her breath. She had no way of knowing how Thomas had taken the news, but suddenly she felt him heave himself from the bed and start fumbling with the matches as he tried to light the lamp. His mission accomplished, Ellie squinted in the sudden glare of the light and found Thomas standing before her, his knobbly knees showing beneath his nightshirt and a look of amazement on his face.

'You mean you're . . . we're . . .' He was flabbergasted about this latest development, viewing it as yet another noose around his neck.

'Aye, that's just what I mean,' she agreed tentatively.

'Oh,' he said flatly, and Ellie chewed on her lip. But then she consoled herself with the thought that he had barely had time to come to terms with the idea yet and no doubt when he did, he would be happier about it.

'So, we're to have another new baby *an'* a new home, eh?' So saying, he blew out the light and climbed back into bed without another word.

Ellie lay staring up at the ceiling of the vardo in the darkness. She was happy about the new baby but her thoughts as they turned to the inn were not so happy. All her life she had enjoyed the freedom of the open road, and the thought of staying put in one place was daunting, to say the very least.

Chapter Twenty

The inn was everything that Thomas had made it out to be; it enjoyed a brisk trade, mainly from the local miners, and was known to enjoy a fair turnover. The back of the inn had sloping lawns that ran down to the canal, which also made it popular with the boat people. Inside, on the ground floor, was a good-sized bar and a comfortable snug. Below these was the most enormous stone cellar that Ellie had ever seen. Above, on the first floor, were the living-quarters, again very comfortable and boasting not only three bedrooms, a kitchen and a living room, but also an inside lavatory, which was Thomas's idea of pure heaven.

By the time the landlord's brassy wife had shown them all the rooms, his face was alight with pleasure, and when she finally left them alone to talk it over, he turned to Ellie and grasped her hands excitedly.

'Ain't it everythin' I promised?' He beamed. 'What do yer think of it then, love? Just say the word and I'll strike the deal.'

Ellie's head was full of her painted wagon, of gambolling along green leafy lanes in summertime, and sitting beside huge outdoor fires on cold winter nights. As lovely as the inn undoubtedly was, compared to the life she had known it appeared as a prison, but then gazing into her husband's eyes and seeing the bright hope there, she knew she had only one choice, for her love for him was such that she would have died for him.

'Aye, it is a fine inn, love,' she said. 'You go off an' strike the deal now.'

Whooping with delight, Thomas almost flew from her to do just that.

Just as Ellie had thought, life in one place was hard to adapt to – although it did have its compensations, for Sassy was a regular visitor now and their friendship deepened. Maisie would sometimes accompany her, and little Florica, who was totally adorable, would follow Maisie around everywhere, much to the little maid's delight.

As Ellie's second pregnancy advanced, Sassy began to feel some disquiet. Whereas Ellie had blossomed when she was carrying Florica, her cheeks now seemed to have lost their bloom and her lovely olive skin appeared sallow.

She also became increasingly tired and left the entire running of the inn to Thomas and David Smith, a local man he had employed to help him.

So concerned was Sassy that one day she actually talked to Thomas about it. 'Ellie doesn't seem to be thriving,' she confided. 'Is there anything wrong?'

His eyes briefly sought hers. 'She looks fine to me,' he mumbled, but Sassy persisted.

'You know that's not true.' She was becoming a little angry now. Because Thomas was happy with his new life he seemed reluctant to admit that anything was amiss.

'She's so quiet,' Sassy went on, 'almost as if she has no interest in anything, and by now she should be gaining weight, not losing it.'

Just then a customer came to the bar, and instantly, Thomas sprang to serve him.

'I ain't got time to talk about it now,' he threw across his shoulder. 'I dare say you're worryin' fer nothin'.' And within seconds he was jovially chatting to his customer. It seemed that he had taken to being a landlord like a duck to water, and even Ellie must take second place to his new status.

Deeply aggrieved, Sassy was left to stare at his back and finally turning on her heel she strode out of the back door and walked down the lawns to where Ellie sat by the canal.

By the time she reached her, she was smiling again. Maisie had Florica by the hands and they were gaily dancing a circle on the grass. *A ring a ring o' roses . . .* the familiar chant brought back happy memories of Sassy's childhood when she, George, William, Jack and Thomas had once chanted the familiar rhyme. She stopped and stared nostalgically for a time and then passing them with a smile and a wave, she continued on to where Ellie sat beneath the shade of a great weeping willow tree on the banks of the canal. Although the day was warm, Ellie had her shawl tightly clutched about her, her colourful skirts spread around her, staring blankly into the gently moving water. Her eyes held a look of such yearning that it caused a stab of fear deep within Sassy's heart, for it was as if the girl wished that she, like the canal, were meandering away.

Hoping to brighten the mood, Sassy sank down beside her and whispered, 'A penny for yer thoughts.'

Ellie turned to her. 'Oh, I were just thinkin' this an' that, yer know.' Her voice was sad. 'It must be nice to be like the canal, always movin' along an' never stoppin' anywhere.'

'You miss the life on the road, don't you?' asked Sassy.

Ellie nodded slowly. 'Aye, I do,' she admitted, 'but Thomas is so happy, I shouldn't complain, should I? As he points out, I have a home to be proud of.' Her voice was so desolate that Sassy's heart went out to her, but just then Florica almost flung herself at her mother like a tiny tornado.

'Hungry, Mammy,' she cried imploringly, and Ellie rose stiffly. 'Aye, all right then, let's be getting yer some tea, eh? An' some o' that nice fruitcake yer grandma sent yer.'

Florica clapped her chubby little hands with delight and scampered off up the lawn, leaving Maisie, Sassy and Ellie to follow with fond smiles on their faces.

A month passed before Sassy next saw Ellie. It was lambing season and at the farm every hand was needed, plus Sassy and Aaron were spending every spare minute they had helping Jack to put his cottage to rights. It was coming along nicely. The slates had been replaced on the roof and Sassy and Miriam had scrubbed every room from top to bottom. Sassy had had to do the lion's share of the work, for before they were halfway through, Miriam was exhausted and the colour had drained from her face. The bed, just as Jack had hoped, did indeed turn out to be solid brass, and by the time Sassy had finished polishing it, it shone like gold. The dresser and table, lovingly polished and rubbed down by Jack, would have graced any home, and now with the walls all newly whitewashed and the stone floor thoroughly swept and washed on hands and knees the little cottage was really beginning to take shape. Jack had managed to find four sturdy oak chairs on a stall in the market, remarkably cheap and needing very little repair, and they were now tucked comfortably under the table. Clara had bought a bale of bright material, and for days had been busily sewing new curtains for all the windows. Much to everyone's amusement, before they did any cleaning, Aaron had spent a whole day sweeping out the chimneys, until he was so black from head to foot, that only his eyes and his teeth showed. Jack was pleased to find that the pump that stood outside the back door was in good repair. Next to the little outside privy, which was also now newly whitewashed, he was building a shelter for the logs that would feed the fires during the bitterly cold winters.

All in all, he was more than pleased at the way his home was progressing, and although he still had a lot to get for the inside of the cottage, the main work left to do was putting the gardens to rights – and this he hoped to have done by the winter.

On Sassy's next visit to the Jolly Colliers, this time un-accompanied as Maisie had chosen to stay at the farm, she was shocked to see the difference a few weeks had made to Ellie. The girl's cheeks had sunk and her long black hair, once so glossy, now hung limply about her shoulders. Her belly protruded in a little round orb, but the rest of her body appeared painfully thin.

As usual she was seated beside the canal with Florica playfully chasing a ball about behind her on the grass. As Sassy descended the gently sloping lawn, Florica spotted her, flew to her and threw her arms about her. After bending to the little girl, Sassy returned the hug and kissed her soundly, but all the time her eyes were fixed on Ellie in horror.

'Ellie,' she greeted her. '*Ellie.*'

Eventually, the gypsy girl turned round, then as if suddenly recognising her, she smiled. 'Oh . . . hello, Sassy. I am happy to see you. It's been a long time, eh?'

'Yes, I'm sorry,' Sassy agreed, and hoping to take the empty look from Ellie's eyes, she launched into an account of all that had been going on at Holly Bush Farm. But her efforts were all in vain. Ellie was once more staring dumbly into the water. Although her head nodded now and again, Sassy had the impression that she hadn't heard a word she'd said. As she stared at the canal, her free hand absently plucked at the butter-cups and daisies that grew in abundance in the grass, and Florica began to gather them together into a tiny bouquet. Just then, Sassy heard a noise, and glancing up the lawn to the back of the inn, she saw Thomas heaving an empty barrel to the rear entrance of the cellar. Gathering up her skirts, she raced back up the garden. By the time she reached him, he was about to enter the inn again, but her hand on his arm stayed him.

'Thomas.' She was slightly out of breath but deter-minedly hung on to his arm. 'Ellie looks so ill – has she seen a doctor?'

He shook his head. 'She won't,' he told her sullenly. 'But don't think fer a minute as I ain't offered to fetch him for her, 'cos I have.'

'Well, *something* has to be done. Surely to God you can see all is not well with her? Why, she looks like a scarecrow!'

Seeing that Sassy had no intention of letting him avoid this confrontation, Thomas's shoulders suddenly sagged and he lowered himself onto the empty barrel. Then, pulling the flat cap from his springing dark curls, he stared at it and began to twist it through his fingers.

'I know she does, lass,' he admitted miserably. 'But fer what is wrong with her I can't offer no cure.'

Sassy frowned at him questioningly.

'It's this place.' He spread his hands to take in his little empire, because to him that was what it had become. 'You'd think as most women would give their eye-teeth to live in a place such as this an' be their own mistress, wouldn't yer? But not Ellie.' His voice now held a trace of bitterness, as his eyes travelled to where his wife sat at the side of the canal. 'She wants me to sell up an' go back on the road.'

Sassy had already guessed that this might be the problem. The girl was pining for her gypsy life.

'I can't do that, Sassy,' Thomas burst out. His eyes were imploring her. '*You* understand, don't yer? In the few months since I've owned this place I've doubled the trade. It's becomin' popular now wi' the passengers from the railway station an' all, as well as the boaties and the miners. Wi' me leg bein' as it is, I can't fight now as often as I once could, an' I need some way o' earnin' a living, what with our Florica and another nipper on the way.'

Sassy nodded, as she felt a little surge of sympathy for him. She could never be angry with Thomas for long because deep down she still loved him. It was more than obvious how much he enjoyed his new life. But even so, her sympathy for Ellie far outweighed all this, for she could see her friend wasting away before her very eyes.

'I do understand,' she said kindly, 'but you know, if Ellie is so unhappy, perhaps you should sacrifice this place? You'd get a good price for it. She is your wife, after all, an' so surely she's worth more than bricks an' mortar?'

He seemed to be weighing her words. 'I'll tell yer what,' he said finally. 'Ellie has another four months till the baby is due, an' come October the gypsies will be back. Happen seein' her family will cheer her up, but if it don't, once the birthing is out o' the way, if she's still o' the same mind, then I'll rethink things. Does that sound fair enough, eh?'

'I suppose so.' Her mind in turmoil, Sassy could see both points of view. If truth were known, although she would never have admitted it to herself, she would have sold her very soul to be in Ellie's shoes. But then again, Ellie appeared to be like a caged bird and part of her told Sassy that Thomas should put his wife before all else.

Still, at least Thomas had promised to review things

after the baby was born, and knowing that this was all she could hope for at present, she turned from him and made her way back to Ellie and Florica as his eyes followed her graceful figure down the sloping lawn.

Thomas's prophecy about Ellie's family's visit was proved to be true, and in October when the Romanies again camped in Gypsy Lane, Ellie seemed to take on a new lease of life. Although now heavily pregnant, she spent most of her time at the camp.

Thomas's trade was so brisk that David, the man he had employed to help out in the bar, now also helped out with the cellarwork. As he saw Ellie slowly returning to her old self, Thomas's spirits began to lift and some of the guilt that he had been feeling slowly shifted from his shoulders. But his peace of mind was to be short-lived, for this year, the gypsies only visited for a few weeks. They then moved camp to be nearer to Lea Gap horse fair, to prepare the horses in readiness for its opening. Ellie was devastated at their going. The birth of the baby was close now and she had prayed that her mother would be present for it. On the day of their departure, she sobbed brokenheartedly, and Thomas was terrified that her state would bring the baby before its time. Nothing he said or did could console her, and eventually, losing patience with her, he stamped off down to the bar.

Within days of the gypsies leaving, Ellie was once again locked in her own little prison of misery. Sometimes when Thomas had seen off the last of his customers and locked up his inn securely, he would climb the stairs to their living-quarters only to find her missing – but he always knew where she would be – shivering at the water's edge, enviously watching the water pass by. With his lantern held aloft and his other arm tight about his wife, he would help her up the slippery canal bank and coax her back to the warmth of their bed, his heart heavy.

On one such night, however, just a week before the baby was due, Thomas's search proved fruitless, and though he held his lantern high and called her name until his voice was hoarse, still he could find no trace of her. All that his lantern showed was the dark, sluggishly moving water and the treacherously slippery canal bank.

It was a bitterly cold night, and although the canal had not yet frozen over, the lawn shimmered with hoar frost and sparkled in the light from the lantern. When he finally accepted that she wasn't there he turned and limped back to the inn.

Once in the warmth of their snug little home, he peeped into Florica's room. Her coal-black curls were fanned across the crisp white pillows, making her look like a dark little angel. She was fast asleep with her chubby thumb jammed in her mouth, and as he gazed down on her, the tears finally began to flow down Thomas's cheeks. In his mind was a picture of Ellie, who must be even now traipsing the lonely roads in search of her gypsy family. In that moment, a cold hand closed about his heart. He pushed the feeling of foreboding away and now a frustrated anger took hold of him. Why did Ellie have to behave like this? He had given her security and a good home, hadn't he? Mixed with the anger was the old sense of guilt. Thomas had always put his own feelings first, and even now that he was a married man with responsibilities, he found it difficult to change. 'She'll be back come mornin' with her tail between her legs,' he assured himself as he headed for their room. 'An' no doubt she'll see how silly she's been, throwin' everythin' I've worked for back in me face. She's married to the landlord of a thrivin' inn now, an' the sooner she settles down to accept the fact, the happier she'll be.' On that self-righteous note he then threw off his clothes and clambered between the cold sheets, and in minutes was sleeping like a baby.

Early next morning, when Ellie had still not returned, he paid a young lad who was passing the inn a shilling to run to the farm and tell Sassy what had happened and ask her to come quickly.

After hastily explaining to her about Ellie's disappearance, she was as concerned as he was.

'She's in no fit state to be trailing the roads!' She exclaimed. 'What if the baby should start to come an' she's all alone? Didn't you go to look for her?'

'How could I?' he snapped, his worry spilling over. 'I couldn't just clear off an' leave Florica all alone, could I? But now that you're here I thought you might watch her while David here sees to the runnin' o' the inn till I get back.'

'Of course I will. You should know that you don't even have to ask,' she replied quickly.

David Smith had just arrived and he said immediately, 'Same goes for me, boss. You get off an' find yer missus,' he encouraged. 'I'll make sure as all's well here fer as long as it takes yer to find her.'

Thomas looked at him gratefully. David was a good, reliable man and he knew that he could safely leave the running of his inn in his capable hands.

Thomas hurried away to get ready as the first customers of the day entered the inn. The boat people often called in early to enjoy a tankard of ale before beginning their day's work and it was as David was serving them that a snippet of their conversation made him prick his ears up.

'Aye,' one was saying sadly, 'they reckon the police

are there now getting a description o' the poor girl to circulate.'

'What's this then?' David asked, placing the frothy glass of ale before the man who had been speaking.

The man leaned across the bar and confided, 'Well, it seems one o' the other bargees pulled a body out o' the canal early this mornin' an' they've took it down to the wharf till it's been identified.'

David was frowning now, as a cold finger played up and down his spine. 'Do they have no idea who it is then?' he enquired.

The man shook his head. 'Only that it's a young woman. Oh, an' they say as she were with child. What a bloody tragedy.' Then lifting his glass and nodding at David, he crossed the bar to sit with his mates.

David gazed at the staircase that ran behind the bar up to the living-quarters above. He knew that he should go up there and pass the news on to Thomas, but in that minute, he would gladly have paid anyone a month's wages not to have to do it.

When he finally plucked up the courage and entered Thomas's kitchen, he found him hastily pushing food into a bag in preparation for his journey. Sassy was sitting with Florica on her lap on a chair at the side of the table. For a moment he was speechless and shifted from foot to foot uncomfortably, then finding his tongue but unable to meet Thomas's eyes, he nodded over his shoulder.

'There's some boaties down in the bar as say a body were pulled out o' the canal this morning,' he mumbled.

Thomas continued to pack his bag before grunting, 'Happen there was, David, an' it's right sorry I am to hear it. But I have more pressin' matters on me own mind at the moment.'

David coughed nervously. 'I don't think you understand,

boss.' He swallowed. 'They're sayin' as it was the body of a young woman who were with child.'

A terrible silence descended on the room as Thomas stood as if carved in stone. Sassy's hand had flown to her mouth, for the thought that was in all their minds was just too frightening to comprehend.

'They say as the body is down at the wharf in the boat house at present,' David finished, and suddenly, as if he had been fired from a gun, Thomas roughly pushed past him and was gone, leaving Sassy to stare after him.

Thomas was becoming a popular figure in the neighbourhood, and many friendly eyes were turned to him as he limped along College Street. But today as he raced headlong he saw no one, and his heart was crying within him, '*No, no!*' In minutes he was at the crossroads, known as the Bull Ring by the local community, and there he turned swiftly and took the downward road, ignoring the curious looks of the people standing outside the workhouse. When he reached the Boot Inn, he hurried across the road with never a look either way and finally entered the wharf yard with sweat streaming from him despite the bitter cold. The whole place seemed to be milling with people, for the wharf boasted a fine boatyard and moorings that the boat people regularly used. Thomas passed them all without a glance until he reached the boathouse, and there he found a policeman at the door, arms behind his back, legs apart, as if he were standing guard. At Thomas's hasty approach the policeman eyed him warily.

'Can I be helping yer, sir?' he questioned.

Thomas said breathlessly, 'I need to see the woman that was pulled from the canal this mornin'.'

Hearing the desperate note in the young man's voice, the policeman frowned.

'Look . . . *please*!' Thomas begged, almost beside himself

with worry, his eyes full of tears. 'Me wife went missin' last night an' she were due to have a baby.'

The policeman's face suddenly wrinkled with sympathy and now his hand came out to grip Thomas's shoulder gently.

'All right, son, in that case you'd best go in, she's in here.' He nodded at the door behind him solemnly. 'Would you like me to come in with you?'

Thomas shook his head. Suddenly his feet refused to move and he didn't want to go in. What would he do if it were Ellie? As if understanding Thomas's dilemma, the policeman patiently waited for him to compose himself.

Thomas was praying as he had never before prayed in his life. 'Please, God, don't let it be her!' He had never been a particularly religious person, but in that moment, if his prayer could have been answered, he would have gladly gone to church every day for the rest of his life.

At last he nodded at the policeman, and as the portly uniformed figure held the door open, Thomas stepped past him and silently entered the boathouse.

A huge workbench stood against one wall and on it lay what appeared to be a body that had been covered with a blanket. Taking a deep breath and grasping one corner of the blanket, Thomas pulled it from the body's face and shoulders.

The sight that met his eyes caused him to enter into silent shock. It was Ellie, even more beautiful in death than she had been in life. Pulling the blanket further down, his hand first caressed her lifeless features then slowly slipped to rest on the swollen mound that was his child. But this time no answering kick met his touch; the child was as dead as its mother.

For an eternity he stood there, drinking in the sight of her and locking it away into his memory, for he knew

233

that after today, memories were all he would ever have of her.

Stooping, he gathered her sodden body into his arms, and as the tears rained from his eyes and fell onto her pale, cold face, he whispered brokenly, 'Oh Ellie, my Ellie, forgive me, my love.' And in that moment his guilt was a terrible thing to bear, for he knew that, had he followed her wishes to return to the road, she and his baby son would still be alive.

The policeman, who had watched all this from the doorway, closed the door on the sad scene and taking a huge white handkerchief from his pocket, he blew his nose noisily. Addressing his colleague, who had come to stand beside him, he said, 'Do yer know somethin', Bert? There's some parts of our job as I really don't like at all.'

Bert slowly nodded in agreement. 'Aye.'

The two Constables had eventually accompanied Thomas back to the Jolly Colliers. Rising from the kitchen table at last, the taller of the two snapped shut his note-book. It was now almost dark and, from the time they had arrived, they had questioned one person after another on Ellie's habits, her routine and her state of mind in general. They had also closely examined the canal bank that she had so loved. Finally satisfied with their investigation, and the fact that everyone bore out Thomas's tale of his wife's depression, he looked down on the young man who sat dry-eyed at the table, with his mother Clara's hand protectively on his shoulder.

'Well, sir, I don't reckon we need to bother you any more. It seems to me that there could have been two possible causes o' death. The first bein' that yer wife simply slipped on the mud an' fell into the canal, the second, according to her mental disturbance, is that she could have . . .' Clara's flashing eyes stopped him in mid-sentence.

'Well, we'll never know will we? But I certainly don't

suspect no foul play, so I reckon we'll just recommend the Coroner finds the cause of death as drowing by accident, eh?'

Thomas said not a word but Clara, highly indignant now, almost spat her words at him. 'I don't know why you've wasted so much o' yer time. This lad worshipped the very ground that lass walked on, an' would never have harmed a hair on her head.'

'I've no doubt he did and I'm sorry, madam,' the policeman replied soothingly. 'But you have to appreciate that in circumstances such as this, we have to investigate 'cos it's our job.'

Clara sniffed loudly, still clearly bristling, and the policeman, lowering his eyes to Thomas, nodded sympathetically.

'Good night then, sir, an' may I just say how sorry I am?'

His eyes dull, Thomas returned his nod as the two policemen turned about and quietly left the room. As they descended the stairs into the dark empty bar, the taller of the two said sadly, 'It surely is a sorry state of affairs, ain't it?'

'Aye it is,' the other agreed. 'It leaves yer wonderin', don't it? I mean, about just what really happened.'

'Well, I've got me own thoughts on that score, but as things stand perhaps it's best as that poor sod upstairs don't know, eh?' And then leaving the inn behind, they parted to make their separate ways to their homes.

Chapter Twenty-One

For the last hour, Sassy had been in Florica's bedroom, trying everything she knew to get the child to sleep, but her efforts had been in vain. The little girl was fretful and wanted her mother. Eventually, Sassy lifted her from the bed and, crossing to the window, she drew back the curtains and stood allowing Florica to stare out at the twinkling streetlights of Nuneaton town centre in the distance. Eventually as she cradled her, she felt the child's head nod, and carrying her back to the bed she gently tucked her beneath the covers and crept from the room on tiptoe.

Ellie's body had been temporarily placed in the morgue of the Cottage Hospital until her coffin was prepared, and next day, once the oak box was delivered by Bob Capener personally, the gypsy girl was brought back to the home that she had come to regard as her prison. It was Clara who tenderly washed her and laid her out in the sitting room, before finally placing two shining pennies on her closed eyelids. It was a chore that almost broke her heart. She had openly disapproved of Thomas's choice of wife in the beginning, but with time she had come to love the girl, and now the sight of her lying there with her unborn grandchild inside her was enough to make her howl. It seemed such a senseless waste of two young lives!

Thomas had not looked on Ellie again from the time he identified her in the boathouse, and although Clara pleaded with him to pay his last respects, he sullenly refused.

'I don't *want* to see her,' he growled every time his mother tried to persuade him. 'I'll thank yer to fix the lid down, an' let me remember her as she was.'

Knowing that it was useless to argue with Thomas once his mind was set, Clara gravely bade Walter to carry out their lad's request.

It was three days later when Ellie's parents' vardo, closely followed by Jez driving a flatbacked cart, wended its way down College Street and stopped outside the Jolly Colliers Inn. At Clara's request, David Smith had gone in hot pursuit of them, until he located their whereabouts. Since then he had been journeying back with them.

Now as they entered the kitchen, Clara immediately rushed to greet them.

'Oh, thank God David found yer!' she said. 'You must be tired to the bone with all that travellin', an' sorely in need of a good strong brew. We've been puttin' off makin' any funeral arrangements, though the vicar's already called in twice, an' we knew we couldn't wait much longer.'

Pearl put up her wrinkled hand and stopped Clara's babbling mid-flow. 'We'll be more than grateful fer the tea, missus,' she said firmly. 'But then we'll be takin' our gel an' be on our way.'

'But why, Pearl? Whatever can yer be meanin'?' Clara gasped.

Pearl's eyes were locked tight on Thomas's. 'You know, lad, as we have our own traditions fer burial, don't yer?'

Thomas nodded. There was no fight left in him.

'Our Ellie may have been yer wife, but she were still a gypsy at heart, an' she would have wished it this way,' Pearl continued.

Just then, Florica burst into the room, like a little ray of sunshine on a dark day, and as her eyes settled on her Grandma Pearl, she let out a squeal of delight and launched herself into the woman's arms. Pearl gazed down on her fondly. Florica was the image of her mother at that age and after fussing the child for some minutes, she said to Thomas, who sat silently watching, 'I reckon as you'll have yer hands full with this little 'un and the inn to run. Would yer like us to take her with us?'

His eyes full of horror now, Thomas said immediately, '*No.*' He was adamant. 'You can take Ellie an' do what has to be done. I accept it's what she would have wanted, but Florica stays wi' me.'

Pearl nodded. 'Well, lad, you're her father, so I'll abide by your wishes,' she conceded. 'But yer know our route as well as anyone, an' if yer ever need us, yer only have to come lookin' an we'll be there for yer.'

Thomas bowed his head in shame as he saw the condemnation in her eyes. Deep down she would blame him for her daughter's death. She had known how unhappy Ellie was trapped in one place. But it was too late to do anything about it now.

Within an hour of Ellie's family's arrival, they departed, this time with Ellie's coffin strapped securely to the flatbacked cart.

It was Walter and Clara with Florica between them who sadly waved them away, while Thomas remained inside staring from the kitchen window, his eyes bleak and his heart heavy with guilt.

The view from this point was breathtaking on a clear day, for beyond the canal that ran along the bottom of the garden, you could see for miles. After standing there for some time, Thomas saw the little procession come into view as it slowly passed beneath the Coton Arches, a huge brick-built three-arched viaduct that allowed the trains access to the pretty little railway station of Trent Valley.

In his mind's eye, all the young man could see was a black-eyed girl in a ruby-red skirt, her ebony hair flying and the golden hoops in her ears flashing as she danced

238

around a campfire, just as she had on the very first night he had seen her and fallen in love with her. Even as his eyes dully followed the wagons, Ellie passed from view, back among her tribe, once again a part of the life he had denied her.

For the first time in many a long year, as Coton Church bells joyously pealed to welcome in the New Year of 1881, the doors of the Jolly Colliers Inn remained firmly shut. There was no one within who felt like celebrating anything at all. The odd merrymaker who passed silently crossed themselves and bowed their heads to the darkened windows as a mark of respect. News had spread quickly through the local community of Thomas's bereavement, and the death of their unborn child too made Ellie's passing even more tragic.

Since the day her daughter-in-law had been pulled from the canal, Clara had seen the inside of her own little cottage only once – and then it was only to collect some clothes. She had barely set foot outside the inn, apart from taking Florica for walks, and had been kept busy seeing to the needs of Thomas and her granddaughter.

It was Thomas who had decided to keep the inn closed over Christmas and the New Year, but now on 1 January she could hear him downstairs, heaving the great beer barrels from the cellar and preparing the bar in readiness for reopening.

Sassy had not long since arrived, and Clara poured them both a hot cup of tea, before placing the tea cosy over the pot.

Sassy was quick to notice that Clara looked tired. 'Are you all right, Clara?' she asked in concern.

'Oh aye, I'm fine, lass, don't yer get worryin' about me.' Clara nodded towards Florica's bedroom door, where the little girl was at present taking her mid-morning nap. 'It's just that I'm out o' the habit o' runnin' round after little 'uns, that's all.' She yawned, then apologised. 'To tell the truth, I'm missin' me own bed an' all. I can't stay here for ever, can I? But then again, I don't want to leave till Thomas has found someone suitable to care fer Florica, 'cos as Pearl rightly said, the lad has his hands full wi' the inn to worry about.'

Sassy sipped at her drink. 'Didn't you say he'd put word out for somebody to live in? Has no one at all applied yet?'

Clara coloured with indignation. 'Oh aye, we've had somebody apply all right,' she almost stuttered. 'Only that *trollop* Moll Twigger. Why, I wouldn't give a dog into her care, let alone me granddaughter. It's a well-known fact that she's had more men than hot dinners.'

Sassy found it hard not to giggle, but somehow managed to keep a straight face, as Clara continued, 'She come here as bold as brass she did, flutterin' her eyelashes an' barin' her bosoms. An' straight off I said to our Thomas, "Lad, if you take her on, she'll eat yer alive in a week flat, an' no mistake".'

A vision of the voluptuous Moll Twigger flashed into Sassy's mind, and unable to hold it back any longer, she broke into a fit of the giggles. Clara stared at her haughtily for a while, but then seeing the funny side of it, she too relaxed and grinned.

'It's all very well you laughin', ain't it?' she scolded, 'but would *you* have taken her on? They reckon she's doing shifts at the brothel in town an' all now. I mean, really . . .'

Sassy shook her head. 'No, Clara I don't suppose I would,' she admitted. In truth, Moll's reputation went before her, and there was many a husband in Nuneaton who'd had the rolling-pin taken to him by an irate wife, just for talking to her, let alone treading the well-worn path to her front door.

Serious again now, she gazed at Clara, saying, 'I wish I could do more to help.'

'No, lass. Yer couldn't do more than yer already doin'. Why, yer must feel as if yer on a piece of elastic, what wi' runnin' between here an' the farm. An' you're doin' the work o' two there, with yer Aunt Miriam bein' unwell.'

They lapsed into a companionable silence for some minutes, each pondering on the problem, until Sassy suddenly sprang up from the table, so quickly, that her cup overturned and poor Clara nearly jumped out of her skin.

'I must be mad!' she exclaimed. 'The answer's been staring me in the face all the time, an' I've only just thought of it.'

Clara's fist was clutched to her chest. 'Eeh, lass,' she cried, 'you nearly give me a heart-attack! Whatever's come over yer?' But her question went unanswered, for Sassy was already clumsily pulling on her boots.

'Where are yer goin' in such a tearin' rush?' demanded Clara.

'I've already told you,' the girl laughed. 'I've just thought o' the perfect person and I'm going to see her.'

'But yer can't, lass.' Clara pointed agitatedly at the window. 'Look at the snow. It's fair blowin' a blizzard out there.'

'That can't be helped. There's no time like the present, an' when I get back I might just have the answer to all your prayers.'

Clara sighed but offered no more argument. Sassy was pulling on her outdoor clothes and obviously had no intention of following her advice.

'You just be careful then,' she pleaded, as Sassy gave her a loving hug.

'I will, don't worry,' she promised. 'Just keep your fingers crossed that my idea's successful, eh?' and with that she was gone, before Clara could even reply.

Once outside, however, before she had taken a dozen steps, the snow had crept beneath her sodden skirts and inside her boot-tops. But determined to go on, she stood for a second, biting her lip and wondering which route to take. She knew that if she took the short cut along the canal towpath, that would remove at least ten minutes from her journey. Deciding that it couldn't be any more treacherous than the roads, she hurried around the Bull Ring as best she could and headed for the Boot Inn. Once there, she slithered down the little path that ran beside it until she came to the canal towpath and there she shook the snow from her skirts and caught her breath. The canal was frozen over in places, particularly at the edges, and it was hard to see where the path ended and the water began. Bowing her head she set off, keeping as close to the hedges as the drifts would allow, and eventually she spotted a huge coal barge being towed along by a great brown horse. A blanket had been thrown across his back, but his mane and tail were white with snow. The owner of the barge raised his hand in greeting and she saw that it was Alf Evans, a regular customer at the inn.

'Happy New Year to yer, Sassy, love,' he shouted cheerfully.

'Same to you, Mr Evans.' Sassy waved and gingerly stepping past the horse she hurried on.

Another twenty minutes brought her within sight of her destination and, sighing with relief, she banged on the door-knocker of her stepmother's house.

The door opened almost immediately and seeing the state she was in, Arthur said, 'Why, Sassy, love, what in God's name are you doing out on a day like this? There's nothing wrong with anyone at the farm, is there?'

Sassy shook her head, unable to speak as yet.

'Come in here and catch your breath and get warm,' he encouraged, but she shook her head firmly.

242

'No, Dad, not yet, I have to see to somethin' first,' she gasped, and taking off her boots so as not to make a mess, she made her way down to the kitchen. When she entered, Ada, who was stoking up the fire, burst out laughing.

'Well, bugger me,' she chuckled, 'I thought yer was the Abominable Snowman for a minute. Get over here by the fire, love, before yer catch yer death o' cold.'

Sassy did as she was told, and finally, divested of her wet coat and hat and stockings, she sat with her bare feet held out to the welcoming blaze. Maisie pressed a mug of steaming soup into her frozen hands.

'You'd have to be mad to venture out on a day such as this without good reason,' Ada grumbled. 'Now put us out of our misery an' tell us why yer here.'

Sassy was beginning to feel almost human again, and looking at Maisie she grinned. 'To tell the truth, it's you I've come to see 'cos I've got a proposition to put to you.'

'Oh, have yer now?' Maisie eyed her warily. 'In that case you'd better tell us what it is, hadn't yer?'

Sassy eyed her friend fondly. 'On the day I left this house, I promised you that one day I'd get you out too, didn't I?'

Maisie nodded.

'Then this might just be the opportunity we've been waiting for. You see, ever since Ellie died, Clara's been living at the Jolly Colliers and caring for Florica. But the thing is, on her own admission she's worn out and needs someone to move in there, so that she can go back to her own home.'

Maisie was listening intently.

'So, Thomas put word out that he needed a live-in help, and up to now the only one who's applied for the job is Moll Twigger. I'm sure you can imagine Clara's reaction to that, can't you?'

243

Ada guffawed. 'Oh dear, I bet she soon left wi' a flea in her ear, if I know Clara Mallabone.'

Sassy nodded. 'She certainly did,' she smilingly agreed.

Maisie continued to stare at her blankly. 'But what's all this got to do with me?' she now asked.

Sassy chuckled. 'Oh Maisie, sometimes you can be as thick as two short planks. Can't you see – you'd be ideal for the job? Florica adores you, an' after working for me stepmother, you'd think you were in heaven.'

As Sassy's words slowly sank in, Maisie asked wonderingly, 'Do yer really think he'd consider me fer the job?'

'Of course he would. You'd be perfect, an' I'm sure that I can speak for Thomas and say that the job's yours if you want it.'

Maisie's whole face lit up. 'Ooh, it would be wonderful,' she cried, but then suddenly her face dropped. 'But what about the mistress?' she whispered fearfully.

'Huh! She's always saying how easily she could replace you, so now let her,' Sassy said scornfully. 'So . . . do you want the job or not? Please say yes.'

With her eyes full of hope, Maisie nodded slowly. 'Yes.'

'Right then, it's done. You'll have to agree a wage with Thomas, but as for her,' she cocked her finger up in the direction of the sitting room, 'you just leave that one to me.' And Maisie was only too happy to do just that.

Some time later, Sassy entered the sitting room and put forward Maisie's new job offer to Elizabeth, and to say that the woman was furious would have been an understatement, for she fairly bristled with rage. 'How *dare* you come in here, poaching my staff?' she snapped as her hands clasped into fists of rage.

Sassy smiled sweetly. 'Why, Stepmother,' she murmured, 'I thought I was doing you a favour. You're always telling Maisie that you only keep her on out of the goodness of your heart, and knowing how dissatisfied you are with her work, and as she's always having to redo it, I thought you'd be pleased.'

Out of the corner of her eye, Sassy could have sworn she saw an amused twinkle in her father's eye as he sank from sight behind his newspaper, but she quickly averted her eyes.

Elizabeth was temporarily speechless and for now could only glare at her.

'Right then,' Sassy said brightly. 'I'll tell Maisie not to leave for a few days till you can find a replacement, shall I?'

'You'll do no such thing!' barked Elizabeth. 'You can tell the ungrateful hussy to pack her bags and get out right now. Her kind are ten a penny.'

'As you wish.' And Sassy left the room, her victory complete.

Once back in the kitchen, as she related her encounter to Maisie and Ada, the homely cook laughed until the tears ran down her face.

'Eeh, I should have loved to be a fly on the wall.' But then as her laughter subsided, her face became sad and she turned to Maisie saying, 'I'm thrilled to bits fer you, pet. But Lord love us, how I shall miss yer.'

Maisie instantly placed her arms as far around Ada's ample waist as they would reach.

'Oh don't take on,' she begged. 'I'll come and see you, I promise.'

'I know yer will, love.' Ada held the girl close to her.

Sassy's eyes were fixed on the kitchen window, where the snow was still falling as fast as ever. She was sitting back at the side of the fire and her sodden skirts were steaming with the heat of the blaze.

'I don't think we'll manage to take all your things today, Maisie,' she muttered. 'I reckon we'll have a job getting ourselves back, let alone all your luggage.'

Ada, who was firmly back in control of the situation now, and who was determined that nothing should spoil this chance for Maisie, quickly stepped in. Crossing to a cupboard in the corner, she drew from it a portmanteau.

'Here,' she said, pressing it into Maisie's arms. 'You slip up an' just pack enough to keep yer goin' for a few days.'

Maisie looked at her questioningly.

'Go on,' ordered Ada. 'And don't worry about the rest o' your stuff. I'll see as it's all packed up, then I'll take it to me room an' yer can pick it up when the weather improves a bit.'

'Oh, bless you, Ada.' Maisie planted a warm kiss on her wrinkled cheek before rushing off excitedly to do as she was told. Ada's eyes followed her fondly and as the door closed behind her, she smiled sadly at Sassy.

'I'm goin' to miss that little madam,' she admitted, 'but still I'm thrilled at this chance fer her to get out of here, 'cos she's a good gel an' deserves better.'

Sassy nodded in agreement. 'I know she is, and if she settles at the inn, it'll be one good thing to come from Ellie's death.' Her eyes filled with tears as she thought of her friend, whom she missed dreadfully.

'Another good thing, o' course,' said Ada with a wicked twinkle in her eye, as a thought occurred to her, 'is that she'll maybe get to see a bit more of Aaron, eh?'

Catching Ada's eye, a grin returned to Sassy's face.

'Why, Ada, you naughty old thing you, I hadn't thought of that.' And then the sombre mood broken, they both dissolved into laughter.

Chapter Twenty-Two

By the time Sassy and Maisie finally arrived back at the inn, they looked a sorry sight indeed. They had chosen to avoid the short-cut along the towpath, as Sassy guessed that parts of it would be impassable by now, and so they had taken the longer route via the roads. This took them at least twice as long as it normally would have, for now they had the added weight of Maisie's luggage to contend with. Although she had done as Ada suggested, and only taken the bare necessities, still this, with the added weight of their sodden skirts and heavy boots, slowed them down even more.

It was Thomas himself who took the portmanteau from Maisie, as the girls staggered into the bar, almost unrecognisable through their heavy coats of snow, and he who without a questioning word ushered them upstairs to the warmth of the kitchen and Clara's kind ministrations. Florica immediately flew to Maisie in delight and refused to leave her side. Eventually, Sassy thawed out enough to explain to Thomas and Clara through chattering teeth the reason for Maisie being there, and then she nervously awaited their reactions. On that score, she need have had no worries. Thomas's face broke into a broad grin, the first she had seen since Ellie's death, and Clara was equally as delighted.

'Why, yer clever little sod, you.' She shook her head in amazement. 'Why the hell didn't I think of it?'

'Are yer quite sure it won't be too much for yer?'

demanded Thomas of Maisie, but as Florica climbed all over her lap, she assured him, 'After workin' fer the mistress, this job will be a pleasure.'

Happy now that her idea had been a good one, Sassy sank thankfully back into her chair.

Not long after, although Thomas and Clara protested noisily, she was once again standing at the door, dressed ready for her final journey home in a dry warm scarf and borrowed thick stockings.

'Oh, lass, *please* don't go back in this,' begged Clara. 'Stay the night here. Miriam and Ben will guess where you are.'

Although she didn't relish the walk, Sassy resolutely shook her head. 'No, I can't. They'd be worried sick and have a search-party out looking for me.'

'Well, at least let me take yer then,' suggested Thomas. 'It ain't fit fer a dog to be out in this.'

'Oh, get off with you,' Sassy grinned, 'I know the way back better than the palm of me hand. I'll be there in no time.'

Knowing that she could be as stubborn as he could, Thomas resignedly shrugged his shoulders.

'You take care now,' yelled Clara as Sassy ventured out into the bitter cold for the last time that day.

Despite her brave talk, by the time she had left the houses and cottages of Coton behind and set out across the fields to take the short-cut to the farm, she became increasingly nervous. The weather had caused a premature twilight to fall, and because of the swirling flakes and the depth of the snow, many of the familiar landmarks and even the low drystone walls had disappeared.

Stumbling on, she had to stop many a time to try and get her bearings, and more than once a dread gripped her heart as she convinced herself that she was truly lost. Once she tripped headlong across some root or branch that was hidden beneath the drifts, and as she lay there, the feeling came upon her that it would be nice to just close her eyes and go to sleep. Realising that she would be buried in minutes if she did so, she wearily pulled herself up and struggled on. Just when she'd convinced herself that she couldn't take another step, she thought she saw a light shining through the blizzard. As the lantern approached, she mustered the last of her strength and managed a weak cry.

'*Hello! Hello there!*' When no voice answered, she sank to her knees in despair and then, laying her head on a thick blanket of snow, she gave herself up to a darkness even deeper than the night.

As her eyelids fluttered open, she blinked, aware that someone was gripping her hand.

'Oh Sassy, thank God.' Casting her eyes about in confusion she saw Jack crying unashamedly as his hand brushed her damp hair from her face.

'Where am I?' Looking about her, she realised that she was tucked up in her own comfortable bed in the farmhouse. But how could that be? The last recollection she had was of lying down and going to sleep in the snow. On hearing Jack's voice, the door was suddenly flung open and Miriam, with Ben and Arthur close on her heels, rushed into the room.

'Oh, Sassy, love.' Miriam was crying too. 'You've given us a rare scare an' no mistake. We thought we'd lost you for sure, an' we would have an' all, if it weren't for Jack who found you.'

A delicious lethargy was creeping through Sassy now, and highly relieved, Miriam bent to kiss her forehead as Arthur looked on anxiously.

'That's it, love, you sleep peaceful now,' she murmured. 'There's plenty of time for explanations later, eh?'

Nodding weakly, Sassy's eyes fluttered shut again, and her last sight was that of Jack smiling down on her.

The next time she woke, it was to find Dr Massey snapping shut his bag. At her slight movement, his eyes flew to her face, and finding her awake, he grinned broadly.

'So, young lady, you've decided to join the land of the living again, have you?' His voice was kindly.

'I fell asleep in the snow coming home yesterday,' Sassy explained in a whisper.

The doctor threw back his head and laughed.

'You fell asleep in the snow nearly four days ago actually,' he enlightened her. 'And if it weren't for Jack, it would have been a very long sleep indeed. All I can say is, you must have had a guardian angel watching over you that night, for how he managed to find you in that blizzard, I'll never know.' He shook his head wonderingly. 'Anyway, you're out of the woods now, and a couple more days in bed and some good nourishing food inside you and you'll be as good as new.' With that, he waved goodbye and left the room, leaving Sassy in a state of wonder. Surely she couldn't have slept for four whole days?

Just as Dr Massey had predicted, within a couple of days Sassy was well enough to sit at the side of the fire in the kitchen. James and Oscar kept her highly amused with their rough and tumble antics, and she had to admit that it was pleasant to be spoiled and fussed over, but as her strength slowly returned, she began to feel guilty.

'Can't I just help out inside a bit?' she pleaded.

Miriam shook the spoon she was in the process of stirring the stew with at her. 'No you *cannot*, young lady,' she said haughtily. 'You've been very ill and you'll not lift a finger till I consider as yer well enough, so just sit there an' do as yer told for a change, eh?'

Her kindly face belied her bullying words and knowing that it was useless to argue, Sassy sank comfortably back into her chair.

'Well, be it on your own head then, 'cos I just might get used to this,' she joked.

Shaking her head in mock-exasperation, Miriam lifted the huge cast-iron cooking pot and carried it to the table, where she began to dish up the evening meal.

Within minutes, almost as if they had smelled it, the kitchen door banged open, and soon Ben, Aaron and Jack were tucking in heartily.

Since the day of her wakening, Jack had studiously avoided her and Sassy was glad of the fact. She could have no way of knowing the long hours he had sat at her bedside, as her chill turned to pneumonia, nor the many prayers he had offered up that her life might be spared. Jack felt that if Sassy had died, he would have had nothing left to live for, but now that his prayers were answered, he felt a deep embarrassment. Since Ellie's death, Thomas was once again a free man and being no fool, and knowing how Sassy felt about him, he wondered what might happen next. He had moved into his cottage some weeks ago and anyone who viewed it now would never have believed how it had looked when he first took it on. For weeks he had scoured the secondhand stalls at the market, and the cottage now looked just as he had imagined it would, even down to the brass fire irons on the sitting-room hearth. He was the first to admit that Clara had had a huge hand in it. She had made all the curtains, the cushions, and the bedspread, and had even re-covered the horsehair couch with a cosy chintz material. Just before Christmas, Jack had felt the happiest man alive as he surveyed his little kingdom, and had almost plucked up the courage to ask Sassy to be his wife. Then came Ellie's death and in a way it had been a double blow to him, for not only had he lost a sister-in-law and niece or nephew, but also he had once again felt that he had to bide his time in speaking to Sassy.

Miriam and Clara had witnessed the extent of his terror when Sassy had lain at her worst at the crisis of her illness, and one day, as they were sneaking a quiet minute together, Miriam had commented on it.

'I feel sorry to me heart fer your son,' she'd muttered regretfully. 'I always guessed he had a soft spot fer her, but he seems beside himself with worry.'

'Aye, he does,' Clara sighed. 'But the trouble is, Sassy don't feel the same about him, an' there ain't nowt we can do about it.'

Nodding, Miriam lapsed into silence.

Just as Sassy had hoped, Maisie was thoroughly enjoying her new role in life and Florica, who adored her, was slowly becoming the happy little girl that she had been before her mother's death. Clara and Walter were now back in the comfort of their own cottage and, although Clara had spent a lot of her time at the farm during Sassy's illness, she was delighted to be back within her own four walls.

'It's true what they say, yer know,' she confided in Miriam. 'Be it ever so humble, there's no place like home.'

Aaron was another who liked Maisie's new arrangement. He was now a regular customer at the Jolly Colliers of an evening, although Miriam knew for a fact that the majority of his time there was spent upstairs with Maisie, which pleased her greatly. She still had high hopes of a wedding in that direction, although it seemed a long time in coming, and sometimes she felt like banging their heads together.

However, there was someone who was not so happy,

as they all found out one day when Ada battled her way through the snow to Holly Bush Farm bearing a huge basket of treats, from rich jellies and brandy-soaked fruitcake to sweetmeats, a sight that made James's eyes bulge with glee.

'Bloody hell,' she gasped on first entering the warm kitchen. 'I reckon I'm too old for all this gaddin' about.' Dropping into the chair next to Sassy's she beamed and said breathlessly, 'So how are yer then, love?'

Sassy was delighted to see her and squeezed her hand lovingly. 'Oh, I'm well on the mend now,' she answered, 'but you shouldn't have come out in this weather. I'll be as good as new in a few more days.'

Ada studied her intently. Sassy did indeed seem much improved since her last visit and, reassured, she leaned back in her chair.

'Right then, if that's the case, I reckon a good strong brew wouldn't go amiss, an' then when I've got me second wind, I'll fill you in on all the gossip, shall I?'

'Well, mind you don't start without me then,' laughed Miriam, and ran to put the kettle on to boil.

Soon they were all holding mugs and Ada started to chuckle. 'I don't suppose I need to tell yer that Maisie's took to her new job like a duck to water, do I?'

Sassy and Miriam's heads wagged from side to side in unison.

'But I reckon as yer stepmother ain't so pleased about her goin' now.' Enjoying herself immensely, the cook looked at the two expectant faces then went on, 'She's had *two* maids since Maisie left, an' she's sacked 'em both.'

Sassy's mouth gaped. '*Two?*' she repeated incredulously.

'Yes. The first were a right little butter-fingers an' kept droppin' everythin' in sight. She went after three days, an' perhaps it's as well, else there wouldn't have been a pot left in the house.'

'Dad never mentioned this when he came to see me yesterday,' Sassy said, and seeing that she was enjoying the gossip Ada continued, 'Well, he wouldn't, would he? He probably don't even know about it. He keeps out o' the way as much as he can. The second maid were a different kettle o' fish altogether. She spent most of her time sat at the side of the fire on her arse, but the crunch came when the mistress noticed one of her figurines missing from the china cabinet.'

Sassy knew the great store Elizabeth set by those ornaments.

'Had she broken it then?' she shivered, imagining her stepmother's rage.

'No, had she hell – though it would have been better if she had.' Ada was well into her stride now. 'Two days later, the missus were walkin' past the pawnbrokers in town with Miss Louise an' two of her posh church friends, an' there it were, displayed bold as brass in the window!' She recalled the scene that had taken place when she arrived back home.

Sassy and Miriam were tittering now and Ada's whole body was shaking with laughter.

'Needless to say, that 'un went out the door faster than she'd come in an' no mistake, an' since then – an' this is the best bit,' she confided wickedly, 'her an' Miss Louise have been havin' to do the work themselves.'

As Sassy tried to picture them doing such menial chores as housework, she started to chuckle. 'Oh Ada, that can't be going down very well, especially with Louise.'

'Huh, that's an understatement if ever there was one. They're at each other's throats like a pair o' fishwives, but I'll tell yer somethin' – it serves 'em bloody well right. Maisie did the work o' two in that house, an' yet neither

254

on 'em ever appreciated her. No, wicked as I am, I'm enjoyin' every minute on it, an' I hope she don't find a new maid fer at least another month. Happen then they'll appreciate her, eh? At one point the cheeky mare told me that it wouldn't hurt me to pitch in an' help, but like I told her, "I'm employed as a cook not a cleaner, so do it yerself".'

At this, the three women's hearty laughter joined and echoed from the beams of the farmhouse.

Another snippet of gossip that Ada passed on that afternoon caused Sassy even deeper pleasure. Matthew had passed the first part of his final exams at medical school, and Dr Massey was considering offering him a partnership at his surgery when he qualified.

'Oh, now that *is* good news.' Sassy's heart warmed; she was fond of the stepbrother who had always been so kind to her. 'It'll be nice to have him back in Nuneaton, won't it?'

'I must admit I'll be pleased to see him back an' all,' Ada admitted. 'If truth be known, I allus reckoned as he were the best of a bad bunch.'

By the time she left later that afternoon, she had lifted Sassy's spirits considerably.

'I'll come and see you as soon as I can,' promised Sassy, but Ada glared at her sternly and wagged a threatening finger in her face.

'You'll do no such thing, me gel, else I'll send you away with a flea in yer ear. You just stay put in the warm until you're properly better.'

'Don't you worry about that,' Miriam said sternly. 'I'll see that she behaves herself.'

Ada nodded her approval and went on her way.

As Sassy's nineteenth birthday came and went, the snow gradually turned to sleet then rain, and eventually to everyone's relief it melted away.

By now Sassy was fully recovered and once more doing more than her fair share of work about the farm. Miriam was far from well and had lost yet more weight. Ben continually pleaded with her to see Dr Massey, but his wife stubbornly stood her ground.

'When I need a doctor, I'll tell you,' she said irritably, but then seeing the anxious look on his face, she teased him: 'Didn't you know it's fashionable to be slim this season?'

And shaking his head in exasperation, he turned from her to go about his chores, muttering all the while, 'Bloody stubborn woman.'

By the time spring arrived, Sassy had resumed her regular visits to the inn. Maisie had gained weight and now wore her hair either loose about her shoulders or pinned up with a pretty ribbon. Sassy was delighted to see the difference in her, especially when she smiled – something that she now did regularly. Florica was flourishing too under Maisie's loving care, and the inn was now one of the most popular in the whole town, a fact which kept David Smith and Thomas running about from morning until night. Sassy loved her visits there and lately, just as Jack had feared, her feelings for Thomas, which had never really died, were rekindled. Although she knew that he was grieving for Ellie, for now she just was content to be in his company. Often, if he and David were busy, she would gladly step in behind the bar to serve the customers or to help out in any way that she could. She loved the atmosphere in the smoky bar and, because of her looks and pleasant nature, was now a firm favourite with the customers – a fact that Thomas hadn't failed to notice. It was one evening as they were standing together, surrounded by the familiar sounds of chinking glasses and the hum of conversation that he commented on it.

'You know, I reckon you have all the makin's of a good barmaid.'

Sassy laughed. 'Maybe I have,' she answered saucily, 'but I wouldn't want to do it fulltime, not unless I were married to a landlord anyway.' Suddenly realising what she had said, she blushed furiously and scuttled away to the sanctuary of the upstairs, leaving Thomas to gaze after her thoughtfully. He was no fool and had guessed, without her saying a word, that she still had feelings for him. She was a girl whom any man would have been proud to claim as his wife – pretty, hardworking, and with a gentle, caring nature. But for all that, Thomas felt reluctant to commit himself again after what had happened with Ellie. He doubted, in fact, whether any one woman would hold his affections for any length of time. Not that Sassy couldn't set his pulses racing. She had turned into a very attractive young woman.

Another regular visitor to the pub since Ellie's untimely death was Louise Bonner. She came along ostensibly to buy ale for the household, since Arthur enjoyed a glass of beer in the evenings, but had made no secret to Thomas of the fact that she was his for the taking – not that he had any inclination to accept her offer. Now there was a spiteful piece of work if ever he'd met one. She wasn't fit to be in the same room as Sassy, from what he could see of it. If he'd any intentions at all of taking up with anyone, it would have been her, not Louise.

As he acknowledged the fact, it brought him no joy. His inn was thriving and his pockets were full, yet his heart was empty and all he could see before him was a long, lonely future. His heart was still heavy with guilt, for when Sassy had pointed out how unhappy Ellie was, he had made excuses and gone about his business, putting his own feelings first as usual. Now he wished to God that he had listened to her. If he had, Ellie and their baby would still be alive, but it was too late to do anything about it now.

One night, not long after Ellie's death, Thomas had broken down in front of Clara.

'Oh Mam,' he had sobbed, 'I wish now as I'd sold this place an' taken her back on the road as she wanted. If I had, she'd still be here, and our new baby with us.'

Clara's heart went out to him as she pulled his shaking head and shoulders into her skinny bosom and held him close to her.

'Well, lad, yer know what they say – if wishes were horses, beggars would ride! It's too late to wish now. What's done is done, but one thing I do know is, yer can't go on punishin' yerself for ever. You've got to make the most o' what yer have, an' get on with yer life as best as yer can.'

Thomas knew that his mother's words made sense, but even so they did nothing to alleviate the guilt he had to carry about like a heavy blanket.

PART FIVE

Spring, 1881

The End of a Dream

Chapter Twenty-Three

One spring evening, Thomas took advantage of a quiet moment at the bar and was busily collecting empty glasses, when a snippet of conversation coming from a group of men sitting in a corner caught his attention. One of them, a regular at the inn, was Jake Stanley, a cousin of Elizabeth's, a fact that shook Thomas to the roots when he had learned of it. The two were as different as chalk from cheese and he found it hard to believe that they were related.

'Ah well,' Jake had laughed, 'I'm from the poor side of the family – the black sheep, if you like. Our Elizabeth don't have much cotter with our lot now. But it weren't always like that. She came from nothing, same as I do. It were me brother as set her up when he made it with his brick an' tile business, an' now you'd think she were a lady born an' bred.'

Jake was a likeable chap, with no airs and graces, almost the same age as Thomas, and since then, he often called in on his way home from his shift at the mine, still decked in his suit of soot. A rapport had sprung up between them and Thomas looked forward to his visits. Jake was a good-looking young man, a bit of a one for the ladies. 'And why not!' he would roar. 'I'm footloose and fancy free, and intend to stay that way.'

As Thomas approached them, his ears pricked, Jake glanced up and caught his eye.

'Hello there, matey,' he greeted him. 'Come and pull

up a chair. I'm just turning me mates green with envy, telling them where I'm off to soon.'

'Oh aye?' Thomas dragged a stool to the table and joined him. 'An' where might that be then?'

'America.'

'*America?*' Thomas repeated in shock.

Jake nodded. 'Yes. I've got me ticket an' I'm off next month.'

'Lucky bugger,' groaned one of his pals. 'If I hadn't got a missus and five kids to feed, I'd bloody go with yer, so I would.'

His words were lost on Thomas, whose eyes were fast on Jake.

'What are yer goin' to America for?' he asked, intrigued.

Jake's eyes twinkled excitedly. 'To make me fortune, o' course!'

'What doin'?'

'Gold prospecting.'

Thomas's eyes almost bulged from his head as Jake leaned across the table towards him. 'It's like this,' he explained. 'Me Cousin Frank has been out there this last year past, an' some right adventures he's had, I can tell you, judging by his letters. He's travelled all over, places as I've only ever read about in books – Virginia, Nevada, Minnesota, Missouri – and he's seen everything from grizzly bears to Red Indians.'

By now Thomas was hanging on his every word, his imagination fired. Enjoying the rapt attention of his audience, Jake continued, 'Well, anyway, in his last letter he'd reached the Rocky Mountains, and it seems he's managed to strike a gold vein there and he's staked a claim on the land it's running on. At present he's building a log cabin and intends to stay there for as long as the seam lasts. It's near a trading post so he's able to get his provisions, and he's asked if I'd like to go and help him with the panning. I ain't got no ties here, see, so I says to me mam, "Why not?". It's got to be more exciting than being stuck down a bloody mine, ain't it?'

Thomas nodded thoughtfully. Somewhere inside him, the wanderlust that had lain dormant ever since he had purchased the inn was slowly reawakening.

Just then a thirsty customer banged his glass impatiently on the bar, and glancing over his shoulder, Thomas sighed and rose reluctantly. 'I'll just go and serve him an' I'll be right back,' he promised, and hurried away. By the time he managed to return to Jake's table, most of his companions had departed and Jake himself was just downing the last of his pint before he too headed off home.

'Will yer not have another?' asked Thomas.

Jake shook his head. 'Thanks all the same, but I'd best be off. I'm black as the Ace o' Spades an' need a dip in the bath.'

'Have just one more on the house.' Thomas was determined to delay Jake's departure as he longed to hear more of America. The offer of a free pint worked, for Jake grinned.

'Aye, go on then,' he said. 'I suppose one more for the road can't hurt, can it?' He followed Thomas to the bar and pushed his empty glass towards him.

It was late that night when he eventually left. The one pint turned to two, then three, and by the time Thomas finally closed and locked the bar door behind him, Jake had a rare old sway on.

'Well, goo'night, Thomas.' He hiccuped merrily. 'I'll see yer tomorrow.'

'Aye, yer will,' grinned Thomas, and then turning he took the stairs two at a time, eager to think on the idea that was fast growing in his mind.

* * *

263

The next day was Clara's day to visit, and she was delighted to see Thomas looking more like his old self than he had since Ellie's death. The familiar cheeky twinkle was back in his eyes and he beamed at her as she walked in.

'Well now,' she said cheerily, 'it's nice to see yer lookin' so chirpy, son. What's put the smile back on yer face, eh?'

Maisie had just walked Florica down to the corner shop, and being as they were on their own, Thomas decided to try his idea out on her.

'What would yer think, Mam,' he asked, 'if I was to say I were thinkin' o' takin' a working holiday?'

Clara stared at him thoughtfully, weighing the idea in her mind. 'It ain't fightin', is it?' she asked warily, and when he shook his head, she let out a sigh of relief.

'No, no, it ain't nothin' like that,' he assured her.

'In that case, I reckon as it could do yer the world o' good.' As her eyes studied his excited face, her heart warmed; she had hated to see him so unhappy. 'So how about yer tell me exactly what yer have in mind?'

He eagerly began to explain and by the time he had finished, Clara was bowled over.

'Well, bugger me,' she whispered. 'You've fair took the wind out o' me sails, lad. Yer certainly don't do things by halves, do yer? How long do yer reckon you'd be gone?'

Thomas shrugged his broad shoulders. 'I ain't sure, to be honest,' he admitted. 'I was thinkin' about a year. But do yer reckon Maisie would be all right wi' Florica, an' David with the inn fer that length o' time?'

Seeing by the look on his face how much this trip meant to him, Clara said, 'I've no doubt that Maisie would be fine with little Flo. I'd keep me eye on her and I'm sure Sassy would help out an' all. As fer David, well,

I reckon as he could run this place with his eyes shut now. But what about yer bad leg? Is it up to a journey like this?'

Thomas slapped it and grinned broadly. 'It's as right as ninepence now. It just tends to ache a bit in the bad weather.'

His eyes lit up with relief as Clara urged him, 'Then go, lad, it might help you to lay a few ghosts. We'll make sure as things are all right here, but you just come back safe now.'

'I will, Mam,' Thomas promised. 'I will.' And taking his mother's skinny little frame into his strong arms, he hugged her to him gratefully.

As the day of his departure neared, it was decided that they would throw a party, and so it was that on the eve of the day Jake and Thomas were due to leave, the inn fair burst at the seams. It was a merry occasion, and although Sassy's heart ached at the nearness of Thomas's imminent departure, she found herself enjoying it. But then, it would have been hard not to. It had been agreed that tonight she would share Maisie's bedroom to save her the trek home in the dark, and now that Florica was fast asleep, she was enjoying a sing-a-long as Jimmy Wainthrop belted out popular music-hall tunes on the piano in the bar.

Maisie and Aaron hardly left each other's side all night and Clara got more than a little tiddly, until eventually Walter managed to encourage her outside into the waiting pony and trap.

At last the door was securely bolted on the last of the merrymakers, and Sassy and Thomas were left to survey the havoc in the bar.

'Come on,' Sassy grinned. 'If we set to now, we'll have it straight in no time.'

'Aw, can't it wait till mornin'?' pleaded Thomas. He had downed more than a few pints that night, and could hardly walk a straight line, but Sassy shook her head.

'No, it can't,' she scolded. 'You should never put off till tomorrow what can be done today.'

'Oh Lord, yer sound just like me mother,' Thomas groaned, but he obediently began to carry dirty glasses to the counter of the bar.

They worked together in companionable silence for some time, and soon nearly all the glasses were stacked neatly, ready to be washed come morning. It was as Thomas was nearing the bar with his hands full of the last load, that Sassy caught her heel on the hem of her skirt. Without thinking, Thomas dropped the glasses and caught her to him, just in time to prevent her crashing to the floor. She looked at him gratefully, as the sound of glasses smashing on the flagged floors echoed in their ears. Then, as their eyes locked, they both suddenly became silent and Sassy's heart began to beat wildly in her chest. She had dreamed of this moment so often since they had come together that one solitary time.

He continued to hold her tightly to him and then slowly his head bent and his lips gently brushed hers. Sassy leaned heavily against him as a whirlwind of emotions swept through her. Then as his kiss became more demanding and passionate, she gladly gave herself up to the joy of being close to him again.

Suddenly Thomas's head snapped away from hers and he gazed at her joyous face in bewilderment. One hand flew to his forehead as the other pushed her almost roughly from him.

'Oh, Sassy, forgive me.' Deeply ashamed, he shook his head. 'I've had too much to drink. I'm sorry, lass.'

Sassy grasped his hand in hers. 'Oh, please *don't* be

sorry.' Her pretty face was alight. 'If only you knew how long I've waited for you to do that. You must know that I've always loved you. After what happened between us that one precious time, I thought we'd be a couple and then you married Ellie and I . . .' Her voice trailed away and sorrow washed across her features, but then fixing the smile back on her lips she said, 'Thomas I—'

'Shush, lass, don't go sayin' somethin' as you'll be sorry for in the mornin',' he pleaded.

'I *won't* be sorry.'

'But, Sassy . . . I'm goin' away tomorrow.'

'I know you are,' she admitted. 'But you'll be back, and after waiting this long I can wait a little longer.'

He bit his lip, horrified at what he had done. The last thing in the world he wanted to do was hurt her. 'Look,' he said gently, 'one o' the reasons I'm goin' is to try and get over Ellie's death.'

Her eyes were full of understanding.

'It might be that when I get back I'll feel different, but I can't promise yer anythin'.'

'I know that,' she said softly. 'But as I said, I'm prepared to wait.' And with that she turned from him and climbed the stairs.

The next morning bright and early, the horse and cart arrived to take Thomas and his luggage to the Trent Valley railway station where he would meet Jake and begin the first leg of their journey that would take them to the ship.

Only Maisie, Florica and Sassy were there to see him off. He had said goodbye to Walter and Clara and the rest of the family the night before.

He pecked Maisie affectionately on the cheek. 'Now you're sure yer have all yer instructions clear?' he asked for the twentieth time that morning.

'*More* than clear,' Maisie assured him with a tolerant grin.

He then turned to Sassy and pecked her on the cheek. 'You take care of yerself now, mind,' he said gently, and she could only nod, her throat was too full to reply. Then leaning down to his bright-eyed little girl he swept her high into his arms. 'An' you be a good girl fer Maisie and Grandma, eh? An' Daddy will bring yer a lovely present.'

Florica chuckled delightedly and threw her chubby little arms about his neck, too young as yet to be sad at a parting. After squeezing her to him for some minutes, he carefully placed her back on the ground, and then turning, swung himself up onto the front of the cart, as the driver clicked his tongue to the patiently waiting horse.

Just before the cart rounded the bend in the road, Thomas turned on his seat and looking back at the three figures, raised his hand in a final salute.

'You all take care now,' he shouted and running a few steps, Sassy called, 'Be sure to write to us often.'

'Aye I will,' promised Thomas, then the horse and cart disappeared around the bend in the road and was lost to sight.

Sassy took his going surprisingly well – a fact that was not lost on Clara the next day when she visited. As Sassy was helping her to polish the brasses, the older woman eyed her suspiciously.

'Thomas got off all right then, did he?' she asked.

Sassy nodded. 'Yes, he did.' She could feel Clara's eyes tight on her, and knowing that she couldn't keep anything from her for long, she confessed, 'Thomas kissed me last night.'

Clara's mouth dropped open and her hands became still. 'He did *what*?'

Blushing furiously, Sassy lowered her head. 'He kissed

me,' she repeated softly. 'An' I think that when he comes back, we might get together.'

Clara was gravely concerned. 'Did he say that?' she asked quietly.

After thinking hard for a minute, Sassy finally shook her head. 'Well, not exactly,' she admitted. 'He said that he couldn't promise anything, but he *did* kiss me.'

Clara gazed at this girl whom she loved as a daughter. 'Look, lass,' her voice was kind, 'a blind man on a gallopin' donkey could have seen our Thomas was way over his limit last night, so don't you go puttin' the cart before the horse now, 'cos it'll only end in heartache if yer do.'

'Don't say that, Clara,' whispered Sassy, since for the first time in her life she had hope.

'I've got to, lass.' Clara was firm. 'Our Thomas ain't a bad lad at heart, but he's . . .' She searched in her mind for the right word. 'Well, I'll have to say it straight: he can be a selfish little bugger. He don't *mean* to be but he has this wanderin' streak in him. He's had it since he were a lad, happen that's why Ellie suited him so well for a time. They were two of a kind, see? An' just look how *that* finished up.' She omitted to tell Sassy that only the week before, Jimmy Wainthrop had seen Thomas leaving the brothel in town late one evening, and she had reason to believe that it wasn't his first visit either.

Sassy's chin set determinedly. She didn't want to hear this, even if it were the truth.

'Don't get wastin' yer life waitin' for him, pet,' Clara pleaded. 'You must know there's a queue o' chaps that would marry yer tomorrow, an' our Jack would be at the front o' the line. I'll tell yer somethin' else an' all, while we're at it. I know I shouldn't say this, fer they're both me sons, but our Jack would see you never wanted for nothin' an' he'd make a far better husband than our Thomas ever could.'

Sassy remained stubbornly silent and, sighing, Clara said no more but bent to finish the brass cleaning, her heart heavy.

Meanwhile, Thomas and Jake had arrived in Liverpool and boarded HMS *Mermaid*, a huge liner which would transport them to New York. This in itself was a great adventure for Thomas. He had never in his life even glimpsed the ocean before, let alone sailed on it. Unfortunately, it soon became apparent that Thomas would never make a sailor. As the ship rolled with the swell of the waves, he turned a curious shade of green and, rushing to the rails, gave himself up to a severe bout of seasickness.

This greatly amused Jake. 'You'll soon get yer sea legs,' he laughed, banging Thomas heartily on the back.

Hanging across the rails, having deposited his entire breakfast into the waves, Thomas shuddered and longed to feel his feet back on dry land.

Chapter Twenty-Four

Life rolled along smoothly in Nuneaton. For the duration of Thomas's holiday it was decided that Sassy would no longer visit Clara at the cottage but would see her at the inn when Clara went to visit Florica each week. She was now doing extra work about the farm and that, added to her visits to the house in Swan Lane, to see Ada and her father, made her feel that there weren't enough hours in the day. During the summer months, Maisie would pack them a picnic basket and they would take Florica off for an afternoon's outing. It would have been hard to say who enjoyed these outings the most, little Flo or the three adults, and very soon a favourite route was established. Off they would go along College Street, then right into Coventry Road until they descended the steep hill and came to the Griff Hollows. There they would veer left to follow the canal that wound through the Rabbit Banks until eventually they would pass the Ladybird Bridge and finally reach the Bluebell Woods. Florica absolutely adored this place, and it was here that they would finally stop, whilst Maisie unpacked the basket of goodies onto a clean white cloth spread upon the grass.

This was a magical place to Florica. It reminded her of the pictures in the fairy storybooks that Maisie would hesitantly read to her. Sassy's lessons had paid off. After gulping a hasty meal, her little legs would be off as fast as they could carry her and she would spend hours peeping under the bluebells and upturning the mush-rooms in search of fairies. Clara too had a soft spot for this wood, but would always insist on setting off before dusk set in. As tranquil as it was in daylight, the Griff Hollows was reputed to be haunted, and Clara, who was highly superstitious, had no intention of ever lingering there after dark to find out if the rumours were true.

Things on the farm were going well. Lately, Ben had called on the services of a solicitor for the making of a Will, and now he owned all the land about for as far as his eye could see – all, that is, except for the small piece of ground that housed Jack's little cottage, the deeds of which Jack now had safely tucked away. All in all, it was a good year. After the terrible storms in the early months, the weather was more than kind to them, almost as if it wished to make up for the wicked blizzards. One idyllic day followed another, offering skies of turquoise blue with silky white clouds slowly drifting across it.

As summer gracefully gave way to autumn, and the leaves turned from green to golden brown and gently fluttered to the ground, Thomas's first letter arrived and caused a ripple of excitement throughout the inn. In it, he wrote of his excitement and relief at leaving the ship and finally docking in New York. From there, he and Jake had taken a train to Chicago, Illinois, and thence to St Louis on the west shore of the Mississippi. It was from there that the letter had been posted and Thomas told them that he and Jake still had many more miles to travel before they finally reached Frank.

He described confrontations with grizzly bears, which made Sassy's eyes bulge with terror. She had seen one once when she was a child and her father had taken her to a fairground in Riversley Park. It had been a huge lumbering thing, fastened to the ground with thick chains and shackles about its ankles. Still it had struck fear into her heart, and the thought of being in an uncivilised place where these great beasts wandered free was frightening. Thomas also wrote of the huge herds of wild buffalo that swarmed across the great prairies, and how sometimes he and Jake had actually dined on them – a fact that had Maisie, Sassy and Clara all shuddering simultaneously.

When she'd had time to think about it, Clara remarked, 'I suppose it's no different to eatin' beef. They're only cows with horns at the end o' the day, ain't they?'

Sassy's greatest fear was that Thomas would be away longer than the year he had intended, and her fear was justified when just after Christmas the carrier cart brought a second letter. In this one he told them that he and Jake had finally reached Frank, who was almost sleeping rough in the wild. His log cabin was nowhere near completed as he spent most of his time prospecting and panning for gold on the piece of land on which he had staked his claim. Thomas told them about fur trappers, and scarce settlements dotted here and there along the banks of the Missouri, and of the Red Indians who dwelled on the prairie lands and depended on catching wild animals for food. He concluded by telling them that he and Jake were lodging with a widow and her son not far from Frank's piece of land on the fringe of the Rocky Mountains – a fact which caused Clara to smile widely.

'Huh,' she chuckled, 'sounds like they still want their home comforts to me, else they'd sleep outdoors with Frank, wouldn't they? Instead o' havin' some widow-woman waitin' on 'em.'

Maisie and Sassy grinned with her, but Sassy's heart ached. Thomas had been gone for almost a year already and there was no mention at all in his letter of his returning. Still, her heart wisely told her, 'Anything worth having is worth waiting for,' and she resolved to be patient, for after all this time, a few more months were but a drop in the ocean. The New Year came and went, much more peacefully than the one before, and soon winter gave way once more to spring and the trees began to sprout their emerald-green coats.

Throughout all this time, Jack had watched and waited and held his tongue. He saw the look that entered Sassy's eyes whenever Thomas was mentioned, and knew now that he had missed his chance yet again. Strangely, he had come to a dull kind of acceptance and felt deep inside that his lifelong dream of claiming Sassy as his wife would never be.

As summer approached, he actually began to walk out with Mary Stevens, who was a bonny lass and the daughter of the owner of the farm bordering Ben's. It was a short-lived thing. Although Mary made it more than clear that she was ready to make a go of it, she seemed dull in comparison to Sassy, and Jack ended it almost before it had begun as his kindly nature would not allow him to hurt her.

The end of this courtship was not lost on Miriam or Clara. One day as they sat together, shelling peas for the evening meal outside the kitchen door with the smell of newly cut hay wafting on the breeze from the field where Jack was busily scything, Clara commented on it.

'I wish our Jack had carried on seein' Mary. She were a nice little lass an' she seemed to think the world of him.'

'Yes, she did,' agreed Miriam. 'But it obviously wasn't meant to be, was it?'

Clara shook her head. 'I know Sassy's still pinnin' her hopes on our Thomas, but I've a horrible feelin' that he'll let her down again.'

'Well, there's nothin' we can do about it,' said Miriam philosophically. 'The heart's a funny thing, an' has a habit of ruling the head.'

'Aye, I'll agree with that,' said Clara. 'You've never said a truer word.' And the two women then lapsed into a comfortable silence and deftly finished the job in hand.

In October, word reached the Jolly Colliers that the gypsies were camped on wasteland in Bedworth, a small town on the outskirts of Nuneaton. Sure enough, within days, Saul and Pearl duly arrived on the doorstep. Florica was delighted to see her grandma and grandpa, and thrilled with the little peg dolls that Pearl had lovingly made for her. There were four in all, each with tiny painted faces and dressed in gaudy scraps of material. Maisie gladly allowed Pearl to take Florica to the encampment whenever she wished, for she trusted her implicitly and knew that Thomas would have wanted it. The little girl loved her visits, so much so that sometimes when they brought her home she would become fretful and slap Maisie's hand away peevishly. 'Want Grandma Pearl,' she would grumble, and Maisie, who loved the child unconditionally, would sigh.

Sassy had become increasingly concerned, for there had been no word from Thomas now for months, and her imagination was beginning to run riot. Then just before Christmas, a much-handled and almost illegible letter arrived and she pounced on it thankfully.

'He's coming home!' she cried joyfully. 'He says that Jake is to remain there with Frank but he feels he shouldn't stay away from Florica any longer.'

'When is he coming?' asked Maisie excitedly and as Sassy quickly read through the letter, she frowned.

'It doesn't say.' She gazed at the postmark. 'It was posted in August, so it could be he's on his way even now.'

'Perhaps he'll be home for Christmas,' said Maisie, and Sassy flushed with delight, for she could think of no finer gift.

* * *

As it turned out, Thomas didn't arrive home for Christmas, but someone who meant just as much to her did.

It was Christmas Eve and Sassy and Miriam hadn't stopped all day. James and Oscar were romping about the yard content in each other's company, and the men were still about their chores. Like the women, they were working extra hard today so that they could have an easy day tomorrow. Sassy had just taken a huge bucket of pigswill to the sties and was crossing the yard when Oscar's frantic yapping caused her to slow her steps.

'Someone coming, Sassy,' shouted James.

Placing the empty bucket down, she went over to him, wiping her hands on her coarse apron. He was staring off down the lane and Sassy's eyes followed his, straining through the deepening dusk. Oscar was growling deep in his throat as he stood protectively in front of his master, his hackles raised and his hair bristling, which told Sassy that whoever was coming must be a stranger.

As the figure approached, she saw that it was a man, tall and broad of shoulder, with what appeared to be some kind of kitbag slung across his shoulder. Seemingly unafraid of Oscar's ferocious welcome, he drew closer and as Sassy stared towards him, something about his walk seemed strangely familiar.

When he was almost within the yard, his steps slowed and James, who was nervous of strangers, crept behind Sassy's skirts, whilst Oscar, as if sensing that the newcomer was no threat, suddenly ceased his yapping and dropped to his belly on the frozen ground.

The stranger stood just outside of the lights that shone from the farmhouse windows, and although Sassy could just make out that his hair appeared to be long and tied into the nape of his neck, she couldn't distinguish his features.

'May I help you?' she asked politely, trying not to show her nervousness.

A soft chuckle came in reply from the darkness. 'Oh, yer can that. Yer can help me by just standin' there and lettin' me feast me eyes on the girl that was once me big sister.'

The man now slowly stepped into the light, and if it hadn't been for James, on whom she leaned for support, she would surely have fallen, for she would have known that voice anywhere, even after all these years. His eyes were still the same soft blue-grey, and his hair still a rich chestnut, but the little boy whom she had missed and grieved for was gone, and here in his place was a great strapping man.

'*William!*' Her voice was choked with emotion. 'I can't believe it's you. I thought I'd never see you again.'

'Aye, well, never is a long time, love,' he replied, and dropping his kitbag heavily to the ground, he held out his arms. Within seconds brother and sister were locked in a firm embrace, each crying unashamedly with delight. There was no need for words; the time for words would come later. For now, all they needed was the warmth of each other after all the long lonely years apart.

Although William now towered head and shoulders above Sassy, for a solid week he followed her about like a motherless lamb. The two of them had a lot of talking and catching up to do.

Clara stood by Miriam's side at the kitchen window, watching the pair as they went about the task of cleaning out the henhouses at the far side of the yard. She beamed fondly. 'Eeh, he's made a fine handsome lad, ain't he?'

'Yes, he has. You know, I don't think they've hardly paused for breath since the second he arrived.'

'Well, that's understandable. Happen they've a lot to

talk about. Yer could have knocked me down with a feather the night he turned up on me doorstep. It gave me a rare gliff, I can tell yer.'

Miriam grinned understandingly. 'I can well imagine.' She pictured the scene in her mind. 'It must have given William a shock too, when he opened the cottage door where he used to live and walked in on a strange family.'

Clara was chuckling now as she remembered the commotion his entrance had caused at her neighbours' house. 'Aye, it certainly did. It's a good job I was at home to back up his story else I reckon they would have called the peelers.'

'I think I would have an' all if I'd been in their shoes.' Miriam began to sharpen a knife. 'But still, luckily you *were* in – so all's well that ends well, eh?'

If Sassy and William could have heard that statement, they couldn't have agreed with it more, for even after their long time apart the bond between them was as strong as ever.

On the night of his arrival, Miriam had insisted that he must stay at the farm, and since then William had shared a bedroom with James, and of course Oscar, who was never far from his master's side.

Arthur had been as delighted as Sassy to see his son again, so much so that he had even stood up to Elizabeth and had visited the farm every day since the lad's arrival. William had visited the grand house in Swan Lane only once, and had obviously felt out of place there, so Arthur told Elizabeth, 'If the mountain won't come to Mohammed, then Mohammed must go to the mountain!'

Unused to Arthur sticking up for himself, she had looked down her nose and sniffed disapprovingly, but for once had held her tongue.

In truth, his father's marriage to the woman he remembered as the Widow Bonner had shocked William to the core, for in his eyes they made an unlikely pair. Clara had told him of it on the night of his arrival, after he had barged into his former home unannounced, and been rescued by her.

It had been Sassy whom William had expected to find married, for by now his sister was almost twenty-one years old and one of the prettiest girls by far in the neighbourhood. The reason why she wasn't soon became apparent to him. The fact that she still carried a torch for Thomas made him feel deeply uneasy, because he remembered his boyhood friend as being a wayward, headstrong sort of lad.

On the first day after his arrival, he had visited George's grave, and memories of the little brother he had adored swept through him. Even now he felt as if a part of him was missing. The graves in the churchyard were decked with holly wreaths befitting the time of the year, but as he stood in the shadow of Coton Church and let the tranquillity of the place wash over him, an inner calm settled on his heart. He gazed at the tiny grave nestled close to that of his mother and baby sister, and when he eventually turned and walked slowly away, somehow he finally felt that George's ghost had been laid to rest.

Sassy was delighted to learn that William was to be with them until early spring when he had to report back to his cargo ship, the *Dolphin* in Liverpool, and she intended to make the most of this time. Each night as they sat around the fire at Holly Bush Farm, he would keep them entranced as he told them of all the places he had visited – especially Sassy, whose eyes would widen in wonder at his tales. She felt that she could have listened to him for ever. William was also proving to be a firm favourite at the Jolly Colliers, for David Smith and the regulars took to him immediately, and William, who accompanied Sassy on her regular visits to see Maisie and Florica, soon looked forward to his sessions in the bar whilst Sassy was upstairs.

In mid-January, Florica developed a heavy cold. When Maisie called Dr Massey out, he assured her that it was nothing to worry about, but the infection was bad enough to keep her indoors for a few days just to be on the safe side.

Sassy immediately volunteered to take on Maisie's shopping while Florica was unwell. As she pointed out, it was no hardship, she had William to carry the extra bags for her now, and so Maisie gratefully accepted.

It was following one of these shopping expeditions as they panted up the hill, fighting against a bitterly cold wind and laden down with numerous bags, that William asked teasingly, 'What yer smiling at then, love? Yer look as happy as a sandboy.'

Sassy laughed at her handsome brother. Since his arrival he had visited the barber and his rich chestnut hair was now cut neatly into his neck. His coming had caused quite a few of the local girls' hearts to flutter.

'I don't know really,' she giggled, and happily shrugged her shoulders. 'I just feel on top o' the world, that's all.'

'Well, long may it last, eh?'

Sassy nodded, and they struggled on until they finally rounded the Bull Ring, and came within sight of the inn. The sight that met their eyes instantly wiped the smile from Sassy's face. A pony and trap was parked at the bar door and as they approached they saw the driver heaving down some trunks from the back of it.

'Hello, I wonder what's going on here then?' William was equally as puzzled as Sassy.

Just then, an idea sprang into her mind, causing her to slow her steps.

'Are you all right, love?' William asked. 'You've gone as white as a sheet.'

For a moment she couldn't answer him. Her heart was beating so fast she felt sure it would burst from her chest. 'Oh, my God,' she whispered finally. 'Do you think it might be Thomas come home?'

William shrugged. 'There's only one way to find out, ain't there? And that's to go an' see.'

Side by side they hurried on again, Sassy almost running now to keep up with her brother's giant strides. When they finally reached the entrance he shouldered the door roughly open for her, for his hands were full of shopping bags, and Sassy almost flew past him.

Within was chaos. There were trunks and valises everywhere. David was piling them against the wall, and as her expectant eyes flew to his face, he dropped his head as if in embarrassment. There was an air of excitement and the buzzing of conversation of the customers, and pipesmoke hanging on the air as she stared at David eagerly.

'It's Thomas, isn't it?' she asked breathlessly. 'He's back!'

David took off his flat cap and scratched his bald head slowly before muttering, 'Yes, love, he is.'

Sassy's face lit up with pure joy. 'So where is he?'

'He's upstairs.' The words had barely left his mouth when Sassy dropped her basket and, lifting her heavy skirts in a most unladylike fashion, went flying towards the staircase.

'Hold up now, love, don't go up just yet. Happen there's somethin' yer should know first,' David shouted after her, but he might as well have saved his breath – she was already clattering up the stairs.

Once outside the kitchen door she paused, her heart thumping as her hand rested on the doorknob. The hum of voices came to her from within, and unable to wait a second longer, she pushed the door open so quickly that she almost fell into the room. Her eyes found him immediately. He was standing at the window with Florica in his arms. The room seemed to be full of people, but for now all she could see was Thomas.

Her bonnet was slightly askew from the wind, her cheeks were rosy, her eyes shining and a few stray curls had escaped from her ribbon and now framed her smiling face. She made a pretty picture as she stood there gazing at him, and as his eyes met hers across the room, something suddenly stabbed at his heart and he flushed a deep dull brickred. She would have flown to him then, but a gentle hand on her arm stayed her flight. Surprised, she glanced to her side to find Clara staring at her, her beloved face wrinkled with concern.

'Sassy, love . . .' She struggled to find the right words. She would have given her life to save this girl any pain but there was nothing else for it but to be truthful and have done with it. Her grip on Sassy's arm remained firm. 'We have someone yer should meet.'

Sassy frowned at her in bewilderment as Clara nodded across the room. At the side of the table sat a woman whom Sassy had never seen before. She was tall – much taller than Sassy was – and muscular too, almost manly. She looked to be about forty or so and could have laid no claim to beauty at all, except for her hair, which was the richest, most beautiful shade of deep auburn that Sassy had ever seen, as was that of the young man who looked to be in his early twenties standing at her side.

'How do you do,' said Sassy quietly.

The woman inclined her head in answer.

Sassy looked enquiringly at Thomas, but as if he had suddenly been struck dumb, he looked away and gazed miserably at the floor.

Coming quickly to the rescue, Clara said, 'Sassy, I'd like yer to meet Daniel an' Faith, his mother.'

A strange feeling had come over Sassy, a terrible sense of misgiving.

'Faith is Thomas's new wife, Sassy,' Clara went on, holding the girl's hand tightly.

Just for a second time stood still and the room seemed to spin around her. If it weren't for Clara, and William, who had come to stand at the other side of her, Sassy was sure she would have fallen. Although the time seemed to stretch to eternity, in truth it was only a moment and luckily all eyes were distracted from her as Florica suddenly let out a peevish cry and demanded to be passed from Thomas to Maisie.

Seizing his chance to save her from further embarrassment, William spun her about. 'Come on, love,' he urged. 'Let's go an' bring the provisions up while Clara puts the kettle on, eh?'

Clara glanced at him gratefully as, without further ado, William gently pushed his sister from the room. Once out of earshot of everyone, he let out a low whistle of relief. Grasping Sassy by the elbow, he steered her down, through the back door and out into the privacy of the back garden, away from the customers' curious eyes. Once there he relaxed his hold as Sassy leaned heavily against the wall of the inn.

William eyed her warily. 'Are you all right, pet?'

Sassy seemed not to hear him; she just stood as if in a world of her own, staring off into space.

'Perhaps a few minutes alone is what she needs.'

William started; he hadn't heard anyone follow them out, but found David standing behind him. Instantly seeing the sense of his words, he nodded.

'I reckon yer right.' He of all people recognised that there were times when you needed solitude to put your thoughts into some sort of order. Turning to Sassy, he told her, 'I'll be in the bar when yer need me, love,' then followed David back into the inn.

For some time, Sassy stood there as if turned to stone, her breath hanging on the frosty air, her still body belying the whirlwind of emotions that were whipping through her.

'Thomas is married *again*!' a silent voice screamed at her, but her heavy heart was struggling to deny it. Thomas wouldn't do this to her a second time . . . would he? And especially not with that plain older woman, who even now sat at his table appearing to be almost twice his age. 'No,' she tried to convince herself. 'I'm having a bad dream. In a minute I'll wake up in my own bed and none of this will have happened.' But even as she tried to convince herself, the initial shock was wearing off and she knew that she was lying to herself. Just then she heard the click of the back door and her heart thumped as she saw Thomas approaching her. They stood in silence for a while, but then her voice hardly more than a whisper, she asked, 'Why?'

He shrugged, obviously deeply uncomfortable. 'I never meant it to happen, Sassy . . . it just sort of came about. I was lodging with her, see? And I was still grieving for Ellie. But she was so kind – she made me feel like a man again. For a long time before she died I knew that Ellie wasn't happy with me or the life we led, but Faith went out of her way to please me and I felt sorry for her. She had Daniel when she was just sixteen and a couple of years after that, her husband was killed in a riding accident. She'd managed for years all on her own earning a living by letting out rooms, and I suppose I admired her for that. And then it came time for me to leave and she was so upset. It had always been her dream to live in England, and before I knew it we were wed. It happened as quick as that.'

'But I thought we had an understanding.' Her voice was full of anguish.

'Not a *firm* understanding,' he said lamely, and the first flutter of rage sprang into life deep within her.

'That's not what *I* understood.' Her voice was harsh now. 'You've made a fool of me *again*, Thomas.'

'No, no, I ain't – or at least I never meant to.' As his eyes held hers she saw the desperation in them.

'Look, love.' He grasped her hands and shook them up and down in his agitation. 'I made a mistake. I knew it the day after Faith and I wed, but I didn't realise just how much of a mistake it was, not until you walked into that kitchen just now. But it ain't too late. There's ways round it.'

She stared at him in astonishment. 'What do you mean?' she gasped. 'Either you're married or you're not.'

'Well, yes, yes, I *am* married, but I've only just realised that it's *you* I should have wed and not Faith.'

Sassy could hardly believe what she was hearing. 'It's a bit late to realise it now,' she said, her voice rising bitterly.

'There's other ways we can be together,' he insisted, and as she gazed at him, her eyes were curious.

'And how do you work that out then?'

'Look . . .' He still had a firm hold of her hands, and his eyes now had an animated look in them. 'I'm a man o' means now, probably as wealthy as any hereabouts.'

'Yes, and what has that to do with anything?' she demanded.

He smiled at her. 'I could set you up in a little place o' yer own, an' visit . . . regular, like. I know it wouldn't be the same as bein' wed, but at least we'd get to be together, an' I'd see to it as you never wanted for nothin'.'

As the meaning of his words sank in, she shrank from him and snatched her hands away from his grasp. When she didn't immediately reply, his eyes became hopeful.

'So what do yer say then, lass?' he asked eagerly.

For now Sassy could say absolutely nothing, for right before her eyes the strangest thing was happening.

The rosy glow of adoration that had always surrounded him every time she had looked at him since she was a child suddenly fell away, and now before her she saw a man of flesh and blood instead of the idol he had always been. Not only that, but she was now seeing him as a selfish, weak man – and for the first time in her whole life she didn't like what she saw. For Sassy, it was the end of a dream.

He was growing impatient. 'Well, come on, lass. I ask again, what do yer say to me proposition?'

Finding her tongue at last, she gazed at him with open contempt. 'You insult me with your proposition, Thomas. I'm no Moll Twigger and I'll not be a kept woman for you nor anybody else.'

'But Sassy,' his voice was pleading now. 'It wouldn't *be* like that. I've told yer, marryin' Faith were a mistake. I don't love her. I realised that the second the ring were on her finger, but it were too late to do owt about it by then.'

'Then that will be your cross to bear. You've made your bed and now you can lie on it. As far as I am concerned, you're dead to me from this minute on. I've wasted enough of my life hanging on your every word, Thomas Mallabone.'

Greatly agitated, he held his hand out to her imploringly. 'Look, lass,' he begged, 'all this must have come as a bit of a shock to yer. You'll feel differently when you've had time to think on it.'

Sassy laughed harshly in his face. 'I can assure you it'll be a cold day in hell before that happens,' she hissed. Then turning from him without so much as a backward glance, she walked away with her head held high.

Thomas stared after her with anguished eyes, for only now did he fully realise what a fool he had been – and just what his foolery had cost him. He had omitted to tell her that marrying Faith had been a calculated move. She had lived in a very respectable boarding-house and he had calculated in his mind that she must be a very wealthy widow and that if he married her, what was hers would be his – only to discover that the house was leased and she didn't have a pot to piss in. And now, yes, as Sassy had said, he would have to live with it.

The fearful rage that was bubbling inside her lent speed to Sassy's legs, and it wasn't until she was almost halfway back to the farm that it began to subside and her steps slowed. Crossing to a drystone wall, she sank onto it and wrapping her arms round herself and rocking to and fro in anguish, she finally gave way to hot, scalding tears. And as they fell unchecked down her cheeks, they slowly washed away the dream that had lived in her heart for as long as she could remember.

Chapter Twenty-Five

Back at the inn, Thomas was in a black mood. Clara, who was sitting at the table with Faith, was doing her best to make small talk, still reeling from the shock of him turning up unannounced with a new wife. She was almost relieved when the kitchen door suddenly banged back on its hinges and Thomas entered bearing a heavy case in each hand.

Looking straight at Faith he nodded towards his bedroom door and told her curtly, 'This will be our room. If you'd like to come through, you could perhaps begin yer unpackin'.'

Faith inclined her head to Clara, then without a word she followed her husband into their bedroom and closed the door behind her, leaving Clara to let out a great sigh of relief. Daniel had gone downstairs some time ago and was already proving to be very popular with the customers, for it wasn't every day that they got to meet a real live American.

For some time, Maisie had been in Florica's room, settling her down for a much-needed nap. The little girl, who usually went down as meekly as a lamb, had taken some quieting today, for she was highly excited at her father's homecoming. Eventually she had succumbed to sleep with the help of Maisie's soothing lullabies, and now lay with her thumb jammed firmly in her mouth and her other hand clasping the beautiful china-faced doll that Thomas had bought for her. Once she was sure that the child was fast asleep, Maisie left the room on tiptoe, and rejoined Clara at the table.

'Well, you've got to hand it to him, ain't yer?' said Clara before Maisie's bottom had barely hit the seat. 'My lad don't do things by halves and that's a fact. Fancy him turnin' up like that out o' the blue, an' with a new wife an' all.' She shook her head in disbelief. 'An' what's even worse, she's years older than him. Whatever was he thinkin' of?'

Maisie was saved from having to reply when Thomas emerged from his room.

'I'm glad I've caught yer while it's quiet, Maisie, 'cos I need to have a word,' he said, looking more than a little uncomfortable. While Maisie sat waiting for him to go on, he nervously strummed his fingers on the table, which had Clara's nerves on edge in no time.

'Go on then, lad, spit it out – the lass is waiting,' she said irritably.

Thomas nodded, still playing for time as his mind searched for the right words. 'First of all,' he said eventually, 'I'd like to thank yer for takin' such good care of Florica while I was gone.'

Maisie flushed with pleasure at the compliment but said nothing, and obviously still very ill at ease, he continued, 'The thing is, now I'm back, Faith's agreed to take over the care of her.'

As Maisie's startled eyes flew to his face he flushed and spread out his hands. 'You can see how cramped it would be with all of us living here, can't yer? It's not that I *want* to get rid of yer, but it seems I don't have an option. Yer don't have to go straight away, o' course. Fer now you can move yer things into Florica's room an' you're welcome to stay fer as long as it takes you to find a new position.'

If he had slapped her in the face, Maisie couldn't have been more shocked, and the colour slowly drained from her face.

Deeply embarrassed, Thomas rose so quickly that his chair almost overturned. 'I'd . . . er . . . best go an' see how Faith's goin' on with the unpackin',' he mumbled, and without another word he scuttled off.

Clara was the first to pull herself together, and hastily leaning across the table, she gripped Maisie's hand tightly in her own. 'Aw, lass, I'm so sorry!' she cried. 'What a rotten homecomin' this is turnin' out to be. I reckon as we must have killed a robin – it's just one thing on top of another.'

Maisie smiled weakly. 'Aw well,' she said sadly, 'I can see his point, in all fairness. Two women in one kitchen would never work, an' I always knew it were too good to last.' But even as the words left her mouth, her heart was crying because the thought of leaving Florica was tearing her apart.

That night as usual, Jack arrived after his day's work with the horse and cart, to take his mother home. By the time he had been reunited with Thomas and introduced to his brother's new wife and her son, he too was reeling with shock.

As the horse gently clip-clopped along the hard-packed earth lanes, he declared, 'That's a turn-up for the books an' no mistake. Whyever didn't he write an' tell us he'd married again?'

'Huh,' Clara tutted. 'Who's to say why our Thomas ever does anythin'. He's a law unto himself, that one is. But I'll tell yer somethin' . . . if I'm any judge, he'll not get all his own way with this 'un, 'cos I reckon she'll give as good as she gets. I think he's finally met his match an' all I can say is, God help him.'

Jack nodded but held his tongue. By now he knew better than to try and stop his mother in midflow.

'It's Maisie as I feel most sorry for,' she continued,

and when he raised a questioning eyebrow at her she told him quickly of what had gone on. 'An' that's not all neither. As if that ain't bad enough, I reckon him an' Sassy had words an' all earlier on, fer she went out o' that door as if the devil hisself were snappin' at her heels.'

Jack could only imagine how betrayed Sassy must be feeling. Eventually he delivered Clara safely back to her door then made the return journey to the farm in record time. Once there, he jumped down from the cart and rushed off in search of Aaron, who listened with a worried frown on his face as Jack related the events of the day to him. Then as Jack headed off to the stable to unharness the horse and settle him for the night, Aaron hurried into the farmhouse for a hasty consultation with Miriam.

Two hours later, when he arrived at the inn with his hair still damp from a quick wash, he went straight to the bar where David was serving a customer with a frothing glass of ale.

'Where's Maisie?' he enquired.

David nodded at the back door. 'Last time I saw her, she was sat down by the cut,' he answered.

Outside it took Aaron's eyes some moments to adjust to the darkness after the harsh lights of the bar, but eventually he spotted her. She was standing with her back to the trunk of the weeping willow tree, and like the aptly named tree, she too was crying. As she heard him approach she quickly wiped away the tears with the back of her hand, and offered him a watery smile.

'I suppose you've heard the news then?'

He nodded. 'Yes I have, but yer know, it's not the end o' the world. When one door shuts another one opens, or so they say.'

'I know I'll get work, if it's only in the laundry at the

workhouse,' she said, 'but it's having to leave Florica that's the worst bit. I've loved caring fer that little one.' Her eyes were full of tears again as Aaron gently raised her chin to look into her eyes.

'If that's the case, perhaps yer should start filling a few cradles of yer own then.'

She frowned at him, puzzled. 'What do you mean?'

Laughing nervously, Aaron began to fumble about in his coat pocket until at last his fingers found what they sought.

'Yer not makin' this easy for me, woman. Yer know I'm no good with words, but perhaps this'll explain what I mean.' So saying, he awkwardly pressed a tiny box into her hand. She opened the lid and what she saw there caused her to catch her breath, for from the darkness a tiny diamond set in a thin gold band winked back at her. Aaron was watching her closely, and when still she continued to stare at the ring in silence, a panic settled on him.

'Look, Maisie,' his voice held a plea, 'I bought that ring fer yer over six months ago, but till now I've never plucked up the courage to give it to yer, 'cos you seemed to go a bit cold on me.'

Still she gaped at him open-mouthed, and desperate now, he continued, 'I wouldn't blame yer if yer didn't want it, 'cos I know I ain't much of a catch what wi' this.' His hand slowly rose to stroke the livid birthmark. 'An' all I can offer yer is the rooms where I live. But I'll tell you this: no one in the world could *ever* love you as much as I do. If you'd only take me for what I am, I solemnly promise I'll see as yer never live to regret it till your dying day. I ain't never had nobody in me whole life before to call me very own. An' if I were to be honest I'd have to admit that till I met you I never wanted anyone. But the truth of it is . . . I love you, Maisie, with all me heart, so I'm asking yer to be me wife.'

Suddenly ashamed of his outburst, he hung his head until Maisie's small hand slowly found its way into his.

'Aaron Lee,' she whispered, her voice thick with emotion, 'you are the handsomest, kindest man I have ever met. The reason I held you at arm's length was because I didn't believe that a man like you could ever love someone like me. But you've just made me the happiest woman on earth and I'd be proud to be yer wife because I love you too. I always have.'

As Aaron's head snapped up he gazed at her in wonder. '*What* did yer say?' he asked, hardly able to believe his luck.

Maisie was laughing and crying all at the same time. 'I said *yes, yes, yes!*' Suddenly they were in each other's arms.

'I . . . I just can't believe it.' He was hugging her tightly.

'Neither can I.' Her laughter and tears joined his. But then a silence descended, for their lips were locked tight together and a wise old owl, perched high in the branches above their heads, hooted his approval.

When at last they made their way indoors to announce their engagement, Thomas insisted on drinks on the house, all round, and glasses were raised merrily to the happy couple.

Maisie could hardly take her eyes off the ring that she now wore on her left hand, and felt as if she were floating on a cloud of unreality. But unknown to her, better was yet to come, for when they had finished the drink, Aaron stood and pulled her to her feet.

'Where are we goin'?' she asked curiously.

Aaron grinned. 'We're goin' to tell Miriam, Ben and Sassy the good news.'

'Ain't it a bit late tonight?' she fretted.

'It's never too late to hear something as wonderful as this,' he whispered lovingly, and within minutes they were headed for the farm with the echoes of the well-wishers ringing in their ears.

They entered the kitchen to find Ben dozing in a chair, and Miriam sewing at the table. Of Sassy there was no sign. Miriam's eyes flew to Aaron's and seeing the joy there she threw aside her sewing and leaped across the room to them.

When Maisie shyly held out her hand, Miriam saw the ring and squealed with delight.

'Well, an' it's about time too,' she laughed. 'Ben, crack open a bottle of that elderberry wine 'cos this calls for a celebration.'

Ben rushed off to do as he was told, and by the time he returned with the bottle and glasses, the women had their heads together talking weddings.

'Now then,' said Miriam, bossily taking control, 'tomorrow, Aaron can have a couple of hours off to help yer bring all yer stuff here.'

When Maisie frowned at her uncertainly, she laughed and wagged a finger in her face. 'You needn't look at me like that, young lady, 'cos you'll be sharing Sassy's room with her till after the wedding. I'll have no hanky panky here.'

Sassy had just appeared from upstairs where she had been since she got home, and Miriam asked, 'Is that all right with you, love?'

'Is what all right with me?'

'Aaron and Maisie here are engaged at last an' I wondered if you'd mind sharing a room with her till after they're wed.'

'Of course.' Despite her own heartache, she was thrilled for her friend. 'That's fine by me.'

Turning back to Maisie, Miriam continued, 'There'll be no need to go out looking fer work. There's far more than Sassy and I can handle here now, so if you're agreeable to helping out, I'm sure Ben wouldn't see you out o' pocket.'

Ben nodded enthusiastically, only too happy to gain an extra pair of hands about the place.

'Right then, that's sorted,' his wife said with satisfaction. 'Now let's go on to the weddin'. When would you like it to be?'

Maisie and Aaron gazed at each other, bemused. They hadn't thought that far ahead as yet.

Seeing their confusion, Miriam laughed. 'Oh dear, it looks like I'm goin' to have to organise everything. How about making it a spring wedding?'

Maisie's eyes glowed and she nodded eagerly.

'Right then.' Miriam was in fine spirits. 'A spring weddin' it is. Just leave everythin' to me, but I think fer tonight we'll just get on with celebratin' yer engagement, eh?'

Ben quickly refilled their glasses and that's just what they did, although every now and again, Miriam glanced towards Sassy and her heart ached for her. She certainly had nothing to celebrate this night, that was for sure.

The next morning bright and early, Aaron harnessed up the horse and after hitching him to the cart, he, Sassy and William set off to bring Maisie back to what was to become her new home.

It was William's suggestion that Sassy should come along. At first she was against it, but as he pointed out gently, 'Look, love, what's done is done. You'll have to face Thomas sooner or later, an' the longer yer leave it, the harder it will be. Don't give him the satisfaction of seeing that he's hurt you.'

Sassy thought on his words and realising that he was right, she finally agreed to go. It turned out to be much easier than she had feared for Thomas and David were busily cleaning the bar and preparing to open. Maisie had been up since first light packing her things and had them all ready to be loaded onto the cart. On their arrival, Daniel kindly began to carry them downstairs for her.

Sassy had hardly noticed Daniel the day before, but now as he smilingly heaved Maisie's cases down the steep narrow staircase, she found herself warming to him. Daniel Jackson was a pleasant young man in looks as well as nature. The smile barely left his face until all the bags were loaded onto the cart. Sassy, William and Aaron had all climbed back aboard by then, thoughtfully leaving Maisie to say her goodbyes to Florica in privacy, and he was chatting to them easily.

Florica was not taking the parting well. 'Want Maisie,' she sobbed, and Maisie, deeply upset herself, did her best to reassure the little girl.

'Don't cry, sweet'eart,' she implored her, very near to tears herself. 'I'll come an' see yer often, an' me an' Grandma will take yer to the market, an' even to the farm to play with James an' Oscar sometimes, if yer a good girl.'

Somewhat comforted at the thought of the promised outings, the little girl eventually quietened and Maisie at last made her way downstairs.

As she crossed the bar, Thomas handed her an envelope that contained her wages and a more than generous bonus. 'Thank you again,' he said, keeping his eyes downcast.

She looked around the inn, which up to now had been the happiest home she had ever known. Then lifting her chin, she walked out to the horse and cart and the start of her new life.

Thomas gazed after her enviously before raising his eyes to the ceiling above, where he could vaguely hear Faith and Florica fratching and arguing. Not for the first time since he had married her, he once again silently cursed himself for a fool and wondered what he had ever seen in her. She had been so attentive back in her own home. Nothing was too much trouble for her, and she had waited on him hand and foot. Added to that, he had thought she would bring him wealth, which in his eyes would more than make up for the difference in their ages. And now he was a laughing stock. He was no fool and he had heard the scandalised whispers of the customers in the bar when they had first set eyes on Faith. Huh! It just went to show how wrong you could be!

Chapter Twenty-Six

A few days later, Miriam insisted on a trip to the market. For some time now Sassy had travelled in with Jack to do the shopping, but this week Miriam wanted to go herself, and Ben decided that he himself would take her.

'I'll tell yer what, love,' he suggested kindly, 'we'll make a day of it, eh? After we've done our chores I'll take yer fer a meal at the Bull Hotel. How would that be?'

Miriam beamed. 'That sounds just what the doctor ordered.' She was like a child in her excitement.

'What are yer goin' to buy anyway?' asked Ben curiously.

Miriam grinned and remained tight-lipped. 'That's fer me to know and you to find out, Ben Ratcliffe. You just make sure as yer bring along yer wallet, that's all.'

Knowing better than to argue with a woman, Ben did just that.

When they eventually arrived home in mid-afternoon, besides the usual shopping and various feeds for the animals that Ben had bought, Miriam had Aaron carry in three parcels all wrapped in brown paper and neatly tied with string. She had him place them on the kitchen table and then waited impatiently for Sassy and Maisie to appear, which they did within the hour.

On entering the kitchen, they eyed the parcels curiously.

'Right then.' There was a twinkle in Miriam's eye. 'Let's show you what I've been off buyin' then, eh?'

Taking up a sharp knife, she carefully cut the string on the middle-sized parcel first, revealing a neatly wrapped length of satin; it was a beautiful shade of cornflower blue. 'There then.' Miriam smiled at Sassy. 'If you're to be bridesmaid, we've got to have yer looking the part, haven't we?'

Sassy's eyes grew moist. She was trying desperately hard to be happy for Maisie, but it wasn't easy when her own heart was breaking. Without further ado, Miriam then proceeded to open the largest of the parcels. Both of the girls became silent as they gazed at a large bale of pure white satin.

'An' if you're to be a bride, then we have to have you looking yer best, don't we?'

Maisie was speechless. Never in her whole life had she known such generosity – and she was lost for words.

'And now,' beamed Miriam, 'for the last one.' Very carefully she began to undo the last parcel, which was the smallest of the three, and gingerly she pulled out a length of the finest gauze net that Maisie had ever seen. It was so beautiful that she dared not touch it, for fear that her work-roughened fingers would snag on it and spoil it.

'No bride is fit to be seen without a veil,' Miriam declared kindly, and suddenly overcome, tears spurted from Maisie's eyes.

'I don't know how to thank you,' she sobbed.

'Yer don't have to thank me, love,' said the older woman. 'Only by bein' the prettiest bride this town has seen.'

Smiling through her tears, Maisie flew into her arms and hugged her fiercely.

Although things were going well at Holly Bush Farm, the same could not be said for the inn. Clara couldn't help but notice that since arriving home, Thomas was drinking far too much and spending more of his time with the customers in the bar than he did behind it. He had also taken to having regular jaunts off into town late at night and she had a horrible suspicion that he was visiting the local brothel again. For now at least she held her tongue, hoping that things would improve. In the meantime, Daniel and William had struck up a friendship and Daniel had become a regular visitor to the farm.

Despite being so sad, Sassy found herself looking forward to his visits. He was easy to talk to and had a lovely sense of humour, and she found his broad American accent pleasing. None of this was lost on William, and he watched with quiet amusement, for just as Miriam had once recognised a spark between Maisie and Aaron, so he now detected the same between Sassy and Daniel, not that Sassy seemed aware of it. She was still grieving for her lost dream and couldn't see what was right under her nose. William just hoped she wouldn't miss her chance. Daniel was a good sort and William could easily picture them as a couple. The way he saw it, Sassy deserved a little happiness after the way Thomas had let her down, so he sat back and waited for the same idea to occur to her. To his mind, it was only a matter of time.

However, Sassy was not the only one who had taken a shine to Daniel. He also had a very ardent admirer in the unlikely form of Louise Bonner, who had transferred her affections from Thomas to him.

Much to everyone's amazement, within days of Thomas's return, Elizabeth's fine horse and trap pulled up outside the inn. Elizabeth was more than happy to be connected with the Mallabones now as Thomas was somewhat of a celebrity in the town these days, and wealthy to boot, although they spent their visits upstairs with Faith, of course. Elizabeth would never have lowered herself to sit downstairs with the working class.

From Louise's first sighting of Daniel, her eyes lit up and much to his embarrassment, she cornered him at every opportunity, which was one of the reasons why he so loved to escape to the farm.

Louise's infatuation was not lost on Elizabeth, and surprisingly she encouraged it. Louise was now twenty-three years old and still unmarried, a fact that worried her mother. She feared that Louise was in danger of becoming an old maid, of being left on the shelf. The idea of an American son-in-law pleased her, and so a friendship of sorts was struck up with Faith, and Louise and Elizabeth became regulars to the inn.

Faith was glad of the distraction of these visits, as married life with Thomas was not turning out to be as she had hoped. He spent most of his time downstairs or out on some jaunt or another. Also, life in England was very different to the life she had known in America and she was finding it difficult to adapt. When he had spoken of his inn, back in America, she had envisaged a beautiful coach house favoured by the gentry, not some small public house that was frequented by working men. On top of all that, Florica hadn't taken to her new step-mother and cried and whined incessantly for Maisie – a fact that almost drove Faith to distraction and tested her patience sorely.

The only time the child ever seemed truly happy was on the days when her grandma paid her regular visits. Faith found herself looking forward to these days almost as much as Florica did, so that she could leave her in her doting grandmother's care. Clara too was unhappy with the way things were going. Lately she had noticed odd bruises on Thomas, usually following one of his outings, and she strongly suspected that he was fighting once again, although he always denied it when she confronted him.

Jack was also worrying her. Sassy had told no one of the proposition that Thomas had put to her, but it was more than obvious that whatever had taken place between them had finally ended her feelings for him. This had caused hope to spring once again into Jack's heart, and fear into Clara's. Like William, she had noticed the way that Daniel looked at Sassy. As yet, Sassy had shown him nothing but friendship, but over the last few weeks she had changed greatly. The happy girl had fled, to be replaced by a solemn-faced young woman, but how long would it be, Clara wondered, before she found solace with the handsome young American? More than anything she longed for Sassy to find happiness, yet again, she could see even more heartache ahead for her beloved younger lad, and her heart cried out at the injustice of it all.

As the day of the wedding approached, a mood of anticipation began to build about the farm. Sassy's dress was finished and now Miriam was busily working, sometimes until the early hours of the morning, on the bride's, sewing with such neat tiny stitches that they were almost undetectable. Maisie was like a cat with two tails. She had never in her whole life owned a dress before that wasn't secondhand, and each time Miriam called her in for a fitting she bubbled with excitement, which endeared her to the woman all the more.

On the Sunday before the wedding, as Maisie and Aaron wended their way home hand in hand from the church where they had heard their banns read out, Aaron suddenly pulled her to a halt.

'Do you have *any* idea at all how very much I love yer, Maisie?' he said.

When she giggled, he went on, 'I have to keep pinchin' meself to make sure that I ain't dreamin'.'

'Why, Aaron Lee, it's *me* as should be *sayin'* that to you!' Maisie exclaimed, and suddenly they both burst out laughing.

'Well, happen then, if yer feel the same, we're lucky that we got to meet, eh?' Aaron chuckled.

As she nodded happily in agreement he gently kissed her, and for now there was no one else in the whole world but each other.

It was the day of the wedding, and all morning the farm had been buzzing with activity. Jack had gone off bright and early to collect Clara and Walter, and on his way back, Ada, whom Elizabeth had graciously allowed to take the day off so that she could help with the wedding feast. Ben had been up at the crack of dawn to see to the needs of his beasts, and just for today that was all the work the farm would see.

Much disgruntled, Aaron had been packed off on the eve of the wedding to spend the night with Jack in his cottage. Miriam insisted that it was bad luck for the groom to see the bride on the day of the wedding before the ceremony, and although he grumbled, he did as he was told.

Now, however, the preparations were done, the animals were fed, the tables were groaning under the weight of a meal fit to set before Queen Victoria herself, and everyone assembled was dressed all in their Sunday best. Sassy looked a picture in her bridesmaid gown, as Clara was quick to comment, but Sassy promised her, 'If you think I look good, just wait till you see Maisie.' She had just left the room where Miriam was putting the final touches to the bride.

At that moment, the kitchen door banged open and

James tripped into the room. 'Jack and Aaron gone,' he squealed excitedly. He had seen them set off for the church some minutes ago, Aaron looking nervous and Jack decidedly proud in his role of best man.

'Right, it's time we were off an' all then,' Clara declared. 'Else the bride will be at the church before we are.' And without further ado, she, Walter, William and Ada hurried out and clambered aboard one of the carts that stood waiting in the yard. In a few minutes, Sassy would follow with Miriam and James, and then Ben would follow on with Maisie, for to him had fallen the honour of giving the bride away.

After waving off the merry guests, Sassy hurried into the bedroom to find Maisie standing before the mirror. The sight brought a huge lump to her throat. Never in her life had she seen a lovelier bride.

'Oh, Maisie,' she said, her voice choked with emotion. 'You look truly beautiful.'

Maisie flushed happily.

'You've made a beautiful job of that dress,' Sassy said admiringly, but her aunt shook her head.

'It's not the dress that's beautiful,' she said softly. 'It's the love that's shining from the bride that's beautiful.'

'Well, whatever it is, she looks radiant,' Sassy said firmly.

Miriam smiled her agreement. 'Yer know,' she agreed. 'They say that true love only comes once in a lifetime, an' it's a sad fact that most people never get to meet the person who was meant for them. But I'll tell yer now, the very first time I saw you an' Aaron together, I knew that yer were meant fer each other, an' I have a feeling that there are only good things ahead fer you two from now on.'

Maisie was deeply touched at Miriam's words and her lip trembled, so quickly breaking the mood, the older woman clapped her hands.

'Now then, I've one last little gift for yer. I'll run and fetch it,' and so saying she hurried from the room. When she returned she held a circle of early spring flowers, all intricately woven one into the other, and as Maisie delightedly bent her head, Miriam placed it gently on her veil. 'There now, that's just finished it off nicely,' she said with satisfaction.

'Whenever did you find time to do that?' questioned Sassy. As far as she knew, Miriam hadn't left the cottage all morning.

'Ah, well,' laughed Miriam, 'I was up at the crack o' dawn, an' that was made before you sleepyheads had even set foot out of bed. What's more, there are two posies in there, one for each of you. But anyway . . . come on, Sassy, it's time we were off, else we'll have the poor bridegroom thinking he's been left at the altar.'

With a wink at Maisie over her shoulder, Sassy hurriedly followed Miriam from the room and within minutes they were on their way.

When some moments later Maisie joined Ben in the kitchen he whistled softly at the sight of her. 'Why, love,' he gasped admiringly, 'you look absolutely radiant.' And she truly did. Her hair, which Sassy had twisted into rags the night before, now lay about her shoulders in soft shining ringlets, and the dress which Miriam had so painstakingly stitched would have graced any bride, and fell about her in folds of pure white. But just as Miriam had said, it was more than just that, for she seemed to be glowing from within and with her sparkling eyes, she was everything a bride should be.

'I'll tell yer somethin', love.' Ben's voice was kindly. 'I've only ever seen one bride to match yer, an' that were my Miriam on our weddin' day.' His eyes misted as his mind drifted back over the years, but then quickly pulling himself back to the present, he caught up her posy and smiling broadly, handed it to her.

'If I'm not mistaken, we have a weddin' to go to, so let's be off, eh?'

Happily taking his arm, Maisie followed him out to the waiting pony and trap.

It was a truly magical day, one that would be long remembered, and to Miriam's delight everything ran like clockwork. As 'The Wedding March' struck up on the church organ, Aaron, who was fairly quaking in his boots at Jack's side, couldn't resist a peep over his shoulder. From that moment on his nerves fled, as Maisie floated down the aisle towards him on Ben's arm.

The church, which was fairly bursting with guests, could have been empty because from then on the bridal pair had eyes for no one but each other. It was a wonderful service, and as Sassy stood behind the bride she felt a huge lump form in her throat. The vows they made one to the other were spoken with such sincerity that she couldn't stop a little pang of envy from shooting through her as she wondered if there would ever come a day when she herself would enter this church as a bride. Glancing to her side she found Daniel's eyes on her, almost as if he could read her mind. She looked away quickly as her heart skipped a beat. With the light from the stained-glass windows shining down on him, turning his hair a fiery red, it suddenly struck her that he was a very handsome young man – but not as handsome as Thomas, of course. Forcing her thoughts back to the service, she tried to focus on what the vicar was saying.

When he at last pronounced them man and wife, Maisie and Aaron embraced each other with such pure joy that there was barely a dry eye in the house.

It was a merry couple indeed who left the church

to meet a hail of rice and rose petals and the joyous congratulations of well-wishers.

Jack was beaming almost as much as Aaron because, as the best man, he had the honour of escorting Sassy back down the aisle on the trail of the newlyweds. As he gazed at her lovingly, he promised himself, 'Tonight I'll speak to her,' and his heart filled with hope at the thought.

By the time the church bells had stopped ringing the majority of the wedding guests had already arrived back at the farm. Then began a party the likes of which had not been seen thereabouts for many a long day. The joy of the newlyweds was infectious and everyone was in high good spirits. Once the speeches had been made and the toasts drunk, the furniture was pushed tight back against the wall and a knees-up began in earnest.

By evening, as the glorious spring day gave up its light to darkness, the laughter and the merrymaking of the people within was echoing around the rafters of the farmhouse and showed no sign of ceasing for some time to come. Sassy's face ached from smiling and her feet were sore, for she had danced until she felt dizzy.

As yet, Jack had had no opportunity to get her alone, and he waited impatiently for his chance. Clara and Ada had sampled more than their fair share of wine and were more than a little tiddly, but in fairness, so were a lot of other people present. Thomas had supplied nearly all the drink as a wedding present to the happy couple, and it flowed freely. Even Elizabeth, who was in a finer mood than anyone had ever seen her in before, was observed at one point to be holding a glass of wine. This caused Ada to raise her eyebrows at Clara, and for them both to giggle like a couple of schoolgirls. Could they have known it, Elizabeth was only there under duress. Louise and Arthur had made such a hoo-hah about attending that she had agreed – and now she was glad that she had.

Thomas was another who watched Sassy closely, and the more he had to drink, the sorrier he felt for himself. Now, too late, he realised what he had lost and the life that stretched before him with Faith appeared like a prison sentence. However, all good things must come to an end and by nine o'clock the first of the merrymakers began to take their leave. It had been a long day. It was then that Daniel seized his chance and, grabbing Sassy by the hand, he pulled her out into the yard. His eyes were alight with mischief as she eyed him suspiciously.

'What are you up to, Daniel Jackson?' she asked.

Laughing, he held his coat pocket open and beckoned her to look inside. Sassy giggled when she saw that his pockets were bulging with rice.

'Look,' he whispered, 'we need to get over to Aaron's rooms and get this lot into their bed.'

Sassy had to hold her hand over her mouth now to smother her laughter. 'You're wicked, that's what you are,' she chuckled.

Beaming, he nodded in agreement. 'I know I am, but are you going to help me, young lady, or what?'

'You just try and stop me.'

'All right then, here we go.' Taking her tightly by the hand, he looked both ways, and seeing no one about, he tugged her across the yard in the direction of the barn. Unbeknown to them, somebody *had* seen them go. At that minute, Jack's eyes were following them, and with each gay step they took, his heart seemed to sink a little lower into his boots. '*You bloody fool, you,*' his heart cried. '*You've left it too late again.*' Turning from the kitchen window, he sank onto the nearest chair, and for him all the joy had gone from the day.

Once inside Aaron's rooms, Sassy and Daniel felt their

way to the bed, giggling with every step, and once it was located, one either side, they quickly pulled back the sheets. 'I can't see a damn thing,' Daniel cursed.

'No, neither can I, but we can't light the lamp or they'll catch us for sure.' Sassy's voice came from the darkness. 'Look,' she urged, 'just throw the rice onto the bed and I'll spread it about.' And for the next five minutes that's exactly what they did.

'Poor devils,' giggled Sassy. 'They won't get much sleep if they try to lie on that lot.'

'From what I've heard, not many people *do* get a lot of sleep on their wedding night.'

As the meaning of Daniel's amused words sank in, she was suddenly glad of the darkened room as she blushed beetroot red, and without another word she hastily put the bedding back as they had found it.

'Right, that's it then,' she whispered. Feeling her way round the foot of the bedrail, she and Daniel crept, like thieves in the night, back down the stairs and out the way they had come. Out in the yard, the silver moon showed them the path to the house, and standing there with the satisfaction of a job well done, they listened to the sound of merriment pouring from within.

It was a beautiful night and, suddenly realising how tired she was, Sassy sighed contentedly and leaned back against the barn door, enjoying the velvety darkness. Daniel was gazing at her. With the moonlight shining down on her, her eyes appeared to be twinkling even brighter than the stars.

'You know, Sassy,' he said, 'you were easily the prettiest girl at the wedding today.'

Flushing at the compliment, she said nothing as he gently took her in his arms. She stared up at him, aware of her heart thumping in her chest – and then slowly his head came down to hers and their lips touched.

Sassy felt like a rabbit caught in a trap. She couldn't have stopped even if she had wanted to, but she *didn't* want to. She had dreamed of Thomas looking at her like this, but knew that would never be now, unless she was prepared to be his mistress – and that was unthinkable. As she returned his kiss, something warm and beautiful suddenly blossomed into life within her.

Just then, however, the farmhouse door burst open and Maisie and Aaron appeared on the step, closely followed by the remaining guests. Guiltily, Sassy leaped away from Daniel and straightened her skirts, then without a word they quickly crossed the yard to join the others.

Elizabeth had noticed them hurrying across the farm-yard, and she frowned suspiciously. A horrible idea crept into her head. Surely Daniel couldn't have designs on Sassy? In her mind's eye she had him earmarked as her future son-in-law, and now as she noted the happy flush on Daniel's face and the twinkle in Sassy's eyes, her heart hardened. '*Right, my girl, if it's a fight you want then you've got it,*' she said to herself. '*You'll have him over my dead body,*' and from that moment on until the time she departed, her eyes never left them.

Meantime the guests had assembled around the newly-weds, and Miriam urged, 'Right, Maisie, turn yer back, love, an' toss yer posy over yer shoulder.'

Maisie laughingly obliged and her posy rose high into the air. Louise and Sassy were standing but feet apart as just for a second the posy seemed suspended in mid-air, then it fell straight into Sassy's outstretched hands, which caused a cheer to go up amongst the crowd.

'There you are then,' laughed Ben. 'It looks like you'll be next, love.'

Sassy's eyes stole silently to Daniel's and seeing the look in them, she gulped deep in her throat.

310

Next minute, Maisie and Aaron made a dash for the barn to spend their first night together as Mr and Mrs Lee and soon after that, the rest of the guests drifted away. Sassy sighed. It had been a truly grand day all round but she was feeling confused. Why had she allowed Daniel to kiss her when she was feeling heartbroken over the way Thomas had treated her? Deciding it was probably just the fact that they had both had too much wine, she slipped back into the house.

But that night as sleep came to claim her, Sassy sighed contentedly and when she finally slept, her dreams were not of Thomas but of a handsome flame-haired young man and the lovely wedding that had just taken place. It had been a wonderful day in all ways.

Chapter Twenty-Seven

Following the joyous occasion of the wedding came a sad one when two weeks later, William had to rejoin his ship. He was heartsore to leave Sassy and his father, but in another way he was ready to return to the sea. It was in his blood now. As he stood with them at the railway station, Sassy sobbed unashamedly.

'Don't cry, lass,' he urged. 'I'll come back again, soon as I can. An' yer know what?' He leaned to whisper in her ear. 'I reckon the next time I do, I could have some red-haired nieces and nephews to play with.'

Sassy pushed him in the shoulder. 'Get off with you,' she scolded, blushing furiously, but then the station-master blew his whistle and with a hasty handshake for his father and a last peck on the cheek for Sassy, he threw his kitbag onto the train and leaped aboard. The train slowly chugged away from the station and within minutes was gone from sight, leaving only a haze of smoke that settled on the station like a fog.

Arthur took her elbow and led his daughter along the platform, and all the time William's words were ringing in her ears. *I could have some red-haired nieces and nephews to play with.*

Sassy had guessed by now that Daniel was fond of her, and if she were to be honest with herself, she was fond of him too. But could he ever take the place of Thomas in her heart? She decided that the only way to find out was to let nature take its course. She was still stinging from Thomas's latest betrayal, though being no fool she knew now that she should have expected it. Now that she no longer saw him through rose-coloured spectacles she could see how selfish he could be, as Ellie had found out to her cost. And now it seemed that Faith was unhappy too. But then, Sassy supposed it was none of her business and she tried to push all thoughts of him from her mind.

As Thomas stood before the fireplace later that night buttoning his coat, Faith glared at him. 'And just where are you going *now* then?' she demanded peevishly.

'Out!' His reply was short.

'I can see that – what I asked is *where*?'

'It's none o' your bloody business, woman. Just go back to bed, can't yer?' Thomas was fast losing patience but Faith would not be put off so easily.

'Look, it's gone eleven o'clock.' She motioned agitatedly towards the mantel clock. 'Wherever you're going, you can't be up to any good.'

Thomas stared at her coldly. 'Why don't yer just go to bed like I said, an' stop yer naggin', eh?'

'Why *should* I?' she spat back at him. 'If you aren't downstairs drinking the profits, then you're off out on some jaunt or another just lately, and I'm about sick to my back teeth of you.'

His eyes narrowed. 'That makes two of us then, 'cos I'm sick o' you an' all.'

Frustrated tears sprang to Faith's eyes but turning from her, Thomas strode purposefully to the door and flung it open with never a backward glance her way.

'I'll have my day with you, man, you just see if I don't,' she threatened, but her words were lost on him, for he was already clattering away down the stairs. Clenching her hands into tight fists, she stared at the empty doorway in frustration.

Anger lent speed to Thomas's legs and in no time at all he was marching down the Griff Hollows hill, his mind angrily going over his row with Faith. His shoulders were hunched and his hands deep in his pockets. The April day had been clear and bright, but the night was bitterly cold and he shuddered involuntarily, for the farther down the steep hill he went the colder it seemed to get. Straining his eyes ahead to the dip at the bottom of the hollow, he noted that a slight fog was hanging there. Off to his left, an owl perched high in a tree was hooting softly, but apart from that, an air of quiet hung in the air. Not a living soul was in sight; most avoided this spot at night as the superstitious of the town swore that it was haunted.

This had never troubled Thomas. He had never been one for believing in superstition, and had been heard to say on more than one occasion, 'It ain't the dead yer should worry about, they can't harm yer, it's the livin' yer should watch out for.' Yet tonight for some reason he felt strangely uneasy.

'Yer silly bugger, you,' he chided himself. 'I'm goin' to have to lay off the beer a bit, happen it's addlin' me brain.' He marched on with determination and just as he reached the mist, the owl suddenly stopped hooting and an eerie silence settled. Just then, the moon peeped from behind a black cloud and Thomas momentarily stopped in his tracks and glanced nervously to left and right. But all he saw was the mist floating about him, seeming to shimmer in the moonlight. Shaking himself, he hurried on. The trees formed a canopy overhead and their branches seemed to be reaching out to each other as he passed beneath them. What small wind there was had suddenly dropped, and now the silence was complete. Not even the whisper of a leaf blowing across the ground could be heard.

He had just begun the steep uphill climb on the other side of the deep dip when something in the mist in front of him caught his nervous eye. A woman was slowly approaching, but strangely she appeared to be almost floating. No sound of footsteps reached his ears and it was too dark to make out her features, so he stood his ground and waited for her to draw nearer, not wishing to give her a fright. The moon had disappeared behind a scudding black cloud again, and as he stood there in the pitch darkness, his heart began to thump like a sledge-hammer.

'Pull yerself together, man,' he told himself fearfully. 'You've done this walk a hundred times – what the hell's wrong wi' yer?' But his words gave him little comfort, and for no reason that he could explain, he began to shake like a jelly. The moon reappeared from behind the dark cloud and the woman in front of him was suddenly illuminated in a wash of moonlight. A strangled cry escaped his lips.

'Oh my God,' he whimpered, for there was Ellie reaching out to him. He roughly knuckled his eyes, and when next he opened them he was alone. She was gone. A chilly finger ran up his spine and, taking to his heels, he ran as if his life depended on it, nor did he stop or even slow his pace until he reached a turn in the lane that led to a farm track. Taking this, he almost flew its length until eventually a large barn came into sight. Gasping for breath now, he tugged the door open and fell inside.

A sigh of relief escaped the man who was standing just beyond the doorway, but then seeing the state of Thomas, he hurried over to him and helped him to a nearby bale of hay.

'Christ, man,' he said. 'What's up wi' yer, Thomas? You look like you've seen a bloody ghost!'

'A drink,' Thomas panted, and one of the many men assembled in the barn, who were all watching him avidly, pulled a small silver hipflask from his trouser pocket and passed it to him. With shaking fingers, Thomas raised it to his dry lips and took a long swallow. The men were all gazing at him in amazement, for it appeared that every hair on his head was standing on end. As the fiery liquid burned its way down his throat, he broke into a paroxysm of coughing, and Jim Temple, who had handed him the flask, banged him on the back. Once the choking fit had subsided, Thomas appeared more his old self.

'Are yer all right now?' asked Jim, and when Thomas nodded: 'What were up wi' yer, man?'

'Oh, nowt,' Thomas lied. 'I'm all right – it's just I knew I were late an' I rushed too much tryin' to get here, that's all.'

Jim nodded, clearly not believing him. 'Well, are yer still goin' to be all right fer the fight?' He had a lot of money riding on Thomas tonight, as did a fair few of the men present.

'Aye, I'll be fine,' Thomas reassured him. 'Just give me ten minutes to get me breath back an' we'll start.' And true to his word, ten minutes later that's exactly what he did, although his gammy leg was aching from the flight up the steep hill.

The next morning, when Clara arrived to take Florica on her weekly trip to market, she knew immediately that all was not well. The atmosphere in the kitchen was so thick that she could have cut it with a knife, and Faith was wearing a face like thunder as she loudly banged the clean dishes into a cupboard.

As Clara entered, she greeted her sulkily. 'Come for Florica, have you?' she said shortly. When Clara nodded she asked, 'Will you be wanting a cup of tea before you go?'

'No, thanks, I've to meet Sassy soon an' if I stay fer tea I'll miss her.' Clara had no wish to stay a minute longer than she had to as she found her new daughter-in-law increasingly hard work. She had never been keen on her, if truth be known, but lately she was beginning to actively dislike her. Clara had the feeling that she could turn out to be a right nasty piece of work, and not for the first time wondered what her lad had ever seen in her.

'Right then, I'll get her wrapped up,' said Faith, and drawing the little girl from the table where she sat beaming a welcome at her grandma, she marched her into her bedroom to get her ready for outdoors.

Glancing across the room, Clara noticed her son's feet sticking out from the fireside chair. Crossing the room, she stood before him – and gasped. He was laid back in the chair with a generous glass of whisky in one hand and his pipe in the other, staring vacantly into the heart of the fire. But it was the state of his face that shocked her most. His lip was swollen and split, and one of his eyes was completely closed and purple with a huge bruise.

'My God, lad, what yer been up to now?' she breathed in horror.

He raised dull eyes to her. 'It's nothin',' he said flatly. 'I just slipped, that's all.'

'Huh, pull the other one.' Clara's voice dripped sarcasm. 'What yer mean to say is you've been fightin' again.'

Thomas looked away as she shook her head in exasperation. 'What's got into yer, lad? Look at the state of yer.' When he still didn't answer, her voice became sharp. 'An' what yer doin' with *that* in yer hand at this time of the mornin', eh?' She stabbed an acusing finger at the

317

whisky in his hand. 'I'm tellin' yer, me lad, if fightin' ain't the death of yer, then that will be, the way you're going on, 'cos yer drinkin' yerself into an early grave, you just mark my words before it's too late.' And so saying she snatched the glass from his hand and banged it down onto the table. Fortunately for Thomas, Faith and the child emerged from the bedroom at that moment, and not wishing to upset the lass, Clara ceased her scolding.

'Are you all wrapped up then, pet?' she asked the child kindly, and when the little girl nodded eagerly, Clara forced a smile to her face. 'Right, well, let's be off then, eh?' Inclining her head at Faith she took her grand-daughter's hand and marched from the room without so much as a backward glance.

Faith immediately disappeared into her bedroom and not long after, she reappeared, also dressed in her best for outdoors. 'I'm off to visit Elizabeth,' she informed her husband, and crossing the room in a swish of bombazine skirts, she banged the door loudly behind her.

Once alone, Thomas leaned forward and buried his face in his hands as he tried to put his thoughts into some sort of order.

Had he *really* seen Ellie last night, or had he just had one too many to drink? He couldn't be sure now. A cold hand gripped his heart as one of his mother's sayings suddenly sprang to his mind. '*Should a loved one come to call, then join them you will before the fall.*' Shuddering violently, he rose and snatching the glass of whisky from the table he swallowed it down in one go, then grabbed the bottle and poured himself another.

Over the next few weeks, Sassy and Daniel rarely got the chance of a moment alone. Since the wedding, Miriam hadn't been at all well, and Sassy and Maisie insisted that she rest more and willingly took on her share of the work about the farm as well as their own.

Back at the inn, Daniel too was being kept busy. Thomas was hitting the bottle with a vengeance now, and most days it was Daniel who helped David to open up while Thomas sprawled in the chair upstairs in a drunken stupor.

Louise Bonner was becoming a real nuisance, visiting the inn at every opportunity. She made it more than obvious to Daniel what she was after, and being the polite person that he was, he was finding the position difficult – so much so that one day he tried to talk to Faith about it.

'Mom.' His voice was tentative, and Faith, who was standing at the table rolling pastry, looked over at him curiously.

'Could you have a word in Elizabeth's ear about Louise following me about?'

She stared at him in astonishment. 'You don't know a good thing when you see it, my lad,' was her response.

'But surely you wouldn't want to see me tied up to the likes of *her*?' he queried.

'Well, put it this way,' she said curtly, 'I'd sooner see you married to class than some I can mention, and while we're on the subject I'll tell you something else as well. Elizabeth has already informed me that whoever marries Louise will find that she comes not only with a good dowry but also with an excellent job in her uncle's works waiting for them too.'

Daniel gazed at her in horror. It was more than obvious that his mother and Elizabeth had already put their heads together. Shuddering at the thought, he left the room.

It was a beautiful morning in mid-June and Sassy was leaving the cowsheds with a large pail of milk in one hand, when a sound from the privy caught her ear. Seconds later, Maisie emerged, her face as white as a piece of bleached linen, wiping her hand across her mouth.

'Are you all right?' Sassy asked.

Grinning sheepishly, then glancing both ways to make sure that they weren't being observed, Maisie pulled Sassy back into the shadows of the cowsheds. 'Can yer keep a secret?' she asked.

Frowning, Sassy nodded.

'Well, I can't say fer sure yet, I'm seein' Dr Massey tomorrow, but I reckon I'm expectin'.'

Sassy's eyes widened in delight. 'Oh, that's blessed news.'

Maisie put her hand over her friend's mouth. 'Shush,' she begged. 'I don't want to say nothin' to Aaron till I'm sure, like.'

Sassy giggled with excitement. 'Don't worry, I'll not say a word,' she promised, and smiling, they both hurried away to their chores.

The next evening, the day's work behind them, Maisie and Aaron were relaxing in their little sitting room, enjoying the view across the fields when Maisie picked up a little carving of a lamb from the sill and stroked it lovingly.

'Yer know, love, you have a gift when it comes to carvin' wood,' she said softly. 'What do yer think you'd be like at carving bigger things?'

He frowned. 'What sort of things did yer have in mind?'

'I were thinkin' of a cradle.'

He stared at her in confusion. 'What would I want to carve a cradle for?' Then the look of mystification slid from his face and his eyes widened with wonder. 'You don't mean – I mean, you're not . . . we ain't . . .' He

320

couldn't find the right words and as he floundered, Maisie gently took his hand.

'Yes, I *do* mean, Aaron Lee.' Her voice was soft. 'In about seven months' time we two will be three.'

'Oh, love.' His voice was thick as his hand slipped to her stomach. 'I can't believe it.'

Maisie laughed. 'Well, I bloody can 'cos the little devil's makin' me sick as a dog already.' With that, she threw herself into his arms, while Aaron, closing his eyes tight, pictured Mrs Lee, the nearest he had ever had to a mother.

'You were right,' his heart told her, hoping that wherever she was, she would hear him. 'You always told me in those long lonely years, that my day would come, and by God it has!'

Miriam and Ben were nearly as thrilled at the news as the parents-to-be.

'Oh, it'll be grand havin' a baby about the place again,' Miriam declared, her eyes shining with pleasure at the thought. 'I'll tell you what,' she said, 'let's have a little get-together, eh – a celebration like. I'll ask Clara and Walter – an' Sassy, you can ask Daniel – and of course, Jack will come. Oh, an' I'll invite yer dad an' Elizabeth, though I doubt she'll want to come.' Miriam did not relish the thought of having to spend time with her sister-in-law, but felt that she should invite her for Arthur's sake. She was getting quite carried away with the idea and the two girls grinned at one another, but Miriam was too busy planning to notice.

'We'll make it Saturday evenin' then, shall we?' she asked, and Maisie happily agreed. With her mind awhirl, Miriam rushed off to begin making arrangements.

Much to Miriam's surprise, when Saturday evening came around, Elizabeth and Arthur were the first to arrive. Not only that, Louise had come with them too, for she had heard that Daniel had been invited and didn't intend to miss out on an opportunity of being in his company.

It was a pleasant evening and passed all too quickly. Miriam had cooked them all a delicious meal, following which the wine flowed freely, for as Ben pointed out, 'We have to wet the baby's head!'

Maisie looked at him and said teasingly, 'I thought that was supposed to be done *after* it was born?'

Ben shrugged. 'Ah well, there's nothin' to say we can't do it before as well, is there?'

Greatly amused, Maisie shook her head.

It was a pleasant evening, but come nine o'clock, Maisie yawned tiredly. 'I'm sorry,' she apologised, 'but I'm dead on me feet. I reckon I'll turn in, if yer don't mind.'

'Of course we don't mind,' Miriam hurriedly assured her. 'You need yer rest now, love, so you go and get yerself off to bed.'

Maisie smiled at her fondly. Ever since telling her of the baby, Miriam had clucked about her like a mother hen and the girl was enjoying the fuss.

Elizabeth also rose from her chair. 'I think it's time we were going too,' she said pointedly to Arthur. She was not at all thrilled with the way the evening had gone. Daniel had barely spoken a word to Louise, which was why her daughter was now sitting in a deep sulk.

Arthur immediately rose and fetched her wrap for her, and within minutes they left too. Jack had retired to his cottage some time ago and James was fast asleep in bed, so now when Ben went out to check on the animals there was only Sassy, Miriam and Daniel left in the kitchen.

'Right then,' said Daniel with a twinkle in his eye as

he turned to Sassy. 'Let's get these dishes out of the way and then you can walk me down the lane.'

'Oh, don't worry about them, they'll wait till morning,' Miriam insisted, then yawning widely she kissed them both soundly and went off to bed.

Within minutes the pots were all stacked to soak overnight in the sink, and the table was cleared and scrubbed ready for breakfast. Taking off her apron and hanging it on a hook at the side of the door, Sassy turned shyly to him. 'Right, I'd best walk you home if you're afraid of the dark then,' she teased.

He returned her smile. 'Yes, you better had, else I might lose my way.'

They stepped out into the balmy night. The fields around the farmhouse were awash with moonlight, and almost as of one mind, they ignored the twisting lane that led to the gate and struck out across the field. They had taken no more than a few steps when Daniel's hand found Sassy's. She could feel the heat rising into her cheeks but said nothing. She had spent so long yearning for Thomas and now here was a man who was showing an interest in her and making her feel special. What could be the harm in it? They strolled along in silence, content in each other's company for a time until Sassy asked, 'So how are you liking it in England then? It must be very different to living in America.'

'It is,' he said. 'But I like it here far better than I thought I would.' When he turned to look at her, Sassy bowed her head to hide her pleasure at the implication of his words.

'Don't you have family or friends that you miss?' she went on.

'Not really. My father died when I was little more than a baby in an accident and I don't really remember him. We do have some relatives still living there – aunts and cousins – but no one I was really close to. And the people here have made me feel so welcome. It's much more civilised here too. Where Mom and I lived in America was in the back of beyond and sometimes she struggled to make ends meet. She let out rooms to gold prospectors.' He chuckled at the memory before going on, 'I tried my hand at that but I was never very successful at it so I earned what I could where I could, working on ranches or helping out in the local saloon bar when they needed me. No – all in all I have a feeling that I shall be making this my home. I have no wish to go back, although I think my mother finds it strange here.'

The sounds of night creatures were filling the air and Sassy's heart began to sing with happiness, for suddenly she felt as if she was floating on a cloud. When presently they came to a large haystack and Daniel drew her into his arms, she offered her lips unresistingly. Eventually he held her away from him and whispered, 'I'm glad I managed to get you to myself, Sassy. You see . . . there's something I've been meaning to tell you.'

'Oh yes, and what would that be then?'

His hand settled on her shoulder and he began to play with one of the dark curls lying there. 'Well . . . the thing is, I think I've fallen in love with you,' he said, then murmured, 'do you think you could ever feel the same about me, Sassy?'

'Well, I . . . I don't know, Daniel. This is all so unexpected.' And yet, Sassy silently asked herself, was it? She only had to see him and she would get butterflies deep in the pit of her stomach. A single touch could make her cheeks burn. But she was terrified of being hurt again as Thomas had hurt her, so she refrained from telling him that she had feelings for him too.

And then his lips came down on hers again and for now she gave herself up to the sensations. His hands were running up and down her spine and slowly the kiss deepened as their passion mounted. When he gently drew her down into the sweet-smelling hay, she lay beside him willingly. Feelings the like of which she had never known were throbbing through her veins, and though her head told her, 'This is wrong,' her heart argued, 'No, no – this is right.' And when his hand cupped her tender breast she gave herself to him with a passion that matched his own, and in that instant the feelings of infatuation that she had felt for Thomas paled into insignificance. At last, Sassy knew that she had found true love – the sort that comes only once in a lifetime – and her heart soared.

Chapter Twenty-Eight

The bar door was wide open. The fine July evening was stifling and the customers were sitting about with their shirt collars unbuttoned as they thirstily supped their pints. Thomas, who sat at the corner of the bar, raised yet another glass of ale to his lips. His eyes were unnaturally bright and his tongue loose, to the point that Ned Chester, a landlord from an inn in Attleborough, a neighbouring village to Coton, was annoying him.

'I can down *any* man,' bragged Ned.

Thomas frowned darkly. Ned was not a popular man, nor was his inn; it seemed to encourage the rougher element of the town and gossip had it that it wasn't doing well.

'I should mind what yer sayin', man,' threatened Thomas, his speech slightly slurred. 'Fer one o' these days you'll meet yer match.'

'Huh!' Ned's voice held derision. 'Ain't *nobody* here as could beat me.'

Thomas shook his head. 'Oh yes, there is. I could down yer in a minute if I had a mind to.'

'Right – well, put yer money where yer mouth is then.' Ned's challenge was out, and leaning across the table, Thomas nodded.

'Very well. Name yer price.'

A silence had fallen around the table and Ned, his mind fogged with alcohol, tried to collect his wits. 'I'll tell yer what,' he said. 'Let's make it worth us while, eh? Your inn fer mine, the winner takes all.'

Jim Temple drew in a shuddering breath. 'Now 'old up, Ned,' he implored him. 'That's high odds yer bettin' by any standards. Why don't yer go home and sleep on it, eh?'

But Ned shook his head. 'No need to,' he said airily. 'The challenge is down, but are yer man enough to take it, eh?' His voice held bravado as Thomas eyed him coldly.

'Aye, I am man enough,' he replied. 'You just name the time an' place, an' I'll be there.' And so the fight was set.

Since Sassy's departure from Swan Lane, Elizabeth had given the girl little thought, but following the night of the party, her hatred for her was reawakened. She had seen the way Daniel had looked at her and now viewed Sassy as the main obstacle against Louise obtaining Daniel as a husband. Somehow, she must do something to prevent it.

Sitting across the table from Faith, she smiled sweetly. 'So how are things then, dear?' she simpered.

Faith sighed. 'To tell the truth, things are going from bad to worse,' she confided.

Her face full of false concern, Elizabeth asked gently, 'Oh, and why is that then?'

'I can't rightly say,' Faith admitted miserably. 'It's just that Thomas doesn't seem to have time for me any more.'

Pursing her lips knowledgeably, Elizabeth said, 'Well, perhaps I know the reason.'

Faith was gazing at her curiously, and sure now that she had her full attention, Elizabeth continued slyly, 'It just might have something to do with Sassy.'

Astonished, Faith repeated, 'Sassy? How do you mean?'

Elizabeth shrugged. 'Just between you and me, it's

common knowledge that since Sassy was knee-high to a grasshopper she's worshipped the very ground that Thomas walked on.'

Faith's shocked eyes flew open.

'But then of course he married Ellie – and that knocked the wind out of her sails.'

Faith nodded, eager for Elizabeth to continue.

'Well, then Ellie died as you know, and Sassy saw her chance again, and from what I can gather they had a kind of understanding that once he came back from America, they'd get together . . .' Elizabeth peeped cautiously from the corner of her eye to gauge Faith's reaction, and noting her horrified face she went on, 'Then he comes back with you in tow, which was a shock to say the least. But I suspect she still has her sights set on Thomas. Does he ever slip away? Could they be meeting?'

Faith was almost gasping with shock now, and thoroughly enjoying herself, Elizabeth delivered the final blow.

'To tell you the truth, the girl's a man-eater – always has been – but I reckon that underneath she still wants Thomas, and intends to have him any way she can. Of course, it hurts me to tell you this, for I love the girl as my own. But to be honest, it was a relief when she left here, for she made my poor Louise's life a misery with her spite and jealousy. Being the sweet nature my girl is, she didn't know how to cope with it.'

Faith was bowled over. 'I can hardly believe it,' she whispered. 'You don't think that's where Thomas has been going of a night, do you?'

'I wouldn't like to say,' Elizabeth said innocently. 'And I'm not one to gossip, but I thought you should know.' She could have told Faith of how she had heard that Thomas was now a regular visitor to the brothel in town, but felt she had delivered enough bad news for one day.

Faith was angry now. 'You did right to tell me,' she said bitterly. 'And if that scheming little minx thinks she'll have my Thomas, she has another think coming. From now on I'll be on my guard, make no mistake about it. She'll have to get past *me* first!' And huffing indignantly, she threw herself back into her chair as Elizabeth sedately poured the tea, a crafty little smirk playing about her lips.

Thomas was now deeply regretting having accepted Ned Chester's challenge, for since that night he had learned of the bloke's reputation as a fighter.

Jim Temple was worried too and said as much to him. 'Look, man, for God's sake call it off. It's a well-known fact that Chester ain't right in the head. He'd slit his own grandmother's throat for a shilling – an' no wish to offend, but yer know, you ain't quite as nippy on yer feet as yer used to be.'

Thomas shook his head adamantly. 'I'll do no such thing!' he snapped, his pride to the fore. 'It were him as threw down his challenge fair and square, an' I accepted it, so that's an end to it.'

'*Listen* to me,' implored Jim. 'He were drunk as a skunk at the time, an' no doubt he'd be prepared to forget all about it if you asked him to. No one would think any the worse o' yer.'

'I ain't never cried off from a fight in me life,' Thomas said stubbornly. 'An' I ain't about to start now.'

Jim had a bad feeling about this fight, and as he mopped the sweat from his brow with a grubby hankerchief, he muttered, 'Have it your own way then, but heed me warning 'cos he's an underhanded bugger.'

'I'm ready fer him,' Thomas said coldly. 'The way I see it, I'll soon be the landlord of *two* inns.'

'I just hope yer right, lad,' Jim said, 'but I'll tell yer

somethin' – I've got a bad feelin' in me gut an' it won't go away. Let's just hope as it don't end up wi' Ned takin' the Jolly Colliers from *you*!' He then lapsed into a subdued silence.

Daniel had made up his mind that the next day, he would speak to Sassy of his intentions towards her. Since the night they had come together he had spent every moment he could with her, and he could truthfully say that he had never been happier in his whole life. He could barely think of anything else and knew now that she was the only one in the world for him. Sadly, during the last week he had seen far too little of her, and even when he had, they had barely managed to steal a moment alone, for Thomas's demands on him were growing by the day as he sank into his alcoholic haze. Faith was also worrying him. She seemed to be deeply unhappy and complained if he so much as set foot outside of the inn. He could see that life in England was not what she had hoped for, and suspected that she would have returned to America in a minute if she could. He also knew that this would never be, for although Thomas's gold strike had added to his already considerable wealth, he showed no sign of wishing to return to America and Daniel doubted that he ever would.

However, the best-laid plans can come undone, and the next day, which was the day of the fight, Thomas waylaid Daniel bright and early. His eyes were shining, as he had tried to convince himself that by the time this day was over, he would be the landlord of yet another inn.

'Ah, Daniel!' Thomas cried eagerly at sight of him. 'I've a favour to ask of yer, lad.'

'Oh yes, and what might that be?' Daniel enquired curiously.

'I wondered if you'd help David out tonight at the bar, as I have some urgent business to attend to.'

Daniel frowned. Tonight he had planned to see Sassy.

Noting his hesitation, Thomas jumped in quickly. 'Look, I know I've asked a lot of yer lately, but I'll make it worth yer while.'

Eyeing him for a moment, Daniel then reluctantly agreed. 'But I'll tell you now, I have matters of my own to attend to tomorrow, so I hope you can give me some free time then.'

Thomas's face lit up with relief. 'Aye I will, lad,' he willingly agreed. 'I promise yer I will.' And smiling broadly he slapped Daniel on the back and disappeared down the roughly hewn stone steps of the dark cellar.

That evening, as the clock struck ten, Thomas ascended the stairs to change. Faith, who was sitting at the table at the side of the empty fireplace, eyed him curiously.

'What are you doing up here so early?' she asked him.

Barely acknowledging her, Thomas crossed to their bedroom door. 'I'm goin' out,' he informed her shortly.

Faith's plain face instantly contorted with rage as Elizabeth's words and a vision of Sassy's pretty face sprang to mind. By now, Thomas had disappeared into the bedroom, where he was hastily changing his clothes, but when Faith came to stand behind him and placed her hand on his arm he became still.

'*Where* are you going again?' Her voice was low and furious.

He impatiently shook her off. 'I've told yer, woman – *out* – an' that's all as yer need to know.'

Faith was not so easily put off. 'I suppose you're going to meet your fancy piece again, are you?' she ground out.

Thomas gazed at her, wondering what she had heard.

'What the bloody hell are yer on about?' he demanded, bewildered.

She sneered. 'Don't think I don't know what you're up to,' she spat. 'It's common knowledge about you carrying on behind my back with that little *trollop*.'

Thomas's face was a picture of genuine amazement. 'Oh, aye, an' what common little trollop might that be?'

'As if you don't know.' Her eyes were flashing. 'I'm talking about Sassy, and well you know it. You admitted to me that you still want her!'

Thomas almost laughed at the absurdity of it as he sputtered, 'Have yer gone completely *mad*, woman? Sassy would never have owt to do with a married man, even if he wanted her to.'

'Well, I'm sure *you'd* be the best judge of that, wouldn't you?' As she eyed him coldly, Thomas's amusement slowly turned to rage as he looked at the plain middle-aged woman before him.

'Perhaps yer right.' His voice was dangerously low. 'Perhaps I *would* know about it, 'cos I'll tell yer now, Sassy is worth *ten* o' you, an' I'd have her any way I could, if only she'd let me.'

Faith reeled from him and leaned heavily against the wall in her shock. 'So it's true then,' she gasped. 'You *do* want her.'

Thomas nodded, his face livid. 'Aye, it's true,' he said. 'For I rue the day I ever wed you, an' if I could turn back the clock, I'd never look the side you were on.'

Tears of humiliation were pouring down Faith's cheeks. 'So you *are* going to meet her then, are you?'

He shook his head. 'No I ain't, more's the pity,' he retorted harshly as he pushed past her. 'But I'll tell yer somethin' – I wish to God I were.' And without another word he strode from the room, slamming the door behind him.

As the sound of his angry footsteps thumping down the stairs receded, Faith stood for some minutes in deep shock. If he had slapped her face it couldn't have shaken her half as much as the admission he had just made. But then as the shock slowly subsided, a cold dark anger gripped her heart, and so hard did her teeth bite down on her bottom lip that they actually drew blood.

'He *is* going to meet her,' she convinced herself. Snatching up her shawl from the back of the easy chair, she flew from the room then quietly crept down the stairs. At the bottom, she paused. The hum of conversation floated from the partially open door of the bar, and she could just make out glimpses of Daniel and David as they rushed to and fro, busily serving the customers. Convinced that no one had seen her, she let herself out of the back door and pulled it to behind her.

She stood for some seconds, her heart pounding, then, quiet as a mouse, she hurried around the outside of the inn and gazed up and down the lane. For a minute, she thought she had lost him, but then as she strained her eyes into the darkness, she caught sight of her husband striding angrily up the lane. Her heart hardened.

'Right then,' she said to herself. 'It's time you got your comeuppance, my man, for I'll play second fiddle to no one, especially a mere slut of a girl.' And then she set out after him, black raging jealousy guiding her footsteps.

Thomas strode purposefully along, his hands thrust deep into his jacket pockets. Despite his brave words to Jim Temple he was quaking in his shoes now, for deep down he knew that he would no longer be a match for Ned Chester. Apart from the injury to his leg, his behaviour over the past months – boozing and carousing, gaining weight and never going for a run or doing his bodybuilding training – meant that he was slow and unfit. The thought of losing his inn was almost more than he could bear, which was why he had devised a plan that would stop the fight taking place without him losing face.

Fingering the cold steel in his pocket he moved on, and soon he was hidden from sight behind one of the drunkenly leaning tombstones in the churchyard of St Nicholas on the border of the town centre. Lately he had made a lot of discreet enquiries and he knew that Ned often took this short-cut on his way to the disused barn in Weddington where many such unofficial fights took place. Blowing into his hands to warm them, praying that Ned would be alone, he settled down to wait.

Shortly afterwards, the sound of muffled footsteps sounded on the grass and Thomas peeped from his hiding-place. A lone figure was striding towards him and he offered up a silent prayer of thanks as his hand closed around the handle of the knife.

He waited until the figure was almost level then stepped from his hiding-place, causing the man to gasp with surprise.

'*Christ*, man,' Ned said with a tremor in his voice. 'Yer nearly give me a heart-attack, creepin' out like that. What the bloody 'ell yer playin' at?'

As Thomas suddenly lunged towards him, Ned saw the knife glint in the light of the moon. ''Ere, what the—' His words stuck in his throat as he felt a sharp pain in his chest, and as his hand strayed to the place he looked down in disbelief. The lifeblood was flowing out of him, warm and sticky on his fingers. Slowly he sank to his knees, staring up at Thomas, then the latter was lunging towards him once more and Ned felt the knife enter his chest yet again. He toppled forward as Thomas stood and drew a shuddering breath. After a moment or two, he rolled the body over with his foot. Ned's mouth was hanging slackly open as blood trickled from the sides of it, and his eyes were staring sightlessly upwards. There would be no fight tonight – nor any other night – for Ned Chester. He was dead.

Thomas's stomach clenched, and holding on to a tombstone for support, he vomited noisily, trembling all over with reaction. But now he must get to the barn and make it look as if Ned had chickened out. He swiped his hand across his brow, which was sweating despite the cold of the night, then suddenly aware of the blood-drenched knife in his hand, he flung it away and stumbled from the churchyard, looking first this way and that to make sure that no one had seen him.

He stood for a few moments, allowing his heart to settle back into a steadier rhythm. If he crossed the Leicester Road bridge he could be at the barn in no time. His mind was in turmoil as he thought of what he had just done to Ned. But it had been necessary, he tried to convince himself. The other man weren't right in the head, and he'd have killed Thomas himself with one savage blow, if he wasn't much mistaken . . . Thomas shuddered. No, Ned Chester had got what he deserved, as far as he was concerned.

Quickly moving along Attleborough Road he then crossed into Riversley Park, past the huge weeping willows that were trailing their branches into the River Anker. Here he hastily washed the dead innkeeper's blood from his hands, and minutes later he again set out for Weddington.

Chapter Twenty-Nine

For the tenth time in as many minutes, Jim Temple stepped outside the barn and gazed up and down the track. Within impatient mumbling had broken out amongst the men assembled there, but Ned Chester's supporters sat quietly smug, their backs against some bales of hay.

'Where have they got to?' one of the men grumbled. 'They must be half an hour late or more by now.'

Jim Temple shrugged. 'I ain't never known Thomas to be late fer a fight in his life before.'

Ned Chester's right-hand man, Bill Bromley, smirked. 'I reckon he's got cold feet.'

Bristling, Jim retorted, 'It would be a cold day in hell before Thomas Mallabone backed down from a fight.' Then, eyeing the man suspiciously, 'An' *you* ain't got cause to be so cocky neither, seein' as Ned ain't here either.'

'He will be, never you fear,' Bill said with certainty.

Jim peered once more into the darkness. 'There's something not right 'ere. I can feel it in me bones,' he muttered to himself, and a cold feeling of dread settled around him like a wet blanket.

When Thomas walked into the barn seconds later, Jim sighed with relief.

'I were beginnin' to think that neither of you were comin',' he ground out.

Thomas frowned. 'What do yer mean – neither of us?

I've just had a right barney with the wife. Askin' me questions, she was, an' tryin' to stop me comin' out. I can tell you, I've had it up to here wi' ruddy women an' their naggin'. That's why I'm late.' Taking off his jacket, he began to roll up his sleeves, as if in preparation for the fight. 'Ain't Ned here yet?'

Jim shook his head. 'There's been no sign of him an' the men are growin' impatient now. Reckon we ought to give it another ten minutes an' then give it up as a bad job.'

'Happen he got cold feet,' Thomas replied innocently, removing his muffler and placing it on a bale of hay, next to his jacket.

Jim stared at him. The bloke was as white as a sheet although he did appear to be sober for a change, which was one blessing at least.

An hour later, the barn began to empty amidst angry comments from the crowd. Wagers had been bet, and the majority of them had demanded their money back.

'Happen we ought to clear off an' all,' Jim said resignedly and nodding, Thomas strode away, his inn still his own.

Faith was in bed when he got in and he slid in beside her, trembling with the knowledge of what he had done. She was pretending to be asleep because she was so angry she knew that if she said so much as one word to him, she would say too much. Somehow he had managed to give her the slip when she'd followed him and now she was convinced that he had been to see Sassy. Lying there in the darkness, she began to think how she might get her own back.

The following day, the town was alive with the news of Ned Chester's death.

'*Stabbed* to death in the churchyard,' a customer told

David the next morning, the second he drew the bolt on the door. Word had spread like wildfire and as Thomas listened to the gossip, he stood amazed, as if taking in every word they said.

Jim Temple arrived shortly before noon, and drawing Thomas to one side he hissed, 'Bit of a rum do, ain't it? No wonder the poor sod didn't turn up fer the fight. I can't say as I had any likin' fer the chap but no one deserves to die like that. Slaughtered like a farmyard animal.'

'Happen it were some tramp after his wallet,' Thomas commented, and as he then turned away to serve a customer, Jim frowned.

When word reached Faith, she too looked at Thomas suspiciously. Through whispers in the bar she had discovered that Thomas had actually set off for a fight with Ned Chester the night before, and not to see Sassy as she had feared. Strangely enough, it had been just before they reached the churchyard that Thomas had managed to give her the slip and now her mind was working furiously. Could he have nipped in there and lain in wait for Ned? If the rumours she had heard were true, Thomas had bet the inn on that fight, and knowing how much he loved this place she wondered if perhaps he had been afraid of losing it? Shuddering, she pushed the idea to the back of her mind. True, her husband had many faults – but surely he would not be capable of committing murder?

The following morning, when Elizabeth and Louise called to see her, Faith was her normal composed self and immediately pushed the kettle onto the fire to boil so that she could make her visitors some tea.

Louise looked about the room expectantly and when she saw no sign of Daniel she asked, 'Is Daniel downstairs?'

'No, he's gone over to the farm to help Aaron move some equipment out of the barn,' his mother told her.

Louise's mouth instantly set into an unbecoming pout as she dropped heavily into a chair and eyed Florica disdainfully. The child instantly snatched up the peg dolls her Grandma Pearl had made for her and scuttled away to the sanctuary of her own room, leaving the women to gossip to their heart's content.

'Isn't it terrible about the landlord that was killed?' Elizabeth said, as she drew off her soft kid gloves and folded her hands demurely in her lap.

'Yes, it is,' Faith answered as she warmed the teapot. 'I thought England was supposed to be a civilised place, but I certainly haven't found it so.'

'And what we were talking about, you know – regarding Sassy – have you given it any more thought?' Elizabeth asked, all sweetness and light and false concern.

Faith eyed the woman with cold contempt, well aware that she knew how distressing she was finding all this.

'Yes, I've given it some thought. But I have to say that I have seen no evidence of my husband having feelings for the girl,' she lied glibly.

Louise's ears pricked up. What was this about Sassy and Thomas? From what she could see of it, it was Daniel who was chasing her hated stepsister now, and causing herself more than a little grief, she might add. But then she was well aware how vicious and vindictive her mother could be when she set her mind to it – and so she sat back and listened.

Over at the farm, Aaron and Daniel were working in the barn side by side when Sassy appeared with two steaming mugs of tea and a plate of homemade short-bread.

339

'I thought it was time you two had a break,' she said with a smile.

The two men sat down on a bale of straw, and gratefully took the mugs from her.

Daniel was beaming from ear to ear at the sight of her, but Sassy avoided eye-contact as she told them, 'I must be off now. I've no doubt Jack and Uncle Ben will be ready for a drink too. They're up in the top field, aren't they?'

'They are that,' Aaron told her, and with a final smile she turned and left them to go and get the can of tea for the other two men from the kitchen.

As she trudged past the hedgerows a short time later her heart was heavy and there was a droop to her shoulders. She knew now without a doubt that she loved Daniel with all her heart. So much so that what she had once felt for Thomas now seemed tawdry and immature. But she was afraid – desperately afraid – that he would betray her as Thomas had. After all, Louise had made no secret of the fact that she had set her cap at him too, and her stepsister was from a good family. Daniel's mother was an ambitious type, much as Elizabeth was, so surely she would steer her son in that direction. Once those two got their heads together, she would stand no chance with him. Faith would frown on him marrying a girl from a farm and it was obvious that Elizabeth was hoping for a match for Louise. Sighing unhappily, she went on her way and soon she spotted her uncle and Jack in the field ahead.

'Aw, lass, yer a sight fer sore eyes,' her uncle boomed, wiping the sweat from his eyes as he took the can from her. He and Jack dropped down onto the grass to enjoy their drink.

Jack patted the grass at the side of him, saying, 'Why don't yer snatch a minute an' come an' join us?'

'I'd love to, but I've work to do in the dairy,' Sassy informed him dully, and with that she turned about and went back the way she had come, leaving Jack to stare after her with misery clear on his face.

'Why don't yer set yer sights elsewhere, lad?' Ben asked softly. It hurt him to see the way Jack yearned for Sassy.

'I wish I could.' Ben had become like a second father to him, and Jack could talk to Ben about anything. The young man would have trusted him with his life. 'Don't think I haven't tried. I even walked out wi' Mary Stevens fer a time but the trouble is, no one can hold a light to Sassy fer me. It's allus been the same fer as far back as I can remember. We ain't all as lucky as you, see.'

'Well, yer right there,' Ben agreed. He knew how lucky he was to have found his Miriam and, much like Jack with Sassy, from the moment he had clapped eyes on her there had never been another for him. It still upset him though, to see Jack pining for someone he couldn't have. Sometimes life could be very unfair.

That evening, as she and Arthur sat together in their smart drawing room, Elizabeth told him, 'I went to see Faith today at the inn.'

'Did you?' Arthur did his best to sound interested although all he really wanted to do was bury his head in his newspaper.

'Yes,' Elizabeth pressed. 'And it seems that she is a very unhappy woman.'

'Oh – and why is that?'

'Well, I believe it could have something to do with your Sassy.'

He sat straighter in his chair now as he stared at her.

Knowing that she now commanded his full attention, she went on spitefully, 'Faith seems to have got it into her head that Sassy still has her sights set on Thomas.'

'What a load of rubbish!' Arthur exploded. 'Sassy's feelings for him finally died when he came home from America with his second wife. If anything, I've a sense that things are developing between her and Daniel.'

'I certainly hope not,' Elizabeth said primly. 'I was rather hoping that Daniel and my Louise would make a match.'

'What you were hoping for and what is likely to come about are two different things,' Arthur told her shortly. 'I sometimes wonder where you get these notions, Elizabeth, and I suggest that you don't try to meddle in other people's lives.'

'How *dare* you!' she cried, jumping up from her seat in a rustle of silk skirts. 'Don't you even *care* about Louise?'

'Aye I do, but I care about Sassy more,' he retaliated honestly. 'In case you'd forgotten, she is still me daughter, an' she's had enough to put up with in her short life from where I'm sittin'.'

As Elizabeth flounced out of the room in a rage, he shook his head in exasperation. His wife seemed obsessed with getting Louise married off, and he worried where it might lead. But at the end of the day there was not a single thing he could do about it.

'So, are you going to walk me to the gate then?' Daniel asked cheekily as he prepared to leave Holly Bush Farm later that afternoon.

Sassy glanced up from the butter she was working with on the dairy slab. 'I'd best not. I need to get this lot finished,' she told him quietly.

With a nod he turned about and set off for the inn but he was heavy hearted. Why was Sassy so cool towards him all of a sudden? Things had seemed to be going so well between them, yet now she seemed to be afraid of being alone with him. Perhaps their lovemaking that night had frightened her. He should have taken things slower. Or perhaps he should have asked her to marry him by now? A horrible idea occurred to him and he frowned. Maybe she didn't feel the same for him as he felt for her! It was a sobering thought, because he couldn't envisage a life without her in it now.

'Mr Thomas Mallabone?'

Thomas nodded warily at the two Police Constables standing across the bar.

'We would like you to accompany us to the station to help us with our enquiries.'

A hush fell on the inn as Thomas stood straight and demanded, 'Regarding what?'

'Regarding the death of Mr Ned Chester, sir. It's been brought to our attention that on the night he was killed, you and he were about to engage in a private fight.'

Thomas remained stubbornly silent as the officer went on, 'Will you come willingly, sir?'

'Aye, I will,' Thomas told him, and turning to David he said, 'Will you be all right here on your own till I get back?'

'O' course I will, boss,' the man hastily assured him.

'Am I allowed to nip upstairs an' get me coat?' Thomas asked.

When the elder of the two officers nodded, he made his way up the steep staircase. As he unhooked his coat from the back of the kitchen door, Faith looked up from her knitting to enquire, 'And just where are you off to?'

'The peelers want me down at the station,' he informed her shortly and then he strode away without a backward glance, leaving her stunned, her needles at a standstill.

It was almost two hours later when he returned,

somewhat subdued, and Faith immediately began to question him.

'So what is happening?'

'*Nowt*,' he growled. 'They just wanted to ask me whereabouts on the night Ned Chester were killed.'

She bit her lip as he slammed off into their bedroom, but she didn't follow him. She had too much to think about.

Elizabeth was like a dog with a bone when she discovered that Thomas had been taken to the police station, albeit disappointed when he was released without charge. She was still smarting from his rejection of her daughter and wished that the police had kept him there and thrown away the key.

As she ranted on about him, Arthur watched from his chair at the side of the fire. His wife seemed almost demented just lately and he wondered if he shouldn't get some help for her. But then he knew better than to even suggest it, for once again he would become the object of her scorn – and he had already had enough of *that* to last him a whole lifetime.

Chapter Thirty

Two nights later, when Sassy turned up at the inn to see Florica, Faith disappeared into her bedroom, hardly able to look at her. Daniel hadn't stopped smiling from the second the girl set foot in the room, and Faith was incensed. Thomas had personally shown her upstairs with a dazzling smile on his face and she began to wonder if the girl was a witch. She certainly seemed to have the ability to make men fall at her feet. Thomas never smiled at her that way. As she sat there in her room, Florica's laughter floated to her and her jealousy deepened. The screaming little brat barely tolerated her, despite the fact that *she* was the one who had to look after her. After half an hour she could stand it no more and stamping into the kitchen she snapped, 'It's time for her to get ready for bed now.'

Sassy and Daniel were down on their knees playing Spillikins with the little girl, but they both instantly rose as Florica began to wail, '*Want Sassy to stay!*'

'Well, Sassy can't stay,' Faith told her firmly. 'Now off to your bedroom with you this instant.'

Too afraid of her strict stepmother to disobey, Florica immediately did as she was told, and as Sassy fastened her bonnet on, Daniel told her, 'I'll walk you back, if you like.'

When Sassy thanked him, Faith was incensed.

'I think you'll find Thomas needs you to help out down in the bar,' she told her son gruffly.

He smiled. 'No, he doesn't, David is working tonight so he'll be fine. I'll see you later, Mom.'

With that he ushered Sassy ahead of him, and Faith's face contorted with rage as she listened to them descend the stairs. She had no way of knowing that Sassy would part from Daniel at the end of the road, insisting that she needed to speak to Clara about something and making it impossible for the young man to say any of the things that were burdening his mind.

Faith's mood had not improved by the time Thomas wearily climbed the stairs much later that night after bolting the door on the last of his customers. There was still no sign of Daniel and she was seething.

As Thomas entered the room he yawned and asked her, 'Where's Daniel then? Is he not back yet?'

'No, he is *not*!' she roared. 'But then it's hardly surprising, seeing who he is with, is it? It seems to me that any man will do for that cheap little trollop!'

'Now hold on a minute,' Thomas said. 'If yer referrin' to Sassy, again I'll tell yer now that she's *far* from bein' a trollop.'

'Oh yes? You would defend her, wouldn't you, seeing as she's one of your whores!'

'Oh, not *that* again,' Thomas sighed, sick to the heart of his wife's moods.

As she opened her mouth to start another tirade, something inside him suddenly snapped, and putting his coat on, he told her, 'I ain't goin' to listen to this tonight. I'm sick of yer naggin', woman.' With that he walked out as Faith's hands clenched into fists of rage. He was going to see her – she just *knew* it. It didn't occur to her that he couldn't, not if Sassy was already with Daniel. She was completely blinded by jealousy.

Deciding to follow and confront him, she once again sneaked down the stairs. The customers had all gone home to their beds but she could see David clearing the empty glasses into the deep stone sink behind the bar.

After letting herself out of the back door, she hurried into the lane, and just as she had on the night he had murdered Ned Chester, she began to shadow her husband.

For some while, Thomas was so angry that he barely knew which direction he was going in. He thought briefly of paying Moll Twigger a visit, but rejected the idea almost immediately. He would have far more choice if he visited the brothel, but first he needed to calm down if he was to enjoy himself. He wandered aimlessly, with no clear direction in mind until he found himself on the Leicester Road bridge that crossed the Trent Valley railway. He could hear a train approaching in the distance and leaned heavily on the low metal railings to watch it go by. Some instinct then made him aware of another sound – footsteps – and they were coming towards him. Turning abruptly, he looked towards the sound and as he did so his mouth fell into a gape as he leaned back against the metal rail.

'What are *you* doin' followin' me?' he asked – and they were the last words he uttered, for as the roar of the train drew nearer, the person he had addressed moved forward, out of the shadows, and gave him a vicious shove in the chest. Taken off guard, he plunged across the railings. Then he was floating in mid-air, his arms flailing wildly. And that was when he saw her – the beautiful angel that he had last seen on the day of Mrs Churm's funeral when he was no more than a boy. She was flying towards him with her arms outstretched, and he briefly wondered who she was coming for. And then all at once he knew. *She was coming for him.*

The loud rapping on the inn door woke Faith from an uneasy slumber. Glancing at the clock, she noted that it was not yet six o'clock in the morning. The first rays of daylight were just filtering their way into the room, and somewhere in the distance a cock was crowing to welcome the dawn. As she hurried down the stairs, the rapping became louder and she shouted impatiently. 'All right, hold your horses, I'm coming, I'm coming.' Feeling her way through the tables and chairs in the bar, she eventually reached the heavy oak door, and after struggling with the bolts, she at last managed to draw them back and threw the door open.

Two policemen were standing on the step – unknown to Faith, the same two Constables who had dealt with the investigation of Ellie's death.

'Mrs Thomas Mallabone?' asked the taller of the two solemnly.

Faith nodded.

'Could you tell us the whereabouts of your husband, Mrs Mallabone?' he continued.

'As a matter of fact I couldn't,' she replied, her heart thumping deep within her chest. 'He left here late last night after an argument, and I haven't seen hide nor hair of him since.'

'Then if you don't mind we'd like to come inside. I'm afraid we have some very bad news for you.'

Without saying a word, Faith drew the door open a little wider and allowed the two policemen to enter the bar.

Once inside, they removed their helmets respectfully and gazed at the ashen-faced woman before them.

'It appears,' said the policeman, 'that some time last night, a gentleman fell from the bridge that crosses the railway station.' Clearing his throat uncomfortably, he continued, 'Early this morning the body was spotted by the driver of the milk train, and we were called out to investigate.'

Faith had slowly sunk onto the nearest chair, and now the officer drew something from his pocket and held it out to her. It was a gold pocket watch with the initials *T.M.* engraved on the back of it.

'This was found on the body, Mrs Mallabone,' he said regretfully. 'And I'm sorry to inform you that we have every reason to believe the body to be that of your husband, Thomas Mallabone.'

She said nothing as she gazed at Thomas's watch gripped tightly in her hand.

Following Thomas's death, Faith insisted that the inn should remain open, and Daniel and David Smith were almost run off their feet. The mysterious circumstances of Thomas's passing drew curious customers from miles around, and the bar fairly heaved with trade from morning until night.

Deep in grief at the untimely death of their beloved son, Clara sobbed to Walter, 'It ain't right. It's bad enough that she won't have his body brought home. The least she could do is close the inn as a mark o' respect.'

Walter comforted her as best he could, though his own heart was broken.

For almost a week the police refused to release the body for burial and Thomas lay on a cold stone slab in the morgue of the local hospital. The whole town was agog, particularly as Ned Chester had been found stabbed to death in the churchyard of St Nicholas Church only shortly before.

During that time, the police questioned everyone they could find who had known Thomas. By the end of their investigations they had formed a picture of a man towards whom many bore a grudge, but with no evidence that could cast any light on his death. At one point the police hinted that he might have committed suicide, as it was commonly known that Thomas's homelife wasn't all it should be, but Clara would have none of it.

'My lad would *never* take his own life,' she swore emphatically. 'Now get yerselves out there an' find the murderin' bugger that killed him!'

Then, of course, there was the remarkable coincidence of Ned Chester's grisly death. Until his own death, Thomas had been their main suspect, but now what? His death could have been accidental, he could have been pushed or, if he *had* killed Ned, he might have taken his own life because of the guilt. They would never know now and eventually the Coroner had no option but to leave the cause of death open, and Faith was allowed to proceed with the funeral arrangements.

And so it was that on a beautiful clear day in late July, as the sun shone down from a cloudless blue sky, Thomas Mallabone was laid to rest in a quiet corner of Coton churchyard in the shade of a great oak tree. Faith stood dry-eyed as the Reverend Rigby intoned the words of the funeral service. It was said later that it was a lovely service, but Clara, as she numbly watched her lad lowered into his early grave, heard not a word of it. Nor, in fact, did she even see any of it, for in her mind's eye all she could see was a bright-eyed, black-haired little scamp forever up to some mischief or other. Visions of him at various stages of his childhood were flitting before her eyes: the day he had been born, and Walter's joy at his first sight of him, the pride at his first unsteady steps, the delight at his first uncertain words – the tears she had cried at his first tumble that had joined his own. And the thrill and wonder in his eyes on the day she had placed Jack, his newborn baby brother, into his arms.

Sassy was unable to comfort Clara, since she had her arm tight about Jack, who was sobbing brokenheartedly. But at last it was done, and the mourners turned slowly from the grave one by one to leave Thomas to spend his first night alone beneath his blanket of earth.

Once outside the churchyard, the mourners solemnly nodded to one another and went their separate ways, for even on the day of Thomas's funeral, Faith had insisted that the inn should stay open. There would be no funeral tea for Thomas Mallabone. In fact, she had not even allowed Daniel to attend the service, saying that he was needed at the inn. Daniel had not been happy about it at all and had pointed out that David could quite easily manage on his own, but Faith had been insistent.

The new widow made her solitary way back to the inn almost impatiently. Now that the funeral was over there were affairs that must be attended to. As she came within sight of the Jolly Colliers, her steps slowed and a frown creased her forehead. Outside was a brightly painted wagon, and if Faith was not very much mistaken, it belonged to Pearl and Saul, Florica's grandparents.

When she eventually entered the inn, which seemed to be packed with customers, and climbed the stairs to the kitchen, she found Pearl with Florica on her lap at the kitchen table and Maisie, who had been left to care for her, filling the kettle at the deep stone sink.

Nodding to Pearl, Faith began to undo the ribbons of her plain black bonnet as Maisie discreetly slipped downstairs to join David in the bar.

'I'm glad you've come,' she said truthfully. 'I was going to try and get word to you of Thomas's death, but I wasn't sure where you would be.'

'We was at Appleby Fair,' Pearl said quietly. 'But never fear, there's nowt much as we don't get to hear of on the grapevine.'

'Will you have a cup of tea?' Faith asked politely as she smoothed her heavy velvet skirts.

Rising with the child in her arms, Pearl told her, 'No, we won't be stayin'.' She eyed Faith curiously. She certainly didn't appear like a woman who had just attended her own husband's funeral. Pearl's dislike of her, which had grown since their first meeting, intensified, and in that moment she was glad that Jez, who had recently married a gypsy girl from another camp, was not with them. She wanted to get this over with as quickly as possible and had Jez been there she had no doubt he would have given this cold-hearted woman a tongue lashing. 'We've come fer Florica,' she informed her bluntly, never one to mince her words. 'Now her dad is gone, we have a right to claim her, so as she can come an' live amongst her own kind.'

If she had been expecting an argument she was pleasantly surprised when Faith nodded immediately.

'I think, all things considered, that would be for the best,' she agreed. 'I'll just go and get her things together for you.' And crossing to Florica's bedroom door, she quietly entered and shut it behind her, leaving Pearl and Saul to raise their eyebrows in amazement at the ease of it all.

It was late afternoon when Clara wearily climbed the stairs of the inn, with Walter and Jack close on her heels. After entering the kitchen she sank into the nearest chair and eyed Faith suspiciously. There was something about her lad's death that most definitely smacked of foul play, despite the open verdict. Faith returned her stare coldly, and Clara, who was just longing for this day to be over, said, 'We've come fer our little lass. Happen she'll be best with me an' her granda now. You'll have yer hands full runnin' the inn.'

Drawing herself up to her full height, Faith tossed her head. 'I'm sorry, Clara, I'm afraid you've come too late.'

Clara glared at her. 'Talk sense will yer, woman? I'm in no mood fer games, this day of all days. What do you mean?'

Faith's face remained impartial. 'Just what I say,' she replied. 'Pearl and Saul were here when I arrived back from the funeral, and they've taken Florica. They felt that she would be best with them. I believed it was what Thomas would have wanted too, so I allowed them to take her.'

Any vestige of colour that had remained in Clara's face now drained from it and she gripped the edge of the table as if for support. '*You've done what?*' she hissed, her voice dangerously low.

Faith stood her ground. 'I've done what I thought was best,' she retaliated. 'And I've no doubt you'll agree, when you've had time to think on it.' For a moment fear entered her eyes, for Clara appeared as a woman possessed as she sprang towards her with her hands bunched into fists and barked, 'You wicked *bitch*! Yer knew full well how much that little lass meant to me. She were all I had left of her dad. I reckon you've got a swingin' brick instead of a heart.' But then as suddenly as it had come, Clara's rage subsided, for this was the final blow. Her shoulders sagged, and the tears that had been threatening to fall all day were suddenly released in a gushing torrent that poured down her cheeks as Walter and Jack solemnly took an elbow each and led her away.

Over the next week, Daniel's frustration mounted. Customers had poured into the inn with no sign of ceasing, and he had no chance to go and see Sassy at all. Worse still, she had made no effort to come and see him, which cut deep. To make things worse, Elizabeth and Louise were calling by almost daily. Elizabeth seemed to have become his mother's closest confidante and the fact concerned him. Also, Louise's unwelcome attentions were beginning to play on his nerves, a fact that caused David much amusement.

'You watch yerself, lad,' he teased. 'I reckon that 'un has her eye on you an' no mistake.'

'I know,' Daniel replied miserably. 'Every time I turn

around she's there. It's getting past a joke now, but what can I do about it without being downright rude?'

'I can't rightly say, lad. But I'll tell yer what – rather you than me.' And David turned and went about his business. Both he and Daniel were missing Thomas, and David was glad of a distraction. For all that had been said about his late boss, he had always found him to be a decent bloke.

Faith had been almost rude to Sassy at Thomas's funeral and had made it more than obvious that she was no longer welcome at the inn. Since hearing of Florica's departure with her gypsy grandparents, Sassy now had no excuse to visit and to her surprise she found that she missed Daniel desperately. For weeks now she had felt under the weather, and Miriam wanted her to visit Dr Massey, but the girl adamantly refused, just as her aunt had refused to go and see him about her own lack of energy.

'I'll be all right,' Sassy assured her. 'It's just the shock of Thomas's death and the fact that I'm missing little Flo.' And with that the woman had to be content.

News came from Matthew to say that he had passed his final exams with honours, and planned to be back in Nuneaton within weeks, working with Dr Massey in his practice. Elizabeth, who was long past the disappointment of him not joining his uncle's firm, was as proud as a peacock.

'Of course,' she said to Miriam confidentially on one of her rare visits to Holly Bush Farm, 'I always *knew* that my son was cut out to be a doctor.'

Miriam was well aware that she had only called in to brag, and catching Sassy's eye above Elizabeth's head, she raised an eyebrow – which caused the young woman to flee the kitchen lest she burst into a fit of the giggles.

It was early in August, as David and Daniel were rushing to see to the demands of the many customers, that a smartly-dressed gentleman in a bowler hat entered the bar. He stood in silence for some moments, eyeing the many clients with satisfaction. Then, slowly approaching the bar, he addressed Daniel. 'I would like to speak to Mrs Mallabone.'

'Who shall I say is calling?' Daniel asked, but before the gentleman could reply, Faith suddenly appeared at the foot of the stairs almost as if she were expecting this well-attired visitor.

'Ah, Mr Boon.' She extended her hand graciously. 'Won't you please step this way?' And ignoring Daniel's amazed stare, the visitor quickly followed her up the narrow staircase.

It was almost an hour later when Mr Boon descended. David and Daniel were enjoying a rare quiet moment, and they watched him curiously as he made his way to the door with a very smug-looking Faith close on his heels.

'I wonder who the bloody 'ell that is,' whispered David.

Daniel shrugged his broad shoulders. 'I can honestly say I haven't a clue,' he replied.

They had no more time to wonder, however, for a deluge of thirsty customers suddenly alighted on the bar, and once again they were busily pulling pints.

Later that evening, as Daniel recalled their visitor of earlier in the day, he asked his mother, 'Who was the gentleman that called this morning, Mom?'

She loaded a slice of hare pie onto the plate in front of him. 'Oh, just someone I had a bit of business with, that's all,' she told him dismissively.

Hungrily tackling his supper, Daniel had forgotten all about it in no time.

Chapter Thirty-One

The following day, Elizabeth's fine horse and trap pulled up outside the Jolly Colliers, and she and her daughter alighted. 'Come back in two hours,' Elizabeth imperiously instructed Isaac, who was also her new gardener-cum-handyman. Nodding obediently, the old chap touched his cap and snapping the reins led the horse back down the cobblestoned lane.

As they entered the bar, Daniel sighed wearily. He was sick to the heart of the sight of Louise. Then just as he had feared, Elizabeth mounted the stairs to visit Faith, while Louise hurriedly joined him behind the counter, which brought a smirk to David's face and another long-drawn-out sigh from Daniel.

'Good afternoon,' she greeted him, eyeing him greedily.

He nodded politely, thinking, I've got to do something about this. Her pursuit of him went far beyond a joke now, and knowing that he had to stop it before it went any further, he said in an undertone, 'Do you fancy a stroll down to the canal? I could do with a bit of fresh air.'

Her face lit up immediately, and so with a nod to David, who was staring at him in astonishment, he hurried out to the garden with Louise hot on his heels.

Daniel's heart was hammering in his chest. He was a kind young man by nature, and not happy about what he was having to do. But then again, he told himself, he had no choice. Resolutely, he began. 'Louise, I have a secret to tell you, and as I feel we're friends, I'm sure I can trust you with it.'

Flushing with pleasure, she inclined her head eagerly.

Searching his mind for the right words, Daniel went on, 'Well, it's like this. I have feelings for a certain young lady, and I'd like to think she returns them, so – do you think I should tell her how I feel?'

'Oh yes, you must,' Louise sighed dreamily as she clasped her hands together.

Daniel cursed himself for his choice of words, as he suddenly realised that she thought he was speaking of her.

'I think you know the girl I'm speaking of,' he hurried on. 'And I'm sure you'll wish us well . . . because it's your sister Sassy.'

When Louise stopped dead in her tracks and gazed at him in horror, it was Daniel's turn to flush.

'You're in love with *Sassy*?' she breathed. Then, as the implication of his words sank in, her face gradually paled.

'Then you are a fool,' she snapped spitefully, 'because Sassy is in love with Jack – and she will *never* look at you!' And then she flew back up the lawn with her skirts billowing in all directions.

When Louise burst into the upstairs kitchen some minutes later, she was obviously deeply distressed.

'Mother, I want to go,' she said, rudely ignoring Faith.

'But, my dear, we have only just arrived.'

'I don't care,' Louise said peevishly. 'I want to go *now* – and if you won't come with me, then I'll go alone.' And so saying she turned about and flounced from the room, leaving Elizabeth and Faith to stare after her in surprise.

* * *

357

The next day, Elizabeth returned alone.

'Have you found out what was wrong with Louise yesterday?' Faith asked curiously.

Elizabeth took a tiny lace handkerchief from her bag and dabbed at her eyes. 'I'm afraid I have,' she sniffed. 'But I don't know if I should tell you, as I'm sure you will be no happier about it than I am.'

Faith was agog. 'Perhaps I should be the judge of that?' she said, and Elizabeth sighed dramatically.

'Oh very well, if you insist. It's like this – my poor Louise is deeply concerned for Daniel.'

Faith frowned. 'Why is that then?'

'It's Sassy up to her old tricks again,' said Elizabeth, and at the mention of the girl, Faith bridled.

'Oh yes, and what's she done now?'

'Well,' Elizabeth's voice was laced with spite, 'it seems that she's playing your Daniel along, when in fact she's actually agreed to marry Jack – though why *he* should want her, I'll never know. He's far too good for the likes of her, as I'm sure you will agree.'

Faith's mouth twisted with hate. 'Is that so?'

Elizabeth nodded.

'Well, don't worry. I'll see that she doesn't sink her hooks into *my* lad.' Faith grinned maliciously. 'I've a few tricks of my own up my sleeve.'

'Really?' Elizabeth was intrigued.

Faith leaned towards her and murmured, 'I'm going back to America. I've sold the inn – *and* may I add I got more than a fair price for it.' She grinned smugly, for Elizabeth was now reeling with genuine shock.

'And after what you've just told me I'll be making sure that Daniel comes back with me now,' she concluded.

'When are you planning on going?' Elizabeth asked faintly.

'Tomorrow. Mr Boon, the new owner, will be moving in and I'll be on my way.'

Elizabeth could hardly believe it. 'You kept that quiet,' she chided.

Serious now, Faith pursed her thin lips. 'I was going to tell you yesterday,' she said, 'but with Louise being so upset, I never got the chance.'

Elizabeth had hoped that Daniel would take to Louise, but her hatred of her stepdaughter went so deep that she would gladly sacrifice the match to hurt the girl.

'Do you think Daniel will agree to go with you?' she asked innocently.

'Oh yes, I'm sure he will.' Faith's voice held conviction. 'To be honest, I've had my suspicions that he had feelings in Sassy's direction, but once he knows that she's planning to marry Jack, I'm sure he'll be only too glad to leave here.' Deep down, the woman was delighted at the gossip Elizabeth had passed on. She had been racking her brains to think of a way to encourage Daniel to return to America with her, and now Elizabeth, albeit unknowingly, had handed her the perfect solution on a plate.

Sinking into her chair, Elizabeth prayed that Faith was right. She was determined that if Louise couldn't have Daniel then neither would Sassy – and she would stop at nothing to prevent it.

That evening, when Elizabeth related Faith's news to Arthur, he frowned deeply. 'You say she and Daniel are going back to America?' he repeated incredulously. 'Then I'm shocked. To tell the truth, I thought there was something growing between Daniel and my Sassy.'

Sensing danger, Elizabeth was immediately on her guard. 'I'm sure I don't know where you ever got *that* idea,' she said sweetly. 'I've certainly never detected anything there.'

'Even so,' he insisted, 'I only called into the farm yesterday on my way home from work and not one of them so much as mentioned that Faith or Daniel was leaving.'

Elizabeth shrugged. 'There you are then,' she said quietly. 'If Sassy were remotely interested in him, she'd have said something, wouldn't she?'

Arthur pondered on her words, then nodding slowly, his eyes returned to the newspaper he was reading. Yet the news failed to hold his attention now, for something, somewhere – and for some reason that he couldn't quite explain – didn't feel right.

Over at the Jolly Colliers, when Daniel drew the bolts on the bar door and climbed the stairs to the kitchen, he found his mother sitting waiting for him at the table.

'Ah, son,' she said pleasantly. 'Come and sit down awhile, I've something to tell you.'

Pulling up a chair, he joined her, stifling a yawn. It had been another long hard day and he was bone weary, and also missing little Florica, who had made their rooms into a real home.

'We're going back to America,' she told him abruptly.

Her words made him sit bolt upright in his chair. 'You what?' he gasped.

'You heard what I said.' Faith began to fold a pile of clothes she had ironed ready to go into their trunks. Avoiding his eye, she went on, 'I didn't want to tell you before everything was signed, sealed and delivered, but now it is. I've sold the inn, son. The new owner takes over tomorrow and I've booked our passages home. It's as simple as that.'

He stood up and began to pace restlessly about the small room. 'But we can't just take off like that, Mom,' he objected. 'And anyway I've no wish to go, if you want

360

the truth. I plan to stay here. There's someone I want to be with. I've been meaning to talk to you about it, and I guess now is as good a time as any.'

He would have gone on, but Faith held up her hand and stopped him. 'Look, dear,' her voice was imploring, 'hold your tongue and hear me out before you say another word, for what I heard today will make you *want* to go home.'

He shook his head in denial but listened nonetheless.

'As you know, Elizabeth was here earlier. I told her that I was planning on going back to America, and she passed a piece of news on to me that might be of interest to you.' Faith was aware that what she was about to tell her son would cause him pain, but even so she delivered the blow.

'Sassy and Jack are to be wed.'

Daniel's eyes started from their sockets. '*No!* It can't be true!'

'I'm afraid it is, son, and you have to accept it,' she said sympathetically. 'It seems that Sassy's a bit of a one for the men, and likes playing one off against another.' She hurried on, 'Look, it's better for you to find out now rather than later, for she'd have made a laughing stock of you if Elizabeth hadn't tipped me off. Come home with me before she makes a fool of you.'

As Daniel screwed his eyes up tight, a vision of Sassy swam before them, a vision of Sassy with Jack beside her – and it caused him so much pain he could scarcely bear it. 'Are you *quite* sure about this?'

Faith gulped. 'Of course I'm sure,' she answered. 'Elizabeth is Sassy's stepmother. Who better than she, to know of the girl's plans?'

'I'm going to go and ask her myself,' he said, suddenly rising, and panicking now, Faith flew around the table to him.

'For God's sake,' she said imploringly as she clung to his arm. 'You can't do that, Daniel. Think of the consequences. You'll look a fool, and Jack will likely down you.'

As the truth of her words sank in, Daniel's shoulders slowly sagged.

Sensing victory, she played her last hand. 'If she'd wanted you, she'd have been to see you, wouldn't she? She knows she's always been welcome here, but has she visited us? Ask yourself – no, she hasn't. Doesn't that speak for itself?' She omitted to tell him that at Thomas's funeral, she had made it more than clear to Sassy that she was no longer welcome at the inn. In truth, her hatred of the girl went as deep as Elizabeth's, but Daniel had not attended the funeral and had no way of knowing that. Now as he slowly sank back onto the chair, his mother tenderly placed her arm around his shoulders.

'I know it's hard now, dear,' she whispered, 'but where there's good there's always better, and this is a new start for us, you mark my words. We're richer now than we ever dreamed of being, and in a few months' time, you'll barely think of her. There's plenty more fish in the sea.'

Daniel felt in his heart that if he couldn't have Sassy then he'd never want anyone again. But then it all began to make sense. The way she had held him at arm's length. The way she had stopped visiting the inn.

'I thought she loved me, Mom,' he whispered brokenly, and gathering him to her breast, Faith smiled over his shoulder, her victory complete.

Chapter Thirty-Two

That night, sleep refused to come to Arthur. The feeling of unease persisted and he tossed and turned restlessly. Elizabeth's news of Faith and Daniel's imminent departure had shocked him to the core. Recently, Sassy had seemed more content than he had ever known her to be, and somehow Arthur had linked that content with Daniel. Now, try as he might, he found it hard to accept that there had been nothing between them. In fact, secretly he had been expecting Daniel to approach him with regards to his intentions. No, there was something amiss somewhere, but as yet he couldn't quite put his finger on it. Elizabeth was snoring peacefully at the side of him, and he gazed at her suspiciously. He, better than anyone, knew that his wife harboured no love for Sassy, and yet what could Elizabeth have to do with Daniel wishing to leave?

Chiding himself for his suspicions, and turning his back on his wife he snuggled down deeper into his pillows. I'll call into the farm first thing tomorrow, just to check she's all right, he promised himself, and somewhat comforted at the thought, he eventually drifted into an uneasy slumber.

The next morning as they sat at breakfast, Arthur glanced across the table at Elizabeth and enquired, 'Will you be going to see Faith off then?'

His wife applied a generous amount of butter to a

363

slice of toast. 'No, I said my goodbyes yesterday,' she informed him.

Arthur frowned. 'It's all a bit sudden, her leaving, isn't it?' he asked.

She shrugged. 'I suppose now that Thomas is dead, she just wants to get away.'

'Yes, well, I can understand that, but I have to say I'm surprised at Daniel going with her.' Arthur stared off into space as his breakfast congealed on the plate in front of him. 'As I said last night, I had the feeling there was something between him and Sassy.'

At his words, Louise stabbed her fork viciously into a thick slice of bacon. Elizabeth glared across the table at her, and then, turning back to Arthur she smiled sweetly. 'I think you must be imagining things,' she said.

Pushing his breakfast away, Arthur stared at her. 'Just the same, I think I'll leave a little earlier and call in at the farm on my way to work to check that Sassy's all right.' Rising from his chair, he was about to do just that, when the dining-room door banged open revealing Ada, who was almost hopping from foot to foot in her excitement.

'Eeh, you'll never guess what,' she cried joyously, but they had no chance to guess because at that very moment, the cause of her excitement suddenly stepped past her.

'Dr Matthew Bonner, at your service,' he introduced himself with a little bow.

Squealing with delight, Elizabeth flew to him.

And so it was that Arthur, instead of leaving the house early, left almost an hour late. He had a great fondness for Matthew and was glad to have him home.

It was almost 9.30 a.m. by the time he arrived at the farm and Sassy, as usual at sight of her father, beamed a welcome. She and James, with Oscar in hot pursuit, had just been to collect the eggs from the henhouse and

James, always delighted to see a visitor, happily skipped to greet him.

Arthur ruffled his son's hair affectionately and followed Sassy into the coolness of the kitchen. Once inside she carefully deposited the basket of eggs onto the table.

'There,' she smiled. 'Now you can tell us what you're doing here so bright an' early. Have you had your breakfast, and shouldn't you be at work?'

Arthur grinned. 'Yes to both questions,' he joked. 'Anyway, I had a bit of news that I thought you'd like to hear,' he continued as Miriam came in.

'So come on then, don't keep us in suspense. Yer know we women like a bit of gossip,' she quipped jovially.

Arthur quickly told them of Matthew's homecoming, which brought exclamations of delight from both of them.

'Well, just fancy that then!' Sassy was thrilled. 'Dr Matthew Bonner, eh?'

'You'd never believe his mother had made all that fuss about him wanting to go to medical school if you could see her now,' Arthur chuckled. 'She's strutting about proud as a peacock.'

Miriam raised her eyes. 'Oh yes I could,' she retorted. 'I don't wish to sound uncharitable, love, but I could well believe anything of your wife.'

At her words, Arthur suddenly became serious. Now his thoughts had turned to his other reason for calling, and he gazed at the table, trying to choose his words carefully.

'Is that all the news you have for us?' Sassy asked quietly, sensing her father's discomfort.

He cleared his throat. 'To tell the truth, I'm not sure,' he said. 'It could be that you know already.'

Sassy narrowed her eyes. '*What* could we know?'

Eager to get it over with now, Arthur continued, 'Elizabeth visited Faith yesterday.'

Sassy lost interest. 'Well, and what's so unusual about that?'

'Nothing,' he replied. 'Except that she told Elizabeth that she and Daniel are going back to America. I just thought it was a bit sudden, that's all.'

As her father's words slowly sank in, Sassy swayed on her feet as the room started to whirl around her.

'What did you say?' she whispered when she could catch her breath.

'I said Faith and Daniel are returning to America, but surely you already know that, love?'

She shook her head in disbelief. 'You must have it wrong,' she said. 'Daniel wouldn't just go off like that.'

'It's no mistake, I promise you,' he said gently. 'Elizabeth was quite sure of her facts.'

A sick feeling had crept deep into the pit of Sassy's stomach as she tried to absorb the news. 'When are they going?' she asked.

Arthur frowned. Her face was grey and he could see that his news had come as a shock to her.

'I believe they are leaving today, love,' he answered.

Sassy reeled, her eyes desperate. 'Then I've *got* to see him!' Grabbing her father's hand, she dragged him towards the pony and trap that Arthur had come in. 'Come on,' she cried desperately. 'We have to get to the inn! I *have* to talk to him!'

Casting a worried glance at Miriam, Arthur hurriedly followed her out.

Mr Boon rocked back on his heels as he proudly surveyed his new empire. Up to now everything had run like clock-work, just as he had hoped it would since his arrival some half an hour ago. His trunks and cases had been quickly carried into the inn, and Faith's and Daniel's then loaded efficiently onto the same horse and cart, ready to carry them to the railway station. Even now, the sound of Daisy, his plump little wife, busily unpacking upstairs could be heard, and he grinned at David, who was still stunned at the speed of it all. He certainly wouldn't miss Faith, though he had been sad to see young Daniel go.

'You needn't worry, lad,' Mr Boon now reassured David kindly. 'There's a job here for as long as you want it. Mrs Mallabone couldn't sing your praises highly enough.'

David's relief was apparent as he eyed the new land-lord cautiously.

'I've got great plans for this place,' Mr Boon confided. 'It's always been me ambition to own me own inn, and now that I do, I have to confess I can hardly believe it.'

David found himself warming to his new boss. 'I'll tell yer what, how about I show you about a bit, before we get busy, eh?' he suggested.

Mr Boon beamed. 'I reckon that's a grand idea, lad,' he declared, so smiling, David did just that.

It was some minutes later, as David was standing behind the bar pointing out the various prices of the spirits there to Mr Boon, that the bar door suddenly banged open and Sassy, wildly dishevelled, flew across the room to them.

'Where's Daniel?' she cried.

'You've missed him, love. I'm afraid he's already gone.'

'Gone where?' she cried.

He pointed towards the open door. 'To the railway station, but you'll have to hurry if you've a mind to catch him. The train's due any time.'

Without another word Sassy spun on her heel and flew back the way she had come, leaving David and Mr Boon to stare after her in astonishment.

The luggage was all safely loaded into the special compart-ment at the back of the train, and dressed in her very best, Faith was settling herself comfortably into a seat in the first-class carriage. The final whistle had blown to herald the train's departure, but still Daniel delayed boarding and stood with one foot on the step, his hand holding the door open as his eyes raked up and down the platform.

'*She'll come,*' his heart cried. '*This* has *to be a mistake.*' But Sassy didn't come and all he saw was an empty platform.

A great burst of steam suddenly rose from the engine, as the train chugged to life, and the station-master, who was standing close behind him, coughed politely.

'You'll have to climb aboard now, sir,' he informed Daniel.

Daniel's eyes scoured the length of the platform for one last time but all they found was emptiness to match the emptiness that was in his heart. Defeated, he slowly boarded the train as the station-master slammed the door shut behind him.

On the short journey from the Jolly Colliers to the station, Arthur urged the poor horse to breakneck speed. By the time they arrived minutes later, the poor beast was sweating profusely and foaming at the bit, but Sassy paid him no heed as she leaped from the cart before Arthur had even managed to pull him to an indignant halt.

As she landed heavily in an unladylike heap on the ground, her ankle twisted beneath her, but ignoring the pain, she was up in a second and holding her hampering skirts high, she limped into the station, her breath coming in great shuddering sobs.

Spying the station-master, who was just about to enter his cosy little office, she sped towards him and grasped his arm.

'The train,' she gasped, her eyes frantic. 'Where's the train?'

'I'm sorry, miss,' he said, sympathy heavy in his voice.

'The train left some minutes since. I'm afraid you're too late.'

Her hand dropped from his arm as his words echoed in her head, and pain such as she had never known pierced her heart.

Too late, too late! And then the words receded, for a warm, deep darkness was enveloping her, and much to the stationmaster's consternation, she sank gracefully into a heap at his feet.

It was now almost a week since Daniel's departure and Miriam, who was standing next to the deep stone sink, watched Sassy's slow progress across the farmyard with a worried frown on her face.

'Just look at her,' she said to Clara, her voice full of concern. 'She's taken Daniel's goin' really badly; it's like having a different girl about the place – almost as if she's lost her spirit.'

Clara nodded sadly. 'Yer right there, lass,' she agreed. 'She must have thought a lot more of him than we guessed.'

Miriam tutted. 'I can't understand him taking off as he did. I'd have staked me life on them two getting together.'

'Eeh, it would be nice if life could run smoothly once in a while, wouldn't it?' Clara muttered.

And Miriam wearily agreed.

On entering the barn, Sassy closed her eyes for a minute and leaned against the wall. As the days passed, what she saw as Daniel's betrayal of her got no easier to bear. Not only that, but she had something else to worry about, for she was almost certain now that she was carrying his child. The thought filled her with dread. The child would be looked upon as a bastard, now that its father had abandoned her. As hot tears of self-pity sprang to her eyes, she angrily swiped them away with the back of her hand.

'Pull yourself together,' she chided herself. 'You've been used again and now you must bear the consequences.' But even as she thought it, her heart cried out in denial; she still couldn't believe that Daniel hadn't loved her. Just then she heard Maisie's door open overhead and within seconds, she was at Sassy's side.

'What yer doin' here all alone?' she asked kindly.

Sassy shrugged. 'Just catching a minute.' Her eyes were dull and Maisie's heart went out to her.

'Look, love,' she said softly, 'Daniel's gone an' yer goin' to have to come to terms with it.'

'I know that,' Sassy cried, 'but it's easier said than done. Why did he leave me, Maisie – *why?* I should have told him that I loved him and then he might not have left me . . . but I was so afraid of being hurt again after all those years of loving Thomas.' When she collapsed into a sobbing heap in her friend's arms, Maisie hugged her and her own eyes filled with tears.

'Oh, don't cry, love,' she implored her. 'You'll have me at it an' all in a minute.'

But almost as if a dam had burst inside her, Sassy sobbed as if her heart would break. Maisie led her gently towards the stairs.

'Come on, Sassy,' she urged. 'Let's go up an' have a few minutes' quiet, eh?'

Once they were seated in the Lees' cosy little sitting room, Maisie went on quietly, 'Is there anythin' else botherin' yer, Sassy?'

Sassy's startled eyes flew to meet hers. 'What do you mean?' she asked warily.

Maisie shrugged. 'Look, love, you an' me have been friends for a long time now, an' I just have a feelin' in me bones that there's somethin' more goin' on than yer tellin' me.'

When Sassy gulped deep in her throat and her eyes

became fearful, Maisie's hand closed over her own. 'Yer pregnant, ain't yer?' she said.

Sassy nodded slowly.

'Aw, love.' Maisie was deeply concerned. 'Is it Daniel's?' Again Sassy nodded and now her friend became angry. 'No wonder you've been so upset at his goin' – the lowdown bugger him.'

Sassy instantly sprang to his defence. 'No, Maisie, it's not like that,' she said desperately. 'He didn't take advantage of me or anything . . . it just sort of happened. He doesn't even know.'

'That's as may be,' Maisie said. 'But it's still you that will be left holding the baby.' She stared at her friend before asking softly, 'What are you goin' to do?'

'There's not much I can do, is there?' Sassy replied. 'But one thing I would ask – *please* don't tell anyone just yet.'

'Of course I won't. But yer know . . . yer can't hide it for ever.'

'I know that,' Sassy replied tiredly. 'But until I get used to the idea myself, I'd rather just you and I knew about it.'

'You have me word,' promised Maisie, and at that, Sassy rose from the table and went downstairs about her business, leaving her friend to stare after her with troubled eyes.

Outside in the yard again, Sassy breathed deeply. Her thoughts were in turmoil but one thing she was sure of. If Daniel's child was growing inside her, then she would keep it. She had seen too many young girls in her predicament tread the path to Grandmother Cox's cottage. The kindly old lady had potions that could rid them of their worry, but Sassy was determined that Daniel's child would be born and it would be loved, whatever the outcome.

As she moved towards the kitchen door she saw Jack

striding towards her with a wide smile on his face, but as he grew closer the smile disappeared. 'Are you feelin' all right, love?' he asked. 'Yer lookin' a bit peaky.'

'I'm fine,' she assured him, and as she went on her way his heart ached for her. He guessed how much she had cared for Daniel and knew that she had taken his leaving badly. But even so, she was footloose and fancy free again now, and he could not stop himself from hoping once more that she might one day look his way.

That night, as Ben lay in bed watching Miriam undress, he too was a troubled man. The weight seemed to have dropped off her and she was as thin as a rake.

'By heck, love!' he exclaimed. 'You'll slip down a crack in the cobbles if you get any thinner.'

Miriam chuckled. 'Oh, don't start on that tack again,' she reproached him. 'I've told you – I'm fit as a fiddle.'

But for once Ben would not be put off. 'I think it's high time you saw the doctor,' he said firmly.

Miriam turned to him. 'If you must know, I already have,' she confessed. 'An' you'll be pleased to learn that he told me there's nothing wrong with me that a good rest wouldn't cure.'

Ben immediately looked guilty, and crossing to the bed, she sat down beside him and took his hand. 'Yer daft ape, you,' she said warmly. 'There's absolutely nothing fer you to worry about. The doctor's given me a tonic, an' I'll be as good as new in no time.'

Ben sighed with relief. 'Are yer sure that's all it is?'

Crossing to the dressing-table, Miriam began to take the pins from her hair.

'I told you so, didn't I?' she said, avoiding his eyes, and nodding Ben settled comfortably down into the featherbed.

Chapter Thirty-Three

Next morning bright and early, Miriam was awakened by a gentle shake of the shoulder. She opened her eyes and saw Ben standing there with a steaming mug of tea in his hand.

'What's this then?' she asked sleepily, pulling herself up onto the pillows. 'Is it me birthday?'

'No, it ain't, it's better than that,' Ben smiled. 'It's yer day off.'

Miriam stared at him. 'Whatever are yer on about, man – me day off?'

'Just what I said,' he told her firmly. 'I got to thinkin'. We don't get to have too much time to ourselves nowadays, so today you and I are off to market. I've cleared it with the others, an' after we've done our shopping we're goin' to sit down for a slap-up meal.'

Miriam gazed at him, her throat full. 'I don't know what I did to deserve you,' she whispered.

Ben winked as he puffed out his chest. 'To tell yer the truth, neither do I. Happen yer just a very lucky woman.' Laughing loudly he then ducked to avoid the feather pillow that came flying towards him.

They were standing at the side of the horse and cart, all dressed in their best, and for the tenth time in as many minutes Miriam asked Sassy, 'Now are yer quite sure you'll manage, love?'

Sassy sighed. '*Yes, yes, yes!* Now will you *please* just get off and enjoy yourselves?'

Miriam's eyes then went to James who was holding Sassy's hand. 'Now you be a good lad for Sassy, mind,' she said, and gave him a last cuddle.

Ben winked at Sassy then leaning over the side of the cart he ordered sternly, 'Come on then, woman, else it'll be time to come back afore we even get there.'

Like a child on a Sunday School outing, Miriam clambered up onto the hard wooden seat at her husband's side. 'We'll be back in time for tea,' she shouted as the cart trundled down the track, and Sassy and James stood waving until they were out of sight.

'Right then,' Sassy addressed him. 'How about you an' me go an' make some jam tarts for when they get back, eh?'

James's eyes lit up. He was now thirteen years old, and appeared as any other boy his age. In fact, he was a handsome lad, but mentally he was much younger, as became apparent by his speech and his behaviour. But for all that he was much loved by everyone, for his kind sensitive nature would have been hard to match and Sassy totally adored him.

'Come on then.' She turned her brother about, and hand in hand they entered the kitchen.

Making jam tarts with James helping was no easy task, as Sassy soon discovered. As fast as they came out of the oven he ate them, but at last she managed to snatch a tray from him and put them to cool on the windowsill.

'There then.' She waggled a spoon at him. 'And don't get touching those, else your mam and dad will have no tea.'

James looked suitably guilty.

'Now we'd better get you cleaned up,' she said. ''Cos from where I'm standing, there's more flour and jam on

374

you than went into the tarts.' And taking his hand, she led him outside to the pump in the yard.

During the afternoon, Matthew came to call and dutifully sampled one of James's jam tarts. 'Mm, they're delicious,' he laughed and the young lad beamed with pleasure.

During his short visit Matthew couldn't help but notice Sassy's pale face, and when James eventually scampered off out into the yard to play with Oscar, he became serious.

'Are you feeling all right, Sassy?' he questioned.

She nodded a little too quickly for his liking.

'Of course I am,' she lied. 'Why do you ask?'

He shrugged. 'Oh, you just look a bit pale, that's all.'

Not liking the road the conversation was taking, Sassy quickly changed the subject. 'How are you settling in, anyway?'

'I'm loving every minute,' he admitted. 'And I reckon I came back just in time, because Dr Massey's run off his feet.'

It was then that Maisie breezed into the kitchen to inform them, 'Clara's comin' down the track.'

Matthew rose from the table and picked up his black bag. 'In that case, I think it's time I was off,' he declared, smiling wryly at them both. 'I know what you women are like when you get your heads together, but some of us have work to do.'

'You cheeky devil,' Sassy scolded him as he headed for the door. 'Come again soon!' she shouted and he raised his hand in reply, blissfully ignorant of just how soon he would be back, and under circumstances that would alter her life for ever.

By the time Clara entered, Sassy was already pouring a cup of tea out for her, and sinking into a chair, Clara sighed contentedly. 'By, lass,' she grinned. 'I'm ready fer this – yer must be one o' them Mesmerists, readin' my mind.'

Sassy grinned. 'Not really, Clara. But I've never known you to refuse a cup of tea in your life, and I think it'll be a cold day in hell before you do.'

'You could be right there, lass,' Clara agreed, and grabbing the cup she slurped at it gratefully.

By teatime, Sassy felt a vague disquiet. There was no sign as yet of Miriam and Ben, and by the time Jack, Aaron and Maisie had entered the kitchen for their evening meal, the couple were still not back.

Clara was also staying for her dinner that night as Walter was off for a rare game of dominoes at the Punch Bowl with Jimmy Wainthrop. Sensing Sassy's unease, she clucked her tongue at her impatiently.

'Eeh, lass, I reckon yer want somethin' to worry about,' she chided gently. 'They don't get the chance of a day to themselves very often, so no doubt they're makin' the most of it.'

Slightly reassured, Sassy agreed. 'Yes, yes, you're probably right. I'll dish ours up and put theirs in the oven, shall I?'

'You do that,' Clara urged. ''Cos I'll tell yer now, me poor stomach thinks me throat's cut.'

Once the meal was over, the dishes washed, dried and put away, Maisie and Aaron returned to their own rooms and Jack, who was to drive Clara home later that night, contentedly settled in the easy chair with his pipe.

Sassy peeped into the oven at her aunt and uncle's dinner some time later. 'If they don't get back soon, these will be so dried up they'll only be fit for the pigs,' she murmured.

Clara was feeling slightly uneasy herself now. 'I have

to admit, it ain't like them to be this late,' she admitted grudgingly. James was yawning tiredly so, going to a cupboard, Sassy took out a clean nightshirt.

'Right then, young man, get yourself into your room and have a good wash now,' she ordered, handing it to him. 'An' mind you do behind your ears.'

Usually an obedient lad, James shook his head. 'I want to wait for Mam an' Dad,' he said sulkily.

'All right then, you can have another half an hour, but no more than that. If they're not back then, it's off to bed, mind.'

James nodded eagerly and snuggled further into the chair, Oscar cuddled on his lap, and long before the half an hour was up, they were both fast asleep.

Darkness was falling when Jack, who had fallen into a doze, started awake. Glancing at the clock on the mantelpiece, he stretched his arms and legs sleepily out before him and asked, 'Shall I take you home then, Mam, afore it gets too dark?'

Clara shook her head. 'No, lad, I reckon I'll wait till they're back,' she answered.

As Jack stared out at the deepening dusk, he frowned before saying, 'I reckon I'll take the lantern an' just have a walk down the track.'

'I'll come with you,' Sassy offered quickly.

Jack knew it would be useless to argue and anyway, he was secretly glad to have a chance to spend a little time alone with her. 'Aye, all right, lass. You fetch the lantern an' I'll get me boots on.'

Sassy hurried to do as she was told, but by the time they had reached the end of the twisting track there was still no sign of Miriam and Ben, and night had fallen around them.

Holding the lantern high, Jack peered into the blackness. 'Let's just go a little further,' Sassy pleaded.

'All right then,' he agreed. 'We'll walk the way they'd take from town.'

Side by side they walked on, carefully avoiding the pot-holes in the rough dirt track. They had gone some distance when Sassy came to an abrupt halt and whispered, 'Hark, did you hear that?'

Jack stood silently at her side. 'Hear what?' he asked presently, but she pressed her hand against his mouth.

'Shush, *listen!*' she ordered and together they stood, their ears straining until suddenly the sound came again.

'Did you hear it that time?' Sassy said fearfully.

'Aye, I did,' he admitted. 'It sounded like a horse in pain.'

The lane they were in was treacherously twisting, with a deep ditch on either side, flanked by high hawthorn hedges. Frightened now, Sassy squeezed Jack's hand.

'Where did it come from?' she asked. A note of terror had crept into her voice and Jack put his arm about her reassuringly.

'Come on, lass, there's only one way to find out and that's to go an' see.' They had gone about 100 yards farther, and rounded a particularly sharp bend when the sound came to them again, but louder this time.

'Come on,' urged Jack, and as one they broke into a run.

The lantern was swinging wildly from side to side as they hurried on and suddenly its light fell on something moving in the ditch ahead of them. Slowing, afraid of what they would find, they cautiously approached.

The sight that met them caused Sassy's hand to fly to her mouth and Jack's eyes to almost start from his head. Deep in the ditch lay the mangled remains of a cart with their faithful old gelding, Brandy, still firmly attached to it, whinnying pitifully. He was lying on his side with three legs wildly thrashing the air above him. The other leg was tucked deep beneath him at an unnatural angle and he was frothing at the bit, his eyes wild and staring. But of Miriam and Ben there was no sign.

'Oh, my God.' Sassy began to sob but for the moment Jack was too shocked to say anything.

'Where are they?' she screamed, and the terror in her voice brought Jack back to himself.

'Here, hold this,' he commanded, and thrusting the lantern at Sassy he jumped down into the ditch and tried to peer beneath the wreckage of the cart. His blood ran cold as he saw what looked like a human hand seemingly reaching towards him. Immediately he began to try and lift the cart but within seconds he realised that he was fighting a losing battle, so trying not to alarm Sassy any more than was necessary, he said, 'Run back to the farm, as fast as yer can, an' get Aaron. There's no way I can shift this on me own.'

For a second she stood as if in a trance staring at him, so harshly now he snapped at her, 'Do as I say, an' be quick about it, fer God's sake. And Sassy – tell him to bring a gun.'

Turning, Sassy flew back the way she had come, and all the time she was crying, '*Oh no, no, please. Let them be all right.*'

It was now the early hours of the morning. Miriam and Ben's mangled bodies lay side by side in the parlour. The horse had long since been put out of its misery but the poor creature still lay in the ditch, for tonight everyone was bone weary. Tomorrow would be soon enough to remove Brandy's carcass. Sassy was in deep shock and sat staring straight ahead. Her father was flapping about pouring tea here, there and everywhere, but no one touched it and gradually a skin formed upon its surface.

Dr Massey and Matthew were now preparing to leave. Although they had both come at speed when summoned, on arriving it had been more than obvious that they were far too late. Miriam and Ben had both been dead for some time.

'How could it have happened?' questioned Maisie yet again, as the tears poured down her cheeks.

Dr Massey sighed. 'It could have been anything that caused it,' he answered. 'A fox could have run before the cart and startled the horse, or maybe Ben just misjudged the turn. It's a bad bend.' His eyes were full of sorrow. 'At the end of the day, accidents happen, and we'll never know the cause – but Miriam was living on borrowed time anyway.'

'What do you mean by that?' Sassy asked.

The doctor shrugged. 'I suppose there's no harm in you all knowing now,' he said. 'Your aunt came to see me over a year ago; she'd lost an unhealthy amount of weight, so I examined her and found a large growth in her chest.' He shook his head at the memory. 'There was nothing I could do except give her something for the pain and tell her to take life a day at a time, but she made me promise then that I'd not tell any of you, because she didn't want you worrying.'

As Sassy screwed her eyes up tight, the tears that had been threatening all this long night suddenly gushed from her.

Dr Massey patted her hand. 'There now,' he comforted. 'Your aunt loved you and James as if you were her own, and you must hold on to that, for she was one of the bravest women I've ever met.' And so saying, he lifted his black bag and wearily left the kitchen.

Miriam and Ben were laid to rest in a double grave, together in death as they would have wished, in Coton

380

churchyard, not a stone's throw from all the others that Sassy had loved who now lay at peace there. As the coffins, with their brass handles gleaming in the sunlight, were slowly lowered into the ground, her lonely heart cried out at the injustice of it. It seemed to her that everyone she loved was being taken from her, one at a time.

'Oh, Daniel,' she cried silently, 'where are you? I need you – *why* did you leave me?' But her heart gave her no answer.

The funeral tea was a solemn affair, made more so by the arrival of the solicitor, Mr Turnbull, who entered the parlour for the reading of the Will. Elizabeth had managed to maintain an outward show of grief, but inwardly she was deeply excited. It was no secret that Ben Ratcliffe had died a reasonably wealthy man and it was obvious that he couldn't leave his farm to James, so her mind had reasoned that his brother-in-law Arthur must be his next obvious choice – after his wife. By this evening, she had greedily assumed that Holly Bush Farm would soon be theirs.

Coughing nervously, Mr Turnbull gazed round at those assembled over the top of his pince-nez, then he carefully opened the envelope that contained Ben's Last Will and Testament, signed and sealed in his presence some months ago.

Clearing his throat, he began to read.

As his voice droned on, Sassy's mind drifted away. The reading of the Will was a lengthy affair and it soon became obvious that Ben had forgotten no one. '"The sum of twenty-five pounds to our dear friends, Clara and Walter Mallabone, forever loyal",' he read out, and Clara bowed her head and quietly cried as Walter's arm came comfortingly about her. '"To Jack Mallabone, my right-hand man, the cottage, the grounds it stands in and the sum of forty pounds with my heartfelt thanks".'

Jack bowed his head.

'"To Maisie and Aaron Lee, who have become a part of our family, the sum of thirty pounds".' And so it went on until Elizabeth feared she would burst with impatience. But at last, the solicitor paused. '"My farm, all the surrounding lands, livestock and monies go to my beloved wife Miriam who has made me the happiest man on earth. If she should pre-decease me, which I can barely contemplate, they will pass to my niece, Melissa Churm, on condition that she agrees to care for James, who has been as a son to us, for the remainder of his life".'

Sassy's startled eyes flew to the solicitor who was smiling at her kindly, but enraged, Elizabeth jumped from her chair. 'What did you say?' she cried harshly. 'Ben can't leave all this to *her*.'

Eyeing her coldly, Mr Turnbull sniffed before informing her, 'Oh, I assure you, madam, *he can and he has* – and in my presence. And if I may say so, I think he made a very wise decision, although none of us could have predicted this tragic development.'

Elizabeth was almost beside herself with rage and as Arthur's hand rested on her arm she shook it off roughly. 'Why, this is nothing short of *outrageous*!' she ranted, red in the face with fury. 'I won't stand for it. Everything should have come to *us*.'

'Everything was done very correctly and above board, madam,' the solicitor assured her with a measure of satisfaction, thinking what a truly despicable woman she was.

Highly indignant, Elizabeth turned on her heel and stormed out of the room.

Sassy, who was still deep in shock, had been ordered off for a lie-down by Clara. The mourners had long since departed with the solicitor, and now she, Jack and Walter sat closely together at the kitchen table.

'Will you be staying on to help Sassy?' Clara asked her son.

He nodded. 'Course I will,' he muttered. 'It goes without sayin'.'

'Thank God for that,' she said. ''Cos I think she'll have need o' yer in the days ahead.'

Jack stared at her curiously. 'What, yer mean with the runnin' of the farm?'

Clara chewed worriedly on her lip before answering, 'Well yes, that o' course . . . but there's somethin' else as is botherin' me an' all.'

'Then spit it out, Mam,' he ordered.

'I could be wrong,' Clara's voice had dropped to a whisper, 'but I have a feelin' that she's with child.'

'Whatever makes yer think that?' Jack croaked, when eventually his voice returned.

Clara pursed her lips. 'I can recognise a pregnant woman when I see one from a mile off,' she said. 'I reckon that's one o' the reasons why she's taken Daniel's leavin' so hard. But yer know, lad, this could work in your favour, fer I've always known that you loved her.'

Bewildered, Jack shook his head. 'I don't understand, Mam.'

Clara sighed again. It had been a long day, a terrible day, and this wasn't proving easy, either. 'Well, it's as plain as the nose on yer face, lad. Do yer need it spellin' out fer yer? The poor lass is pregnant if I'm any judge, an' the baby's goin' to need a father an' a name, ain't it?'

Still he stared at her.

'Perhaps this is yer chance; I always told yer that yer day would come. What you have to do is ask yerself, do yer love her enough to marry her, knowin' she's carryin' another man's child? An' if the answer is yes, then now's the time to speak up.'

Jack's hand moved to his brow and he stroked his

forehead in great agitation, his mind awhirl. *Sassy pregnant*. He could barely take it in, and yet he set great store on his mother's wisdom, and knew she would never suggest such a thing unless she was fairly convinced of it.

Sensing the mixed emotions that were tearing through him, Clara soothingly patted his hand. 'I know it's a lot to take in, pet,' she said softly. 'But they say that everythin' happens fer a reason, an' as one door shuts another one opens.'

Still Jack said nothing, but sat staring numbly ahead, and it was Walter now who butted in.

'Look,' he pointed out sensibly. 'It's been a long hard day for all of us, so get yerself off to bed, lad, an' sleep on what yer mam's told yer. But heed this: you don't *have* to do anythin' yer don't want to do, an' whatever you decide, me an' yer mam will stand by yer.'

Jack gratefully squeezed his father's shoulder, then without a word, he left the room and went over the fields to the sanctuary of his cottage, to think on what his parents had said. This latest shock had set his mind a-spinning, and he knew there'd be no sleep for him, this night.

PART SIX

Summer, 1885

'Behold, I make all things new'

Revelation, 21; 4

Chapter Thirty-Four

Although the sun shone, the days that followed were dark indeed. Besides having to come to terms with the loss of Miriam and Ben, those that were left were also having to cope with the extra workload, and every night they dropped into bed, weary in mind and body. Usually such a happy lad, James cried repeatedly. Though they had all tried to explain to him that the people he had known as his mam and dad were not coming back, his poor mind could not accept it, and he spent hours in the yard, straining his sad eyes up the track for a sign of their return. When he was not doing this, he followed Sassy about like a shadow to the point that he would panic and cry fearfully if he so much as lost sight of her. The nights were now drawing in and had grown cooler, and each evening when Sassy had tucked James into bed she welcomed sleep as a blessed relief.

For weeks now she had been violently ill each morning, and though as yet she had managed to hide her condition by loosening the waistbands of her skirts, she knew that she wouldn't be able to conceal it for much longer.

Maisie on the other hand looked just as Sassy had always imagined a pregnant woman should look. She seemed to be positively glowing with health, her eyes sparkled and her hair shone. Her midriff had suddenly exploded out of shape and she now proudly carried a round belly before her.

Sassy would watch enviously as Aaron's face lit up with

pride when he looked at her and her own heart would cry. Daniel should be looking at her like that. But then once again it would hit her that he never would – and she would bow her head in shame.

The September nights were becoming colder, and tonight, Sassy had built a fire that roared up the chimney, to try and expel the draughts that were finding their way into the room past the window- and doorframes. She had long since seen James off to bed, and was sitting in her cocoon of loneliness staring miserably at the flames, when the kitchen door opened and Jack walked in. He had washed and changed and his black curls were still damp. Sassy smiled at him, glad of his company.

As he stood there seemingly ill-at-ease, she patted the chair at the side of her. 'Come an' sit down,' she offered. 'I'm glad to see you. It gets lonely of a night.'

He nodded as he plonked himself down beside her.

'And to what do I owe the honour of this visit then?' she asked.

Avoiding her eyes, he shrugged. 'Just thought you might be glad of a bit of company, that's all.'

'You know,' she confided sadly, 'I reckon this is the worst time of the day, 'cos when all the work's done you have time to think on things.' As her eyes filled with tears, Jack patted her hand.

'I know yer miss Miriam and Ben,' he said softly, 'but life has to go on. What's done is done, an' they wouldn't have wanted us all to be miserable, would they?'

Sassy sniffed loudly. 'I know that, Jack, but I'm *so* lonely.'

'Aye, well, that's why I'm here,' he confessed, suddenly nervous again. 'I . . . er . . . I have a proposition to put to yer.'

Sassy eyed him curiously, as Jack gazed into the fire

wondering how to start. He had been rehearsing what he would say to her all day long, but now for the life of him he couldn't remember a word of his speech.

'Well, go on then. What is this proposition?' Sassy finally asked as curiosity got the better of her.

'All right then.' Jack cleared his throat. 'There's no easy way to ask yer, so I may as well just say it straight out. Sassy . . . will you marry me?'

The look of shock that crossed her face caused a red flush to spread up from his neck and across his face.

'I bet yer think it's 'cos you own all this now that I'm askin' yer, don't yer?' he said, spreading his hands. 'But I promise you, Sassy, it ain't. As far as I'm concerned, the farm is yours an' always will be. Should yer ever wish me to leave, I wouldn't ask fer a single brass farthin'.'

Stunned at his proposal, Sassy said, 'I didn't think it was that at all, Jack. And I'm flattered that you should ask me, but I have to say no. You see . . . I can't marry you or anyone.' And burying her face in her hands, she began to cry.

Jack's arms came around her trembling shoulders. 'If it's 'cos yer with child,' he said quietly, 'don't let that stop yer 'cos I already know.'

Her amazed eyes flew to his face. 'How?' she demanded.

'Me mam,' he admitted. 'She's had her suspicions fer weeks, but don't worry, she's told no one, only me an' me dad.'

Sassy let out a deep breath. 'Oh well, I knew I couldn't hide it for ever,' she said. It was a relief to have the truth out in the open.

Jack took her hand and squeezed it gently. 'Look, love, won't you at least consider it? You're goin' to need someone to look out fer you.'

'It wouldn't be right, Jack, you having to bring up

someone else's child,' she protested. 'And anyway, I have to be honest – I've always cared for you, you know I have, but I don't love you.'

Jack was desperate as he saw his chance slipping away yet again.

'All right then,' he cried. 'Just hear me out. I don't *care* if yer don't love me. I have enough love in me fer the both of us. I've loved you fer as long as I can remember, an' you'd *grow* to love me, I *know* yer would – if you'd only give me a chance.'

Shocked at the sincerity of his words, Sassy gazed at him open-mouthed. 'B . . . but the baby?' she whispered falteringly.

He gazed deep into her eyes. 'Aye, the baby. Happen that's another reason yer should consider me, 'cos I'll tell yer now, this child deserves a father, an' from the minute it's born I'll love it as me own I promise yer.'

As Sassy remained silent, he continued, 'Look, lass, you ain't the first this has happened to an' yer won't be the last. But think of the little 'un, for God's sake. *Surely* it deserves a dad, an' I'd be a good dad an' all. I'd see as neither of yer ever wanted fer anythin' as long as I had a breath left in me body. I swear it.'

When Sassy still didn't answer, he slowly dropped his head, defeated.

As Sassy stared at this kind, gentle man before her, she considered his proposal. She truly believed every word he had said, and knew that there were many girls hereabouts who would jump to be in her shoes.

'Jack.' Her voice was thick with tears when she eventually addressed him, and she saw that his eyes were full of anguish.

'I thank you for the honour you have just paid me. I know I don't deserve it, but,' his eyes held hers, 'if you're sure, then yes . . . I'll marry you.'

Time seemed to stand still for Jack. 'Did you just say *yes*?' he breathed eventually, hardly daring to believe his ears.

Grinning through her tears, Sassy nodded, and suddenly he was kneeling before her with his arms tight about her waist.

'Aw, lass, I promise yer, yer won't regret it.' Tears were pouring unashamedly down his face. 'I'll love you an' this little 'un till me dying day, an' I'll tell yer somethin' else an' all. From now on, things will get better.'

And strangely, though her heart still ached for Daniel, she believed him.

So it was that in the first week in October, Sassy once again entered Chilvers Coton Church, this time as a bride. It was a sober affair as weddings go. So soon after the deaths of Miriam and Ben, no one was in the mood for celebrating, even at a wedding.

Sassy wore a plain blue costume, her only decoration some late-flowering roses that Clara had pinned to her bonnet. But for all that, the look of pure adoration and love that shone from Jack as he gazed at his bride was touching to see.

Just for a second as they stood at the altar, a stab of despair shot through Sassy, as she pictured Daniel standing beside her. But then, after blinking rapidly, it was Jack's face that she saw, and she solemnly took her vows.

Although the couple had declared that they wanted no fuss, Clara and Ada had insisted on laying on a small wedding feast. Compared to Maisie and Aaron's reception, it was a quiet affair, and even before it was over, Jack slipped away with the horse and cart to fetch the rest of his belongings from his cottage.

Shortly afterwards, the wedding party departed and

by teatime they were all going about their chores as if it were any other day.

As night fell, Sassy tucked James safely into bed and once she was sure that he was settled, she left the room to join Jack in the kitchen where he was sitting at the side of the fire contentedly puffing on his pipe.

As bedtime approached, her heart filled with dread. Eventually, knowing that she could put it off no longer, she rose from her chair.

'I'll be off to bed then,' she said nervously.

Jack nodded and smiled. 'Aye, all right, lass. I'll join yer in a minute.'

Trembling now, Sassy almost ran to the bedroom. Once there, she threw her clothes from her and with shaking fingers poured cold water from the jug into the bowl, and hastily washed. Seconds later she pulled her nightgown over her head, and leaping into bed, she lay shivering, the covers pulled up tight to her chin.

Below, she could hear Jack bolting the doors and extinguishing the lights, then eventually came the sound of his footsteps on the stairs. Her heart began to thump within her chest as she eyed the door in terror.

On entering the room, he crossed to the chair and began to undress, but when he reached his longjohns she screwed her eyes up tight, and then she felt him lift the blankets and slide into bed beside her.

For some moments they lay side by side in silence then his arm came across the pillows and gently pulled her to him. 'Sassy,' his voice came to her from the darkness, 'I just want yer to know that today you've made me the happiest man on earth.'

'Oh Jack,' she cried brokenly, but his finger pressed against her trembling lips and silenced her.

'Shush, love, an' listen a minute,' he said softly. 'Stop yer trembling. You've nothin' to fear from me, ever. I'll never lay a finger on yer, not unless yer want me to. An' if yer never do . . . well, that's all right an' all. I'm happy to have you as me wife any way I can. I know yer don't love me, but happen that'll come with time. For now I'm happy as I am.' And true to his words, he planted a gentle kiss on her lips then turning from her, he left her to her thoughts.

As Christmas approached, Maisie began to resemble a duck as she waddled about the place. She was now heavily pregnant and becoming impatient for the birth. Sassy, however, had never got over the sickness and became tired easily, and so Clara now came almost daily to help with the chores, which gave Jack an idea.

'Look, love,' he said to Sassy one evening as they were sitting companionably at the fireside, 'I've had an idea.'

'Oh yes, what's that then?' Sassy looked up from her darning.

'Well, the thing is, me mam an' dad ain't getting any younger, as yer know. I reckon me dad's finding his shifts down the pit hard goin' now, an' me mam's already here most days, ain't she?'

When Sassy nodded he hurried on, 'I got to thinkin'. Seein' as how my cottage is standin' empty like, how would you feel about them movin' in there, an' *both* helpin' out about the place?'

Sassy's face lit up with pleasure at the thought. 'Why, I think it's a fine idea!' she said eagerly. 'Do you reckon they'd come?'

Jack shrugged. 'We won't know if we don't ask them, will we?' he laughed.

'Then let's ask them right away, eh?' she cried, and the very next day that's exactly what they did.

Clara and Walter could see the sense in Jack's proposition and after giving it some thought, they readily agreed to it. And so it was that just a week before Christmas, much to everyone's delight, they left their own cottage in Tuttle Hill for the last time and moved into Jack's former home on the farm. Walter was only too glad to be leaving the pit and spending his working life outside in the fresh air.

Within days the couple had become invaluable about the place and for the first time in months, laughter returned to the farm.

Christmas came and went, and as the year 1886 approached, they woke up one morning to find the landscape hidden beneath a thick blanket of snow. Aaron had made James a sturdy wooden sledge for Christmas and the boy was delighted with the turn in the weather, as he had been longing to use it. The lad was slowly returning to his old happy self, and Clara felt a sense of hope blossoming in her heart.

As she pointed out to Walter one evening when they were sitting at the side of a roaring fire, 'I don't think I've ever seen our Jack so happy in his whole life, an' what with two new babies on the way, I reckon things are finally lookin' up.'

Walter squeezed her work-worn hand lovingly. 'Aye, let's just hope yer right, love,' he said, and Clara happily returned to her knitting.

One day in late January as Maisie waddled into her sitting room, an object in the corner of the room caught her eye. It was covered with a sheet and she pointed to it curiously.

'What's that?' she asked Aaron.

Grinning, Aaron gently pushed her in the back. 'Why don't yer go an' have a look?'

Maisie eagerly puffed across the room and grasping the sheet, she pulled it away, then looked down on a rocking cradle the like of which she had never seen in her life before.

'Oh Aaron,' she breathed. 'It's really beautiful.'

And indeed it was. The inside of it was so smooth that it reminded Maisie of silk as she ran her hand around it. All along its edge he had painstakingly carved tiny flowers and leaves, and as she gazed at it enthralled, in her mind's eyes she could imagine a tiny child laid within it beneath a pretty soft eiderdown.

'Thank you,' she said, her eyes full of happy tears.

'Don't thank me,' Aaron grinned. 'Just give me somethin' to put in it.' And exactly one week later, that's just what she did.

It was almost lunchtime and Maisie was crossing the yard with a wicker basket full of eggs she had just collected from the henhouse when the first pain gripped her. It was so sharp and severe that it almost bent her double. But then, as quickly as it had come, it was gone. She sucked in her breath as she cautiously straightened.

My God, this is it, she thought and hurried on to the kitchen door, but she had barely closed it behind her when another pain tore through her.

Sassy and Clara rushed to her as one, and immediately in control, Clara began to bark out orders. 'James,' her voice brooked no argument. 'Run outside now like a good lad an' fetch the men. They're gettin' the cows into the barn.'

Sensing that something important was about to happen, James immediately rushed away.

'Sassy, boil some water, an' lots of it, an' fetch some clean sheets and towels.' All the time she was leading Maisie towards the stairs and they had almost reached the foot of it, when the door banged back on its hinges and, white-faced, Aaron ran into the room, closely followed by Jack.

'Right, Jack!' she barked. 'Get yerself off, quick as yer can, an' fetch the doctor.'

Turning about, Jack hurried out as quickly as he had come in.

'An' you, young man,' her eyes went on Aaron, 'sit yerself down at that table an' don't move.'

Aaron, who was too afraid to argue, dropped onto the chair like a stone, and taking pity on him, Walter went to brew some tea.

One hour later, as Aaron anxiously paced the floor, a terrible scream rent the air and he stopped mid-stride. His eyes flew to the ceiling above, and as he stood staring, an uncanny silence settled on the room.

'I can't stand this no longer,' he said suddenly, and turning on his heel he headed for the staircase.

Walter gripped his arm. 'Hold on, lad,' he urged. 'Yer can't go up there just yet.'

Aaron shook him off roughly, but Walter was saved from further argument as Matthew and Jack rushed in through the kitchen door.

Matthew beamed broadly at Aaron's ashen face and patted him on the shoulder. 'Don't look so worried, man,' he smiled reassuringly. 'This is your first, she could be *hours* yet.' But the words had scarcely left his lips when another sound brought them all to a standstill as the plaintive cry of a newborn baby floated down the stairs.

'It seems I'll have to eat my words,' Matthew chuckled as he banged Aaron on the back. 'Someone obviously couldn't wait for me to get here.' And grinning broadly, he rushed away upstairs.

Twenty minutes later, he reappeared and nodded delightedly at Aaron. 'There's a young man upstairs waiting to meet his dad,' he informed him.

Aaron's eyes stretched wide. 'Is it *really* a lad?' he asked shakily.

'It most certainly is, and a fine bonny lad he is as well, if I may say so.'

Aaron didn't hear him. He was already taking the stairs two at a time.

When he entered the bedroom seconds later, Clara straightened her back from the bed where she was leaning over Maisie.

'Come on, lad,' she encouraged. 'Come an' meet yer new son.'

Aaron didn't answer her. He was too busy gazing in wonder at the sight before him. Maisie was propped back against the pillows, and no one would have believed that she had just given birth, for her eyes were sparkling and at her breast his new son was snuggling.

'Come an' see him, love.' She grinned happily as he approached the bed.

'Are you all right?' he asked emotionally.

Maisie giggled before telling him, 'I'm better than all right. I feel *wonderful*, Aaron. I don't know what all the fuss is about – it were easier than shellin' peas.'

He was sitting on the side of the bed now, gazing in awe at his perfect little son. Maisie then became serious and looked into his eyes.

'I were thinkin' we might call him Benjamin Aaron, for Ben and for Mrs Lee who gave you yer name. What do yer think?'

He nodded, his heart full of love for this remarkable young woman he was privileged to call his wife. 'I think that's a fine idea,' he agreed, and not wishing to intrude, Clara went out quietly and left the new family to themselves.

Benjamin was such a lovely baby that he was soon much adored by everyone. Clara in particular doted on him. He was a hungry little mite, always ready for a feed, and when she cuddled him, he put her so much in mind of Thomas that she could almost imagine it was him, once again a baby, whom she held.

Maisie astonished everyone, for after three days she flatly refused to lie in bed a moment longer and within a week was back in her old routine.

Sassy was now highly impatient for her own baby to arrive, but whereas Maisie had sailed through her pregnancy and the birth, Sassy was still having a hard time of it. Most of the time she was so exhausted that she only had to sit down and she would fall fast asleep.

'I don't know,' Clara confessed to Walter one evening. 'That lass ain't well, far from it, an' I have a bad feelin' about this baby.'

'Now that's enough o' that talk,' he scolded her. 'I reckon as you just want somethin' to worry about. Sassy will be fine, you'll see.'

Still Clara fretted. 'Aye, well, let's just hope yer right,' she muttered, and chewing on her lip, she let the subject drop.

Chapter Thirty-Five

Some days later, Clara stood in the market, carefully choosing some soft linen to make some more nightgowns for the baby. Benjamin already had a beautiful shawl, knitted by her, and now she was furiously knitting another one, ready for the arrival of Sassy's baby. She was just about to pay for it when a tap on her shoulder made her turn. Elizabeth was standing at her elbow.

'Good day, Clara,' she said coolly.

Clara inclined her head. Elizabeth had not set foot on the farm since the day the Will was read, and that suited Clara down to the ground. It was common knowledge that there was no love lost between Elizabeth and herself.

'So, how is *she* then?' Elizabeth asked, a slight sneer on her face.

'Who is she – the old cat's mother?' Clara bristled.

Elizabeth grinned maliciously. 'I think you know who I mean – *Sassy*.' Her voice held scorn. 'From what I hear she's about to give birth. And so soon after the wedding, eh? I mean, one minute Daniel deserts her, then she gets the farm left to her, *then* she snares poor Jack – and next thing you know, she's *expecting*. Mind you, I suppose it's no more than we should expect from the likes of her, is it?'

Clara gazed at her with contempt. 'Now, now, dear, put yer claws away.' Her voice was dangerously low. 'If you ain't careful, you'll have folks thinkin' yer jealous o' the lass. After all, she did, as yer put it, snare a husband, which is more than can be said of your Louise, ain't it? But still, don't worry too much. I'm *sure* you'll find someone daft enough to take her off yer hands – if you pay 'em enough.' And turning from Elizabeth she walked away, leaving Elizabeth to stare after her, red in the face with rage.

True to his word, not once since the day they had wed, had Jack placed a finger on Sassy, other than to give her a cuddle and a kiss. This had more than endeared him to her. Somehow she felt that, although they were married, it wouldn't have seemed right while Daniel's child was growing inside her. And yet she found herself looking forward to him coming in from the fields and enjoyed their cosy evenings together by the fire, and all things considered, she realised that she was very lucky to have him. None of this was lost on Clara, and sometimes when she saw them together, she would smile to herself.

'You know,' she commented to Walter one day, 'I've a feelin' that if we can just get this birthin' safe behind us, those two are goin' to make a go of it.'

Walter nodded in agreement. 'Well, *now* yer talking sense, woman.' He smiled. 'Everythin' has a way of comin' out right in the end, you'll see.'

Clara closed her eyes tight, and prayed that he might be right. But deep down she knew that Sassy still missed Daniel, for sometimes she would catch her staring off into space with a sad look in her eyes.

It was a fine clear morning early in March. There was more than a hint of spring in the air, and all about the farm primroses, crocuses, snowdrops and early flowering plants peeped from beneath the hedgerows. Jack was in fine high spirits and went about his chores humming happily to himself, and why shouldn't he? he asked himself. He finally had Sassy as his wife and in a few short weeks he would be a father. It was strange, but since the day he had placed the wedding ring on Sassy's finger, he had never thought of the child growing inside her as anything other than his own, and now he was looking forward to the birth impatiently.

In an alcove at the side of the fire in the kitchen stood a fine wooden cradle. It was almost identical to Benjamin's, which had been much admired by all, and Aaron had worked long hours deep into the night to ensure that he finished it on time for them. His gift had caused Sassy to cry with pleasure, and now every time her eyes lit on it, she would stroke her huge stomach lovingly.

Today, however, she was feeling far from well and went about her chores slowly. She had a niggling ache deep in the pit of her back and a feeling of complete exhaustion. Still, at least the child inside her was calm for once, and for that she was thankful. During the last two days she had felt it turning somersaults and it was a relief to have a rest from its constant kicking.

Clara entered the kitchen mid-morning, to find Sassy and Maisie busily baking. Benjamin was wrapped in a warm shawl, and was fast asleep propped on the rocking chair.

'Are you all right, lass?' she asked Sassy, thinking that her daughter-in-law looked even paler today than usual.

'Oh yes, I'm fine,' Sassy said. 'It's just a bit of back-ache, that's all, but I expect that's normal, lumping this lot around.'

'Aye, well, that's as may be.' Clara was unconvinced. 'Have you had any pains?'

'No, I haven't,' Sassy grinned. 'Now stop fussing and put the kettle on. I reckon me and Maisie are due for a tea break, and the men will be in soon wanting theirs, so make yourself useful.'

'Huh! Cheeky young bugger, you,' said Clara, then smiling she turned away to do as she was told.

The men had been in for their midday dinner and returned to their chores about the farm, and now Sassy was becoming extremely uncomfortable. Today the weight of the child seemed unnaturally heavy and as the day wore on, the pain in her back was becoming stronger. For some reason, she kept feeling the need to rush to the privy, and it was following one of these frequent visits, as she re-entered the kitchen, that a warm gush came from between her legs. She gazed in horror at Clara. 'I've wet myself!' she whispered in shame.

'No, you ain't, lass,' Clara reassured her calmly. 'Yer waters have broken.'

Sassy stared at her fearfully. 'You mean the baby's coming?'

'Aye, that's just what I mean.' She chuckled at Sassy's horrified expression. 'But don't look so worried. It can't stay in there for ever, yer know? An' happen now's as good a time as any. So come on, let's be havin' you. Up to bed, young lady, an' we'll get you prepared.'

Sassy nodded and was just about to do as she was told when the first breathtaking pain caused her to double over. When it eventually died away, she slowly straightened and gripped the edge of the table. She was sweating and hugging her swollen stomach as Clara crossed to her and placed her arm about her.

'Come on, lass,' she encouraged. 'Let's get you upstairs, eh?'

Sassy allowed herself to be led to the foot of the staircase.

'Shall I run an' fetch Jack?' questioned Maisie.

'No, lass, there's no need to go worryin' him just yet,' Clara said. 'They ain't all as quick as you, yer know. Happen when he comes in at teatime will be soon enough. In the meantime, you make us all a nice sup o' tea, eh?'

Maisie hurried away to do as she was asked.

Just as predicted, late afternoon, when the men entered the kitchen tired and hungry after their day's work, there was still no sign of the baby, although Clara was not unduly worried as yet. To her mind things were progressing nicely. Sassy's pains were now a few minutes apart and she was bearing up bravely.

Jack's eyes, however, were terrified as he gazed on his wife. 'Why didn't yer fetch me, Mam?' he scolded.

Clara looked at him fondly. 'There weren't no point, lad. She's doin' well, an' if I had fetched yer, what could you have done?'

'Shall I go for the midwife or the doctor?' His voice was fearful as Sassy writhed on the bed, deep in the grip of a contraction, but Clara shook her head.

'No, lad, there ain't no need for that yet. She's comin' along just fine and it shouldn't be too long now. But in the meantime, you get off an' have yer meal an' leave us to it. This is women's business, an' we can well do without you frettin' about us, now be off with yer.'

Even as she said it, she had him firmly by the elbow, propelling him towards the bedroom door. 'Go on, love,' she urged. 'Don't worry, I'll call if we need yer.'

With a last backward glance at Sassy, Jack slowly descended the stairs.

As darkness fell, the first misgivings began to flutter in Clara's stomach. By now, Sassy's pains were coming short and fast, but as yet there was no sign of the child. Hastily making a decision, she ran downstairs and beckoned to Aaron. 'Get yerself away, lad, an' fetch the doctor.'

Jack caught her arm. 'Is somethin' wrong, Mam?'

Clara patted his hand. 'No, lad, no, don't worry,' she soothed him as best she could. 'I'm only goin' on the cautious side. Better to be safe than sorry, eh?'

Jack nodded numbly as Clara turned from him and hurried back upstairs to Sassy.

The next hour was one of the longest Clara could ever remember, for in that time Sassy deteriorated rapidly. Unbidden, Clara's mind flew back across the years to another bedroom, another birth, in the cottages in Tuttle Hill. As she gazed on Sassy's pain-wracked body, she prayed as she had never prayed in her life before that Sassy would not go the same way as her mother.

After what seemed like a lifetime, Matthew entered the room and as he saw the seriousness of the situation, he flung off his coat, rolled up his sleeves and washed his hands thoroughly. Then he began to gently prod around Sassy's swollen abdomen, causing her to arch her back in agony. Eventually he straightened and looked at Clara with a deep frown creasing his forehead. 'It's breech,' he said.

Clara caught her breath. 'Can yer turn it?' she asked.

He sighed deeply before answering her truthfully. 'I'm not sure,' he said, and then bending back to the bed, he took Sassy's wrist and felt for her pulse. It was thready and irregular, and deeply concerned now, he stared up at Clara.

'Take her hands,' he ordered firmly. 'I'm going to try.'

Quickly she grasped Sassy's hands in hers and pressed them firmly into the mattress, and bending low now, Matthew carefully felt for the child. Sassy's scream was earsplitting and before it had even died away, the door banged back on its hinges and Jack fell into the room, but Matthew didn't even notice him. All his attention was firmly fixed on Sassy.

'It's no good,' he muttered in despair. 'I can't turn it, it's too far down.'

Clara stared at him angrily. 'Well, yer have to do *somethin*',' she snapped. 'An' quick, by the look of it.'

'There is something I could do,' he said, as he stroked his chin thoughtfully. 'But I have to warn you, it's not without risk.'

'What is it?' Jack's eyes were wild with fear as Matthew eyed him miserably.

'I could cut her and bring the child out in no time, but doing it that way, there's a risk that the shock could be too much for the child. We could lose it.'

Screwing his eyes up tight at the thought, Jack asked, 'What's the alternative?'

Matthew sighed. 'I can leave things to take their natural course, but to be honest, Sassy's at the end of her tether and I think if we do that, there's a very strong chance we could lose them both.'

'*No!*' Jack was so horrified that Clara leaped towards him and clutched him to her.

'Come on, lad,' she scolded him. 'Hold yerself together, we ain't got a choice. Look at her – she's slippin' away. At least the first way there's a chance.'

As the truth of his mother's words sank in, Jack bowed his head and said brokenly, 'Do it then.'

Taking up his bag, Matthew drew from it a wickedly sharp knife and gulping deep in his throat, he then took a deep breath to compose himself and bending to Sassy, he deftly did what had to be done.

For a second her agonised body seemed to rise from the bed, and in that instant, Matthew grasped the tiny foot now showing and gently pulled it. Within seconds the rest of the baby slithered out to lie between its mother's legs, unmoving on the bed as Matthew hastily cut the cord. He then turned his attention back to Sassy as she suddenly let out a great sigh and dropped back onto the pillows.

'Oh my God,' Jack gasped as panic flooded through him. 'Her heart's stopped.' He was trembling from head to foot. '*Do* somethin',' he implored Matthew, and as Clara snatched up the silent child, Matthew began to pump her chest relentlessly.

As the child was released from her body, Sassy suddenly had the sensation of being freed from the pain. Sighing gratefully, she closed her eyes and welcomed it, for after the long agonising hours she had just endured, this pain-free state was a blessed relief. She kept her eyes shut tight, fearful that at any second the pain would return, but after what seemed like an eternity, she cautiously opened them and gazed about her in delight. She was floating in a warm bright light. It was unlike any light she had ever seen, for its warmth seemed to envelop her. She was hovering there contentedly when a soft hand slipped into hers, and turning she found her mother Sarah standing beside her. It seemed right that she should be there and Sassy welcomed her lovingly. Sarah was just as beautiful as she remembered her, and her presence only added to the young woman's sense of blissful well-being.

Something in the brightness behind them caught Sarah's attention and she slowly turned. As Sassy's eyes followed her mother's, they came to rest upon George, who held a tiny bundle close to his chest. Her heart filled with love at the sight of him as he returned her smile. 'Look there, love,' said Sarah. Sassy looked – and to her surprise found herself looking down into her bedroom.

Matthew was bent over the bed, sweat pouring from him as he furiously worked on what appeared to be a body lying there. Sassy gazed curiously, but try as she might, she couldn't make out who the body was, for

Matthew was blocking the face from her sight. Clara too was trying to blow life into the body of a tiny baby, but it was the sight of Jack that held her attention, for he was standing to the side of the bed, his face stricken.

Her heart went out to him in pity. 'Who is it?' she asked curiously.

'It's *you*, my pet,' her mother answered.

Just then, Matthew slowly rose from the bed and to her amazement, Sassy saw her own body laid beneath her.

'You *have* to go back, Sassy,' her mother whispered urgently.

Tears squeezed from the corner of Sassy's eyes. 'No, Mam. I want to stay here with you.'

'You can't, love – it's not your time yet,' her mother told her. 'You have your whole life before you. You must go back and live it.' Sarah pointed to the room below them once more. 'Look at Jack,' she said. 'He loves you *so* much – he always has. If you leave him now, his life will be over too. Not only that, there's someone else who needs you now.'

A thin wail suddenly pierced the air, followed by Clara's cry of triumph as she held aloft a tiny, flame-haired infant.

'It's a girl!' Clara cried exultantly, and Sassy's heart suddenly flooded with love.

'It's *your* little girl.' Sarah's voice came to her. 'Now you *must* go back. But never fear – I'm always near you.' Even as she spoke she was stepping away from Sassy, and as Sassy watched her, she took George's hand and she, her son and her still-born daughter, James's twin, slowly entered what appeared to be a long tunnel, from which the warm light seemed to be spilling. 'Goodbye for now, my love,' her mother whispered. 'You will have a good life, I promise.' She was drifting further away and now, Sassy could see other beings gently joining her in the light.

'Goodbye, Mam,' she whispered, and as the tears poured down her face she found herself all alone, and the glorious light began to fade.

As her eyes jerked open, a joyous shout echoed about the room and Jack pulled her into his arms, hugging her fiercely. 'Oh lass,' he cried, sobbing unashamedly. 'Don't ever scare me like that again. I thought I'd lost yer then fer sure.'

She offered him a weak smile and looking like the cat that had got the cream, Matthew wagged a finger at her, beaming all the while. 'I'll second that,' he said, exhausted, but then Sassy's weary eyes fell on Clara, who was offering her a tiny bundle wrapped in a shawl.

'Here you are, lass.' She sniffed as she struggled to keep her emotions under control. 'Here's the cause of all the trouble. She's a scrawny little mite, but there's nowt wrong with her as a bit o' fattenin' up won't cure.'

As Sassy stared incredulously at her tiny little daughter, her heart overflowed with love. 'I want to call her Rose, and her middle name can be Sarah after my mother,' she whispered.

With the tears still wet on his cheeks, Jack nodded in delight. 'I think that's a lovely name,' he agreed and smiling, Sassy drifted off into a peaceful sleep, the first step on her long road to recovery.

Although it took Sassy many weeks to recover from Rose's birth, still she would come to remember it as a happy time. She could never have too much of her perfect little daughter, and like Jack she spoiled her unashamedly. She was a beautiful baby, with flawless ivory skin and flaming red hair that framed her face in wispy little curls. At first sight of her hair, Sassy feared that it would remind

Jack of the fact that Rose was Daniel's child, but she needn't have worried, for Jack totally adored her. Unlike Benjamin who could often be heard screaming lustily for a feed, Rose was an undemanding child. James was completely besotted with her and when allowed he would spend ages cradling her in his arms, content to simply hold her.

As Sassy watched Jack's devotion to the little girl grow, so her fondness for him increased. Occasionally her heart would fill with pain when she imagined Daniel in his place, but then it hardened as she remembered the way he had used her, just as Thomas had before him, and she would try her best to put him from her mind and be thankful for Jack.

It was Clara who suggested a double christening, and the idea was met with enthusiasm from all sides. And so it was that in the first week in June 1886, on a fine Sunday afternoon, a merry party set out for Chilvers Coton Church, where Benjamin Aaron Lee and Rose Sarah Mallabone were duly baptised by a delighted Reverend Rigby.

For the first time since the reading of the Will, Elizabeth reluctantly set foot on the farm. Arthur had made it more than clear to her that if she didn't wish to attend the party following the christening, then he would go alone. Not wishing to lose face, she begrudgingly consented. Just like everyone else, Arthur was completely enthralled by his little granddaughter, but at first sight of her, Elizabeth's heart contracted, for the child's flaming red hair caused a shock to course through her.

What have I done? she thought to herself, as she remembered the lies she had told to Daniel and Faith, but then she pushed the thought to the back of her mind. At present she had more pressing things to worry about, namely Louise.

Much to Elizabeth's shame, the girl had recently been seen in the company of a miner who worked at a local pit. The fact had caused Elizabeth to cringe, for the lad came from the poorer part of the town and she considered him to be far beneath her daughter. Still, when confronted, Louise had adamantly refused to stop seeing him and now Elizabeth could only pray that the affair would sizzle out. It never occurred to the woman that she herself had come from humble beginnings and that Arthur had been a miner too when she married him.

The party that followed the christening was a joyous occasion, and by the time the last of the guests had departed, Sassy and Jack were in fine spirits. Maisie and Aaron had taken Benjamin, screaming lustily for a feed, back to their own rooms, and Clara and Walter had returned arm-in-arm to the cottage.

Sassy was sitting next to Rose's cradle where the child lay fast asleep, exhausted but content, and Jack gazed on his little family thankfully. It was a beautiful evening, and after a while, he stood and drew Sassy gently to her feet.

'Come with me, lass,' he said, his eyes full of love. 'I have somethin' to show yer.' He led her around to the back of the farmhouse, her hand still fast in his. Then he guided her through the orchard until at last they came to the vegetable patch.

'Now then,' he commanded, 'close yer eyes till I tell yer to open 'em.' Sassy obediently screwed her eyes tight shut and trustingly allowed Jack to lead her along.

'Where are you taking me?' she asked, but Jack was determined to keep his surprise a secret until the very last minute.

'Never you mind,' he said, his voice happy. 'You just keep yer eyes shut and do as yer told for once.' Presently he drew her to a stop and told her, 'All right, lass. Yer can look now.'

Sassy opened her eyes and gazed round incredulously. Before her was a circular flowerbed, full of roses, exactly as her mother's had been so many years ago.

'Do yer like it?' he asked, his voice anxious, but for now Sassy couldn't answer him; she could only stare in awe.

'I did it as near to the one yer mam had as I could remember. I knew you missed seein' yer mam's an' thought perhaps you'd like to have a rosebed of yer own.'

As Sassy thought of all the hours he must have put into the making of the rosebed, a little corner of her heart that had been firmly shut since Daniel's betrayal slowly opened and allowed him in. He was staring at her, waiting nervously for her reaction, and tearing her eyes away at last from the multi-coloured rosebushes, Sassy took both of his hands in her own.

'It's the most beautiful, thoughtful gift I've ever had,' she told him.

Delighted with her reaction, Jack gathered her into his arms and as she nestled against his broad chest, unbidden, Sarah's words came back to her on the night of Rose's birth. *You will have a good life, I promise.*

That night, as usual, Jack carefully carried Rose, still in her cradle, into the bedroom and placed her at the side of the bed.

'I'll just go an' lock up, love,' he whispered.

When he returned, some time later, his eyes stretched wide with astonishment, for Sassy was sitting up in bed waiting for him, her breasts bare. He quickly lowered his eyes in confusion, but her voice came to him clearly from the dimness.

'I think it's time, Jack,' she said.

He shook his head. 'Now, lass, yer don't have to do nothin' yer don't want to do. I told yer that on the day we were wed an' I meant it.'

'I know you did,' she murmured. 'But I *do* want to.'

His heart beating wildly in his chest, he lifted the covers and crept in beside her. 'Are yer sure about this?' he asked, and drawing his lips down to hers, Sassy nodded.

'I've never been more sure of anything in my whole life,' she whispered, and as the darkness wrapped itself around them she finally became Jack's wife in every sense of the word, although part of her heart would always remain with Daniel.

Chapter Thirty-Six

Much to everyone's delight, almost a year to the day following Benjamin's birth, Maisie presented Aaron with a fine healthy daughter. Her birth, like her brother's before her, was swift and easy, and they called the little girl Katie.

An air of well-being seemed to surround Holly Bush Farm. Clara and Walter were settled contentedly into their cottage, where Florica stayed with them whilst her gypsy family were in the area, and Rose was growing into a bright-eyed, mischievous little imp. Unlike Benjamin, who was a chubby little lad, Rose was delicate and petite, but what she lacked in size she more than made up for in energy.

Sassy had just come from Aaron and Maisie's living-quarters, and dropping down beside Jack, she said happily, 'Katie's a lovely little girl, isn't she?'

He nodded in agreement. 'Aye she is, lass, though not as lovely as our Rose.'

She thumped him playfully on the arm. 'Oh, you're just biased. You spoil her,' she scolded.

He grinned and her heart warmed with gratitude as she gazed at him. Over the last months she had come to be at ease in his company and now had a great fondness for him. True, it wasn't the breathtaking love and passion that she had felt for Thomas and Daniel, but a joyous feeling all the same, and every day she thanked God for him and counted herself lucky to have him.

'You know,' she said, thoughtful now, 'I hope we have a baby one day – a son for you.'

At the thought, a mixture of emotions crossed Jack's face. As much as he would have loved a son, he had never forgotten how close he had come to losing Sassy when she gave birth to Rose, and the thought filled him with fear.

Gazing into her serious face he told her, 'If it's meant to be, it'll be. But yer know, love, I've got you an' Rose, an' that's all I need.'

They became silent for a time as he watched the firelight playing across her face, and then he said, 'I've been thinkin', it's goin' to be mighty cramped fer Maisie and Aaron in those rooms now that Katie's come along.'

'I've been thinking the same,' Sassy said. 'They barely have room to swing a cat around now.'

'So why don't we build them a cottage then?' he suggested.

Sassy's eyes lit up at the idea. 'Oh Jack, you're so clever!' She clapped her hands in excitement. 'Why didn't I think of that? We could build it somewhere close to Clara and Walter's.'

'That's what I were thinkin'.' He pulled her into his arms for a cuddle, and for the rest of the evening they could talk of nothing else.

The very next morning, bright and early, they put the idea to Maisie and Aaron. Maisie cried with delight at the thought, but proud to the end, Aaron shook his head adamantly.

'Yer can't do that, man!' he exclaimed. 'We've barely time to do the work about the farm as it is let alone find time to build a cottage.'

But Jack stood his ground. 'Don't talk so daft,' he argued. 'We'll do it in our spare time between us. An' anyway, think on. Once it's done we can take on another

414

pair o' hands, for your rooms will be empty – so you'll be doin' us all a favour in the long run.'

As the sense of Jack's words sank in, Aaron chewed his lip thoughtfully. 'You're on then,' he agreed, and Maisie let out a whoop of delight.

The very next week, the bricks were delivered from Elizabeth's brother's brickworks and from then on Jack, Walter and Aaron spent almost every spare minute they had on digging the foundations and erecting the cottage.

It was a fine summer's evening. The men as usual were busily building, and the women, with the children all safely tucked into bed, were enjoying a restful hour's gossip. Ada, a frequent visitor, was gleefully filling them in on the latest news from Swan Lane and all eyes were on her agog, for news it was indeed.

'Aye,' she grinned at their staring faces. 'It was a right to-do, I don't mind tellin' yer. Miss Louise comes in bold as brass an' tells the mistress she intends to wed the miner she's been walkin' out wi', an' the mistress were yellin' like a common fishwife.'

They were all grinning now at the picture she had conjured up, and well in her stride, Ada continued, 'I thought she were heading for a seizure, I tell yer, an' she told Miss Louise in no uncertain terms that she would never consent to having a miner fer a son-in-law after all she's spent on her education.'

Unable to help herself, Sassy was giggling as she enquired curiously, 'And what did Louise say?' Her father never passed on any of the household gossip when he called but then, that was men for you. Thank goodness they could rely on Ada.

The cook lowered her voice, almost as if her mistress could hear. 'She said what were so wrong wi' her marryin' a miner when Elizabeth had done exactly the same when she married Arthur? The mistress hadn't got no answer to that, she just sat there wi' her mouth gawpin' open an' then the gel just turned on her heel an' stormed out o' the room. Red in the face she were, an' she ain't hardly left her room since.'

Clara tutted. 'Huh, I should think Elizabeth'd be grateful there's someone to offer, fer they ain't exactly queuing up fer her, are they?'

Sassy slapped her hand playfully. 'Now then, Clara,' she grinned. 'Don't be spiteful.'

'I'll tell yer somethin' else an' all,' Clara went on. 'It could be the makin' of that lass if she did wed him, fer Elizabeth's given her ideas above her station ever since she could walk.'

Ada nodded, setting her chins wobbling. 'Yer right there, pet,' she agreed. 'But the mistress is so against it, she's told Miss Louise she'll cut her off wi'out a penny if she so much as even sees him again.'

'Aye well, that's as maybe, but if I know Louise she'll have her own way in the end, and good luck to her, that's what I say. It's about time somebody brought Elizabeth down a peg or two!' And so saying, Clara lapsed into a thoughtful silence.

The new cottage came on in leaps and bounds and by the end of July, after hours and hours of hard toil, the inner and outer walls were finished and they began on the roof. Like Clara and Walter's cottage it was built all on one floor and as it began to take shape, Maisie would wander from room to room excitedly. It was somewhat larger than Clara's and once finished it would boast three bedrooms. Maisie could barely wait for its completion.

It was Arthur who furnished the women at the farm with the next instalment of Louise's predicament. He was sitting at the side of the table bouncing a joyous

Rose on his knee when he said casually, 'Louise is gone, you know.'

'What do you mean, *gone*?' Sassy asked.

Her father shrugged. 'She's left home,' he said. 'She didn't come down to breakfast this morning, an' fer a start Elizabeth thought she were sulkin', so she left her to it. Eventually she went up to Louise's room and there weren't a sign of her.' He couldn't help but grimace as he remembered his wife's rage.

'Where do you think she's gone?' asked Sassy.

Arthur tickled Rose beneath her chin, setting her giggling with delight. 'I ain't got a clue,' he said. 'But I'll tell yer what, I'm keepin' well out o' the way till Elizabeth has calmed down a bit, fer there's no talkin' to her at the minute.'

Sassy stared at her father, deeply concerned. 'Will you be all right, Dad?' she asked.

'Oh yes, I'll be all right,' he chuckled. 'To tell yer the truth, I'm so used to Elizabeth's moods now, they just flow over me like water off a duck's back.' And so saying he gave Rose his complete attention and for now the subject was dropped.

For months it was almost as if Louise had dropped off the face of the earth. Although Elizabeth made a few discreet enquiries, pride forbade her from prying too deeply and she continued about her business with her head held high as usual. Unbeknown to her, she was in fact the subject of much gossip, for Louise's whereabouts were common knowledge to many, and those who knew where she was waited in gleeful expectation for the day that Elizabeth would find out.

Arthur's life during that time was barely worth living. With Louise gone and Matthew hardly ever in the house, he was the one who took the full brunt of her moods, so much so, that eventually he began to call in at the farm almost every evening on his way home from work. Elizabeth suddenly found herself a very lonely woman.

It was one afternoon following a visit to one of her influential friends, who, the maid had informed her, for the second time that week, was out, that she decided to take a short-cut through the marketplace. She didn't normally take this route but today, following what she felt sure was a snub, she was eager to get home and hurried along, rage lending speed to her daintily shod feet.

She was just rounding the bend of Abbey Street when she almost collided with a group of women who were standing in a tight group on the cobbles laughing uproariously. As Elizabeth quickly moved aside to avoid them, a hush fell on the little group. She gazed at them superciliously and was just about to go on, when one of the women stepped out from the rest and stood in her path.

'What's up?' sneered the woman, who was Moll Twigger. 'Afraid to touch us commoners, are yer, for fear you'll catch sommat?' She planted her hands on her hips and stared with dislike at Elizabeth, but the latter returned the woman's stare unflinchingly.

'Kindly move out of my way,' she said coldly.

Moll's lip curled with contempt. 'Ooh, 'ark at 'Er Ladyship – *kaindly move hout of my way*,' she mimicked, and the group of women began to giggle, for they were enjoying themselves immensely. Moll's ample bosom was almost falling over the low-cut neck of her blouse and Elizabeth eyed her disdainfully.

'I suppose you think you're being funny,' she quipped, 'but you know, I do have better things to do than stand here with the likes of you.'

A little group of curious passers-by was now assembling about them and Elizabeth felt a flush of embarrassment flood her face, but Moll, now well in her stride, laughed harshly.

'I don't know 'ow yer can say the likes o' *me*,' she goaded. 'After all, now yer daughter's wed to Charlie Duffy an' livin' in the slums, I'd 'ave thought as you'd class *me* as well off.'

The other women were laughing openly now, and as the meaning of Moll's words sank in, Elizabeth's face stiffened. Moll noted this with satisfaction, and determined to sink the knife even further in, she cocked her eyebrows and went on, 'What's up, gel, didn't yer know? Well, well . . . 'appen yer didn't – but then they say as pride comes before a fall, don't they? An' 'appen yer gel couldn't 'ave fallen much lower than Charlie, for even I, who's known for not bein' fussy, wouldn't take money from the likes o' *him*.'

Moll viewed Elizabeth's chalk-white face with mock concern. 'Eeh, don't look so shocked, gel,' she chided her. 'Happen when yer see yer first grandchild you'll forgive 'er, eh? An' judgin' by the size of 'er you'll not have to wait long, 'cos she's as big as the side of a house – not that she weren't already afore she fell fer the nipper.'

This final blow was just too much for Elizabeth, and dignity suddenly forgotten, she gathered her skirts into an unladylike bunch and fled unsteadily across the cobbles, never once stopping until she reached the privacy of her own four walls.

When she almost fell into the hallway, dishevelled, sobbing and breathless, Ada was dumbfounded, for never once in all her years of employment there, had she ever seen her mistress in such a state.

'Eeh, whatever's happened?' she said, taking Elizabeth firmly by the arm. 'Come wi' me now an' let's make yer a nice strong cup o' tea.'

Elizabeth meekly allowed herself to be led to the

kitchen, where she sank slowly onto a hard wooden chair. Ada put the kettle on and once the tea was placed before her mistress, she asked softly, 'What is it? What's upset yer so?'

Elizabeth gazed back at her from anguished eyes. 'It's Louise.' Hot tears had sprung to her eyes. 'I've just heard from Moll Twigger that she's wed Charlie Duffy from the slums.'

Ada nodded slowly. 'Well, to tell the truth, I've heard the same,' she admitted.

'Then *why* didn't you tell me!' Elizabeth rasped.

Ada shook her head sadly. 'It weren't my place,' she said. 'But if it's true, then yer have to accept it. It's no use cryin' over spilled milk. What's done is done, an' at the end o' the day, Louise is old enough to please herself.'

Ignoring the tea, Elizabeth rose slowly from the table and left the room without a word.

'Poor woman,' Ada muttered to herself. 'I can't help but feel sorry fer yer. But the truth of it is, you've been settin' yerself up for a fall fer some long time now, wi' all yer fancy airs an' graces. Happen now yer must face the consequences.' And lifting Elizabeth's cup from the table, she tipped the contents into the sink.

Chapter Thirty-Seven

The cottage was finally finished and Maisie was beside herself with excitement as she and Aaron and the children prepared to move in. The fields were too uneven to allow a horse and cart to pass over them, so Jack, Aaron and Walter laboriously transported each piece of furniture there by hand.

As they delivered each piece, puffing and panting, Maisie determined where they would put it, and slowly the empty cottage began to resemble a home. Clara was close at hand, helping to hang curtains at the windows, and after the delivery of the handsome oak dresser, Maisie started filling it with china and gazed at Clara happily, her eyes alight.

'Yer know,' she confided when the men had departed to fetch the beds, 'it's a good job we had three bedrooms.'

Clara paused to eye her fondly. 'What yer sayin, lass?'

Maisie giggled. 'Well, I reckon I'm expectin' again.'

'Bloody 'ell, lass!' Clara chuckled. 'An' Katie not nine months old yet – yer goin' to have yer hands full, fer sure.'

'I know,' Maisie said with a contented sigh. 'That's why I had the cottage built so close to yours, so you could help out.'

'Yer cheeky young bugger, you,' Clara grinned, but inside her heart turned in her chest. She of all people knew how much Sassy wanted to give Jack a son, and she wondered how she would take the news of Maisie's latest pregnancy.

She needn't have worried, however. Being the generous nature she was, Sassy was delighted for her friends, though she openly admitted to being more than a little envious, and said as much to Clara.

'Do you think Jack an' I will *ever* have a baby?' she questioned wistfully.

Clara stared her straight in the eye. 'I can't answer that, lass,' she said. 'I'm a firm believer that our destinies are all writ in the stars afore we take our first breath. But what I will say is this; if it's meant to be, then it'll be, an' if not, then yer should be thankful fer what you've got.'

As the truth of Clara's words, by which Sassy set great store, sank in, she nodded thoughtfully. Then as her eyes lit on Rose happily charging about on her unsteady little legs in hot pursuit of James and a wildly excited Oscar, the smile returned to her face. She had a lot to be thankful for. Rose was now a beautiful flame-haired toddler, and on top of that she had a doting husband, although she still sometimes felt Daniel's loss and suffered all manner of guilt because of it. 'Clara's right,' she said to herself, but yet for all that, her heart still yearned to present Jack with a son. She felt that she owed him that much at least.

Maisie and Aaron were well settled into their new home when she gave birth to yet another bouncing baby boy. Little Rose was totally in awe of the new addition and would sit at the side of the cradle, so lovingly carved by Aaron, for hours. They called the new baby George for Sassy, and because of this, Sassy had more than a soft spot for him, but still for her and Jack there was no sign of another child, and deep in her heart she began to despair.

They had been married for just over three years, when Sassy awoke one morning and rushed off to the privy to be violently sick. She welcomed the nausea joyously, for it helped to confirm what she had scarcely dared to believe for the past two months. Yet still she didn't whisper a word to Jack until after she had paid a visit to Matthew.

'Yes, you're pregnant all right,' he told her, 'but you must promise me after the last time that you'll take it easy.'

'Oh I will, I promise!' she exclaimed as she pressed her hands tight together with delight, and Matthew couldn't help but grin. Already she was hovering at the door, anxious to be gone and pass the good news on to Jack.

Once the initial sickness of the early months passed, almost as if someone had suddenly waved a magic wand, to everyone's relief, Sassy blossomed and the rest of her pregnancy passed uneventfully. It was one evening as she and Jack were approaching their fourth wedding anniversary that Sassy went into labour, and Jack flew into a high panic. Matthew was sent for post haste, but by the time he arrived, it was all over bar the shouting. Sassy was already red in the face and bearing down, prompted by Clara, and Matthew saw at once that he was only just in time for the birth.

Within minutes of his being in the room, Sassy suddenly gave an almighty determined push, and a beautiful black-haired boy almost catapulted from her into Clara's waiting hands.

When all was clean and tidy, and the new mother had been given a cup of tea, Jack was allowed to come into the bedroom. Beside himself with joy, he gazed at his new son in awe. The child was a tiny mirror image of himself, from his black springing curls to his deep blue eyes.

Sassy viewed the scene with high elation as Clara threw her apron across her face and tears of relief sprang from her eyes.

Oblivious to the rest of the people in the room, Jack

carried his son to the window, and drawing back the curtains, exposed him to the perfect starlit night.

The stars were uncommonly bright and seemed to twinkle a welcome to the child, as Jack planted a tender kiss on his still damp forehead. 'Look, son,' he whispered. 'This is where you'll live with me an' yer mam an' Rose, an' one day all this will be yours.'

As if understanding his father's words the baby gazed up at him silently for some moments, then suddenly let out a lusty yell.

Her heart full at the sight of father and son, Clara beamed before ordering him, 'Get your son and heir back to his mother. Happen right now he'd sooner have a suckle than view his inheritance.'

Jack tenderly handed Sassy their newborn son.

'How can I ever thank yer, lass?' His voice was full of emotion.

'You don't have to, Jack,' she whispered. 'It's *me* that should be thanking you.'

She knew that all Jack longed for now was to hear her tell him that she loved him. He was a wonderful husband and father, but still her heart belonged to Daniel and she couldn't bring herself to say it, although she did have a great fondness for him and counted herself a lucky woman to have him.

Clara grabbed Matthew by the hand and pulled him towards the door. 'Come on, lad,' she urged. 'They don't need us any more.'

Matthew glanced over his shoulder. 'Do you know, Clara,' he smiled, 'I think you're right.' And gently pulling the door to behind him, he left the little family to become acquainted.

Arthur was as pleased as Punch with his new grandson, but underneath, Elizabeth was seething. It all seemed so pointless now, the way she had managed to talk Daniel into leaving Sassy. The girl had still managed to come out on top in the end. There she was, the owner of a fine farm, with a doting husband, a daughter, and now a fine healthy son, whilst Louise lived in little more than a slum dwelling, with nothing but a common miner for a husband. She still flinched every time she thought of it, for Moll Twigger's words had cut deep, and even when news reached her that Louise had given birth to a little girl, still she adamantly refused to see her or the child. She was bitterly disappointed with her daughter's choice and could never forgive her for the humiliation she had caused her.

All her hopes were now firmly pinned on Matthew making a good marriage, but as yet that seemed a long way off. As Dr Massey's practice flourished, her son spent more and more of his time working, and was hardly ever in the house – apart from when he came back to sleep. Even so, she had at least three possibilities lined up for him, since some of her wealthy friends had not snubbed her, and three of those families had daughters of a marriageable age. She pushed him in their direction at every opportunity.

However, unbeknownst to Elizabeth, Matthew already had his eye set firmly on the girl of his choice, and knowing that she wouldn't meet with his mother's approval, he wisely held his tongue.

Sassy and Jack had named their baby John William, but from the day of his birth he became known as 'Little Jack', for in every way he was a miniature copy of his father. An easy child, he seemed to gain weight by the day, and was much adored by everyone, particularly Rose who could hardly bear to let her little brother out of her sight.

It was a bitterly cold night in the first winter of Little Jack's life when Matthew called into the farm on his way home for a warming cup of tea. As usual his welcome was hearty, and he sat contentedly at the side of the flickering fire. Rose and Little Jack had long since been tucked into bed and he, Sassy and Jack were chatting away happily.

Sassy was laughing, telling him of Florica's mischievous antics that day. Just as she did whenever her gypsy grandparents were in the area, the child was staying with Clara and Walter in their cottage at present for a few weeks. She had done this regularly since Thomas's death and Clara delighted in having her. James and she seemed to get up to all sorts of mischief during these visits, yet for all that, they all looked forward to her coming, and always felt her loss sadly when she departed.

Sometimes Sassy would pinch herself to make sure that she wasn't dreaming, for life now was better than it had been for many a long year.

Her children were a constant source of joy to her, even if she felt a pang sometimes when she looked at Rose. The lass was so like her father that Sassy couldn't help but regret that Daniel wasn't even aware of her existence.

The rose garden Jack had created for her flourished, and she never grew tired of tending it, just as her mother had tended hers all those years ago in the garden of the cottage in Tuttle Hill. During the summer months there was always a vase of roses in the middle of the table, but now, as winter closed its icy arms about the farm, the rosebed lay sleeping beneath a thick blanket of snow.

Matthew and Jack were each enjoying a large glass of cider made from the apples in the orchard, and a companionable silence had fallen on them. However, glancing at Matthew, Sassy noted his frown and asked, 'Is there anything troubling you, Matthew?'

Feeling that he could trust these two, he nodded and sighed, 'Yes, there is.' His voice was low and Sassy, instantly concerned for this man whom she loved as a brother, urged him on.

'Is it something we can help you with?'

'Not really,' Matthew told her, 'but thank you, all the same. You see, for some time I've been seeing someone – a young lady – and I have to admit that I've come to love her and want to marry her. Today I asked her – and she said yes.'

Sassy was beaming with delight. 'Why,' she cried, 'that's *wonderful*! What could possibly be wrong with that, if you both feel the same about each other?'

He laughed bitterly. 'It's *who* she is, that's what's wrong with it, for I know my mother won't approve and I don't know what to do about it.'

Jack stepped in now. 'Do yer want to tell us who it is?' he asked, unable to contain his curiosity.

Matthew shrugged. 'It's Victoria, the vicar at Coton's daughter.'

'But Victoria's a lovely girl,' Sassy said, puzzled. 'What could Elizabeth have against her?'

'My mother had her mind set on me marrying one of her high-falutin friends' daughters,' Matthew said bleakly, 'and after Louise marrying Charlie, she'll never consider Victoria. Her father is as poor as a church mouse, even though she has had a genteel upbringing. But I'll tell you now, there's more to that girl than meets the eye. She's kind and loving and generous, and she'd give away her last penny, if anyone needed it.'

Sassy and Jack glanced at each other, and then leaning towards him, Jack gently squeezed his arm. 'Take my advice, man,' he said quietly. 'Follow yer heart, an' don't give a thought to what yer mam thinks. You have yer own life to lead, an' if yer give Victoria up now, you'll regret it fer the rest of yer life.'

Matthew thought on Jack's words for some minutes

then raising his eyes, which now held hope, he asked, 'Do you really think so?'

Jack nodded firmly. 'Aye I do,' he said. 'Life's too short to miss out on the things that are important, so go with yer heart an' shame the devil, that's what I say. For what my opinion is worth, I think you've made a wise choice. Victoria's a fine lass so don't let anythin' yer mam says make yer think any different. Though I have to admit, yer could knock me down wi' a feather. I had no idea yer were even seein' the lass.'

Sassy was in complete agreement with Jack. 'He's right, Matthew, an' don't worry if your mother turns her back on you like she did Louise. There's Aaron an' Maisie's living-quarters standing empty above the barn, an' you'd both be more than welcome to use them till you found something more suitable.'

As Matthew gazed at these two dear friends, his throat was full. And then a slow smile spread across his face. 'You're right,' he decided. 'I'll do it and I thank you both from the bottom of my heart.' And so saying, he rose quickly. 'There's no time like the present,' he grinned. 'And no sense in stalling so I'll go and talk to my mother right now.'

Jack thumped him heartily on the back. 'That's the spirit, man! Nothin' ventured, nothin' gained, eh?'

'Wish me luck, both of you,' Matthew said, as he gathered his things and drank the last of his cider. 'I'm going to need it!'

When he arrived home and confronted Elizabeth with his news, she almost choked with rage.

'You bloody *fool*, you!' she stuttered furiously. '*Victoria!* Her father couldn't even afford to settle a dowry on her. What are you thinking of, Matthew? You could have anyone you choose.'

Matthew's rage was rising to meet hers. 'I suppose you'd sooner tie me to one of those damn snobby daughters of your friends.'

'Yes, I would,' she snapped. 'At least they have class in their favour.'

'Huh,' Matthew grunted. 'Then I'm sorry to disappoint you, Mother. I have no intention of paying court to any of those flibberty-gibbets. Victoria *does* have breeding – and if you don't bloody like it, then you'll bloody well have to lump it!' And with that he turned on his heel and marched from the room.

The very next day, Matthew packed his bags and moved into the rooms above Dr Massey's surgery nearby, and five weeks later, after the Banns were read, he and Victoria were wed in her father's church.

For weeks Elizabeth barely left the house. Matthew's marriage was the talk of the town, and to her this was the final straw. She was a laughing-stock amongst her friends. They all knew how much she had wanted her son to marry a girl with a title at least, so now with her pride in tatters she avoided them studiously. Luckily, it was she and not Arthur who managed the household accounts, for from then on, the wine bill came to more than the food bill each week. Ada found this strange, because until then Elizabeth had adamantly refused to have alcohol in the house. Yet now she seemed unable to face the day without it. Realising that it was her mistress's only pleasure now, like Arthur Ada chose to ignore it, watching helplessly as Elizabeth slowly slipped into an alcoholic decline.

Chapter Thirty-Eight

Sassy was busily washing the Sunday dinner pots on a bitterly cold day in January 1892 as four-year-old Little Jack climbed impatiently over his father, who was sitting to the side of the fire. She smiled indulgently as she heard him say, '*Please*, Daddy.'

Rose, now a bright eight year old, immediately added her pleas to those of her brother.

'Come on, Daddy,' she begged him. 'Let us take our sledges out.'

'But the snow's a foot thick,' Jack objected. 'We'll freeze to death.'

'No, we won't – we can wrap up warm.' The girl sensed her father weakening, and picking up on it, Little Jack too gazed at his father imploringly.

Sassy grinned, guessing that they would soon get their way. Jack could never deny them anything for long, and sure enough, she was proved right.

Laughing, he rose from the chair. 'All right then,' he said. 'But take heed, it's only fer half an hour now.'

The children danced with excitement before rushing off to the cupboard to pull out their warm coats.

'Do you fancy a stroll, love?' he asked Sassy.

'Not on your life,' she shivered. 'I'll stay in the warm, thank you very much. It's freezing out there. You must be mad, giving in to them.'

He grinned sheepishly back at her. 'I dare say you're right, but like I said, it'll only be for half an hour.'

Minutes later, they all stood warmly clad at the door and the minute Jack opened it, the children scampered off eagerly to drag their sledges from the barn.

Jack watched their progress before turning to Sassy and planting a tender kiss on her lips. 'Have I told yer lately, lass, how very much I love you?'

He was serious now, and poking him playfully in the ribs, Sassy replied, 'Well, not since this morning.' She pushed him gently out into the cold. 'Now be off with you, an' leave me in peace.'

When Jack had crossed the yard to join Rose and Little Jack he suggested, 'How about if we call an' see Aaron an' the kids an' Grandad Walter to see if they want to come with us?'

The children squealed their approval and when they were halfway across the first field and the cottages came into sight they whooped with delight and ran off ahead. A smile played about Jack's lips as he watched them. Smoke was spiralling from the chimneys of the cottages, and nestled in the snow they reminded him of a picture he had once seen on a big box of chocolates. He could never remember a time when he had felt so content. Life is just about as good as it can get, he thought to himself, and his smile stretched even wider.

Soon afterwards, the menfolk herded the children away amidst joyous shouts while Maisie and Clara made their way to spend a peaceful hour with Sassy back at the farm.

'Ah peace, perfect peace,' Clara sighed happily as they struggled through the deep snow.

Maisie grinned in agreement. 'Aye, well happen we'd better make the best of it while it lasts.' Arm in arm, they battled on.

It was a merry party that wended its way through Bermuda village. Jack was pulling Rose's sledge behind him. She had already become tired of sledging and was now bombarding everyone with huge fluffy snowballs.

'I want to go slidin' on the ice, Dad!' she cried, and the children all shouted in support of this. They were approaching the canal basin and Rose would have jumped onto the ice there and then, but Jack caught her arm firmly.

'Not here, lass,' he ordered. ''Tis too far across an' happen the ice won't be thick enough to take yer weight.'

Rose pouted with disappointment. 'Well, where *can* we do it then?' she asked.

Jack smiled at her patiently. 'I know just the place,' he said, winking at her, and taking her hand firmly in his own he moved her on.

'Where yer got in mind then, lad?' asked Walter as he breathlessly struggled to keep up with them.

'I were thinkin' of the pond on the outskirts of the Arbury Estate,' Jack answered, and so saying the little group set off up the farm track that led to South Farm. Soon they changed direction and entered the grounds of the estate through a fine wrought-iron gate, and after slipping and sliding down a gentle incline, they came to the edge of the pond.

Jack tentatively stepped onto the ice to make sure that it would take his weight, then content in his mind, he watched as the children careered onto the frozen water. Jack, Aaron and Walter were much amused at the youngsters' antics, and Jack found it strangely touching, for in his mind's eye was a picture of himself and Thomas sliding about on the canal, back in Tuttle Hill when they were children.

After some time he was brought back to the present by Walter, who was stamping his feet and blowing into his hands.

'By heck, lad!' he exclaimed. 'It's freezin' – ain't they had enough yet?'

Jack grinned at Aaron. 'We'll just give 'em another five minutes, then we'll set off back,' he promised, but the words had barely left his lips when an ear-piercing scream filled the air. The men's startled eyes all flew towards the children and Jack gasped with horror when he saw Benjamin, who was only feet away from Rose, pointing fearfully at the ice beneath his feet.

It was Walter who took control of the situation. Keeping his voice as calm as possible, so as not to panic the children further, he said, 'Children, I want you all to walk this way *now*. No matter what happens, just keep walkin' – an' be quick about it!'

All the children except one immediately began to do as they were told. But Rose seemed to be frozen to the spot as she gazed at the ice beneath her from terrified eyes.

As the children approached the pond's edge, eager hands reached out to snatch them to safety. Only Rose remained in danger now as Walter's voice took on a desperate edge. 'Rose, *listen* to me!' he commanded, and the tone of her grandad's voice made Rose raise her fearful eyes to his.

'Walk to me *now*. Do as I say, lass. Don't look down . . . just walk!' His hands were held out to her and she nodded slowly, but just as she was about to obey him, a terrible cracking noise hung on the air, and the ice beneath her feet opened up. For what seemed an endless time the child seemed suspended there, her eyes locked tight on Jack's, and then suddenly she sank out of sight beneath the ice. Jack stood as if rooted to the spot gazing in horror at the gaping hole that had swallowed up the child that he loved as his own. Then with a heartbreaking cry, he flung himself onto the slippery ice and slithered his way to where she had stood. Once there he dropped onto his belly and plunged his arms into the freezing water, but though he felt this way and that, his desperate hands felt nothing.

'Be careful, man, come back,' implored Walter. 'There's nowt yer can do, lad.' Tears were streaming down his wrinkled cheeks, but Jack refused to heed him, and to everyone's horror he swung himself round, and with not a word dropped into the hole himself and disappeared from sight.

'No, Jack, *no!*' Aaron screamed, and would have followed him, had Walter not hung on to his arm.

'Don't be a bloody fool,' he shouted. 'There's nowt we can do now but pray.'

Aaron was sobbing unashamedly. Jack was like the brother he had never had, and as he gazed at the yawning hole, he felt more useless than he had ever done in his whole life.

Suddenly ripples appeared on the water and seconds later Jack's head appeared. His lips were blue and he was gasping for breath, but before they could urge him out, he took a deep gulp of air and again disappeared from sight.

Next time he reappeared, his face was triumphant and as they looked on, he pulled with all his might with the hand that wasn't gripping the ice and Rose's flame-red curls suddenly appeared beside him. Jack was obviously weakening but to everyone's profound relief they heard the child coughing and spluttering, and even as she did so, Jack managed to heave her from the freezing water onto the ice with one last almighty effort.

'C . . . crawl to yer grandad, pet,' he ordered her in a trembling voice. 'An' be sure to stay flat on yer belly now.'

Weakly, the little girl began to do as she was bid, as impatient hands reached out to pull her to safety.

Clinging onto the ice, Jack watched her progress with

his heart in his mouth. But when at last he saw that Aaron had her shivering little body safe in his arms, he let out a shuddering sigh of relief.

All eyes now returned to him. 'Come on, lad,' Walter urged frantically. 'Get yerself out o' there now, fer God's sake afore it's too late.'

Jack was trying but his frozen limbs would not do as they were told and a terrible numbness was creeping through him. Then as his fingers lost their grip on the ice's edge, he slowly sank from sight for the last time.

Aaron was almost beside himself with grief. '*We need a rope!*' he cried desperately, and after pushing Rose's shuddering little figure into Walter's waiting arms, he began to sprint towards South Farm. Minutes later he was back, dragging behind him a thick length of rope and a long wooden stick.

Tying the rope hurriedly around his waist, he threw the other end to Walter. 'Give Rose to the kids an' get them to warm her up. I need you to hold on to that,' he commanded. 'Now – pull when I tell yer to. An' for God's sake, pull hard.'

Knowing there was not a second to be lost, Aaron slithered across the ice. Once at the edge of the hole in the ice, he dropped onto his belly and thrust the wooden rod into the water, then furiously thrust it about, this way and that. At first he felt nothing, only the pull of the icy current, but then the wood made contact with something, and manoeuvring the stick about, he slowly drew it towards him. Once the object was within his reach, he dropped the wooden pole, grasped the mass firmly and pulled it toward the surface. When Jack's wet black curls emerged from the murky water, Aaron gasped with relief, and holding fast to the precious burden, he shouted urgently over his shoulder, '*Pull, Walter, pull!*'

The farmer from South Farm had now joined Walter

at the edge of the frozen pond, and at Aaron's command, they began to heave on the rope as one. Sweat was pouring from Aaron despite the bitter cold, but he heaved with all his might until at last Jack's inert body lifted from the water and slithered onto the ice beside him.

Fearful now that the ice would give way beneath the combined weight of the two men, Walter and the farmer renewed their efforts and within minutes they had pulled Aaron and Jack to the pond's edge.

The farmer's wife had joined them by now and hastily gathered the half-drowned child into her chubby, comforting arms.

'Come on, me darlings,' she said to the terrified group of children about her. 'Let's get you all into the warm, eh?' And so saying, she hastily shepherded them up the slippery incline, casting a last concerned glance over her shoulder at Jack's still body.

Dropping the rope, Walter fell to his knees on the snow beside Jack and quickly pushed his trembling hand into his son's shirt to rest it on his chest.

'There's no heartbeat.' His voice was tormented.

Aaron dropped down beside him. Lowering his lips to Jack's, he attempted to blow air into the drowned man's lungs, but despite his very best efforts, Jack lay cold and unresponsive beneath him. On and on Aaron went, with no sign of ceasing, until eventually Walter's hand on his shoulder stayed him.

'It's no good, lad,' he said brokenly. 'It's too late . . . he's gone!'

'No, no, he can't be,' Aaron croaked, but then as he looked at Jack's peaceful face, he had to accept that Walter was right, and lowering his head to Jack's chest, he cried as if his heart would break.

The farmer was greatly distressed at the scene before

him, and rested his hand on Walter's arm as he sought for something to say.

'I'll go and fetch something we can carry him back on,' he said eventually, but Aaron's head snapped up.

'There's no need,' he wept. 'I'll carry him meself.' And hoisting Jack's limp body across his shoulder, that's exactly what he did. Walter was to wonder afterwards how he had ever managed it, for Jack was no lightweight. But if truth were known, the dead weight of Jack's body was nothing compared to the terrible weight in Aaron's heart, and throughout the journey to South Farm, not once did his steps falter.

Once there, the farmer led them towards the barn and quickly pushed two nearby hay bales together. 'Here you are, lad,' he said to Aaron. 'Lay him down on there.'

Aaron obeyed.

'Right, now let's go into the warm and get a hot drink inside of you, eh?' The farmer's offer was kindly but Aaron shook his head.

'I'm stayin' wi' Jack.'

The man nodded understandingly. 'Aye, all right, lad. Shall I hitch up the horse an' cart so you can get him home?'

It was Walter now who shook his head. 'No, it's all right, man,' he said throatily. 'Happen I'd best take the children an' break the news to the womenfolk first.'

'That might be best,' the farmer agreed, and leaving Aaron to keep his vigil, he led Walter from the barn to the warmth of the farmhouse kitchen.

Rose was sitting at the side of a roaring fire, and although she was snugly wrapped in a huge blanket, she was shivering uncontrollably. The farmer's wife had stripped her sodden clothes from her, and they were now steaming on an enormous wooden clotheshorse. As Walter entered the kitchen, the little girl's frightened eyes flew to him.

'Granda, where's me dad?' she asked fearfully.

Unable to answer her for the moment, for fear of bursting into tears, Walter bowed his head.

Sizing up the situation in a moment, the farmer's wife hastily stepped in. 'Hush now, sweetheart,' she soothed the little girl. 'We'll talk about that later. For now you just snuggle down and get warm, eh?'

When Walter flashed her a grateful look she smiled sadly. 'Will you have a nice hot cup of tea?'

Walter shook his head. 'No thanks, missus. I reckon I should be getting the little 'uns home an' speakin' to the women.'

At his words the rest of the children, who had been sitting at the huge oak table in silence, went and huddled about him.

'Leave the little girl here for now,' the woman told him. 'Don't worry, she's in shock, but if she's kept warm she'll be right as rain.'

Walter turned about and quietly left the kitchen with the subdued children close on his heels. Aware that something was very wrong, Little Jack clung fast to his grandad's hand. They were barely out of the farmyard when Benjamin asked, 'Where's me dad, Walter?'

Gazing down at the child, Walter chose his words carefully. 'He's stayin' here fer a time, lad, till I can come back with the horse an' cart to fetch him.'

Benjamin nodded solemnly as the sad little group continued their journey in silence.

When Holly Bush Farm came into sight, Walter began to quake in his boots. How could he tell the women that what had started off as a pleasant Sunday afternoon outing had ended in tragedy? His footsteps slowed but then realising that it must be done, he forced himself to go on.

When the kitchen door banged open and the children trooped in one by one, the women turned smiling faces to greet them, but then as they saw the pinched little faces, the smiles vanished.

It was hard to believe that this was the same merry party that had set out less than two hours ago. All their faces were solemn and frightened, and even Oscar, who usually bowled people over with his tail-wagging welcome, slouched to the fireside and dropped down onto his belly.

Walter stood just inside the doorway, twisting his cap nervously in his hands.

'What's up, man?' Clara asked. 'Yer look like you've lost a bob an' found a tanner. An' where's Rose an' our Jack an' Aaron?'

Gulping deep in his throat, Walter raised his eyes to hers, and the women were deeply shocked to see tears glistening there.

A cold hand suddenly closed about Sassy's heart. 'Yes, where are they?' she whispered fearfully. Maisie came over and the two young women clasped each other in support.

'Th . . . there's been an accident,' Walter explained gently, and as a look of panic filled their faces, he quickly held out his hands.

'Rose is all right; she's back at South Farm. Aaron's there an' all. She fell through the ice while she were playin' on the pond, but Jack managed to pull her out.'

Sassy and Maisie hugged each other with relief. 'Thank God,' Sassy said shakily. 'So where is Jack then?'

At her question, tears started to pour down Walter's cheeks. Guessing that there was bad news to come, Maisie hastily ushered the children into the parlour out of earshot.

'He's back at the farm an' all . . . But, lass, I have to

tell yer . . .' At this point, Walter went to his wife and took her in his arms. 'After Jack managed to get Rose out he went under himself, an' though Aaron pulled him out, it were too late. He'd gone.'

'What do you mean, *gone*?' demanded Clara.

Unable to bear the torment in his wife's eyes, Walter hung his head before muttering, 'He's dead. We did everythin' we could, but it were too late.'

Sassy's face was whiter than the snow that lay on the ground as she stared back at him incredulously. 'He *can't* be gone, he *can't*,' she said, shaking her head from side to side. But even as she denied it, Walter's weary face and Clara's heartbroken sobs told her that it was true, and sinking slowly onto a chair, she stared numbly ahead.

Some short time later, Jack's body was brought home and laid in the parlour and that evening, as Clara and Maisie saw to the needs of the children, Sassy slowly entered to stand beside him.

His face was peaceful, so much so that she could almost believe that at any minute he would wake up and smile at her. But then as she took his icy cold hand in hers, it suddenly struck her that he would never smile on her again, and the tears that had refused to fall throughout the long afternoon, suddenly gushed from her eyes.

Only now, when it was too late, did she realise just how much he had meant to her, and she cursed herself for a fool.

'Oh Jack,' she whispered brokenly, as guilt flooded through her. 'I'm so sorry that I never loved you the way you deserved to be loved. But I was very fond of you and I hope you knew it. I did *try* to make you happy.' As her scalding tears rained down onto his face, Sassy gently kissed them away.

'Sleep tight,' she said softly. 'You were the best husband a woman could ever wish for, an' I'll never forget you.' Then turning about, she slowly left the room, leaving Jack to his long sleep.

The funeral was a solemn affair. It had taken the grave-diggers all morning to dig the grave, for the ground was frozen solid.

Jack's body lay in the finest coffin money could buy. Sassy would settle for nothing less. It was transported to Chilvers Coton Church in a glass-sided hearse, drawn by two perfectly matched black stallions, sporting high black feather plumes above their manes.

News of Jack's death had spread around the town like wildfire and the church was packed to overflowing with people who wished to pay their last respects. Jack had been a much-loved and respected member of the community, and he had died a hero. Yet none of this brought even an ounce of comfort to Sassy, for she was wrapped in a blanket of misery and struggling to envisage her life without him.

When the service was over, the mourners sadly wandered away from the graveside until only Clara and Sassy remained, each clinging to the other for comfort.

'I never told him that I loved him,' sobbed Sassy.

'Don't whip yerself on that score, lass,' Clara comforted her. 'He had enough love in him fer the pair o' yer. An' I'll tell yer somethin' else an' all – he was happier with you fer the few short years yer had together than he could have been with anyone else for a whole lifetime. So put yer guilt away, pet. My son died a happy man.'

Clara hugged her lovingly. 'Now come away, lass,' she said. 'It's time we left him to rest in peace.'

Sassy stared down at the shiny brass name-plaque on the coffin for one last time and then she and Clara picked their way through the tombstones back to the waiting cart.

Chapter Thirty-Nine

'So how is she then, Maisie?' Arthur asked as he stepped in through the kitchen door and out of the strong July sunshine.

Looking up from the dough she was kneading, Maisie gave him a welcoming smile.

'Not good, to be honest,' she answered. 'She's still working far too hard, but you know what she's like – she won't listen unless she's a mind to. I think she does it for a reason. While she's busy, she doesn't have time to think – and that's the way she likes it.'

'I can understand that.' Arthur sighed heavily as he sat down at the table. 'When you think of all she's been through – what we've *all* been through, these past few years – it's a miracle she's coped as well as she has.'

'Aye.' Maisie covered the dough with a damp cloth and left it to rise, then clapping the flour from her hands she wiped them on her apron and hurried away to fetch the jug of lemonade from the thrall in the pantry.

After she had poured them both a glass she went on, 'She's been working in the dairy all morning, but she should be done soon. Between you and me, I think it's only the children that keep her going. But then that's hardly surprising, is it? Little Jack gets to look more like his father every day. It's funny really . . . What I mean is, life goes on just the same – the farm is still prosperin' an' the children are thrivin' – but without Jack, Sassy's lost all her sparkle. The only time she really smiles is when she's tending the rosebed that he planted for her. Soon as ever they come into bud, she picks 'em an' takes 'em down to the churchyard to put on his grave.'

'He was a good man,' Arthur said solemnly. 'And a brave one. If it wasn't for him, it would be Rose's grave Sassy was putting the roses on.'

'You're right there.' Maisie took a swallow from her drink and looked to where the children could be heard playing in the yard. 'I wish there was more I could do to help her,' she muttered sadly.

'You couldn't do more, my dear.' Arthur reached across the table and squeezed her hand affectionately. 'I really don't know what Sassy would have done without you over the last months. You've all been a tower of strength to her, and I know my lass appreciates it.'

'Even so, I hate to see her so changed.' Maisie plucked at her apron. 'Do yer know, I ain't seen her shed so much as a single tear since the day o' Jack's funeral? It ain't natural, to my way o' thinkin'. Sometimes I wish she could let it all out instead o' bottlin' it up inside her. She's had it really rough from the word go, ain't she? Three men she's had, an' she's lost the lot of 'em, one way or another.'

'That's life, I'm afraid,' Arthur replied philosophically. 'But happen things can only get better from now on.'

And Maisie silently prayed that he might be right, because from where she was standing, Sassy had sunk just about as low as she could get.

At that very moment in the dairy, Sassy was gazing from the open window across the fields and her heart felt as heavy as lead. With each day that passed, the burden of guilt she carried seemed to grow heavier. Sometimes she longed to confide in someone – Clara or perhaps Maisie? – but each time she tried to summon

444

the words they lodged in her throat and threatened to choke her. 'Oh Jack, I'm *so* sorry,' she cried, as she clutched the edge of the deep stone sink. She missed his company more than words could say, and every waking minute she regretted that she had not been able to love him as he had deserved. But it wasn't that which was eating away at her – it was the fact that even though she had grown fond of Jack for his kind and gentle ways, it was Daniel who owned her heart and always had. Now, more than ever, she realised that he had been the love of her life, which explained why she had never been able to give herself wholly to Jack. But it was too late now. Too late to tell Daniel or Jack what they had both meant to her in their different ways.

Lately, Clara had been dropping hints as big as house bricks about the possibility of her marrying again. 'You're only a young lass still, wi' the rest o' yer life stretchin' ahead of yer,' she had said. It was so kind of her. She had always had a heart as big as a bucket.

Sassy had listened but said nothing. How could she tell Clara that the love of her life had come and gone? She knew only too well that her friend and former mother-in-law was hurting too. She had never got over Thomas's death – nor the fact that no one had ever been brought to book over it. And then she had lost her second son too, in tragic circumstances. And so one lonely day stretched into another and Sassy knew that if hadn't been for the children, she would not have wanted to go on.

As she thought of them now, she smiled sadly. They were each so like their fathers. Rose's hair was the same flame-red as Daniel's. She knew that there had been talk about that when she was first born, and had worried at the time about how Jack would react to it – but she needn't have worried. From the second the child had drawn breath he had taken her as his own. And then there was Little Jack, so like his father and uncle that it was almost painful every time she looked at him. Although he had the same black curly hair and deep blue eyes as them, more importantly, he had Jack's gentle nature. Somehow she knew that while she had Little Jack, she would never really lose his father.

'*Sassy, yer dad's here!*'

Maisie's call brought her thoughts sharply back to the present and so, after quickly smoothing her skirts and patting her hair into place, she hurried across the farmyard.

Some days later, when Sassy and Maisie were again working in the dairy, they became aware of the children shouting excitedly in the farmyard.

'Hey up, what are them little devils up to now?' Maisie grinned.

'I have no idea,' Sassy answered, walking towards the door. 'But I'd better go and see.'

The chickens in the farmyard scattered in all directions, clucking indignantly as she marched through them to demand, 'What's going on here then?'

The men were still busy at work in the fields, but seeing the giggling group of children clustered round the open kitchen doorway, Sassy frowned suspiciously. I smell mischief afoot here, she thought.

'All right then, you lot, what have you been up to?' she demanded.

Unable to contain his delight, James hopped from foot to foot.

'It's a surprise!' He could barely contain his excitement. 'Look!' he cried, happily pointing into the open kitchen doorway, and following his finger, Sassy saw a large kitbag leaning against the doorframe. Her heart began to pound within her chest.

'*Go in, go in,*' chanted the children in unison, and hardly daring to hope, she slowly stepped into the kitchen. It was then that a voice she had been longing to hear came to her from the shadows.

'How yer doin' then, gel?'

Sassy threw herself into the tall man's strong arms. '*William.*' She was laughing and crying all at the same time. 'Why didn't you let us know you were coming? We had no idea.'

William grinned mischievously. 'Well, yer know me,' he told her. 'I always turn up like a bad penny when yer least expect me.'

She shook her head vehemently. 'Oh, don't ever say that,' she begged. 'You know you're always welcome. And you look so tanned. Where have you been?'

Maisie had followed Sassy across the yard and witnessed the reunion from the doorway. 'Come on, you lot,' she ordered the over-excited children. 'We'll go back to my cottage fer a nice cool drink an' some ginger buns, eh? I reckon Sassy an' William have a lot o' catchin' up to do, an' they could do without you little whipper-snappers rampagin' about the place for a while.' So saying, she ushered the children away as Sassy took William's hands in her own and gazed up into his eyes.

'I got off the ship from Australia a week ago in Southampton, and I've been sorting out my affairs and making my way here since then. I have gifts for you in my bag somewhere, but never mind that for now. Tell me what have I've missed out on?' William urged, and hardly knowing where to begin, Sassy led him to a chair and began to tell him of all that had gone on since his last visit.

When she finally told him of her marriage to Jack and the way he had died saving Rose, her brother shook his head in disbelief. So much had happened since his last visit that he could scarcely take it all in. Rose was the only one of the children he hadn't yet met as she was presently helping Clara with her baking, just as Sassy had used to do when she was a child.

'Well, bugger me!' he exclaimed, scratching his head. 'Yer could knock me down with a feather 'cos I could have sworn when I left that it were only a matter o' time before you an' Daniel got wed.'

Sassy's face clouded. Even now, after all this time, the mention of Daniel's name could still cause her hurt.

'What went wrong, love?' he asked gently.

Sassy shrugged. 'I don't know,' she said. 'I thought he loved me, but the next thing, he'd upped and gone back to America with his mother, without even saying goodbye.'

William stared at her with concern. 'You loved him, didn't yer, gel?' he asked.

'Yes, I did,' she gulped, then went on, 'but don't get me wrong. No one could have wished for a kinder husband or a better father for their children than Jack.'

William smiled at mention of the children. 'I've met Little Jack,' he said. 'He's a fine little lad, no doubt about it.'

Sassy nodded proudly. 'Yes he is,' she agreed. 'And you'll think the same of Rose when you meet her. She'll be back soon.' And then as they sat side by side with their hands locked tight, she quickly continued to tell him of everything else that had happened since his last visit.

When Arthur called in on his way home from work later that evening, he was equally as delighted to see William as Sassy had been and he wrung his son's hand warmly, tears of joy in his eyes.

For the first time since Jack's death, the crowd that sat down for their evening meal was merry, and Sassy felt her spirits, so long dampened down by grief, begin to rise.

As yet, Rose still hadn't put in an appearance but Sassy wasn't concerned. It was usual for Rose to spend a lot of time with Clara, and to have her supper with her grandma. They were almost at the end of the meal when the child suddenly skipped into the kitchen only to stop and stare at the stranger seated at the table.

William turned in his seat to look at her, and when he saw her flame-red curls, his mouth gaped open in astonishment, for never before in his whole life had he ever seen anyone with hair that colour, apart from Daniel. His eyes turned questioningly to Sassy, and she flushed deeply and dropped her eyes.

When at last the children were tucked into bed and darkness was setting in, brother and sister sat together by the empty grate.

'Rose is Daniel's child, isn't she, Sassy?' William asked eventually.

'Yes, she is.' Sassy bowed her head. 'I found out I was carrying her just after Daniel left me.'

'So he didn't know yer were with child?'

'No. I never told him because I wasn't sure until after he had left.'

Something didn't feel quite right here, and her younger brother chewed on his lip thoughtfully.

'Have *you* met anyone special yet?' questioned Sassy, hoping to break his chain of thought, and sure enough, a wide grin appeared on his face.

'Aye, I have,' he laughed. Then: 'There's someone special in every port – an' that's the way I like it.'

Punching him playfully on the arm, Sassy rested her head on his shoulder and for now the subject of Daniel was dropped.

William's visit went a long way to lifting everyone's spirits. He spoiled the children shamelessly and they adored him. He soon became their chief supplier of candy and would play with them for hours on end. He had to confess to having a huge soft spot for Rose. The more he got to know her, the more she reminded him of Daniel, and soon a special bond grew between them.

During his visit, he called in at the Jolly Colliers one day and received a warm welcome from Mr Boon and David Smith. But the latter could throw no more light on Daniel's hasty departure than Sassy could.

'I don't know why he left so sudden,' he said. 'To tell yer the truth, it shook me to the roots. One minute he were keen as mustard on your Sassy, an' the next minute he were gone.'

William nodded, but then as a thought occurred to him he asked, 'Did he leave a forwarding address?'

'Yes, he did, as a matter o' fact,' David said, 'though to tell yer the truth I've never been in touch 'cos I ain't much of a letter-writer.'

'Right then,' William said. 'I'll have that off yer afore I go back to sea, if yer don't mind. Yer never know, I may just be in his neck o' the woods one o' these days, an' if I am, I'll call an' pay him a visit.'

His next call was to Elizabeth and Arthur, and he was shocked to see the change in his stepmother. She rarely ventured from the house now, and if possible, seemed even more bitter than he remembered.

'It's strange, ain't it,' he said to her when Arthur had bustled off to order a pot of tea from Ada, 'the way that Daniel and Faith suddenly shot off back to America, I mean.' For a second he detected a frightened look in her eye, but then she shrugged.

'Why shouldn't they return to their homeland?' she said imperiously. 'With Thomas gone, there was nothing to hold them here.'

Suddenly suspicious, William said slyly, 'I suppose yer right. But yer know, I were sure as he an' our Sassy had somethin' goin' between 'em.'

When Elizabeth answered, her voice was full of contempt. 'What if they did?' she spat. 'Your sister still dropped on her feet, didn't she, what with being left the farm and landing Jack as a husband.'

Something about her cold eyes made William shiver involuntarily.

'Still,' the woman went on, 'she didn't have a happy-ever-after ending, did she? Both Thomas and Jack are gone now, and it's too late for her and Daniel even if there *was* ever something between them.'

William was shocked at the malice in her tone, and his voice was as hard as hers as he replied, 'We'll 'ave to see about that, won't we? 'Cos to my mind, it's *never* too late.'

They eyed each other with open hostility, until Arthur re-entered the room carrying a tray. Beaming at William, he asked, 'Have you time for a cup o' tea, lad?'

William's expression eased as he smiled fondly at his father. 'Aye, that's just what the doctor ordered.'

Oblivious of the tense atmosphere, Arthur set about pouring the tea.

As Sassy had come to know all too well, all good things must come to an end, and as August drew to a close, so did William's visit. In the time he had spent with them, he seemed to have blown a breath of fresh air back into the farm, and for the first time in months, Sassy now felt that she could again look forward.

Every single one of them accompanied him to the Trent Valley railway station to see him off, and the little platform was fairly bulging. The children were all greatly upset at their Uncle William's going, but Sassy was dry-eyed. She had shed too many tears in her life, she thought, and would not do so now. As she held both his callused hands in hers, she smiled on him fondly.

'You take care now,' she whispered.

This time it was William who had tears in his eyes, for knowing how life had let her down at every turn his heart was heavy with guilt at the thought of leaving his sister.

Sensing his mood, she told him, 'That's enough o' that now. I don't want you worrying about me. I've got more than enough to keep me occupied, an' every minute I'll be looking forward to your next visit.'

As the final whistle blew, she drew him into a last fierce hug. Once aboard, he peeped out of the open window. The train was pulling away now, and he gazed back at the little group on the platform. The children were waving excitedly, and he waved back at them. Clara and Walter were waving too, as were Maisie and Aaron, but his last sight was of Sassy, seemingly all alone.

'It's a cryin' shame,' he muttered to himself. 'If ever anyone deserved a happy endin', it's her.' And as she disappeared from sight, an idea was born in his mind.

Once he got to Liverpool he made his way to his ship, the *Mermaid*, and went straight to the Captain's cabin.

The Captain welcomed him warmly with a firm hand-shake. Over the years he had seen William rise from being a mere cabin boy to one of his best sailors, and he valued him highly.

'What can I do for you then, man?' he asked graciously.

Pulling off his cap, William looked him straight in the eye. 'It's a favour I'm after actually, sir,' he stated frankly.

The Captain nodded.

'I were wonderin' if yer wouldn't mind me missing this voyage as I know we're bound for the Indias an' I have business to attend to in America.'

The Captain frowned. William was one of his most trusted hands, and he would be sorry to put to sea without him. Even so, in all the years that William had sailed with him he had never once asked a favour of him before, and being known as a fair man, the Captain had no wish to refuse him now.

'Is your business urgent?' he enquired, and as a vision of Sassy's lonely face floated in front of his eyes, William firmly nodded his head.

'Right then, that's good enough for me, and I might even be able to help you get there.' So saying the Captain crossed to his desk and hastily scribbled a note, then standing again he handed it to William. 'Take that to the Captain of the *Dolphin* – she's due to leave for New York with the turn of the tide. Tell him I sent you, and you have every chance of joining their crew.'

William smiled at him gratefully. 'Thank yer, sir,' he said.

The Captain nodded. 'Safe voyage,' he said kindly and turning about, William left the cabin.

Chapter Forty

Once the *Dolphin* had docked in New York it took the crew two days to unload the cargo, and only when this task was done, were they given leave to go ashore. After descending the gangplank, and standing on dry land for the first time in four weeks, William hastily pulled out the screwed-up address that David Smith had given him from his pocket.

After making enquiries of passers-by, he found that the address was, in fact, only a few streets back from the dock. He knew from David that it was a hotel owned by a relation of Faith's, so following directions he headed there immediately.

The Liberty Hotel was hardly more than a lodging-house really, but clean and comfortable for all that. After banging on the bell that stood on the desk in the entrance hall, William gazed about himself with satisfaction.

The proprietor's wife, when she finally came in, eyed him with suspicion. After his weeks at sea, he was sorely in need of a shave and a bath, and was looking far from his best.

'We don't usually take in sailors,' she said hesitantly. 'We run a respectable house here.'

'I'm sure yer do,' William said, flashing her a smile full of charm. 'An' I must say yer establishment does yer credit. I apologise fer the state I'm in, but I've only just docked.'

Pleased at the compliment, the woman blushed, and

deciding that he appeared to be a cut above in manners, she enquired, 'Was it a room you were wanting, sir?'

'Well, yes, I am lookin' fer a room,' William said, 'an' I doubt I'd find anywhere better.'

Now falling completely under the spell of this handsome young sailor, the woman smiled in return.

'In fact, there's somethin' else yer could perhaps help me with as well,' he continued. 'I believe yer related to a friend o' mine an' his mother. They left this address with us in England, an' I'm hoping to catch up with 'em again.'

At his words, the plump little woman went pale. 'You must be talking about my sister-in-law, Faith Mallabone and her son Daniel Jackson,' she said quietly.

'That's right,' he confirmed, delighted at how easy it had been.

'You don't know, do you?' she asked sadly.

William raised his eyebrows. 'Know what?'

'Poor Faith has been dead these last two years,' she informed him.

'Oh, I'm terribly sorry,' William said immediately. 'An' Daniel?'

A small smile returned to her face. 'Oh, my nephew's all right,' she assured him quickly. 'but he isn't here at present. He's off on some jaunt somewhere – he comes and goes as he pleases.'

William asked politely, 'Do yer happen to have any idea where he might be?'

Her head wagged from side to side. 'I'm afraid I haven't,' she sighed. 'He's been very restless ever since they came back from England. When they first got back, Faith and he bought a small ranch, but when she died, he sold up and came back here to us – though I must admit, he's away more than he's here.'

At sight of the perplexed look on William's face, she

455

hurried around the desk to him. 'You must be very tired – you look dead on your feet. How about I find you a room? Then you can have a good hot bath. There's a barber just around the corner, who'll shave you and cut your hair, – and then I'll have a hot meal ready for you. My other guests eat at six – I'll save some dinner for you at seven, and then we can talk. My husband's gone a-visitin' this month – doing some trading business on the Hudson – so I'll be glad of the company.' Heartened at this proposal, William obediently followed her to his allocated room.

By the time he had bathed, changed his clothes, visited the barber and got a hearty meal inside him, William did indeed feel much better. He chatted to the woman easily.

Mrs Laplante, as her name was, was a homely person, married to Faith's brother, Nat, and obviously more than a little fond of Daniel. Regrettably, she had never had children of her own and since Faith's death, she had looked after Daniel possessively.

'How long do yer reckon he might be gone?' enquired William, after he had done justice to the delicious sweet potato and steak meal she had set before him.

The woman could only shrug. 'It's hard to predict. As I said earlier, he's never really settled since he came back from England.'

She leaned towards William, and whispered, 'I have a feeling he was crossed in love while he was there and he's never got over it.'

William stared at her in astonishment, and enjoying his rapt attention she hastily continued, 'The girl's name was Sassy – an unusual name, isn't it? From what I can gather, he was all set to ask this Sassy to marry him, but then a friend of Faith's – Elizabeth, I think he said her

456

name was – informed him that Sassy was going to marry someone else.'

William had flushed with rage, and now it was Marion Laplante's turn to stare at him.

'*I knew it!*' he said angrily. 'I smelled a rat from the start, fer I knew them pair were meant to be.' He banged the table with frustration, setting the pots and the cutlery rattling as the landlady looked startled.

Apologising, he hastily explained to her who he was, and as his story unfolded, Mrs Laplante looked unhappy.

'So, it was this Elizabeth who kept them apart then, was it?' she asked.

'Aye, that's how it's lookin',' William agreed. 'But our Sassy thinks that Daniel betrayed *her*!'

Mrs Laplante shook her head in disbelief. 'This Elizabeth must be a very cruel woman,' she decided.

'She is that,' he agreed. 'But I never thought as even *she* would sink to that depth.'

His companion sighed. 'Well, son, it's water under the bridge now. What's done is done, and there's no turning the clock back. But I'll tell you something. Knowing my nephew as I do, I can promise you that he loved your sister with all his heart, for he's never so much as looked at another girl in all these years. So, perhaps it's as well he isn't here, because if he knew how this Elizabeth had kept them apart, I reckon there'd be blood on the moon.'

William thought on her words, and for the first time he wondered if he had been right to make this journey. But then a picture of little Rose flashed into his mind and his shoulders sagged despondently.

'It ain't as simple as that,' he said quietly. 'For it ain't just Daniel an' Sassy that's involved.'

As the woman stared at him curiously, William continued, 'The thing is, when Daniel came back to America, Sassy was carryin' his child, but she never got

457

the chance to tell him. Daniel has a fine little girl back in England called Rose.'

As the shock of what he was telling her registered, Mrs Laplante's hand flew to her mouth. 'A little girl . . . Oh, dear God love us,' she whispered fearfully. 'What's this news going to do to him?'

It was more than obvious from the way she spoke of Daniel that she loved him as the son she had never had. 'I don't know how he'll take it,' William answered truthfully. 'But I came here 'cos I felt he had the right to know about her, even if he decides to do nothing about it.'

Her mind was in turmoil, but then suddenly noticing how weary her visitor looked, her kind heart went out to him. 'Why don't you go and get a good night's sleep and we'll talk more about this tomorrow?' she said.

'I reckon I will,' William yawned, and wished her a good night as he slowly rose and made his way to his room.

Once he had gone, Daniel's aunt sat on, her mind spinning, for she of all people knew how much it had hurt Daniel to leave his love in England. She had an inkling that when he found out about Elizabeth's trickery, he might well make his way back there, and loving him as she did, she didn't know how she could bear to lose him again.

'Perhaps it's just as well he's not here,' she told herself. 'It seems to me he's suffered enough, and at least whilst he's here I can look out for him.' And she sat on as night fell, wrestling with her conscience.

William only had three weeks' shore leave, and during that time he acquainted himself with the sights of New York city, including a visit to the Statue of Liberty which stood proudly on Bedloe's Island. William was totally enthralled with it, and could speak of nothing else to Mrs Laplante over his evening meal. She informed him that the statue had been a present to the city from France. Auguste Bartholdi, the sculptor, wished it to be erected there as a symbol of welcome to the many thousands of immigrants who were flooding into the country at the time.

William also rode across the Brooklyn Bridge and was in awe at the gothic towers and steel wire cables that had gone into its construction. Mrs Laplante was able to tell him that it had been designed by John Augustus Roebling, who was considered to be an engineering genius of his time. The bridge spanned 1,600 feet and was the widest bridge in the world.

William went to a music hall and visited the theatre in Manhattan, but each night when he returned to the hotel he looked eagerly for a sight of Daniel, only to be disappointed. As his leave drew to an end, he began to give up hope. At one stage, out of sheer frustration, he almost decided to go in search of him, but as Mrs Laplante pointed out, it would be like looking for a needle in a haystack. Daniel could be anywhere, and America was a vast place. Recognising the truth of her words, William accepted that perhaps his journey had been a waste of time. But at least he could let Sassy know that Daniel hadn't betrayed her, and as he posted the letter in which he told her of Elizabeth's trickery, it gave him some measure of comfort.

It was the morning of his departure. Still there was no sign of Daniel, and he stood at the Liberty Hotel doorway with Mrs Laplante, saying goodbye.

'Thank you,' he said sincerely. She had promised to tell Daniel of his visit, and he believed that she would. The rest would be in the lap of the gods.

There were tears in her eyes as she gently shooed him

away. 'Hurry along now, son,' she urged him. 'Else you'll miss the tide.'

Bending, he planted a gentle kiss on her cheek, then strode away, turning once to give her a final wave. Then, hoisting his kitbag further onto his shoulder, he made his way back to the *Dolphin*.

Two weeks after William had set sail, Daniel returned to the hotel. His aunt was sorry to see that he appeared to be in no better spirits than when he had left, for although since Faith's death, he was a man of considerable means, his eyes always looked sad and empty.

Over the last two years she had watched a string of women set their caps at him, but Daniel flatly refused to consider any one of them.

The news Mrs Laplante had to impart to him was weighing on her heavily. For two days she kept the secret, giving herself the excuse that she was waiting for the right moment to tell him. But eventually her conscience began to plague her until finally she could bear it no more, and so sitting him down one evening she related the whole of William's story to him.

Sassy and Clara were busy at work kneading dough in the farmhouse kitchen when the carrier cart delivered William's letter. Whooping with delight when she spied the foreign post-mark, Sassy hastily wiped her hands on her apron and excitedly tore open the envelope.

'Is it from William?' asked Clara.

'Yes, it is,' Sassy told her, and eagerly began to read. However, she had barely finished the first page when she sank unsteadily onto the nearest chair.

'Whatever's up, lass?' asked Clara. 'Yer look like you've just seen a ghost.'

'Oh Clara,' she gulped, tears trembling on her lashes.

460

'I can't believe what William's telling me.' She began to read the letter aloud. By the time she had finished, Clara too was fuming.

'I bloody well *knew* it,' she said angrily. 'I always felt that bitch had a hand somehow in Daniel goin' – an' all these years we've thought he walked out on yer.'

Sassy was crying openly now, as Clara pulled her into a warm embrace. 'Hush now, love. Things will come right in the end, you'll see.'

But Sassy shook her head. 'No, they won't. It's too late now,' she sobbed.

The older woman was beside herself at the injustice of it all. She knew that Sassy had found a measure of peace with her Jack, but she was no fool and had always known that underneath, Daniel had been her true love.

'Ah well,' Sassy said eventually through her tears, 'at least I know now why he left as he did.' And this knowledge brought her comfort of a sort.

The next night when Arthur called in on his way from work, he found his daughter strangely subdued. Clara, by contrast, was in a fighting mood.

'It's about time as yer put that bloody wife o' yours in her place,' Clara said before he was properly in the room, and although Sassy frowned at her, she refused to be silenced.

'Read that!' she ordered, and snatching William's letter from the mantelpiece, she thrust it into his hands. Arthur sat bent over it, quietly reading for some time, and when he finally raised his head, his rage was terrible to behold.

'Right, this is the *last* straw,' he spat, and with the letter still clutched tight in his hand, he strode out of the cottage.

'Oh Clara, what have you done?' Sassy was deeply distressed, but Clara was unrepentant.

'It's about time somebody knocked that bloody

461

woman off her pedestal,' she sneered. 'An' if yer ask me, it's long overdue.'

Some time later Arthur stood, hands on hips, surveying Elizabeth's impressive residence in Swan Lane, and it suddenly came to him that in all the years he had lived there, he had never once considered it to be his home.

Without even bothering to fumble in his pocket for his key, he banged loudly on the great brass knocker, and when the latest in a long line of maids opened the door, he thrust past her unspeaking and stormed into the sitting room.

Elizabeth's blurred eyes were already on the door at all the commotion and as Arthur marched into the room she glared at him. 'What the—' she began, but shoving the letter roughly into her lap, he cut her words short. A glass decanter stood on a table at her side, and he could see that she had been drinking.

'Read that,' he commanded, and too amazed to argue, Elizabeth narrowed her eyes and holding the letter at arm's length, did as she was told.

'Is it true?' His voice was ominously quiet.

'What if it is?' she said, regaining her composure. 'Daniel should thank me for saving him from that little trollop. Look how she always comes out on top. She got the farm, didn't she, and tricked Jack into marrying her into the bargain!'

Now that the truth was out, Elizabeth sneered, 'I wonder if Jack knew when he married her that she was carrying a *bastard*.' She laughed spitefully at Arthur's shocked face, and would have gone on, but suddenly he caught her by the shoulders and shook her hard.

'You wicked woman,' he said, and for the first time panic gleamed in her eyes. 'You've always had it in fer my Sassy, ever since she were just a poor, motherless little girl, but this time you've gone too far. As far as I'm concerned, you ain't fit to lick her boots, fer all yer fancy airs an' graces.'

'How *dare* you say that to me!' Elizabeth cried haughtily, as she shrugged his hands off. 'I took you from a slum cottage and gave you all this – *and* a fine job!'

He laughed bitterly. 'Aye, yer did that,' he agreed. 'An' I've never known a single happy day since, 'cos I'll tell yer now, you ain't a *quarter* o' the woman my Sarah was, but it's took this for me to realise it – and I'll tell yer now, it's finished 'cos I'll not stay in this house one day longer.'

By this time, Ada had come to stand in the open doorway and was twisting her apron in consternation, for she had never seen Arthur, who was usually so placid and subservient, so upset.

'I don't regret what I did,' Elizabeth said, her lips twisted with contempt. 'Even on the first night of our honeymoon it was Sarah you cried out for, and then I had to come back to live with that *slut* of a daughter of yours who was the spit out of her mother's mouth. What chance did our marriage ever stand, with her here as a constant reminder to you, eh? So I decided I'd get my revenge on her one way or another. And I did just that. Oh yes, I did that all right. I managed to get rid of *two* of her beaus, didn't I? I'd have got rid of Jack as well, if he hadn't met his death in a watery grave!'

Arthur had paled. 'What do you mean . . . *two* of her beaus?'

She laughed harshly and the sound grated on his nerves. 'Daniel and Thomas. I got rid of them both.'

His face wreathed in confusion and dawning horror, he took a step back from her as she sprang to her feet.

'It was *me* that pushed Thomas from the Leicester Road bridge onto the train track,' she told him smugly, and when his hand covered his mouth in horror, she laughed dementedly in his face.

'B . . . but why?' Arthur managed to stutter.

'*Why?*' She threw back her head and laughed maniacally. 'Because he spurned my daughter's advances when Ellie died, for your slut! Louise was his for the taking, but oh no, Master Thomas only had eyes for Sassy!'

Full of righteous anger, Elizabeth rushed on, 'If it hadn't been for Sassy, my girl might have married Thomas and never have even met the scum she is married to now!' Grabbing her wine glass, she emptied it in one swallow, and filled it again, while Arthur and Ada watched paralysed.

'Everyone suspected that Thomas was responsible for murdering Ned Chester, so all I had to do was wait for my chance to kill him, then make it look like a possible suicide, or revenge by one of Ned's friends. I took to hanging about the inn each night for half an hour, and following him, if he should come out. That night, I was on my way there, when by some lucky chance, along comes the great man himself. I hid until he was on the bridge, and then I crept up and pushed him. It was so easy. You should have *seen* the look on his face when I lunged at him.

'Ha ha! It was *his* turn to die.' Grabbing the glass from the table, she took a long swallow then continued, 'And Daniel – well, you know what happened there. Every man my Louise was interested in, Sassy stole away, so I had to get rid of him too, didn't I? Because of *her*, my only daughter is lost to me – and even Sassy thinks she is too good to speak to me now just because she owns the farm!'

'Y . . . you're completely mad, woman,' Arthur breathed as he pulled at his collar. 'And I'll tell you now, I'll not stay another night in this house with you.'

Suddenly realising that she had said too much, Elizabeth slammed down her glass and clutched at his arm. 'You can't leave me,' she cried. 'You've nowhere to go.'

He roughly shook her off. 'That's where yer wrong,' he replied. 'I'm goin' to move into Aaron's old rooms above the barn at Holly Bush Farm. An' as fer me job . . . well, yer can stick that an' all, fer they'll be more than glad of an extra pair of hands at the farm.'

Even as he spoke he was striding towards the open doorway, where the maid and Ada were hovering with their mouths agape, for surely this was not the man who had bowed down to their mistress for as long as they could remember.

'Expect a visit from the police,' he told Elizabeth with no trace of emotion, and now she flew at him and began to pummel his back with her clenched fists.

'I'll deny everything!' she screamed. 'It will be your word against mine.'

'I hardly think so,' Arthur replied, as he gestured towards Ada, who had witnessed the whole exchange.

'Ada, send the maid for the police and tell Isaac to keep guard outside,' he instructed her, then turning at the door, he eyed his wife's white face coldly and delivered his last parting shot. 'An' don't think I ain't known you've been hitting the bottle neither,' he sneered, '"cos I have, an' fer all I care, yer can drink yerself to death, though I think there's very little chance of that where you'll be going.' And then without so much as a final backward glance, he banged the door behind him, locked it, and went to wait in the kitchen with Ada until the police arrived.

Many traumatic hours later, Arthur was welcomed at the farm with open arms, and when he told them of the developments back in Swan Lane, Clara had sobbed in Walter's arms as if her heart would break.

'Our poor lad can rest in peace now his murderer has been found,' she said, and Arthur nodded solemnly, omitting to tell them exactly why Elizabeth had done what she had. From where he was standing, Clara had suffered enough, losing both her boys. Sometimes, he decided, ignorance was bliss. It would be enough for Clara to know that Thomas's murderer would finally stand trial – and would then be hanged by the neck until she was dead.

Chapter Forty-One

It was a fine July day in 1894 and as the train chugged into Chilvers Coton station, everything looked exactly as he remembered it. He had read the news of England avidly in the American newspapers since he had left and knew that a lot had happened since he had last been here, including the opening of the Manchester Ship Canal in May. Two further engineering achievements had also been accomplished that year. First, the Tower Bridge in London had been opened and secondly, Blackpool Tower, which at 518 feet was reputed to be little more than half the height of the Eiffel Tower in Paris, but the tallest building in England nonetheless. William Gladstone had retired from his post as Prime Minister earlier in the year, after a brief audience with Queen Victoria, who had recently become a great-grandmother for the first time when the Duke and Duchess of York presented her with a fine baby boy. But despite all these happenings, Nuneaton looked just the same.

As the flame-haired man stepped down from the carriage onto the platform, lugging his heavy trunk behind him, the stationmaster touched his cap respectfully. There was something about this passenger, he thought, that was vaguely familiar.

'Good day, sir,' he welcomed him.

Daniel inclined his head in reply. 'Is there anywhere I can leave my trunk for an hour or two?' he enquired, and at the sound of his American accent, recognition dawned on the stationmaster's face.

'Course there is,' he said jovially. 'You can put it in my office, sir, and may I say it's good to see you back.'

Daniel returned his smile, and as he pressed a half-crown into the man's hand, the stationmaster's smile became even broader.

'Why thank you,' he beamed. 'Will you be staying for long?'

Daniel shrugged. 'That all depends,' he replied, and although he didn't say it out loud, his heart cried, *I hope so!*

As he strode past the Jolly Colliers Inn a short time later, memories of the brief time he had lived there flooded into his mind, but as much as he would have liked to see his old friend, David Smith, there was someone else whom he was longing to see even more and so, without slowing his step, he resolutely strode on.

When he eventually reached the entrance to the track that led to the farm, he stopped to gaze at the sign that was gently swinging in the warm breeze above the gate. *Holly Bush Farm*, he read, and smiled.

He walked on, his steps slower now, for suddenly he was afraid. Very soon he would behold the child who, until recently, he hadn't even known existed. But better yet, he would see Sassy, and the thought caused his heart to begin to hammer within his chest.

Unknown to him, his progress was being watched by curious eyes. Arthur was working in the hayfield that bordered the farm track, and as he suddenly recognised Daniel, he almost flew across the field to greet him.

'Why, Daniel, lad,' he cried, when finally they were face to face. 'I can't tell yer how pleased I am to see yer.' He was beaming as he shook Daniel's hand firmly in a warm grip. 'This will mean so much to Sassy,' he added, and Daniel blinked nervously.

468